EXISTENTIALLY CHALLENGED

EXISTENTIALLY CHALLENGED

YAHTZEE CROSHAW

Book Two of
The DEDA Files

DARK HORSE BOOKS

Cover art by Ethan Kimberling.
Cover design by Ethan Kimberling and May Hijikuro.

Published by Dark Horse Books
A division of Dark Horse Comics LLC
10956 SE Main Street, Milwaukie, OR 97222

DarkHorse.com

First edition: March 2023

Library of Congress Cataloging-in-Publication Data

Names: Croshaw, Yahtzee, author.
Title: Existentially challenged / Yahtzee Croshaw.
Description: First edition. | Milwaukie, OR : Dark Horse Books, 2023. |
    Series: The DEDA Files ; Book two | Summary: "With magic declassified in
    the UK, the fake psychics and fraudulent healers are running amok, and
    it's up to the Department of Extradimensional Affairs' newly appointed
    Skepticism Officers to crack down. But when they set their sights on
    Modern Miracle, a highly suspicious and fast-growing faith healing cult
    with remarkably good social media presence, even their skepticism is put
    to the test. Is Modern Miracle on the level? Is Miracle Meg's healing
    magic real? Why do dead bodies keep showing up on their doorstep? And
    just what is Miracle Dad's preferred flavor of crisp? In Existentially
    Challenged, the sequel to Differently Morphous, the men and women of the
    Department of Extradimensional Affairs continue their struggle to
    uncover the motives of the Ancients under the ever-present threat of
    death, insanity, and sensitivity training"-- Provided by publisher.
Identifiers: LCCN 2022032374 (print) | LCCN 2022032375 (ebook) | ISBN
    9781506733593 (trade paperback) | ISBN 9781506733609 (ebook)
Subjects: LCGFT: Fantasy fiction. | Humorous fiction.
Classification: LCC PR9619.4.C735 E95 2023 (print) | LCC PR9619.4.C735
    (ebook) | DDC 823/.92--dc23/eng/20220909
LC record available at https://lccn.loc.gov/2022032374
LC ebook record available at https://lccn.loc.gov/2022032375

10 9 8 7 6 5 4 3 2 1
Printed in the United States of America

Mike Richardson President and Publisher • Neil Hankerson Executive Vice President • Tom Weddle Chief Financial Officer • Dale LaFountain Chief Information Officer • Tim Wiesch Vice President of Licensing • Vanessa Todd-Holmes Vice President of Production and Scheduling • Mark Bernardi Vice President of Book Trade and Digital Sales • Randy Lahrman Vice President of Product Development and Sales • Ken Lizzi General Counsel • Dave Marshall Editor in Chief • Davey Estrada Editorial Director • Chris Warner Senior Books Editor • Cara O'Neil Senior Director of Marketing • Cary Grazzini Director of Specialty Projects • Lia Ribacchi Art Director • Michael Gombos Senior Director of Licensed Publications • Kari Yadro Director of Custom Programs • Kari Torson Director of International Licensing • Christina Niece Director of Scheduling

(Names redacted)

K—— G——:
Attention, Acton Road Neighborhood Watch! Does anyone recognize the old man in the denim jacket standing outside Mrs. Klebold's house? He's leaning on her hedge and staring into her front windows. He's been there for the last hour.

J—— S——:
No, I don't recognize him. Didn't Mrs. Klebold just get home from her bladder surgery? I can't imagine she appreciates people nosing in on her private business.

E—— B——:
I've been watching him for two hours now. It's disgusting that nobody's done anything about him yet. So much for community.

J—— S——:
I know. Did you know somebody stole the post out of my letterbox two weeks ago? This whole country's been going downhill ever since all that magic stuff came out.

D—— N——:
J——, please don't turn this into yet another rant about the new corner

shop owner. I keep saying, if you took the time to get to know Mr. Shgshthx, you'll find he's actually very polite for a slime monster.

J——— S———:

All I know is, a year ago there weren't any slime monsters, nobody was getting their minds wiped by evil wizards, and my post wasn't getting stolen from my letterbox.

K——— G———:

You won't believe this, but I just went and looked at the old man again and he's actually leaning over Mrs. Klebold's fence and smelling her front lawn. Has anybody called the police?

E——— B———:

No I have not because we shouldn't have to. The whole point of neighborhood watch is to let everyone in the community live in peace without having to worry about things like police and mad people sniffing our grass.

K——— G———:

Well, if he's still there in another hour I'm going to give him a piece of my mind.

K——— G———:

Small update: turns out he was dead. Police en route.

J——— S———:

Once again I bring up my letterbox, and once again this group chat finds a way to change the bloody subject.

OFFICIAL MINISTRY OF JUSTICE TRANSCRIPT

SPEAKER 1: Hello, coroner's office?

SPEAKER 2: Is this the pathologist who submitted the report on the Acton Road body?

1: This is she.

2: This is Detective Brady of West Mercia Police. I was wondering if I could confirm a couple of the points on your report.

1: Oh yes.

2: So just to confirm: you noted that the body was identified as one William Harold Shaw, of Worcester?

1: I did.

2: And you also reported that Mr. Shaw's cause of death was old age.

1: I did.

2: Did you know that Mr. Shaw's birth certificate shows that he was twenty-six years old at the time of his death?

1: I did.

2: Right.

1: Was there anything else?

2: Uh. Frankly, I was expecting a little more than "I did" from you at this point.

1: Well, he was definitely twenty-six, and he definitely died of cardiovascular issues related to advanced age.

2: So . . . did he have some kind of condition . . .

1: No. Mr. Shaw had no history of progeria or any other kind of wasting illness that might appear to accelerate his physical aging. But he did die of old age.

2: Right. That didn't strike you as odd?

1: It might have done a year ago, Detective, but I've had to stop thinking about that sort of thing. A few weeks ago I had to write up someone who died of respiratory failure after their right lung spontaneously transformed into a bat.

2: [*sighs*] I was afraid you'd say something like this.

1: Was there anything else?

2: No. I suppose I'd better call the purple ponces.

01

"Purple," said Elizabeth Lawrence.

She put no expression into the word, and yet, in her characteristic manner, with which her colleagues had become extremely familiar, she somehow conveyed entire paragraphs of meaning. It had come across as both a question and an expression of disapproval, and was more than a few steps on the way to becoming an insult.

Dr. Nita Pavani repeated the "ta da" gesture she had made toward her recently unveiled whiteboard. "Yes, the designer is going with purple," she said, with unshaken confidence. "The feeling was that we needed a specific color for the public to associate with the new magical emergency service. Just as the police are associated with blue, and the ambulance service with green . . ."

"No, they aren't," said Victor Casin. This caused heads to turn, as it was his very first contribution to the meeting, which he had thus far spent buried in the upturned folds of the unseasonably warm black trench coat he stubbornly insisted on wearing. "I've never seen a green ambulance. They use red. Like the Red Cross."

"Erm, red is for fire engines, surely," said Alison Arkin, who was sitting to his left.

"Yeah, to be fair, I think she was right the first time," said Adam Hesketh, who was on Victor's right, wearing a trench coat that would be identical were it not about a foot shorter and a foot wider. "Green is for first-aid kits. The first-aid kit in the toilet is green."

Victor pouted as he considered these points, then extended a long index finger toward the whiteboard. "All right. Can we agree that that looks completely stupid?"

"This is the uniform design that tested most positively with the focus group," said Nita, dismissing the ongoing commentary by flicking her ponytail in a manner that Alison found quite inspiring. "It rated highest in creating a sense of reassurance and professionalism in a hypothetical extradimensional-emergency situation."

"Purple," repeated Elizabeth in precisely the same tone as before, nevertheless adding another four or five chapters to the established subtext.

Nita quickly puffed out her cheeks for a moment before replying, as if attempting to physically reinflate her mood. "Yes. The focus group scored purple the highest in its associations with extradimensional physics and, ah, neomysticism."

The slight hesitation made Alison wonder if *mysticism* was a new addition to the growing list of words Nita and her cultural sensitivity network disapproved of, and if *neo* had been the agreed-upon bandage for that particular wound.

"If I could shift topic from the color to the style . . ." said Richard Danvers, who was at the head of the meeting table.

"Ah yes," said Nita, turning back to the whiteboard with a spin that made her ponytail bounce like a circus seal being promised a fish. "The cut of the jacket and shirt have been influenced by popular cultural associations with magic and magic users, blended with the style of conventional police uniforms."

"Right," said Danvers. "I'm seeing that. It does explain the sleeves. But I have concerns about the hat."

"Oh yes, me too," said Adam, relieved to have a senior voice to which he could add ditto marks. "I think we might possibly want to shelve the hat for now."

"With some force," added Victor.

"That's fine," said Nita quickly, this being the one area of ground she had already decided to concede with very little fight. "Although the designer asked me to stress that this design is exactly the same height as a traditional policeman's helmet."

"It's not so much the height," said Danvers, "as the . . ."

". . . point," said he and Adam together.

"Let's move on," said Elizabeth, again with no expression but with such commanding power that Nita was already returning to her seat at the meeting table before her conscious brain had fully registered the words.

As senior administrator, Elizabeth was, by all practical metrics, the person in charge of the Department of Extradimensional Affairs, but no one acknowledged that out loud. As an official government department, DEDA was technically headed by an appointed cabinet minister, whose name very few of the staff had committed to memory. The man had showed up at the office precisely once, and only to pick up his new business cards.

"Richard?" she prompted.

Richard Danvers was the most senior member of the Department's operations division, in every sense of the word. He was well past the point that his gray hairs had taken over the parliament of his head, but it was still only a minority government. "Okay," he said, consulting the paperwork before him. "If there are no further questions about the new uniform policy . . ."

Victor's hand shot up.

". . . bearing in mind," stressed Richard, "that special agents and senior field agents based out of the Department building in London are considered equivalent to detectives in the police force and are permitted to operate in plainclothes . . ."

The hand descended again, returning to its dark burrow in the folds of Victor's coat. Richard hadn't even paused.

". . . I can finish going over the official restructuring. I'd like to thank you all for your 'patience' while Ms. Lawrence, Ms. Pavani, and I have been finalizing the details on this." He passed a glare around the room. "In brief, Operations is being split into subdivisions, with each one to be represented by one of our existing special agents. From now on, Adam will be permanently attached to the Identification and Investigations Office, and Victor to Control and Pacification."

"We're being split up?" asked Adam, starting with sudden concern.

"Only as an official partnership," said Richard, with fatherly reassurance. "I'm sure your work will continue to very frequently overlap."

"Yeah, calm down, Adam," said Victor contemptuously. "I'm not your security teddy."

Richard consulted his agenda, then made a show of eyeballing the room again. "I notice that our other special agent has not graced us with his presence."

"Erm, yes," said Alison as several sets of eyes turned to her. "I think Doctor Diablerie wants me to represent him at these meetings."

"You think?" asked Elizabeth, one eyebrow twitching the slightest amount.

"I think that's what he was saying. His exact words were that he would have me act the Huginn and Muninn to his Allfather Odin as he sits astride his throne of intrigue, probing the uncanny realms of the inner-most." Privately, Alison suspected that making it possible for him to barely show up for work was the main reason Doctor Diablerie had finally accepted her as an assistant, or at the very least, stopped actively trying to get her killed during assignments.

"Well, he's certainly putting your memory to work," said Danvers, bored. "In any case, please inform your mentor that he and, by extension, you are being assigned to the Office of Skepticism." He paused in antic-ipation of the obvious response.

"Skepticism?" repeated Alison.

"The remit of the Office of Skepticism will mainly be to debunk claims of magical ability," said Elizabeth.

"But magic does exist," said Victor flatly. "Last I checked."

"Yes, which is what has made skepticism all the more important," said Nita, growing suddenly heated. "All those fake palm readers and crystal merchants didn't go away just because real magic came out of the closet."

"Quite," said Danvers, attempting to head a rant off at the pass. "Emboldened them, if anything."

"It's disgusting," continued Nita. "It's literally magical blackface, and we're finally doing something serious about it."

"Yes, well." Danvers eyed the clock. "A lot of that will depend on how this afternoon's vote turns out."

"Oh, is that today?" asked Alison. "I thought things seemed quiet." Being in a government department, in the same building as several other government departments, Alison was used to seeing a steady trickle of politicians, their aides, and their aides' aides, but none of them had been around that day. There was an eerie, anticipatory stillness hanging over Whitehall, through which all the civil servants were moving like grazing wildebeests waiting for the first sign of a lioness.

"They delayed it long enough," said Nita spitefully. "Maybe the government can finally stop talking about supporting extradimensional rights and actually put some policy behind it."

"*If* it passes," said Elizabeth, the emphasis on the first word as heavy as a stone slab.

"At any rate," said Danvers, sharply moving some papers around to punctuate the change of topic. "All of our current in-house operatives will be divided among the three teams. We've already gone through the staff and tentatively assigned everyone to the subdivision best suited to their personal skill sets." He took up a stack of identical pages and dealt one to each person at the table with rapid sweeps of his arm. "I think you'll all agree that we made fair assessments; if there are any specific individuals you'd like to request for your division, then please submit them by tomorrow. If no one has questions, we can—"

"Why does Adam's list have so many more names than my list?" interrupted Victor.

Danvers wrestled his tongue back under control and sighed through his teeth. He followed Victor's gesturing hand and pretended to notice for the first time that the Investigations list was three times longer than the Pacifications list. "It's nothing to take personally, Victor. The amount of manpower—"

"Personpower," said Nita.

"Personpower, thank you, assigned to each subdivision reflects which . . . official procedures will have the greater emphasis, going forward."

"And what does that mean?" probed Victor, his upper lip curling like an unfolding flytrap.

"Well, what it means is that the Department is still going to be doing a lot of investigating and tracking down of extradimensionally gifted persons and nonperson entities," said Nita, eyes condescendingly wide. "But what we don't intend to do as much of is setting them on fire and blowing them up."

Victor's mouth tightened like the chains on a torture rack as he fixed his gaze upon Nita. "I happen to identify as someone who sets things on fire and blows them up," he intoned.

"Come on, Victor," said Adam, after a cough. "She's right, you haven't had much to do lately. And look, your team still has Reinholdt, and Stoke, and Stewart . . . they're all good people. At least you're not . . ."

He had been about to wave his pudgy hand over the minuscule third column on the page, which had only two names: Doctor Diablerie and Alison Arkin. But then he accidentally caught Alison's eye, and his hand returned immediately to his lap like a startled badger to its sett.

"Not . . . dying of cancer," he concluded.

02

"Extradimensional rights," muttered Victor as he wore a furrow into the cheap carpet of the corridor outside the meeting room. "Next they'll be saying we can't stop them murdering people anymore 'cos that would be oppressing their identities as transdimensional death monsters."

Alison gave up trying to speed walk past without making eye contact, and offered him a wincing smile. She reminded herself to try to see the scrawny, shaggy-haired, emotionally vulnerable human being, rather than the tenuously stable fire-summoning pyrokinetic with the hypothetical destructive yield of a ten-kiloton nuclear bomb. "Everything okay?"

Victor scowled, jerking a thumb at the meeting room door. "What the hell do they expect me to do the next time some possessed bastard tries to kill me?"

"Person of dual consciousness," said Alison, before she could stop herself.

"Perthon of dual conthiouthneth," repeated Victor, with his tongue pressed to his teeth. "Seriously, what do I do? Ask a few probing questions to ascertain its position on the kill-all-humans issue in the three seconds before it bites my legs off?"

An unexpected wave of sympathy washed over Alison. She and Victor had recently encountered a person of dual consciousness that had come close to killing them both. Still, Alison was pretty sure that Jessica Weatherby–Shgshthx had been an outlier, even for the usual standards of people sharing their bodies with Ancients, the ancient godlike beings from another dimension.

Victor read her expression. "Yeah, remember the salt bitch? What do you think she'd have done if we'd stood around worrying about politics?"

"I . . . don't think politics mattered much to her," conceded Alison diplomatically, drawing a circle on the floor with one foot. "Unless wanting to kill lots of people counts as politics."

"What is even the bloody point of having a ministry for magical defense if it's just going to open the door to the next Ancient attack?"

Alison grimaced and quickly glanced around for anyone who might be listening. She was rarely one to openly disagree, but Victor's language was making her more uncomfortable by the second. In the age of smartphone surveillance, careless talk cost social lives. "Victor, there are loads of dual-consciousness people coming out now, and most of them are normal people who aren't trying to murder anyone."

"Oh. Right. Sorry. I guess I'm just making knee-jerk presumptions about Ancients based on an unrepresentative sample of every single sodding time I've ever had to deal with one."

"That's not true . . ."

He splayed out a pale, bony hand and counted off the fingers. "One, the salt bitch. Two, the shadow thing that tried to eat the country ten years ago. Three, oh, almost forgot, the one that lived in my head for my whole teens trying to convince me to melt everything fleshy. Hey, Adam!"

Adam Hesketh had just tottered out of the meeting room with his gaze locked firmly onto his phone. "Mm?"

"Adam, think about it. When was the last time we had to deal with an Ancient that didn't come across as even slightly kill-all-humans curious?"

"Yeah, probably," said Adam, not looking up.

Victor let out an angry sigh, letting his hands drop to his sides. Then his hands almost immediately came back again to gesture at Alison's face. "Remember I said all this."

He turned on his heel and began to stomp away, but stopped after a few yards, one boot hovering a foot above the floor. He peered over his shoulder and frowned at Adam, who hadn't moved an inch. "Adam?"

"Mm?"

"We going to lunch or what?"

Adam finally looked up, blinking in confusion, like a parakeet in the moment after the cover is yanked off its cage. "What? Oh. Sorry. I can't right now. I'm supposed to be meeting with the new team to go over all the outstanding cases. Don't you need to meet with your new team?"

Victor groped the outside of the coat pocket where he kept his phone. There was a distinct lack of vibration ensuing. "Apparently not," he spat.

"Oh," said Adam. "Well. Your work is probably a bit less . . ." His mouth tried in vain to shape the right word, and he struggled to avoid breaking eye contact as his phone vibrated yet again. "A bit less."

"Meaning?"

Adam finally succumbed to his new text. "Oh. Ugh. I really have to go now, actually. Mr. Badger wants to know when I can come down to the school and look over the students." He caught Alison's eye, gave an embarrassed shrug, then shuffled away.

Victor tapped his foot three times in a slow, measured fashion, then turned to Alison. "You want to get lunch?"

"Erm. I think I'm supposed to meet with Ms. Lawrence in a minute. It's that thing where I explain how our last assignment went. Debrief? Is that it?"

"Yes, that's what actual professionals call a debriefing," he said, nodding sarcastically. "Say no more. The Dread Pirate Pegleg says jump, so it's all hands on deck . . ."

He trailed off as he saw her expression change. She reddened, her eyebrows came together, and the corners of her mouth stretched out in an urgent grimace, so if her nose had been an exclamation mark she would have been doing a convincing impression of a triangular warning sign.

Elizabeth Lawrence wasn't physically built for looming over people, but nevertheless a shadow seemed to fall over Victor's face as he sensed the presence behind him. Slowly, carefully, like a minesweeper suspecting that the thing his foot just nudged might not have been a manhole cover after all, he looked around. And down.

"Mr. Casin," said Elizabeth, her walking stick rhythmically tapping the floor between them. "Go to lunch."

03

"Ms. Lawrence, Victor didn't mean anything," said Alison, one nano-second after the door of Elizabeth's office finished closing.

"Hm?" said Elizabeth, taking her seat.

"What Victor was saying? He—"

Elizabeth pinned Alison to her own seat with a look. Between her large, professional desk and high-backed executive chair, she looked like a lost baked bean peering out from between two sofa cushions, but the effect of her gaze was unmitigated. "Victor Casin is one of the most powerful magic users in the country," she said. "I can't imagine why he would think he has anything to fear from me."

She paused slightly, as she always did when she thought Alison needed a few seconds to digest the usual heavy dose of subtext in her words.

"Your last outing with Diablerie," Elizabeth said, jabbing a few keys on her laptop to bring up the relevant email. "Someone called the new emergency line and reported that magic rituals were being conducted on Tooting Bec Common at night. Diablerie was dispatched to make an assessment."

"Um, yes," confirmed Alison.

Elizabeth closed her laptop and got comfortable, letting her back muscles melt into the chair's cushioning. "Give me a detailed account of what happened."

"We left the Department in Diablerie's car at 7:17 p.m.," began Alison promptly, sitting up. "The drive took twenty-four minutes and eleven seconds, engine start to—"

"Please stick to the most relevant points on this occasion," interrupted Elizabeth, not unkindly.

Alison nodded. Working full time with other people, she had gradually come to understand that most people didn't have eidetic memories, but she was still having trouble grasping the nuances of what they meant when they asked for a "detailed account."

"We arrived after dark," she summarized. "Parked near the lake and continued on foot. We saw three people gathering in a patch of grass surrounded by trees . . ."

"How long did it take you to find them?" asked Elizabeth, brow furrowing slightly.

"Diablerie went straight there practically," said Alison, uncertainty slipping into her tone as she analyzed her own words. "I mean, he was doing that thing he calls 'channeling' where he holds one hand out and puts the other on his head and makes lots of silly noises with his lips, but I'm pretty sure he wasn't doing anything actually magic related."

"You don't say," droned Elizabeth. "The three people you saw?"

"They were wearing robes with hoods," said Alison. "They were standing in a circle in the middle of the clearing with their hoods low over their faces and their hands together. There was a bag on the floor between them, like a duffle bag. And they were chanting."

"What were they chanting?" As Alison's eyes rolled back and her mouth formed a narrow O, Elizabeth felt moved to add: "Just a general impression, please, don't repeat it."

"Well, they were all chanting different things," said Alison. "And they weren't repeating chants. It sounded a lot like Diablerie's chanting, actually, like they were making it up as they went along. I thought they might have been making fun of him, but they hadn't noticed us arrive."

"Did Diablerie intervene?"

"Not straightaway. They chanted for a while, then they stopped, and one of them kicked the duffle bag a few inches along the grass, and that was when Diablerie . . . intervened."

"What level of flamboyance?"

Alison winced in memory. "Probably up to a seven. It wasn't just a smoke bomb. He dropped one of his flashy ones as well, one that makes a big noise and sprays glitter everywhere. Then when everyone was looking he said, 'I am Diablerie, and I would know the nature of this magical mischief.'"

"And how did they respond to that? General impressions again."

"Well, they were shocked. The one on the left was terrified. The other two were more confused. Then the one who had been chanting the loudest said that they were devotees from the Cult of Bathorax, and they had come out to Tooting Bec Common to commune with their Ancient."

"Were they magically infused? Dual consciousness?"

"They all *looked* human," said Alison, faintly worried that her emphasis was insensitive in some way. "Diablerie asked what they wanted from their Ancient, specifically, on that occasion."

"I see."

"And then the middle one, not the frightened one, said that this was just a general worship-and-praise sort of situation and they hadn't thought that far ahead. Then the first one got quite aggressive and told us to leave them alone because we had interrupted their Holy Communion, which was blasphemy against Barothax."

"Barothax," said Elizabeth flatly.

"Yeah, that's when I pointed out they'd pronounced the name of their god two different ways. Then they went quiet for four seconds, and then the one who hadn't spoken yet, the one who looked scared, he made a sort of panicky noise . . ." She demonstrated.

"'Pleh'?" echoed Elizabeth.

"It was most like a 'pleh,' yes. He made that noise, and then tried to run. And after he did that, one of the other two tried to grab the duffle bag, but Diablerie was holding the bag down with his cane and they fell over when they tried to run away with it."

"And the contents of the bag?"

"Drugs," said Alison, with a little shrug. "Turns out it was just a drug deal. We called the local police and left them to it, really."

"The one that hadn't tried to run, didn't he give you trouble?"

"No . . . he surrendered. I think he got scared when the other person—the one who'd made the noise and tried to run first—ran into the invisible barrier and knocked himself out." There was an awkward pause. "Oh. Sorry. I thought that was one of the details to leave out. While we were watching them chant, Diablerie set up a couple of rune circles around the exits from the clearing that created invisible barriers. Then he sort of waved his hand and said, 'Fazoom,' like, at the exact moment the first guy ran into the wall. That was what frightened them."

Elizabeth frowned. "He set up rune circles? Openly? In front of you?"

"Yes. He told me to keep watch while he did it." She found herself mimicking Elizabeth's frown. "Isn't that good? It means we know he's still using runes."

"And he must know that we know." Elizabeth cradled her chin in her hand and thought aloud. "It disturbs me that he sees no need to hide it. He had a reason for hiding his use of rune magic from me. Now it appears that it no longer matters. Whatever his real agenda is, it appears to be progressing."

"I still wonder how he got his rune circles made," said Alison. "Since, you know, writing down runes usually makes people's brains explode."

"Not important," said Elizabeth brusquely, still lost in thought. "What matters more is the extent of what he can achieve with them."

Light depression settled on Alison's shoulders like a pair of fat gray slugs. Archibald Brooke-Stodgeley, the Department's senior researcher and resident doddering-uncle figure, had once said to her that an eidetic memory was a sign of incredible, almost superhuman, genius. He had probably meant it as a compliment, but if anything it had only highlighted how unlike a genius Alison felt.

She boggled at people like Elizabeth who could instantly zero in on the most important facts. To Alison, the facts, perfectly recalled as they were, were like three jumbled-together jigsaw puzzles with no edge pieces.

"Those drug dealers, the way they pretended to be Ancient worshipers," said Alison. "That's been happening more and more, hasn't it?"

Elizabeth caught her inquiring look and snapped out of her pondering. "Yes. The anti–extradimensional discrimination laws were rushed through and badly phrased. Certain kinds of opportunists have been exploiting them."

"Is that what the new Office of Skepticism is for?"

Elizabeth very nearly smiled. Alison might later have convinced herself she had imagined it if it weren't for the perfect-recall thing. "No, Alison, I very much doubt the Office of Skepticism will have much effect on anything."

"It won't?"

"You still have a very important role," added Elizabeth quickly. "Your continued monitoring of Diablerie will be all the more vital. Because when Diablerie is stuck in a position with little influence, he'll get frustrated. He'll make a play. Make a mistake."

"Oh," said Alison, trying to sound convinced.

The fat gray slugs of depression on her shoulders gained a few pounds. Back in the meeting, after hearing about the Office of Skepticism, Alison had had a vision of herself in dark glasses, confidently crossing the perimeter of a crime scene. She imagined a uniformed police officer trying to stop her, and her pace not slowing as she flashed an ID badge and said, "Arkin. Office of Skepticism," in a tone of voice implying that the conversation had begun and ended in those four words. It had been an empowering thought. Now, she felt stupid.

There was no doubt in her mind that Elizabeth was right about Doctor Diablerie having a secret agenda, possibly a dangerous one. After all, this was a man who dressed like a Victorian-era stage magician, spoke in melodramatic pseudomagical nonsense, and put more effort into feigning incompetence than most people put into the things they were actually good at, and no one with entirely harmless intentions would devote that much energy to obfuscating them. But she also wanted to make a difference, and it was hard to think that Diablerie could be more of a threat than half of what the Department had to deal with most days.

She tried to resist it, but the memory of Jessica Weatherby–Shgshthx and their—for want of a better phrase—fight to the death on the beach rose to prominence in her mind. She didn't want to think about that, because then she would have to think about how Diablerie had technically kinda-sorta saved her life.

"But, the new law they're voting on today," she said. "Isn't that supposed to . . ."

"It isn't going to pass," said Elizabeth bluntly. "It's even broader and more exploitable than the existing law. The government will . . ."

She paused and looked Alison up and down. The girl was, by now, sitting with her spine practically curving ninety degrees, and was looking at the floor as if she was expecting it to split open and devour her, and wouldn't blame it if it did.

Elizabeth sat forward and clasped her hands before her. "Alison. I'm being honest with you, and you've been honest with me. You remember our deal." It wasn't a question. "Since you're doing your part, anything you want to know about the Department, its history, its operations, I will tell you to the best of my ability."

Alison perked up, but the question at the top of her mind froze on its way down to her tongue. Even with Elizabeth putting on her approachable face, it was a question Alison wasn't sure she had the courage to ask.

"What would you like to know?" prompted Elizabeth as the silence drew on, Alison's jaw hanging like the handset of an old-fashioned phone left off the hook. "Ask anything."

Alison took a deep breath, finally deciding that enough things had disappointed her that day, and she didn't want to add herself to the list. "Ms. Lawrence," she said, "what's the history between you and Doctor Diablerie?"

Elizabeth's approachable face froze, and her two index fingers unfolded from her clasped hands like the questing feelers of a spider. "Anything at all," she said, tightly.

Alison rested the tips of her fingers on the edge of the desk, as if it were the first handhold of a long climb. "I know that you and he have been working for the Ministry since before anyone else. And I know you suspect him because . . . well, because he's really suspicious, obviously, but I think you have other reasons." She scrutinized Elizabeth's unblinking face. "You did say anything."

"I know, Alison, I know." She broke eye contact as her index fingers tapped gently together. "But I may need more notice to prepare my answer to that question. In the meantime, is there any other information I could satisfy you with for now?"

"Oh," said Alison, with a little start. She had been briefly mesmerized by the older woman's rare display of uncertainty. "Um. How about the shadow thing?"

"Hm?"

"The thing ten years ago, when the skies went dark for a few days? They told everyone it was a volcanic ash cloud, but Adam told me it was actually—"

"Ah yes," said Elizabeth, a fresh coat of unpleasant memories fluttering across her expression. "That would be easy. You should certainly be brought up to speed on that story. Anything else?"

As she mentally sorted her priorities, Alison's gaze couldn't help falling upon Elizabeth's walking cane, still leaning against the armrest of her chair. Here came a question that Alison could only ever have asked now, while dizzy drunk on a heady mixture of imagined power, despair, curiosity, and encouragement. "I've been wondering . . . if I could ask . . . what happened to your leg."

Elizabeth followed her gaze to the handle of the cane, and this time, allowed herself to smile properly. A small, sad smile, born partly of the relief that might be felt by an overworked mother when one of her children offers to carry one of the shopping bags from the car.

"That is even easier," she said, before meeting Alison's stare. "Because it's the same story."

She mulled things over for a few more seconds, jaw moving as if physically testing the words, then opened her mouth to speak again.

A hubbub suddenly rose in the corridor outside, and both women turned to look at the door. Through the frosted glass, they could see indistinct heads peering from cubicles like bubbles of marsh gas. Several phones started ringing. Something Nita Pavani shaped ran past, emitting a prolonged high-pitched squeal like a flatlining heart monitor.

Alison and Elizabeth exchanged a baffled look, and at that moment, Richard Danvers appeared, knocking twice on the door's glass before opening it without waiting for a reply. He was wearing his typical work-wear—no jacket, tie askew, sleeves rolled up, thin layer of sweat.

"It passed," he said.

"It what?" said Elizabeth.

"It passed."

"What passed?" asked Alison.

"*It* did," said Richard and Elizabeth together.

Excerpt from the Extradimensional Appropriation Act:

2. False claim of extradimensional ability or effect

(1) It is an offense for any Person to attempt to profit from any false claim that they or any Entity they claim to own or associate with are in possession of extradimensional capabilities, or that any extradimensional incident or effect was caused or influenced by an unrelated Entity.

(2) In paragraph (1): "Person" refers to:

I.   Any individual human, male, female, or gender neutral;

II.   Any fluidic or other sentient nonhuman individual;

III.   Any incorporated entity composed of multiple individuals, including corporations, partnerships, and hive minds.

(3) In paragraph (1): "Entity" refers to:

I.   Any Person as defined by paragraph (2);

II.   Any animate being, including animals, artificial intelligences, and enchanted furniture;

III.   Any inanimate object;

IV.   Any intangible matter, including: thoughts, dreams, noncorporeal beings, or any Entity as defined above made intangible by virtue of being confined to extradimensional territories other than our own plane of existence (as defined in section 5), real or imagined.

(4) In paragraph (1): "Profit" refers to the acquisition of any kind of material or nonmaterial gain acquired in exchange for the alleged extradimensional service, entity, or any associated peace of mind or benefit, including:

I.   Physical or digital currency;

II.   Goods or services;

III.   Any increase in reputation or esteem in the eyes of another Person as defined in paragraph (2), real or imagined;

IV.   Any kind of legal defense or alibi;

V.   Any promise of hypothetical future assets, such as firstborn children.

THE NEXT MORNING

04

Adam Hesketh was no stranger to death. In the years before declassification, when the Department of Extradimensional Affairs had still been a secret and called the Ministry of Occultism, he'd had to deal with many of his fellow agents dying at the hands of one magical being or another, and he and Victor had barely been out of high school, at first.

So as he entered the church where the funeral service of William Shaw was being held, and he felt the strange looks he was attracting from the collected mourners, he wondered—not for the first time—if his experiences had given him an unusual attitude about death. He had consciously made the effort to dress entirely in black, including his black jeans and blackest Slayer T-shirt, and he still felt he was blending in about as well as a giraffe in a crowded cinema.

He quietly took a seat in an unoccupied pew near the back and, after letting the droning voice of the skinny vicar wash over him for a few moments, decided to go over the case file on his phone again.

William Shaw had been found dead in someone's front garden in Worcester, and despite being only twenty-six, he had had the body of a ninety-year-old, with the cause of death listed as old age. The local police strongly suspected extradimensional influence, but their small detachment of extradimensional investigators hadn't been able to confirm that, mainly because they lacked any agents with the supernatural ability to sense magic.

Hence Adam's presence. Adam had already switched on his "special vision," and sure enough there were telltale pink wisps floating around the coffin, indicating as much as he would have expected—that the body within had been the victim of vampiric magic. If the body had been fresher, and if Adam could have gotten closer, he might have been able to divine some other details, and possibly even recognize the perpetrator's handiwork if they struck again. But that wasn't possible, because in the time it had taken for the local police to admit they needed help, and for Adam to get around to the case, the family had kicked up enough of a stink to get the body released from the morgue.

Adam switched to his messaging app and thumbed out a reply to Sumner, the member of the Investigations team who was in charge of this case. *At funeral. Definite vampire traces. Need fresher body for more information.*

While he waited for Sumner to reply, he thought about the vampires he and Victor had dealt with in the past. Mostly possessed animals, but not always. He thought of Rachel Grice, who had manifested vampiric powers in a big way before agents could get her to the Ministry's magic training school in Devonshire, and who had ended up getting possessed. He had used his senses to track her down to an old farmyard, and Victor had blasted her until no trace remained but a slightly greasy sheen on a combine harvester.

She had been as hostile as they come, but he now had to wonder. If that had happened today, now that dual-consciousness persons had rights and official policy was no longer to kill or forcibly separate, maybe there would have been room for negotiation. Maybe a lot of people would be alive today, on account of not having been killed. By him.

He felt wretched. Then he felt good about feeling wretched, because that was definitely in line with how you were supposed to feel at funerals. He glanced around to see if anyone had noticed his developing funeral prowess.

Sadly, at that moment, Sumner replied to his text, and the alert sound drew a few more dirty looks. Adam had even made the effort to replace the default text alert sound with that of a sonorous bell ringing. It definitely felt as if everyone else in the world had gotten a different memo regarding this whole mourning thing.

That was all I needed, read Sumner's text. *Will come down to investigate tomorrow. You can come back.* After a few moments of staring at the words, a second message popped up. *Good job!*

Adam pouted, letting his hands drop into his lap. There it was again. The feeling that he was being left out. The other members of the Investigations division were always very welcoming every time he entered the office, with the forced smiles and awkward stances of schoolchildren who have been asked to welcome a special-needs student.

And he knew exactly why. Because they didn't see him as an equal. They saw him as the fragile receptacle for a mind-bogglingly useful magic power, and intended to handle him as gingerly as possible so they could keep enjoying the benefits.

He could hardly blame them. For almost his entire career, Adam's role had been to act as a targeting system for the human drone strike that was Victor Casin. But he was determined to prove that he had a lot more to offer. He had no intention of coming straight back to the Investigations office yet. He was going to investigate.

To that end, he waited a dreary hour for the service to end, and then held back as a queue of mourners lined up at the church entrance to take turns saying a few comforting words to the two people who could only have been William Shaw's parents. The father was tall and rigid, with a dusting of silver stubble on a face like a stone slab, standing with hands clasped loosely before him and offering only token nods to the mourners as they passed. The mother was short and round, and every hand she was offered to shake she clutched with trembling gratitude. She was holding a handkerchief to her pink face that she had been steadily loading with tears and mucus to the point that Adam was sure it would stay there if she took her hand away.

Inadvertently, Adam found himself swept up into the informal queue as the last few dregs of mourners were being filtered through the doors, and then being presented before the grieving parents ahead of a small pack of distant cousins or neighbors who were occupied with discussing their lunch plans. Before Adam knew what was happening, he felt a moist hand encasing his.

"Um, s-sorry for your loss," he said, struggling a moment to recall the phrase.

"Bubba lubber gubber du woo," acknowledged Mrs. Shaw, through wet, vibrating lips.

"Um!" added Adam as he felt himself being gently pushed along the human conveyor belt. "Actually. My name's Adam Hesketh. I'm a . . . special agent for the Department of Extradimensional Affairs. Could I ask a couple of things about your son?"

"Buh hurber du gunnu huh?"

"We spoke to the police already," said the father gruffly, laying out his words like bricks in an impassable wall. "We'll tell you what we told them. We don't know where he went that night, and last we saw him he weren't ninety years old."

"Okay," said Adam. The next person in line was already extending a hand to shake. He was getting pushed along like a sack of oranges at the supermarket checkout. "Could I just ask . . . if . . . he'd made any new friends lately? Taken up any new interests?"

"Oh yeah," said the father, now shouting at him over the heads of the group of mourners currently being acknowledged. "Go hassle them Internet Miracle types. Much good it'll do."

With those perplexing words, both parents very determinedly forgot about Adam's existence entirely. He drifted out into the churchyard, where he joined the dissipating crowd of mourners that were still milling around, uncertain of how long they needed to remain visible before it would be socially acceptable to head off and get on with their day.

The various family and friend groups clumped together and closed ranks through a complex series of subtle unspoken movements, and Adam was gently shunned. Drifting through the swarm of indifference, he found himself naturally gravitating to the side of the other odd man out: the vicar. The two of them stood side by side, casting overseeing eyes upon the masses.

"Did I hear you say you're from the Department of Extradimensional Affairs?" asked the vicar softly, steadily picking his way through the awkward string of syllables. He was a thin man with a prematurely white bristle of upward-pointing hair and eyebrows permanently raised in polite interest, giving him the air of a man who had been recently electrocuted but didn't want to kick up too much of a fuss about it.

"Yes," said Adam, glad of the human contact. "Special investigator. Did you know the deceased?"

"Oh, I'm afraid not. It seemed like a very grim business, though. It must be jolly interesting work."

"I suppose," muttered Adam gloomily.

"I was reading about the new law, the X-Appropriation Act?" Again, he took the time to make sure he pronounced every syllable, eyes searching Adam's face for any sign of disapproval. "I think it's a wonderful step."

"Really," said Adam, trying to not sound interested, apparently in vain.

"Oh, I know you think that sounds strange, hearing it from me." He fiddled pointedly with his dog collar. "But you might be surprised by how up on current thinking the modern church is. I had a parishioner,

Mrs. Klebold; she was totally taken in by one of those fake psychics. Paid thousands of pounds for energy crystals to save her from extradimensional forces. Turned out to be rock salt."

"Salt does actually work on some things," muttered Adam.

"Well, this is why we need experts like you, I suppose. It's just nice to see something being done about those terrible people out there who want to frighten us into believing some nonsense so they can exploit people and tell them what to do. I really think the church could be doing so much more to help with that."

Adam had been visually scanning the churchyard, looking for Shaw's parents to see if he could grab them in a less distracted moment, but they were nowhere to be seen. Perhaps they had gone inside the church to do whatever the funeral equivalent of signing the marriage certificate was. Or they had snuck out the churchyard through the back to avoid the crowd. Either way, he resigned himself unhappily to the fact that he had done all the investigating he was likely to get done.

"Don't suppose you know what 'Internet Miracle types' might be referring to?" he asked.

The vicar blinked a few times, his smile unchanging. "I'm not sure. But it really is a miracle, isn't it? Just yesterday my nephew was showing me this delightful video of a young man attempting to eat seven Creme Eggs in less than a minute." He shook his head happily. "Truly, the good Lord has blessed us with an age of wonders."

THE FOLLOWING EVENING

05

Alison Arkin pushed open the door to the new Office of Skepticism, and took a moment to examine the room beyond. This did not take very long. Standing there in the entrance, she was using up about a quarter of the available floor space.

The office was buried in the middle of the ground floor of the building, in the bureaucratic no man's land where the space designated for Extradimensional Affairs blurred with the borders of the Department of Business. The room was a windowless cube whose bright fluorescent ceiling light gave its solitary desk the air of a gallows platform at high noon.

Alison made a token effort to brush the dust off the desktop, but after one swipe her arm was so caked with it that she realized she wasn't so much cleaning as taking the dust for a ride. She released a sigh and flopped into the hard metal chair.

It seemed that Elizabeth's plan to isolate and frustrate Diablerie was still in action; even now the new law meant that the most she could do was deny him a nice chair in which to sit. The Department's official skepticism officers now essentially had the power to arrest anyone they felt particularly skeptical about.

Alison had briefly been pleased that her and Diablerie's new roles could actually be effective, until she had seen the dire look on Elizabeth's face, and things never turned out well when Elizabeth's emotions rose above the usual flat line. Even without knowing Diablerie's history, Alison had a clear sense that he could be trusted with power as much as one could trust a naughty dog with a string of sausages.

It was possible that Diablerie didn't know about any of the recent developments. The niceties of newly enacted parliamentary legislation might take a while to penetrate his weird bubble of delusion, which might at least limit the damage he could cause. She had only come here to confirm the meagerness of the facilities they had been assigned. There was nothing else to do until she could return with a vacuum cleaner. She opened the door to leave, and found Doctor Diablerie standing right there in the hallway.

Alison's hope that he might not have learned the full extent of his new powers was immediately dashed. He was wearing his top hat at its most rakish angle, which was always a sign that he was in his best possible mood.

But it was the expression on his face that removed all remaining doubt. Or more accurately, the fact that he was revealing the expression on his face and not walking around with his cape covering all but his eyes. His smirk combined with his thin mustache looked like stark black arrows pointing to his ears.

"Ah, girl," he said with relish. As ever, Alison was only partly certain that he remembered what her real name was. "Excellent timing. Your calling in life awaits. Diablerie requires his assistant."

"He does?" asked Alison innocently. "What for?"

He cut short his dramatic, thoughtful stare into the middle distance and gave her a look of mock affront, letting his cape billow around him. "Have you not heard? Do you young people never emerge from your bubble of Beatlemania and malt shops? Diablerie has been judged worthy of a most vital task. Diablerie is to shine his terrible light upon the charlatans that scavenge in the wastelands at the fringes of Eternity. To finger their hidey-holes until they squeal for succor."

That was that, then. "Oh yeah," said Alison. "I think I heard something about that."

"Then we must make haste!" He took a step back and pointed smartly down the hall, causing his flowing cape to hit a passing civil servant in the face. "To the place of transference!"

Alison followed the pointed finger. It seemed to be indicating the elevators. "Do you mean the car park?"

"Yes, I mean the car park," said Diablerie quickly, not moving.

"But . . . we don't have any assignments at the moment."

"Pah!" A single droplet of spittle fired across the hall with the force of a bullet, seriously upsetting the passing civil servant who was still trying to gather the armload of papers he had dropped. "The hawk needs not the blessing of any master to begin the hunt for scurrying mice. And Diablerie has had the scent of vermin for some time."

"Really?" said Alison, suddenly interested.

"Yes! Servants of ignorance, dancing their provocative dances before Diablerie's stony glare, assured of their safety while Diablerie is bound by the laws of Man." He waggled his eyebrows. "The time is nigh to unleash the fury of righteousness."

Alison followed as he half strode, half jogged away, one pointed finger held aloft. It was just possible that Elizabeth's plan was working in ways she hadn't anticipated. She had assumed that frustrating Diablerie was the key to getting him to play his hand, but it seemed that making him drunk on fresh power might be achieving that result a lot faster.

Elizabeth had a habit of taking the slower, more considered option, Alison realized, possibly to a fault. When the Department had still been called the Ministry of Occultism, it was ostensibly run by the Hand of Merlin, a group of aristocratic old men who liked pretending to be wizards. Elizabeth, as their chief underling, had spent ten years gradually persuading them to modernize. That was until magic had been forced to go public, at which point the man from Downing Street achieved the same result inside a week by kicking in the door, swearing a lot, and throwing the Hand of Merlin out a figurative window.

Admittedly the sudden change had been rather traumatic for the staff and for various other people, and Alison had to remind herself of that. It was hard not to get swept up in Diablerie's excitement as he hurried down the stairwell three steps at a time, having once again refused to do anything so mundane as ride down in the lift.

By the time they burst into the car park, Diablerie was at a full sprint, his cape fluttering behind him like the wings of a diving bird of prey. He vaulted over the door and into the back seat of his open-top car. Alison tried to follow suit, swept up in the high of feeling like Batman and Robin, until she banged her ankle on the car's wing mirror and lost faith in the attempt. She sheepishly opened the door and slid into the driver's seat under Diablerie's withering glare.

"Where are we going?" she asked, gripping the steering wheel. Diablerie never drove if he could help it, or did any other manual task that meant he couldn't use his hands to make dramatic gestures throughout.

"To the serpents' nest," he declared, sitting back and placing his hands to his temples. "Our destiny awaits within the arms of the Builders."

"Right." She gunned the engine, then let her hand hover awkwardly over the satnav interface for a moment. "But, you know, in terms of number and street name?"

Diablerie didn't reply. He was "channeling" again, closing his eyes, holding his palms either side of his face, and making a prolonged braying sound with his lips. On a hunch, she tried keying in the words *serpents*, *nest*, *arms*, and *builders*. A few false starts later, she discovered that the Builder's Arms was the name of a pub in London's West End, one that appeared in the list of recent destinations.

She set off, pulling out of the car park and into the streets of London, where the slow drift into evening was just beginning to turn the shadows long and stringy. As the distance between them and the Department grew, Diablerie's gibberish became less hearty as he realized that Alison was concentrating on the road and not paying much attention.

"So, in this new Age of Awakening, as magic clumps, cheap mascara–like, upon the eyelashes of the world, our masters in government would seek to strengthen the border between the realm of that which Is and that which Can-Never-Be," he said eventually. "And Diablerie is appointed the champion that shall guard the wall."

The fact that Diablerie was actively trying to initiate conversation pointed to just how gigglingly excited he must have been. "Er, yeah," said Alison. "It's funny."

Diablerie's defiant smirk faded instantly as he locked his gaze onto Alison through the rearview mirror. "Why is it funny?"

"Erm, you know," stammered Alison, caught off guard. "It's funny that they chose you for the Office of Skepticism. Of all people."

His eyes narrowed. "And pray, what do you mean by that?"

Alison coughed. "Nothing. I was just thinking, the job is to debunk fake psychics and stuff and . . ." A keener instinct than the one she had been allowing to speak thus far kicked in and her words died, leaving her mute and with hands splayed over the steering wheel in a frozen placatory gesture.

"Your inarticulate blitherings are as chaff upon stony ground," growled Diablerie, his upbeat mood vanishing by the moment. "But I read from your aura the sense that you struggle to associate the figure of Diablerie with the concept of incredulity. Would that be so?"

"I . . . genuinely don't know what you mean."

Diablerie snorted. "Rest assured, girl, Diablerie's grip on reality is as firm as any man's. I am assured of such by my daily tarot."

Alison tapped her fingers against the steering wheel a few times. "Do you think these red lights are taking longer than they used to?"

MEANWHILE

06

At the same time that Alison and Diablerie were making their way to the West End, Adam Hesketh and Victor Casin were being transported to a destination neither was entirely clear on in an old police van that had been refitted for use by the Department of Extradimensional Affairs. The process of this refitting had largely involved putting purple tape over the recognizable parts.

"You know what 'Internet Miracle' is?" asked Adam.

Victor had been sitting with arms folded and his head to one side, his cheek resting on the cool metal of the van's interior. In reply, he slowly let his head rotate and flop into withering eye contact. "No, I don't know. Tell me all about it."

"I don't know either. I was hoping you would. It might help an investigation I'm doing."

"Oh." Victor rested his face on the wall again. "Well. Why don't you ask all your amazing new friends in the Hinvestigations Hoffice. I'm sure they'd be much better qualified."

"I did," said Adam. "They said I shouldn't worry about it."

Victor whistled. "They really are a smart bunch."

Adam sighed, and let a few minutes pass in silence, listening to the van's engine and letting the warm atmosphere of convivial reunion between two old friends continue failing to occur. "So. You handling your missions all right by yourself?"

Victor didn't look at him. "I'll let you know when they give me one."

"Oh. They not keeping you busy?"

"No, they are not. I've spent the last three days in the cafeteria beating all my *Joogie Bounce* high scores."

"Oh." Adam stared at his feet knocking together. "Still, you're on a mission now."

"Yeah. Remind me where we're going?"

Adam referred to the printout he had been handed on his way into the van. "Some kind of warehouse in the docklands. Destructive magic in use. Perpetrator unknown and still on the scene. Situation not secure. Not much detail. Apparently the phone call to the emergency line was a bit panicky before it cut off."

Victor punched his palm with slow deliberation, letting a little wisp of orange flame escape. "Right then."

"Standard procedure for unknown threats. Locate, identify, if necessary pacify."

"I know. I know. The usual. LIP."

"L, I, and *if necessary*, P."

"Not quite as snappy, now, is it. Come on. We've been sent after this sort of thing millions of times, right?"

"I guess."

"So what's with the babysitters' club?"

Adam followed Victor's glare in the direction of the van's front, where Agents Rawlins and Black from the Investigations Office were taking care of the business of driving and navigating, respectively. "You know why," he said.

"Assume I don't."

Adam sighed. "Because this could be a human with a dual consciousness. And the more people we have on the ground, the more likely we can keep things under control."

"You mean keep *me* under control," said Victor sulkily.

"Look, you don't need to take it personally. The Department's making everyone roll back the extreme force. They want to avoid another media pile-on like what Alison got last time."

Victor cocked his head, a wistful expression crossing his face for a moment. "That was classic, wasn't it. We spent years and years killing hundreds and hundreds of monsters before magic went public, and the very first time a stink is raised, the new girl gets all the blame." He shook his head. "Funniest shit."

"Didn't you almost die?"

"Almost died of boredom, yesterday." Victor bowed his head and folded his arms, then glared at Adam through his shaggy fringe. "While you were out doing investigations and getting pats on the head for being a good boy . . ."

Adam was pinching his eyes. "Victor, what exactly do you want me to say? I'm sorry that you haven't had a chance to kill anything lately?"

Victor held out both hands and delivered his words slowly and measuredly as he felt his irritation—and, relatedly, the ambient temperature—rise. "I. Am capable. Of more than just killing things."

"Like what?" said Adam. Then, as Victor pressed his lips together to pronounce an *m*, he quickly added: "And don't say maiming things. Or traumatizing them in any way."

The awkward silence that followed ended when the van pulled to a halt, making both men rock sideways like a pair of oil pumps. "We're here," said Rawlins, punctuating his statement with a yank on the hand brake.

Adam and Victor emerged into the docklands around Tilbury, in the middle of a flat expanse of concrete where a scattering of large cargo containers didn't so much break up the emptiness of the scenery as highlight it.

A warehouse with a slanted roof hugged the area to the north like a gigantic hibernating bear slumped forward on all fours, a mountainous black silhouette against the darkening evening sky. The four men began to walk tentatively across the concrete toward the steel double doors of the entrance.

"It's quiet," said Rawlins. The only sound was the gentle sloshing of the river Thames from just over the horizon.

"There's traces everywhere," said Adam, squinting as he applied his special vision to the building's entire frontage. "It's like a frozen ticker tape parade. Someone or something has definitely been throwing a lot of dangerous magic around recently."

"No bodies," added Rawlins, who had acquired a reputation for terseness among his peers that he now felt somewhat pressured to live up to.

"Yeah, that's a bit weird," said Black. "Maybe the local authorities got things under control?"

"Ha!" barked Victor. "Good thinking, Black. Defuse the tension with a joke." He looked to Adam. "What sort of dangerous magic is it, anyway?"

"Um."

As if in reply, a shattering BOOM rang out that made all four men simultaneously drop into crouches. An elongated orange fireball emerged from one of the upper windows like the unfurling tongue of a hungry beast. A moment later, a brief shower of small glass fragments made the agents cringe in an attempt to will themselves thinner.

Adam waited until the last tinkle of falling glass faded away into the silence. "Um. Pyrokinesis," he said.

"Victor, maybe you should take the lead," said Black, not rising from his crouch.

Victor turned a slightly manic smile on him. "Aren't you supposed to be trying to talk to them at this point? Isn't that the policy now?"

"So talk to them," said Black. "You're pyrokinetic too. That's a conversation starter."

"Oh sure. I'll just flash my club membership card." Victor stepped gingerly through the broken glass and pressed himself against one of the double doors, preparing to push them open with one hand while readying a fierce orange glow in his other. He glanced back at Adam, who hadn't moved. "Got their position?"

Adam threw several glances of his special vision around, looking like a nervous hen trying to remember where it had laid its eggs that morning. "They're a ways inside the building. Door should be clear."

Victor pushed the door. The heavy metal only moved a couple of inches, but it was enough to spill a line of illumination from the building's watery exterior lights across a stack of nondescript cardboard boxes. They were, all things considered, probably not hostile.

"Hello?" called Victor. "Department of Extradimensional Affairs!" Silence. "I'm not going to hurt you. They say I can't anymore, so I genuinely mean it this time."

"Victor!" hissed Adam.

"There's no one around. I'm going in." Victor turned back to the door. "I'm coming in!"

He pushed the door open the necessary two or three inches to admit his skinny form, and inched through the gap with his glowing hand forward. Partly to illuminate the room beyond, partly to give any waiting ambushers second thoughts.

The stack of boxes he had seen earlier was actually an entire wall of boxes running parallel to the door, obscuring most of the warehouse's interior. Victor glanced left and right, but the light from his glowing hand couldn't penetrate more than a few yards of the dusty black. He took a more confident step into the building.

"Careful," said Rawlins.

"Oh, suck it up, Team Courage," said Victor, with withering spite. "Adam already said they're a ways inside."

"Yeah," said Adam. "But they might still have set up a—"

A metallic crash to Victor's left made him jump, and he instinctively projected flame in that direction. The corner of the warehouse was bathed in orange, illuminating an extremely unsteady stack of corrugated metal pieces and scaffolding poles for just long enough to reveal that it was in the process of toppling over.

Victor flung himself against the wall of cardboard boxes as the pile of rusty metal clattered to the ground with an aural catastrophe, an ear-splitting wall of groans and clangs that clenched every sphincter within a fifty-yard radius. When the last metal object had tinkled into place and Victor finally unscrewed his eyelids, he found the door being firmly held closed by several tons of scrap, cutting him off from his allies outside.

"Trap," he muttered.

07

Alison had certain associations with the word *pub*. Especially pubs with names like the Builder's Arms. It came of having grown up in a house where the adults had an insatiable appetite for banal teatime detective shows set in country villages, and a permanent death grip on the television remote. She pictured mock Tudor, wooden shingles, and a bartender who wore braces and was forever behind on keeping his glassware polished.

Absolutely none of which was the case with the Builder's Arms, whose car park she found herself pulling into. It was a brutal concrete building on the blurring border between an expanding commercial district and a run-down industrial zone for some kind of heavy concern that must have fallen out of favor in more environmentally conscious times. Some modernish black windows had been installed in the frontage to give a more welcoming vibe, but they clashed somewhat with the heavy entrance doors, which would have looked more appropriate admitting clusters of hard hats than the evening hipster crowd.

The effect was only barely reduced by the neon sign above the door, which read "The Builder's Arms" in a flowing cursive style, alongside a piece of imagery that Alison found utterly baffling, until she realized that it was supposed to be a flexing muscular arm. For a moment she had thought it was an advertisement for fried chicken.

Diablerie had regained his cheerful mood over the course of the mostly silent car journey. He even opened his car door himself and posed briefly under a streetlight before confidently sauntering toward the main doors like a traffic policeman approaching the window of a pulled-over motorist.

Then, just a few yards from the entrance, he lifted one foot, spun smartly on the other, and began heading to the side of the building. Alison watched him, confused, then noticed a prominent poster in the window near the door.

"Amateur Magic Night at the Builder's Arms!" it read, in lurid pink text surrounded by white stars. "See the latest new magic in a showcase of up-and-coming talent!"

Alison might not have had much faith in her deductive abilities, but she knew even before checking that the date at the bottom of the poster was that day's date. She felt a complex blend of disappointment and fore-boding, as if she had just witnessed a single baby spider emerge from the wrapping of an unusually weighty Christmas gift.

Meanwhile, Diablerie had traffic-police-sauntered all the way to the side door of the venue, onto which someone had airbrushed a large star. Its intended effect was fighting a losing battle with the smell rising from the nearby drains and dustbins.

Diablerie rapped his knuckles three times upon the door, then took a step back, clasping his hands behind him. An impish smile was fixed upon his face.

The door opened to reveal a thin man wearing large spectacles, a cream-colored shirt, and a matching pair of trousers that seemed, to Alison's eyes, to have been pulled up alarmingly high. He froze for a second at the sight of Diablerie, then threw out his hands and put on an impressively convincing show of delight.

"Doctor Diablerie! I haven't seen you in so long!" he exclaimed. He shifted forward uncertainly, trying to gauge if this was a hug situation, and rebounded off Diablerie's glare. "Super, super good to see you. Agh, it's such a pain, if only you'd warned us, we could have left a slot open for you, but the whole evening is booked up . . ."

"Fret not, *Terence*," boomed Diablerie, pronouncing the man's name as if he were disdainfully biting the end off a cigar. "Diablerie has no intention of sharing the mysteries of the inner realms this night."

"Oh, good," breathed Terence, before tensing up again. "I mean, oh dear, that is a shame. You've got a super, super act. It's . . ." He made an indistinct shape with his hands as he sought the right word. "Super. But the audience, bless them, have never really . . . got it, have they?"

"That is of no concern," said Diablerie, gathering up his cape. "My companion and I are present tonight only as observers."

Terence stared at Alison over Diablerie's shoulder, then looked back to Diablerie, his mouth going through a little ballet of pouts and confused smiles, as if he was having to reassess certain things. "Oh, of course. Super. Thank you so much for taking the time to say hello first." He pointed vaguely toward the front of the building, already preparing to shut the door with his other hand. "If you could just go in the front entrance, there are plenty of seats, and I'll ask Jenny to—"

"Yes, observers," clarified Diablerie at the top of his voice. "In our capacity as skepticism officers for the Department of Extradimensional Affairs."

"Oh?" said Terence, feigning interest, already going through the motions of closing the door. But then Diablerie's words seemed to sink in, and he froze, his face still smiling desperately in the middle of the eight-inch gap. "Oh."

"Yes, I'm sure you have been made aware of the new legislation that empowers us," continued Diablerie, rocking back and forth on his heels with an undisguised glee that Alison had never seen in him before. "And I'm sure that a fine hostelry such as this is not enabling any activity that might earn the ire of justice."

"Um, no, of course not," said Terence. The door he was holding began to wobble back and forth rapidly. "As I say, front entrance, talk to Jenny, super to see you, goodbye." The door snapped shut. Diablerie turned around slowly, to give Alison the full effect of the smirk that had unfolded across his face.

"What are we actually doing here, Doctor?" asked Alison flatly.

The smirk widened. "Nothing more nor less than our sacred duty to the rule of law, my girl. Come! Let us find a suitably foreboding corner in which to lurk."

08

The moment Victor realized that he was cut off from his colleagues, all hell began breaking loose outside. Great roars and hisses swept through the building, chasing the silence to the furthest corners as flashes of orange and yellow lit up the murky glass of the unwashed windows.

Victor hurried over to one and rubbed a clear circle out of the grime just in time to see Adam and the others sprinting behind the nearest cargo container, pursued by tongues of fire that moved like caffeinated snakes. After the three of them were out of sight, the deluge of fire halted. An indistinct head peered around the corner—Victor couldn't make out whose—and an extremely precise blast of fire lasered out and splattered into sparks on the corrugated metal mere inches away. The head ducked back out of view.

Silence fell again, but for the slightly festive crackling of distant burning debris. Victor leaned back. This had all rather conclusively removed the possibility of this being a possessed animal. Something sentient was acting very deliberately here.

The pyrokinetic power he'd seen on display so far had already told him he was dealing with a heavy hitter. Possibly as powerful as him, which suggested a demonic possession (Victor was loath to use the phrase "dual consciousness" even in his internal thoughts). And if they were as powerful as Victor, then they could have melted straight through that cargo container even at this distance. Which meant they weren't trying to kill the others, just hold them back. Because whatever they were intending was intended for Victor alone.

He struggled to think. It was always a lurch for Victor, being in a situation where his powers didn't immediately outclass everything else in the room. Suddenly having to formulate a clever strategy was like being tasked to complete a coloring book with a paint roller.

Now that the fireworks had stopped, Victor's eyes were adjusting to the gloom. There was no one around, but the ceiling was flat, rather than angled, like the roof. Therefore, there was an upper level. That must have been where the suspect was throwing magic from. Ergo, locate a staircase. He nodded to himself. Solid strategizing. Focus on one thing at a time; that was the trick. He headed into the maze of boxes, holding out his glowing hand.

Victor himself had no explanation for why his level of power was so high. It might have been because he had started young. His fire had first manifested at the age of eleven, on that fateful night when his family had been staying with Uncle Jim and Auntie Val and the young, hormonal Victor had stumbled upon Jim's collection of vintage *Playboys*.

The boxes were laid out like a maze, possibly intentionally, but after a few turns Victor spotted a set of metal steps leading up to a mezzanine overhead. He was squeezing himself halfway through a narrow gap between boxes to get to it when there was another lash of magical fire at the front of the building, bathing the warehouse's interior in orange again. Presumably Adam and the others were still being kept at bay.

Victor placed a hand on the steps. He could already see that the mezzanine led to the upper level of the warehouse's front section, where the hostile pyrokinetic was almost certainly waiting for him. Blundering into line of sight didn't strike Victor as wise, since he was clearly expected, but his enemy probably couldn't watch him and the agents outside at the same time. Victor crouched and hugged the steps, waiting to scamper up them the moment he heard another magical blast. He felt the heat throbbing in his palms in anticipation.

It was doubly strange that Victor's power outclassed even demonically possessed pyrokinetics. He had never succumbed to Ifrig, the Ancient from which his power derived, even for a moment. He had been fighting to block its malevolent voice out of his head even before the Ministry's magic school took him in and showed him the most efficient way to do so. More than one Ministry expert had speculated that his increased resistance to Ifrig may have been the cause, counterintuitively. Perhaps his resilience made him all the more interesting to Ifrig, and drew the Ancient's power into closer reach.

For his part, Victor had simply concluded that Ifrig wasn't the smartest monstrosity in the Ethereal Realm. It had been frightening at first, that dark, smoky voice in his head commanding him to burn and kill, but it had never had a convincing argument. After two weeks of commanding Victor to boil the milk and atomize his breakfast cereal every morning, it had been hard to take seriously.

There. After a minute or two of waiting, there was another *schwoof* of magical energy igniting, and Victor threw himself up the steps as another insane display of orange light outside sent a spiderweb of shadows dancing through the warehouse.

The mezzanine platform led, via a second set of steps, to a network of metal walkways that ran over the box labyrinth below. In the forward corner, Victor could see a little enclosed office, ideally positioned to oversee the warehouse, and therefore probably belonging to the overseer. Next to that was a walkway that ran along the windows in the front-facing wall, and on that . . .

Victor quickly dashed forward and hugged the next set of steps, then carefully raised his head to look again. There they were. The hostile, with their back to him, still silhouetted against the conflagration outside. They were humanoid, but that much Victor was expecting. Every other identifying detail was lost in the flickering light.

As Victor watched, the stranger sent another barrage of fireballs across the car park with a casual sweep of the hand. This was the . . . fifth or sixth excessive display of pyrokinesis in about ten minutes? And who knew how many before the DEDA agents had arrived. If this had been Victor, he'd be at least staggering at this point. But the figure in the window up ahead was throwing out fire as if they were flicking bogeys. Looking closer, Victor was pretty certain they were propping up their chin with their free hand.

All of which pointed to this individual being possessed. If not, then using that much of an Ancient's power in such a short time would make them a prime candidate for possession in the very near future.

Victor felt a thrill. Possession or near possession plus demonstrated hostile intent equaled a justifiable use of extreme force. But this didn't seem like the average chump, and Victor's usual method—extend a hand

and wait for the squealing to stop—wasn't going to work. Still, his strategizing hadn't failed him yet.

He checked the terrain again. Yes, this seemed doable. All he had to
do was wait until the target was distracted again. Then just stand up,
dash up the steps, across that section of walkway, kick off the handrail
there, swing off *that* overhead pipe, land on the opposite walkway, and
blast the suspect's head off his shoulders before he can react. Easy.

The target was distracted again. Victor stood up, dashed up the stairs,
caught his foot on a handrail, and fell flat on his face with a loud clang.

"Victor?" said the suspect, turning from the window.

The voice had that strange layered effect that openly possessed people
have, but there was something familiar about it. Victor frowned in confusion, which made it all the more difficult to peel his face off the steel
grating. "Grnph?" he said, looking like an angry pug trying to extract
itself from a chainlink fence.

"You're Victor Casin, aren't you?" The stranger moved along the
walkway with an airy manner, as if their body weighed nothing at all
and was simply being pushed through the air by a breeze. "I wasn't sure
they'd actually send you. I didn't think this would work so well."

Victor finally pulled himself into an all-fours position thanks to a
nearby handrail and stared at the encroaching figure. Now that they had
moved away from the window, he could see that their face was half
covered in chin-length blond hair, and the other half was a mass of black
leathery skin, lined with glowing orange cracks.

"Do you know who I am?" they asked, the human side of their
face smiling.

Victor squinted. Somehow he did. He knew who they were. It wasn't
the face—he couldn't even tell if the human part was male or female—but
he recognized the voice. The growling, smoky tone of the Ancient. It
wasn't precisely how he remembered it, but . . .

". . . Ifrig?" he asked.

09

The interior of the Builder's Arms had a much more welcoming appearance than the outside, but that may have been because most of it was shrouded in darkness. There was a bar, behind which a young woman in a collar and tie stood in an arms-akimbo pose suggesting she didn't expect to have much to do tonight, but the most prominent feature was the semicircular stage and its purple curtains patterned with reflective stars. A couple of spotlights were angled toward it, along with every table and booth in the place.

A rather eclectic audience was dribbling in. About half of them were locals, old people with little else to do with their evenings and much younger people desperately hoping that their air of aloof maturity would stave off requests for their IDs. In short, nobody who had to be at work in the morning.

The other half of the crowd was what Alison assumed to be the "hardcore" audience, the real amateur-magic enthusiasts. Most of them looked like anyone who describes themselves as a "hardcore" fan of anything looks: lots of acne scarring, spectacles, and tightly cinched cargo shorts losing the battle with expanding guts.

But scattered among them Alison spotted members of another subgroup. They were all men in their late twenties or early thirties, and all dressed in accordance with a very specific style. Some of them wore turtlenecks, some tight leather trousers, some had silk dress shirts unbuttoned far enough to show off the chest hair, but there was one clear connecting factor: every single thing they wore was black. Also, while the other demographics congregated in little groups of their peers, these men were invariably alone, or dragging along an openly uninterested girlfriend or boyfriend, and were watching the stage waiting for the event to begin with narrowed eyes. Although many of them had offered respectful looks to Doctor Diablerie.

Alison took all of this in as she picked her way between the chairs and tables carrying the drinks back to their booth. Diablerie had wanted a red wine, and for herself she had gotten a bottled vodka drink the color of an attention-starved teenager's dye job.

Diablerie had carefully chosen a booth near the stage, and was currently sitting in the exact center of it, leaning back in satisfaction as if soaking in a hot bath. He was holding his walking cane between his legs, clasping his fingers over the skull-shaped decoration on the top.

Alison set the drinks down. "Sorry it took so long. They didn't have any obsidian goblets, so I had to go back to the car."

"No matter," declared Diablerie. "You have my thanks." Between the low light and his top hat, his face was hidden in shadow, but Alison could tell that he was grinning from ear to ear.

Alison sat down on the furthest edge of the booth seat, took a sip from her own drink, and idly bobbed her head back and forth in time to the generic rock music that was rolling in from some distant unseen speaker. She had come to terms with the fact that Diablerie hadn't brought her here for anything more important than settling some grudge he had with an amateur stage magic group that had shunned him, but despite everything, she was having a better time than usual.

Part of that might have been Diablerie's good mood rubbing off on her. She was aware that she was the kind of person who couldn't smile or laugh without self-consciously glancing around the room to make sure someone else was doing the same, and she occasionally fretted that people thought less of her for it.

But she was also a little stoked that she was "going out." Taking part in the "nightlife." It was foreign territory to her, one that had held a certain mystique ever since her mother had made it perfectly clear that if she so much as indulged the thought of staying out a single nanosecond past eight, then she would return to find the locks changed, a binful of burning documents, and a houseful of people denying that any person named Alison Arkin had ever lived there.

So a little campfire of gleeful rebellion was burning in the pit of Alison's stomach as she bobbed and sipped on her extremely colorful vodka drink that tasted like melted-down Skittles. When she thought about it, this was also the first time she had ever been on anything one might interpret as a "date" . . .

She glimpsed Diablerie out of the corner of her eye and consciously screeched that thought to a halt. In that direction lay madness. She took a longer sip and fixed her gaze on the twitching stage curtain.

"Drinking it all in, girl?" boomed Diablerie, somehow sensing the opportunity to stoke the awkwardness. "Storing away the details?"

"Um. Yes, Doctor," said Alison, not looking away from a particularly poorly cropped half-moon in the middle of the curtain pattern.

"Thinking of how you will word it when you report back to our mistress?"

Alison coughed on a throatful of her drink. It was like being briefly strangled by a gummy bear. "You know about that?!" she sputtered.

Diablerie cocked his head in poorly feigned confusion at her reaction, smiling broadly. "Know about what? It is the way of things that our superiors expect debriefings from their agents, and I know they have not been getting them from Diablerie himself."

"Oh yeah," said Alison. "Debriefings. That's all."

"Tell me, girl," said Diablerie, drumming his fingers on the top of his walking cane. "Has she enlightened you as to the full history of our dealings?"

"Um, no. Not yet."

"Not. Yet," repeated Diablerie, biting his *t*'s with loud clicks of his tongue. "Hmm. How elucidating."

Alison was getting that familiar feeling that she had just stepped in the kind of mess that was going to be rubbing off everywhere she walked for a while yet. Fortunately the music stopped and the lights began to turn down at that moment, so Diablerie left her in her little private cringe and leant forward eagerly.

After a recorded snatch of introductory music that sounded to Alison like someone trying to re-create the *Doctor Who* theme song by smashing the keys of a cheap electronic organ with a theremin, the spotlights on the stage intensified and the man Diablerie had addressed as Terence emerged from the curtains, smiling nervously like a man in the headlights of a car that may or may not be coming to a stop.

"Hello, everyone," he said, into a waiting mike. "Thank you all for coming to another night of amateur mag—er, sleight of hand and optical trickery entirely unrelated to extradimensional forces. Here at the Builder's Arms!"

He raised his voice slightly to provoke a round of applause, and the resultant smattering was clearly briefer than he would have liked. He peeled a piece of paper out of his sweat-sodden shirt pocket, absent-mindedly mopped his brow with it, then squinted at the handwritten words.

"Our first act tonight is . . . oh. Um." He adjusted his spectacles. "It's the . . . entirely mundane . . . feats of spiritual . . . guesswork by the ever-popular Blake Shadow!"

Another token round of applause went up, with a noticeable increase of enthusiasm among the elderly component of the audience, and Terence retreated behind the curtain, to be replaced with another man. This one had a shaved head and a triangular beard, and was dressed in accordance with the style of the magic hipsters—black suit with black polo neck, and a single red rose stuck into his lapel to indicate his higher status.

"Thank you, Terence," said Blake Shadow, a little sarcastically. His fists were clenched and his posture was somewhat uptight, giving him the air of a man who had just been the subject of a very severe talking-to. "I am Blake Shadow, and tonight I will guide you once again on a spiritual voyage to the other side—"

"NO HE WON'T!" yelled Terence, barreling back out onto the stage and grabbing the mike. "He's just going to do some cold reading! Nothing magical at all!"

Blake wrestled the mike back. "Yes, fine, it won't be magic the way the government officially defines it these days," he said quickly, before returning to a more pretentious, airy tone. "But with an open mind, perhaps you'll discover a new kind of magic—"

Terence yanked the mike back. "YOU WILL NOT! NO KIND OF MAGIC AT ALL! IT'S—"

A brief scuffle broke out between the two men before Blake pushed the microphone out of the range of both mouths, and an angry exchange of whispers took place. Terence seemed to finally impart something important, and Blake looked worriedly into the audience, directly at the booth where Diablerie and Alison were sitting.

Alison risked a quick look at Diablerie. He was still smiling at how much chaos he had caused with such a small amount of effort, but there was impatience in his eyes.

Some kind of agreement appeared to have taken place onstage, and Terence retreated through the curtain. Blake coughed to silence the murmur of the increasingly confused crowd. "Um, yes. As I was saying, I will now astound you with . . . some cold reading. Which doesn't involve magic at all." He placed a hand to his forehead and closed his eyes with a mixture of fake mysticism and despair. "I am getting the letter *H*. For no particular reason I am thinking about the letter *H*. Does that mean anything to anyone here?"

"Yes!" came the cry of an elderly woman not far from Alison. "My husband's name was Harold!"

"That's an interesting fact, madam, thank you for sharing," said Blake. "It is, however, a complete coincidence. Would I be right in saying that Harold passed away recently? This is entirely an assumption on my part."

"Oh yes," said the audience member sadly. "Is he in a better place, Mr. Shadow?"

"I have no idea, and no way of finding out," said Blake through his teeth. "But I don't think anyone could possibly object to you assuming as much. Unless they could?" He directed the question to where Diablerie was sitting. "Are we going to have a problem with that? Maybe assume the opposite as well, madam, just to be safe."

"Thank you, Mr. Shadow," said the woman. "Could you let him know that we all miss him?"

"I am completely unable to do that," said Blake, apparently gaining confidence. "But I can wildly guess on a basis of nothing at all that he either is or isn't aware of your feelings. Shall we move on?"

The woman sat down, and Alison overheard one of her nearby friends whisper excitedly, "He's very good, isn't he?"

Diablerie kept up his faint smile through the rest of the act, which continued along the same lines for the next ten minutes, but the drumming of his fingers on his walking cane became more and more heavy and deliberate, until it sounded like someone was repeatedly throwing basketballs down a wooden staircase.

Blake Shadow's act seemed to be targeted squarely at the elderly locals, as everyone else in the audience had settled into a patchwork soundscape of disinterested murmurs, but this began to abate as the ten-minute mark rolled around and Blake had to hurriedly wrap up his segment, cutting short a moment wherein a father either was or was not reassured that his estranged son was still alive or dead but who could say.

An extremely mixed round of applause saw Blake back behind the curtain, and Terence came out again. His skin was by now extremely flushed, and his pink face and hands poking out from the ends of his cream-colored shirt gave him the appearance of an undercooked sausage roll. "Erm, thank you, a big hand for Blake Shadow," he said, prompting a brief upsurge of the dying applause that failed to get it off life support. "I think our second act is ready, now, so please enjoy the . . . uh . . . mundane activities of Abdul the Astonishing!"

Terence darted offstage as the curtain was whipped aside to reveal a stage with a table covered in standard magical props—cups, rings, playing cards, a white bird in a cage, swaying under some kind of heavy sedation—behind which stood a man whose appearance drew a gasp of shock from the younger sector of the audience.

He had black hair and a coffee-colored skin tone, and since that apparently hadn't been enough to establish his Middle Eastern background, he was also wearing a turban the size and color scheme of a beach ball, a glittering sleeveless robe, and sandals whose toes curled so deeply that they came back around to pointing forward again.

"I am Abdul the Astonishing," he said, throwing wide his arms. He had a curly black mustache that Alison felt sure she could have wound around her hands twice, and he spoke in a comically overdone Arabian accent worthy of a production of *Aladdin* in a particularly out-of-touch part of the country. "And tonight, I shall astound you with feats of magic and mysticism from the East."

Alison heard a strangled noise that sounded like it was coming from Terence's throat, and caught a glimpse of a cream-colored figure sprinting toward center stage.

Abdul simply clapped his large hands, and a ring of fire burst into life around him and his table, immediately climbing to several feet high and stopping Terence in his tracks. An appreciative gasp went up.

"Yes, expect nothing less than the true magic, the old magic," continued Abdul, flexing his fingers over his table of apparatus. "Real magic, like the supernatural mystery of the rings!"

He grabbed a trio of metal rings and launched into an extremely fast routine, during which every part of his body other than his arms remained ramrod stiff and unmoving. It wasn't a very good version of the interlocking-rings trick, as it ended with only two of the rings interlocking, and the other one rattling to the floor somewhere near Abdul's feet. But his face wore an expression of such furious concentration that when he thrust the rings forward with a grunt of triumph, half the audience burst into applause just on reflex.

"How can it be explained?" He threw the rings to one side with a clatter, then pulled a line of colored scarves from thin air. At least, Alison assumed that was the intended effect. In reality, she could clearly see that they were coming out of the back of his robe. "It cannot be explained! Surely I must possess powers beyond the wit of mortal man! It is the only explanation!"

A shrill "NO IT ISN'T!" rang out from the direction of Terence. Abdul simply clapped his hands again, prompting another surge from the ring of fire that still surrounded him, and Terence was drowned out by the earthshaking sound of a gong.

"Yes, it is!" affirmed Abdul. He pulled one of the scarves off the string and tucked it showily into his closed fist. Then he tapped the hand once, twice, three times, and opened it to reveal that the scarf was gone. Although something looked very much as if it fluttered to the floor behind him and was set alight by the ring of fire. "Tremble before my mystical power!"

He continued in this vein, quickly rattling through extremely standard tricks performed very shoddily while aggressively asserting his magical power. Going by the increasingly absent applause and the open mouths around her, Alison got the sense that the audience had no idea what to make of this.

She glanced at Diablerie. His grin had returned in full force, and the tapping of his fingers upon his walking cane had upgraded to a full-on grope. He was shifting in his seat like a famous actor at an award ceremony in the pause before a name gets read out.

Abdul fanned out a deck of cards, picked one, and showed it to the audience. "This is your card!" He then placed it back on the top of the deck and proceeded to slowly and fumblingly shuffle, in a way that made it extremely obvious he was keeping the audience's card on the top of the deck. Then he passed it behind his back a couple of times and threw all the cards in the air, leaving only the top card in his hand. "Is this your card?" he exclaimed in triumph as the scattered cards started a few additional fires around the stage.

Alison looked at Diablerie again, and somehow, at that moment, the situation made sense to her. This wasn't an attempt at a serious conjuring act. This was a protest. This was a challenge. And Diablerie had the look of a career duelist who had found a worthy opponent.

"It's magic!" reiterated Abdul. He had thrown his hands wide again and was now staring directly at Diablerie's booth. "It's real magic from the unknown realms of mystery, and there is not a man here who can say otherwise!"

That felt suspiciously like a cue. Diablerie slapped his hands upon the tabletop, making the drinks rattle, and began to rise.

"BOOOO!"

Diablerie hesitated in surprise. The boo had come from another part of the seating area, in a deep shadow near stage left. Abdul seemed to have been caught off guard as well, as he had paused his act to stare at the source of the voice with boggling eyes.

After the kind of pause that holds the entire room on tenterhooks waiting to see what would break it, Terence burst onto stage one last time clutching a fire extinguisher, with which he proceeded to douse the burning ring with several white coughs of carbon dioxide. At the same time, the theater lights came on and the soundtrack was abruptly silenced. Abdul's spell was well and truly broken.

"Boo! Disgraceful!" came the voice again. With the lights up, Alison could now see that it belonged to a woman wearing a khaki T-shirt and a red beret. She was advancing on the stage in a fighting stance—fists clenched and elbows apart as if she was carrying two rolls of carpet under her arms. "Boo! Magic appropriation! Boo!"

She placed one foot on the stage, then turned to address the person directly behind her. He was a man with a similar T-shirt and long hair in dreadlocks, who was holding out a phone to record.

"We've just interrupted a so-called magic act that was being blatantly X-ist," she said, in the kind of hushed tone that was clearly audible right to the back rows of the theater. "Excuse me, sir? Are you aware that you claiming to be doing real magic is extremely offensive to extradimensionals and persons of extradimensional infusion?"

Robbed of his special effects, his stage lights, and his backing track, Abdul the Astonishing had been reduced to what he was—an ordinary man of Indian or Pakistani descent, dressed like a pantomime genie. Still, he drew himself up to his full height and folded his arms with dignity. "Abdul claims nothing," he boomed. "I say that I am in command of magical forces, and this is no lie."

"Ooh!" barked the girl, stepping further onto the stage. "Ooh! Did you get that?" She addressed her camera operator again. "That was live!

Someone clip that! I am now admonishing Abdul the Astonishing." She turned, then almost immediately turned back. "That's good. Clip that as well. That's a meme. Well, Abdul the Astonishing, which I do not believe to be your real name, were you aware that X-appropriation is now an actual crime with a real, actual law against it?"

If he wasn't, Abdul let the news wash over him like low tide over a half-buried stone. He made a show of glancing around. "I see no police."

The girl was trying to step into his personal space, but his folded arms and proud stance didn't crack, so in the end they were making nose-to-nose glaring eye contact. "Well!" she said. "You'll be in real trouble when the Department of Extradimensional Affairs hears about this!"

"Erm, perhaps we should . . ." whispered Alison to Diablerie, or rather, to the space that Diablerie had occupied the last she had checked, because only then did she notice that Diablerie had since vacated it.

She was still processing this when she heard a familiar hissing noise and saw a spherical smoke cloud burst into existence on the other side of the stage, mingling with the wisps of smoke and fire extinguisher exhaust that were still drifting around. Alison hissed a demure little oath and began the process of working her legs out from under the table.

"The summons is issued!" announced Diablerie, his voice carrying easily throughout the room. "Let they who invoketh the name of the Department of Extradimensional Affairs behold the form of Diablerie!"

It was one of his better entrances. He timed the flash and the burst of glitter perfectly to cast his body into silhouette just as the smoke had died down enough to reveal it. It was slightly spoiled when, as the smoke was fully clearing, Terence ran up and blasted Diablerie's shins with the fire extinguisher, leaving a white powdery residue on his black silk trousers.

"Sorry," said Terence, running back. "Panicked."

"Who are you?" demanded the girl in the red beret.

Diablerie pulled his signature move: gathering up his cloak and flinging it around himself, covering all of his face but his eyes. "You are addressing none but Doctor Diablerie! Known by mortal agencies as the Department of Extradimensional Affairs Officer of Skepticism!"

There was another of those tense silences that are defined by the thing that breaks them. In this case, it was the man in dreadlocks peering out from behind his phone camera to simply say, "Bollocks you are."

"I am!"

"Erm, he is," called Alison, still picking her way through the chairs and tables to the stage. "Sorry, sorry, excuse me, sorry. We are from the Department. I've got our IDs here." She was holding out the laminated identity cards for both herself and Diablerie, the new ones with the purple stripes. Diablerie never kept his own on him, because a self-styled "man of mystery" carrying an ID card was completely off message.

The activist girl squinted as she read the cards. "Oh. Okay then." She uncertainly moved into the kind of stance that one associates with the phrase "officers, arrest those men" but then came out of it and inspected the cards again. "Wait a minute. Alison Arkin?"

"Yes?"

"Arkin the Mind-Taker?"

Alison sagged. Danvers had reassured her some time ago that the media would move on to the next scandal and it was only a matter of time before everyone forgot about how she had used a magic-cancellation ritual on a dual-consciousness person and reduced them to a drooling vegetable, and she'd made the mistake of believing him. "That was an accident."

"So we're now seeing exactly who your kindly government thinks is appropriate to send after harmful X-ism," said the girl to her cameraman, pointing a finger into Alison's face. "The mind eraser from the news and"—she waved a hand at Diablerie and let her jaw flap for a moment as she sought the words—"and him. We've found an actual breach of the X-Appropriation Act that everyone witnessed, and the people want to know if you're going to do anything about it?"

"Er, yes, of course," said Alison.

"Well?!"

Alison looked back and forth, feeling pressured. With Diablerie and Abdul on one side of the stage and the activists on the other, they rather looked as if they were squaring off for a volleyball match, in which Alison had just volunteered to be the ball. "We . . . we can probably arrest him," she hazarded, looking to Diablerie for support. "Can't we?"

She had to do a double take, as Diablerie was staring at the floor with an expression of wonder on his face. He took a moment to process Alison's words, then turned his widened eyes to her.

Then he began to laugh. It began with a breathy "Hm, hm, hmm" and quickly expanded along with his mouth to become a hearty cackle that would not have been out of place being delivered over a stitched together corpse on a laboratory slab. "I'm afraid we must disappoint, girl," he announced, eyes twinkling. "We have no power here."

Alison frowned, then stared down at the stage. Diablerie tapped his foot to indicate where she should be looking.

It was the circle that Abdul had used to create his ring of fire. It wasn't a gas pipe or anything like that. It was a simple loop of plastic tape, upon which was inscribed a repeating pattern of hand-drawn black symbols.

"It's . . . a rune circle," she realized aloud.

"Rune magic!" said Diablerie, laughing anew. "Skepticism is confounded this day!"

"What the hell's going on?!" demanded the girl in the red beret. "What does that mean?"

"Um." Alison turned, feeling like a volleyball again and sensing a vicious spike in the near future. "He's a runecrafter. He used rune magic to make the fire appear. So we can't arrest him for magic appropriation because he's using actual magic."

The girl stared at her, jaw slack, then at Abdul. The pointing finger came out again. "Can you arrest him for the hat?"

10

"Ifrig," repeated the possessed person, whose gender, if they even had one, Victor still hadn't figured out. They drifted closer with uncertain steps, staring into the middle distance thoughtfully. "Ifrig. Ifrig. That's what I'm called in your head? I like it."

"Stay back!" Victor was on his feet by now. He backed away as fast as the stranger was approaching, and the two began a lazy pursuit around the catwalk.

"My name was Leslie. I suppose I might as well be Leslie-Ifrig now."

"Yeah, don't care," said Victor. He summoned fireballs to both his hands without even shaking them free of his sleeves first, and the air was filled with the scent of singed leather. "What do you want?"

Leslie-Ifrig cocked their asymmetric head, smiling vacantly with what parts of it were capable of doing so. "There's no need to be afraid of me."

"I'm not afraid!" spluttered Victor, on reflex.

"I think you are. I think you're very afraid and threatened, and that's why you're about to hurt me."

Victor froze for a second, then shrugged. "Eh. Can't fault your intuition." He threw out his arms and let loose.

A tornado of orange fire burst into life, filling the triangular area directly in front of him, roaring and swirling like a stampede of blazing tigers in a kaleidoscope. It was only when the afterimages faded that he noticed that Leslie-Ifrig had moved out of the way, and was watching it with professional interest.

Victor gritted his teeth, moved his arms as if hauling on an invisible tow rope, and the tornado swung like a gigantic baseball bat. Leslie-Ifrig hopped out of its way with astonishing speed, and a puff of magically conjured hot air swept Victor's hair back like a lover's hand.

He dropped his hands in exasperation and the tornado scattered. The catwalk in front of him was a lot more warped and twisted than he remembered, not to mention a lot more orange and sizzly, and Leslie-Ifrig was inspecting it with mild interest.

"Why are you doing this?" asked Victor as he took some deep breaths.

Leslie-Ifrig seemed genuinely baffled. "I didn't do that. You did that just now. I saw."

"I meant, in general!"

"I can do something like that. It looks a little bit different to yours. Want to see?" They held out their own hand.

Victor flinched. "Uh . . ."

Leslie-Ifrig's fire tornado was indeed different; it was narrower and slightly yellower. Victor only had a moment to appreciate this, as he then had to fling himself out of its way. He ended up lying full length on the glowing orange gantry he had already superheated.

He felt a warmth across his leather-covered shoulder blades that was rather pleasant, at least compared to the searing pain he felt in his uncovered hands a moment later. He scrambled to get his bare flesh off the red-hot metal, and some important part of the softened catwalk chose that moment to collapse.

The floor tilted sharply, and Victor descended the newly created slide onto a pile of boxes, where the yielding cardboard slowed him down just enough to make his impact with the concrete ground painful rather than immediately lethal.

He lay on his back for a few moments, wincing as he made a mental checklist of his bones, then slowly opened his eyes. Directly above, the murky silhouette of a misshapen head and shoulders was peering down at him through the smoking ruins of the catwalks.

They tilted their head like a playful dog wondering if they had just imagined their owners briefly uttering the word *walk*, then brought their hand up.

Victor saw the glow in time and rolled to one side, his smoking trench coat fluttering around him as another cone of fire splattered against the floor where he had been lying. Somehow he was on his feet—the instinct to stand up hadn't even registered with his conscious mind—and then he was sprinting into the relative shelter of the box labyrinth, throwing mushroom-shaped blasts of magical fire in all directions to cover his movement.

He headed deeper into the warehouse, away from the front section that the gantry oversaw, and where Leslie-Ifrig had the high vantage point. He turned a few more corners and ran along a long tunnel of boxes, only to find that it led to a dead end.

Which was exactly what he wanted. Above him, there was nothing but distant ceiling. So with his back to the end wall, there was only one route to get to him, and he'd see them coming. He planted his feet and held as still as he could, listening for the slightest sound.

He heard a harsh, ringing sound of something tapping metal, then the flutter of soft soles landing on concrete. Leslie-Ifrig must have come down to ground level. "Victor?" Their strange, layered voice carried even from a distance and through several walls of cardboard. "Why are you scared?"

Victor frowned, confused. "Because . . . you're trying to kill me?" he called back. He was giving away his position, but at least it would get this over with faster.

"I meant, in general." There were a few mysterious movement sounds, and then Leslie-Ifrig's voice seemed to come from a completely different direction. "Why are you so hostile?"

"Are you serious? You're Ifrig!" Something clonked to the floor less than ten feet away and Victor flinched. "You spent years trying to possess me. Trying to make me burn and kill things."

"You *do* burn things." The voice was very close now, possibly even just on the other side of the wall to Victor's left. "And kill things. It says on the wiki."

Victor tried to peer through the cracks between the boxes, but there was no sign of movement. It was still too gloomy in the warehouse, even with the ever-increasing number of burning things inside it. "Yeah," he conceded. "But I'm capable of other things."

"Why do you need to be?"

Leslie-Ifrig was definitely close by. Victor ground his teeth for a few moments. "Tell you what. Come around the corner and talk to me face-to-face and we'll have a proper conversation about it."

"Okay. I'm going to do that."

Victor tensed and held his arms forward like a conductor, staring at the corner ahead where the passage turned ninety degrees, ready to unleash at the first sign of movement.

Then the entire wall exploded.

A blizzard of boxes flew through the air like a cloud of buckshot, each one with enough sharp corners that, however heavy their contents, anything on the receiving end was in for a miserable evening. Victor's fight-or-flight instinct kicked in, and took the usual option.

Everything within his field of vision disappeared behind a wall of yellow-orange, angrily writhing and fluctuating like television static. Ifrig's power flowed through him like water through a sieve, filling his body with a tingling sensation to the ends of every nerve. It was unpleasant, but at the same time, satisfying, like the feeling of finally getting to a urinal after a long car journey.

When the conflagration faded, all the boxes that might have been flying toward him were reduced to a coating of ash upon the ground, along with every other box in a radius of a hundred yards. The interior of the warehouse was now almost entirely transformed into a smoking black fan-shaped scorch mark, still hissing and tinkling where parts of it had turned to glass.

Victor tottered. His entire body felt hot and tingly, and he was hyperaware of everything touching it. All his clothes felt too big and itchy. His pulse thumped in his ears, and something dark and unnatural added a pounding bass to it. But it seemed that Leslie-Ifrig was finally . . .

"That was interesting."

. . . behind him. Victor spun around, reflexively throwing out fire again, but this time it sputtered like the last moments of a catherine wheel, and his aim was thrown by another blast of hot air that lifted him off his feet. He landed in a pile of unburnt boxes that had been slightly behind him, and the moment he had settled, his legs made it quite clear that they were not going to be moving again until after a union-mandated coffee break.

Leslie-Ifrig, still unharmed and unsmoking and wearing that damn smile, came forward with hand outstretched. Victor was spent. He couldn't even lift his arms. All he could do was stare, panting.

Then the hand became a finger gun, which Leslie-Ifrig "fired." "Pow! I win." Their smile broadened even further. "That was fun. We should do this again. Can I friend you on Facebook?"

11

"Make yourself at home," said Abdul the Astonishing, now talking in the accent of a man born and raised in London.

He held the door of the tiny dressing room open to allow Diablerie and Alison inside. Alison guessed that the room had been converted from a spare toilet, and going by the smell, probably still moonlighted as one. A musty old office chair was set up in front of a sink with a mirror, and Abdul sat there to start busying himself with the removal of his costume and makeup.

After peeling off his absurd mustache and removing his turban—which, when put aside, took up a good percentage of what little floor space was available—Alison could see that he was, indeed, a completely normal man in his late thirties, with a boyishness to his features that she thought made him quite handsome—although it was hard to tell, as he was still wearing black eyeliner that looked as if it had been applied with a spoon.

"So . . ." he began.

"Enough small talk!" barked Diablerie, slamming the door closed behind him. "You stand accused of flagrant violation of the law. What say you in your defense?"

"I thought we'd cleared that up," said Abdul.

"Oh?" Diablerie took up his traffic-policeman saunter again, pacing meaningfully around Abdul's seat with hands behind back. Alison had to flatten herself against the closed door to give him room to do so. "Confident, are you, that your little technicality will not crumble under higher scrutiny? Mayhaps your true calling lies in tightrope walking, for the line ye tread is near as thin."

Abdul rolled his eyes. "Oh goodness. Looks like you have me bang to rights." Alison had seen many people's reactions to Diablerie's performances, usually somewhere on the spectrum of fear and confusion, but Abdul's show of bored tolerance was something entirely new. "Have mercy, milord, for I am but a small fish, and if you would overlook my transgressions just this once, I can give you information on someone higher up the ladder."

Diablerie paused in his pacing. "Your craven wriggling in the light of Truth fills me with contempt. But Diablerie may yet be open to your proposal."

Abdul snorted. "It's nice to see you again, by the way, Doctor. Feels like it's been too long."

"You . . . know him?" said Alison, taken by surprise.

Abdul stopped cleaning off his eyeliner for a moment to offer her a look of pity. "And you haven't clued your assistant in. Of course you haven't. Why would you?" He held out a slightly mascara-stained hand to shake. "Rajesh Chahal. Scholar of the occult."

Alison let him take her unresisting hand and wobble it up and down a couple of times. "So this whole thing was a setup?"

Rajesh looked to Diablerie, saw that he was standing stiffly with his lips pursed and showing no signs of replying, and sighed. "He called me a few hours ago. Told me he was coming here, about the new skepticism laws, and asked me to give him a reason to come backstage and talk. A nice public, easily explained reason, so no one would suspect we were doing business. I hadn't even planned an act for tonight, I had to throw together—"

"Diablerie has considered your proposition," shouted Diablerie, who had gone quite red. "You shall be permitted to submit your intelligence for consideration."

Rajesh offered him a patronizing little half smile, then very pointedly turned his gaze back to Alison. "I had to throw together that disaster you saw back there. Those hecklers weren't part of the plan, but it was nice of them to help our cover."

"So you're, like," said Alison, drawn by the encouraging twinkle in Chahal's eye. "One of those people who . . . tell . . . people . . . things? Important things?"

"Informant," he said, gently. "I think the word you're looking for is *informant*. My main interest is trends in magical subculture, and Diablerie and I—"

"Diablerie has no more patience for this prattle," interjected Diablerie, spitting his *p*'s with visible bursts of droplets. "Elucidate us! Or contemplate a stay in Diablerie's most dismal oubliette!"

"He doesn't change, does he?" sighed Rajesh as he leaned over to fish around in a small backpack that was wedged between the sink unit and the wall. "All right. I've got something here that should fit into the remit of government skepticism officers. Check it out."

He produced a small tablet computer and woke up the screen. A web browser was already loaded with a paused video, currently displaying what looked like a conjoined kitchen and dining area in an average middle-class home.

When Rajesh unpaused the video, a pudgy man with a colorful T-shirt and an infectious grin stepped into frame. "All right, Miracle Mob!" he said, bobbing left and right excitedly. "I'm Miracle Dad, and welcome to another stream! First thing today, we're going to reward another lucky subscriber with the blessings of our lady, El-Yetch."

The camera turned slightly to reveal a pale young man sitting at the breakfast bar, wearing a T-shirt identical to the first man's. He wrung his hands and smiled nervously, his confused eyes focused squarely on the first man the way a zebra on the Serengeti keeps an eye on a suspiciously quiet patch of long grass.

"Your name?" asked Miracle Dad, now out of shot.

"Um, online I'm StonyTuna," said the man, embarrassed, in some kind of European accent that Alison couldn't quite place.

"And StonyTuna's come all the way from the StonyTunaGaming YouTube channel to be here," said Miracle Dad. "And you're having a problem with your wrist, you said?"

StonyTuna held up one skinny arm and let the hand flop over pathetically. "Um. Yeah. The doctor thought it might be tendinitis, but none of the exercises she gave me have been doing anything . . ."

"Okay, great story!" said Miracle Dad, jumping back into shot. "So, will the powers of our lady El-Yetch be enough to relieve StonyTuna of his pain? Only one way to find out! Time to take the Walk of Worship!"

The camera rotated again until it was pointing down a darkened hallway, at the end of which lay an open door, and beyond that a small bathroom, from which bright fluorescent light was spilling. The sound of angelic choirs began playing as StonyTuna, having been awkwardly prodded into place by the hand of Miracle Dad, uncertainly began to walk toward the light, the camera following shakily.

"And remember, like this video and subscribe to our channel if you'd like to be in with a chance to win the blessings of El-Yetch, the Mother Goddess, and get Miracle Meg to personally heal your bodily injuries. Here she is now!"

StonyTuna was now close enough to the light that the camera could adjust and finally reveal the bathroom's interior. It was an ordinary sub-urban bathroom with white fittings, and there was a young girl of around ten years old sitting on the toilet. She was wearing yet another T-shirt identical to the others, albeit child sized, with a long white skirt that rippled as she absent-mindedly kicked her legs. She was holding a hand-held gaming system as close to her face as a jeweler would hold an intricate piece of work.

"Meg?" hissed the voice of Miracle Dad from behind the camera.

The girl quickly stashed her device by the side of the toilet, then looked to StonyTuna with a very well-rehearsed expression of messianic calmness. She took StonyTuna's unresisting hand and clasped it between both of hers.

The handheld footage was very poor quality, but something was defi-nitely happening; whether it was magic or an understated video effect, Alison couldn't have said. StonyTuna's body trembled, and his skin became flushed pink with supernatural speed. When Meg let go, he staggered back and collapsed, presumably into Miracle Dad's arms, judg-ing by the way the camera shook like amateur UFO footage and, after some confused movement, started capturing footage of the skirting board.

In short order Miracle Dad's round face returned, and after he had corrected the angle, he was standing with an arm around a dazed StonyTuna. "All right!" he said. "How's the hand, Stony?"

StonyTuna gawped at Miracle Dad as if he'd just been shook awake, then at his own wrist, clutching it in his free hand. "It . . . wow. That really worked." He wobbled it back and forth. "It doesn't hurt!"

"That's the magic of Miracle Meg!" announced Miracle Dad, squeez-ing the other man chummily. "Are you a believer in the wonderful power of El-Yetch now?"

"Well, yeah, I mean, I was already, that's why I subscribed . . ."

"Yes!" Miracle Dad centralized his own face in the shot, bisecting StonyTuna's with the edge of the frame. "And you too could receive the blessing of El-Yetch and Miracle Meg if you subscribe to the Modern Miracle channel. There's also a new range of T-shirts . . ."

Rajesh suddenly paused the video, fixing Miracle Dad's expression at a moment when he looked particularly pleased with himself. "So, they call themselves Modern Miracle, and they're one of the fastest-growing magic-focused streaming channels right now."

"Faith healers," intoned Diablerie ominously with a curl of his upper lip, pronouncing it the way one would pronounce a phrase like *train station lavatory*.

"Well, that and playthroughs of popular video games, but the faith healing stuff is starting to take over. They seem to be trying to establish a religious cult, and not without success. That little girl, Miracle Meg, she's the figurehead." He pointed to the corner of the frame, where Meg's face was still visible. She appeared to have gone back to her game console. "Her father claims that she's in a dual consciousness with El-Yetch, which you may have gathered is the Ancient they claim to worship as a god, and that she's capable of magical healing."

"Is she?" asked Alison.

Rajesh and Diablerie both turned to her wearing capital-L Looks of condescension. "No," said Rajesh slowly. "Obviously not."

"Does *that* look like one possessed by demon spawn to thee, girl?" said Diablerie, pointing to the distracted but unbesmirched face of Miracle Meg.

"Well, I guess she doesn't . . ." murmured Alison, going red.

". . . doesn't have a face like a bag of spanners covered in sick," offered Rajesh, turning back to the screen. "Still, they've done their homework. El-Yetch is an Ancient on record, and those infused with her have tended to manifest healing abilities. Anyone could have found that out from the Ancients Wiki, of course, but then there's this."

He brought up a surprisingly professional website, headed with the words "MODERN MIRACLE!" and "ARE YOU WORTHY OF THE BLESSING?" in an elegant cursive typeface. Rajesh highlighted a paragraph of small print on a lengthy FAQ.

"See? 'No cancer patients.' It's not common knowledge that magic healing doesn't cure cancer. For a scam, it's doing a very good job of looking legit."

"Oh yeah, I heard about the cancer thing," said Alison, recalling a passage she had read during her short education at the government magic school. "The magic mistakes the cancer for part of the organism and makes it worse, right?"

"They're based out of Worcester," said Rajesh, not acknowledging her. Alison was feeling increasingly shouldered out of the conversation. "They don't make a secret of their street address, in case you want to pay your respects. Apparently they do regular services in their front garden."

"THIS is the intelligence with which you would buy your freedom?" roared Diablerie, straightening up. "The niceties of small-time salvation salesmen?"

Rajesh half turned in his chair, resting one elbow on the backrest, continuing his show of being absolutely unperturbed by Diablerie. "There are a lot of eyes on this, and the interesting part is that none of them have been able to figure out how they're pulling the scam." He lowered both his head and the tone of his voice to emphasize the gravity of his words. "Testimonies all state that real magical healing is going on. At least two of our peers went to investigate and are now evangelical El-Yetch converts."

Diablerie harrumphed. "So it falls to Diablerie, as master of skepticism, to succeed where our more credulous fellows have fallen. Very well!" He snapped his cape around himself. "We shall journey to Worcester, and quest to drag these shysters into the light of truth."

"So, um, question," said Alison, sensing a gap in the discourse. "How do you know she doesn't have actual healing powers?"

Rajesh and Diablerie turned those capital-*L* Looks on her again, now both with an extra dollop of aghastness. "So Diablerie's supposed to be mentoring you, did I get that right?" asked Rajesh.

"'Tis a gradual process," said Diablerie moodily. "One can hardly expect fast results when one leashes a sloth."

12

The warehouse had gone quiet. The cargo container behind which Adam was hiding with Black and Rawlins was still providing cover, and the side closest to them was intact, but it had been making some very disquieting creaks and pinging noises, and none of them had risked peering out since the last salvo of magical fire. Instead, they were trying to keep abreast of the situation with Adam's magical senses, but at a distance, and amid innumerable traces of the magic that had already occurred, his ability to pinpoint specifics was severely reduced.

"There's still . . . two blurs," he reported, squinting with all his might. "Maybe one blur now. They still haven't thrown any more magic around since the last time."

"Moving?" asked Rawlins.

"No." Adam's face twitched. "Wait. Yes. I think."

"This is pathetic," said Black, who was sitting on the concrete with his back to the cargo container. "We know the perp isn't watching the windows now. We should be backing Victor up."

"After you," grumbled Rawlins.

"Something's coming," reported Adam. "They went blurry for a bit then came back. I think they must have gone out the rear exit and are coming around the side."

"Is it Victor?" asked Black.

"It's . . . definitely a pyrokinetic." He snapped out of his squint. "Did you guys bring weapons?"

Rawlins wordlessly reached into his back pocket and produced a stun gun. The kind that was useless at anything further than handshake range.

"I think I might start writing my report, now, since we're about to die," said Black, digging his phone out of his jacket. "What's a more heroic way of saying 'stood around like frightened prannies'?"

"Watching the six," suggested Rawlins.

"Wait, they're close enough now," said Adam, squinting again and pressing his face right into the side of the cargo container. "It's Victor."

"You sure?" asked Black, clambering to his feet.

"Unless there's someone else infused with the same Ancient in there," said Adam, before stepping out from cover. He was momentarily distracted by the sight of the other side of the cargo container, which now closely resembled a gigantic wad of chewed gum, some parts of which were still dripping.

A figure appeared at the side of the warehouse, walking in the calm and measured way of someone who intends to collapse onto the first surface they can find that's even mildly softer than a bed of nails. Ash and soot had turned them into a black silhouette, and there was still smoke rising from the folds in their clothing.

"Victor?" said Adam, hesitating.

The figure paused, tottered back and forth for a moment as if about to fall flat on their face, then snapped out of it and took several rapid strides forward. "Where the hell were you?!" spat Victor, shaking burnt ends out of his shaggy hair.

"Uh, watching the six," said Adam. "How did it go?"

Victor's lips silently formed a number of different shapes for a few moments as he considered possible replies, before settling on "It's sorted."

"What was it?"

"Possession. Pyrokinetic. Hostile. I sorted it."

"Right. Sorted it," said Black. "So how much of them is left?"

Victor glared at him through his singed bangs for a moment, then, to Adam's enormous surprise, broke into a smile. "In there? Not much at all."

"Figures," muttered Rawlins.

"Might as well leave it to the cleanup crew," said Black, eyeing the melted cargo container and adjusting his collar self-consciously. "Come on. Back to the van."

"Oh sure," said Victor, lazily falling into step behind Black and Rawlins as they began to walk. "Guess I've got quite a long report to write, huh. Don't expect you lot will have much to add, unless you can think of lots of things to say about the side of that cargo container."

"Is that your phone?" asked Adam, walking beside him.

Victor slapped his buzzing coat pocket. "No."

"Pretty sure it is."

Hastily, Victor pulled out his phone wallet—the custom one he'd had made that was lined with Teflon—and thumbed the cover open. He glanced at the illuminated screen for less than a second before theatrically rolling his eyes and slapping it closed again. "Ugh. Just, er, someone messaging me on Facebook. Ah! Here's the van." He jogged ahead a couple of yards, pulled open one of the rear doors, and gestured to the interior. "Our carriage awaits."

Adam didn't get in. "Are you all right?"

"Yeah!" Victor's pocket buzzed again, and his free hand snapped over it. "Yeah."

"You seem a bit . . . hyped up."

"No! I mean, of course I'm hyped up. I just got to scorch an entire warehouse. They haven't let me do that in ages."

Adam stepped forward and placed one pudgy leg on the van's bed, before hesitating and peering at Victor again. "You didn't overdo it with the magic?"

"I'm not hearing voices, if that's what you're asking," said Victor, dropping his arms in exasperation. "I was in absolutely no danger of losing myself back there. Trust me. Maybe Ifrig had other things to worry about."

"Okay," said Adam distrustfully, before carefully climbing into the back.

In short order the four of them were back on the road, leaving the devastated warehouse to smolder and generate angry phone calls to and from the Department and the Department's preferred professional cleaning service. After five minutes of silence, Adam found himself examining Victor, who was staring at the ceiling with his arms folded and one foot tapping rapidly on the floor. He heard Victor's phone buzz again.

"That Facebook friend seems to have a lot they need to say to you," he said, picking what he thought was a nice, neutral conversation starter.

"Yeah, maybe," said Victor. He silently stared back at Adam, who was staring expectantly at him for a few seconds, then tutted and dug his phone out again. "Yeah, it's not important. They're just . . . trying to invite me to this message board social network thingy they're on."

"Oh."

Victor peered closer to the screen and frowned. "Don't suppose you know what Modern Miracle is?"

Adam began blinking rapidly as every single other muscle in his face suddenly froze solid. "I'm sorry, what?"

13

"So do you trust him?" asked Alison as she and Diablerie filed through the narrow back passages of the Builder's Arms, looking for a door that led outside.

"Chahal is a snake," growled Diablerie. "He slithers about the darkest cracks of the occult underworld, in pursuit of the Ancients know what. Diablerie trusts his information. His motives, less so."

"Right," said Alison. She found a door with a crossbar that gave her a good feeling, and sure enough, pressing it in brought on a refreshing blast of night air and electric streetlight. "So, this might sound like a stupid question . . ."

"There they are now!" cried a familiar voice. Alison turned to see the activist girl in the red beret and her phone-wielding cameraman standing near a gray van in the car park. They jogged over as soon as Alison appeared from the pub's rear exit, the girl clutching a cheap microphone the way a natural historian wields a pin with which they intend to attach a butterfly to a board. "Alison Arkin! Will Abdul the Astonishing answer for his blatant display of X-ism?"

"Um," said Alison, leaning back a good twenty or so degrees as the microphone was thrust under her chin. "He's . . . promised not to do it again?"

"But what about justice? Have you and your partner made an arrest?"

The use of the word *partner* derailed Alison's train of thought into a mixed flurry of emotions, but she eventually managed to stammer her way into coherence. "Sorry, we, we, like I said, sorry, we can't arrest him, because he was using runes. Which is actual magic. So a crime wasn't being—"

"And what are these 'runes'?" asked the girl. She wasn't looking at Alison, but deeply into the camera phone with set jaw and furiously interested eyebrows.

"Runes?" Even taken by surprise, Alison had enough sense to realize that saying too much about runecrafting in a public forum would be a very bad idea. "It's . . . a way that some people can do magic. Not many people."

"And there you have it," said the girl to the camera. "Once again, a privileged minority weasels out of consequences by exploiting technical loopholes while their government friends look the other way—"

"It's not a privilege!" protested Alison, before she could stop herself. "Runecrafting makes you go insane!" Specifically, attempting to draw runes temporarily gave one's mind a direct line to the Ancients, and the Ancients didn't understand that they had to take turns to speak. Alison had only attempted to copy down a rune once, and had spent the remainder of the night hallucinating non-Euclidean geometry on a bedroom floor.

The girl looked at Alison in shock for a brief second before turning back to the camera, her disapproving mouth tightening even further like the coils of a python. "And now the official DEDA representative has just equated magic users with the mentally ill. Look at this face!" She thrust out a pointing finger that came dangerously close to going right up Alison's nose. "Look at and shame this face! For this is the face of government failing its people! This has been Beatrice Callum for LAXA Updates. Remember to like, subscribe, and donate for more great activism like this." She maintained her fiercely righteous expression for a few seconds of silence. "How was that?"

"I think we can call it a video," said the dreadlocked cameraman, finally lowering his phone and poking at the screen.

"Whew." The girl who had called herself Beatrice relaxed, letting all the tension out of her face and lowering her height by about two inches. In an instant, Alison was addressing an actual human being just a couple of years younger than her. "Cool! Thanks for this. Good episode. I think people are really gonna engage, y'know?"

"LAXA?" was all Alison could say.

"League for Advancing Extradimensional Acceptance," explained Beatrice, smiling with a hint of embarrassment. "I just joined them actually. I've been, like, planning to do some activism for my gap year, and this is where the really interesting stuff's happening right now. Especially with the new law. Do you need a lift somewhere?"

She was pointing to the gray van she had come from. Her cameraman hauled open the side, and a large brown shaggy dog bounded out, brimming with surprise and delight at the cameraman's extraordinary door-opening prowess.

At the same time, a face appeared at the driver's-side window. It was a boy of about Beatrice's age, wearing a red beret identical to hers. "Bea, you said we could get burgers now," he whined at full volume. "I'm hungry. This is abusive."

"I'm networking, David! Stop abusing me!" yelled Beatrice, with quite astonishing venom. "Sorry, that's my brother. He signed up as well so he could drive the van, but all he does is complain. We're investigating a feng shui consultant in Oxford tomorrow, and I just know he's going to complain all the way through that, too, snotty little dick."

The off-camera version of Beatrice spoke like an unsupervised factory production line, words pouring unconcerned out of her as if from the end of a conveyor belt. Alison had to wait for a gap as if trying to cross a busy motorway. "You go all around the country in that van?"

"Yep," said Beatrice proudly. "Well, it's not our van . . ."

"With a dog?" said Alison. Beatrice's cameraman was still trying to pet the dog while simultaneously disentangling its excited paws from the front of his jeans.

"Yes."

Alison coughed. "Solving mysteries?"

"Yeah!" A moment's doubt flashed across Beatrice's features. "Why does everyone keep saying that like it's weird? Anyway, did you need a lift?"

"No, er . . . we came in Doctor Diablerie's car."

"Doctor who?"

"No, Doctor . . ."

An important fact suddenly dropped into Alison's conscious mind like a rhinoceros from a set of bomb bay doors: the fact that Diablerie hadn't spoken or done anything to draw attention to himself since they had left the pub.

For the second time in one night, Alison looked around for Diablerie and saw only empty, unchewed scenery. "Oh, *nuts*," she swore, before jogging back toward the pub, listening intently for the sound of smoke bombs going off.

14

Rajesh Chahal was still hunched in front of the mirror in the pathetic dressing room of the Builder's Arms. He had successfully wiped off the eyeliner, and was now struggling to scrape the last few flecks of glitter off his cheeks. There was a quick, businesslike knock on the door, and he turned to see a darkened figure in a top hat and cloak enter.

"Diablerie," he groaned. "You forget something? I've got no more intel."

The figure let the door close behind them, then stepped forward into the light, removing their top hat and setting it on the repurposed bathroom counter. Rajesh stared at it, then up at its prior wearer. His hand froze in the act of rubbing the swab on his cheek.

"Well," he said, with fascinated caution. "It's been even longer since I last saw you."

The man wearing Diablerie's clothes ran a hand over the door. "Is this room safe for talking?" he asked, in a soft voice.

Rajesh watched him carefully. "I suppose. Didn't expect you'd want to talk in person anytime soon."

The man continued his way along the walls, feeling for gaps or anything out of order. "Internet chatrooms aren't as secure as they used to be, 'Priest.'"

Rajesh pretended to go back to rubbing his makeup off, but he was only making pointless strokes of his hand as he scrutinized his visitor through the mirror. "So. You call me up out of nowhere and pass me information about Modern Miracle. And then you instruct me to feed that information back to you when you come here as Doctor Diablerie. Hm. Obviously I don't expect you to explain—"

"Modern Miracle is the opportunity we've been waiting for," said the man, finally turning from the wall. "A chance to prove the Third Way theory. But the situation needs a lot of massaging first. I need the Department's eyes on it."

Rajesh met his gaze through the mirror. "'We'? That's a big word. The last time we talked in person, you were kicking me out of the band."

"You showed me you were unwilling to change. Unwilling to learn. There was nothing more we could do for each other."

"And now?"

"Now, everything's changed." He leaned against the wall comfortably and displayed his hands. "Magic is public. Our previous disagreement has become moot. I need your help pulling things back from the abyss."

Rajesh wasn't even pretending to clean his face anymore. He was only partly aware of how tightly his fingers were clenching around the swab. "And this is what all that theatrics was for? An excuse to hang out?"

"Perhaps. It was also for the girl's benefit."

An absurd smile forced its way across Rajesh's face. "Weren't you trying to get her killed, last I knew?"

"At that time, her death would have served a purpose," said the man dispassionately. "Now, she would be more useful brought into the fold."

"She's spying on you for the Department," Rajesh pointed out.

"Exactly. She's already a spy. Half the work's been done. Now it's just a matter of turning her around." He allowed Rajesh a few seconds of skeptical silence. "She's willing to learn. That gives her potential. She's driven by curiosity. Lawrence understands that. She's buying Arkin's loyalty by promising information. And we have far more of that to barter with."

"Okay," said Rajesh flatly. "Now I know you haven't changed. You only ever explained your plans when you were hoping one of us had a better one."

"Do you?"

"No, not at all," said Rajesh, with negative enthusiasm. "It's certainly an improvement on the previous plan to actively murder an innocent girl. You mess with your assistant's head all you like."

"In any case," said the man, with just the merest hint of testiness, "this is a side project for the longer term. Modern Miracle is the next point on our graph. Find out as much as you can. Maintain observation. Infiltrate if possible."

"Aren't you forgetting something?" said Rajesh as the figure began to drift toward the door like a shadow moving with the passing of the sun. "You haven't actually asked me to come back yet. You haven't asked if I even want that."

The man shifted his weight. "Do you need me to?"

The pregnant pause that followed was interrupted by a genteel knock upon the door and the voice of Terence. "Um, sorry, Raj, Diablerie's girlfriend is back looking a bit of a fright. Don't suppose you'd know where he'd be?"

"Yeah, hold on, I'll be out in a sec," called Raj, before giving his visitor the side eye. "You should probably get back in character."

The man took up Diablerie's hat. "I'll check in soon. Assuming that you're in?"

Rajesh looked down at the absurdly large turban resting beside his leg, and at the ridiculous curls on his slippers. He smiled the kind of smile worn by people who are feeling every emotion other than the ones usually associated with smiles. "You know, when you went dark for so long, I actually assumed you were dead." He shook his head. "Like the human race could ever get so lucky."

From the Modern Miracle forum front page:

> Welcome to the Modern Miracle community! This is a fun place for fans of the Miracle Meg streams to hang out and make friends. As well as a place for general discussion about extradimensional topics and providing resources for extra-dimensionally gifted individuals. Please keep things light!

Trending topics:

Why normal people should be killed (17864)

Dual consciousness: next evolution for humanity? (81929)

New infusion! How to avoid going to DEDA school? (9124)

Terrorism: a logical response to discontent (4678)

Post your DEDA memes (39159)

Miracle Meg is the best religion (41532)

If you are infused but not dual consciousness, then please just die (73632)

Does anyone know how runes work? (8262)

My Ancient could beat yours in a fight, prove me wrong (7032)

Calling people extremists is oppressive (29034)

Need someone to use telepathy on my girlfriend (812)

MIRACLE DAD PLEASE READ MY GRANDMA HAS CANCER (532)

The new Interstellar Bum Pirates sucks (-27) (this thread has been locked for hate speech)

THE FOLLOWING DAY

15

The elevator in the Department of Extradimensional Affairs building stopped on the lowest basement level, and the doors trundled open. Alison stood where she was, squaring her shoulders and taking deep breaths to build up her determination. Then the door started threatening to close again, so she hurried the process up and trotted forward.

She had come to a capital-*D* Decision. It had become clear to her that learning the ropes of occult investigation was never going to happen from just hanging around waiting to absorb passing tidbits like a basking shark; she was going to have to seek out answers to her questions. And she had reluctantly decided that Archibald Brooke-Stodgeley was the best place to start.

It wasn't that he was unapproachable. Quite the opposite. To Alison, he was by far the most approachable of the Department's senior staff. But he hadn't quite figured out when was and was not a good time to let himself be approached, such as while elbow deep in the guts of a magically mutated animal corpse he was finding particularly enlightening.

He had made an effort to make his laboratory in the converted car park a little more organized over the last few months, so the piles of ancient books on magical theory were very deliberately placed on the opposite side of the room from the stacks of pet carriers full of magically infused animals, and anything else with a reasonable chance of accidentally setting things on fire, but otherwise things were as chaotic as ever. The portly form of Archibald himself was sitting at the central lab bench with his back to Alison, hunched over some work or other.

She began to walk toward him, then stopped in her tracks when he produced a wet crunching, cracking sound that immediately caused her lunch to sit up and register its presence in her stomach. "Mr. Brooke-Stodgeley?" she said, in a weak voice.

He turned to reveal surprised eyes and a torn hunk of baguette sandwich protruding from his mouth. "Mmph?" he said in greeting, the syllable gaining a strange musical quality as it passed through a cylindrical curl of bacon.

"Is this a bad time?"

"Nnph, no!" He recklessly pushed his sandwich wrapper into a nearby pile of experiments and turned around, shaking something off his hand that Alison sincerely hoped was piccalilli. "Not at all. Lovely to see you, my dear. Come in."

Alison was already in, and opted not to come any farther. "Could I ask you a question about healing magic?"

Archibald's attitude changed instantly. A pained look flickered across his eyes, and his shoulders and knees sagged as the enthusiasm was pulled out of his muscles. "Oh. Well. I suppose."

Alison cocked her head. "Would that not be all right?"

"No trouble at all!" He tried to perk himself up again, then gave up and sighed. "I'm sorry, my dear, it's just . . . us magic know-it-alls, we don't really like talking about healing magic."

"Why?"

He winced and waggled a stained hand. "Because it's so . . . unscientific." He caught her frown. "Life essence manipulation is what we call it. That's the school of magic that healing and vampirism both belong to. But . . . no one has been able to figure out what life essence is, exactly. Even with all us brainy types working together."

"But magic healing is a thing?" pressed Alison. "It does exist?"

"Oh, it is, as you say, a thing," said Archibald. "There are people who can make another person's natural healing ability get temporarily boosted to superhuman levels. And there are vampires who can make your body age prematurely and generally break down. But 'life essence' is still only a penciled-in theory to explain this. No one's been able to detect any actual substance passing from the one person to the other. For all we know there really is some cosmic cupboard full of hourglasses marking each person's time on earth, and life essence manipulation is the ability to move the sand around."

"Right," said Alison, finally breaking a word in edgeways. "It's just, there's this video online of someone doing healing magic, and everyone in the Department who's looked at it just seems to instantly know that it's fake. Like, it's really obvious. But nobody's explained to me why."

"Hm. I suppose I'd better take a look."

Alison took out her phone and played the video of Miracle Meg apparently healing her devotee's wrist. Archibald leaned in to watch, and Alison tactfully leaned back slightly to escape the upsetting smell of death and sandwich condiments.

"My word," he said, leaning back after the healing had finished and Miracle Dad had moved on to shilling T-shirts. "Fake healing seems to have come a long way since the days of snake oil and carnival barkers."

"But how do you know it's fake?!" gasped Alison, holding up two clawed hands in frustration.

Archibald smiled in bafflement. "Because . . . she's still alive."

"What?" said Alison, her arms falling limply by her sides.

"Oh dear, I can't have explained this very well," said Archibald, scratching his head. "Did I forget to say that healing and vampirism are from the same group of powers?"

"No . . . Life essence manipulation, right?"

"Transfer. Sorry, I should have said life essence transfer. You understand that vampirism is the power to drain another life form's essence and add it to your own?"

The temperamental outboard motor that was Alison's mind finally started after a third determined yank on the pull cord. "Oh. Oh! So healing . . ."

". . . is the opposite," said Archibald, with a proud smile.

"Magical healers have to give up their own life?" Alison's expression cycled through a complex sequence of surprise, horror, and realization.

"Mm. And they often don't realize they're doing it, if the school doesn't get to them in time." He poked at the frozen image of Miracle Meg with a hairy finger. "There's no way that girl would be looking as healthy as she does if she's a practicing healer."

"I . . . suppose not," said Alison, feeling stupid.

"Yes, this is why life essence transfer is so poorly understood," said Archibald, folding his arms, shifting his gaze to the middle distance, and slipping back into know-it-all mode. "We so rarely get a chance to examine it in use. The educated ones are very firmly taught not to use it at all, and the rest just don't live very long. The healers die from using the power, the vampires generally from angry mobs with pitchforks."

"Wait a second," said Alison, looking at the image of Miracle Meg again. "They say she's a dual consciousness. Wouldn't that give her more control over—"

"Oh, no no no no no!" said Archibald, stopping her short with a concerned look and two wobbling hands. "Possessed healers have even shorter life expectancies."

"They do?"

"The Ancients . . . have a couple of blind spots when it comes to corporeal life," he explained uncomfortably. "You have to remember, these are immortal entities that live beyond time. They don't understand our concept of mortality. Healing Ancients go through hosts like a snotty nose through tissues. Goodness, I'm popular today."

He was looking over Alison's shoulder. She turned to see Adam Hesketh coming off the elevator. He wobbled out into the lab and paused for a split second when he noticed her, after which he resumed approaching with several degrees of casual saunter artificially injected into his gait.

"Hey, Alison," he said, with overdone nonchalance. He turned to Archibald, then did a double-take back to her. "Oh. The administrator's looking for you."

"Ms. Lawrence?" Alison checked her watch. "Oh . . . bother, it's brief o'clock. Erm. Thanks, Mr. Brooke-Stodgeley."

"Anytime, my dear," said Archibald. He waved as she jogged to stop the elevator doors before they closed, then turned to Adam the instant she was out of sight. "Lovely girl. Bit dim. What can I do for you, Mr. Hesketh?"

"I, er, had a question about healing magic."

Archibald sighed. "What is it with all you young people and healing magic today? Is this one of those meme things?"

"Um, no," said Adam, eyes darting like a confused actor at a rehearsal who was on the wrong page of the script. "I wanted to ask about this online faith healing outfit?"

Archibald put up his hands as Adam made to unpause the video on his phone. "I've actually seen that video before, Mr. Hesketh."

"You have?"

"It's that Miracle Madam girl or whatever she calls herself, yes?" He took a moment to drink in the look on Adam's face. "Don't look so surprised. A good wizard does their part to stay updated on modern lore, too, dear boy."

"All right," said Adam. "Did you know someone turned up dead in Worcester from a vampire attack? Modern Miracle is based in Worcester. I've reason to think there might be a connection."

"That's . . . I don't think that's even circumstantial evidence, Mr. Hesketh."

"Just hear me out. The vampire victim, William Shaw, he was interested in Modern Miracle. His parents said so. I think he was part of their, you know, congregation." He reached into the back of his trench coat and produced a creased and sweaty manila folder. "And look at this. The place where his body was found? It's closer to Modern Miracle's headquarters than his own house."

Archibald didn't reply, but smiled and nodded charitably, making prompting motions with his hands to try to coax a point out of Adam.

"Okay, so, I know everyone says it's got to be fake healing because she still looks young and isn't dead, but there are so many testimonials online, so I was thinking, what if it is actually real? And what if she's still alive because she's a vampire as well as a healer? It's possible to have more than one power from the same group of powers, isn't it?"

"Ah," said Archibald, nodding as the penny dropped. "You think she might be a conduit."

Adam brightened. "There's a word for it?"

"Yes, but there's a word for unicorns and Mr. Spock and lots of other things that don't exist. Conduits are only theoretically possible with our current understanding of magic. There's no actual record of any existing."

"But it is possible," pressed Adam.

Archibald glanced mournfully at his unfinished sandwich. Its lack of presence inside his stomach was beginning to gnaw at him. "Yes. It's possible. She'd definitely have to be possessed to have that level of control, but—"

"She is!" announced Adam with growing confidence. "That's what they say! She's in dual consciousness with El-Yetch."

An increasingly weary Archibald looked at the paused frame of video on Adam's phone again, then back at Adam. "She doesn't look possessed."

Adam was smiling with slightly worryingly widened eyes. He snapped his fingers. "Neither did Jessica Weatherby. Until the last part."

"Well. That was a rather unique situation."

"Is it me, or have there been lots of 'unique situations,' lately?" said Adam. "Maybe other things are changing. Maybe now magic's gone public, the Ancients are starting to feel differently about our world. Now that we don't just suppress and kill them the instant they pop up."

Archibald frowned at the video again. "So you're suggesting that the Ancient possessing this girl has somehow opted not to physically mutate her."

"Is it possible?"

Archibald was a scientist, and enjoyed a good thought experiment as much as any, but more and more of the processing power of his mind was being turned over to assessing the smell of uneaten lunch. He sighed in irritated tolerance. "I feel like we'd need to pile a lot of assumptions on top of each other for this theory to work, Mr. Hesketh. First we're assuming this person is a possessed healer who isn't being consumed by their own power, which would require an Ancient that understands the concept of mortality. On top of that, we now also need to assume that this Ancient understands the concept of vanity as well. And that Ancients can somehow opt not to physically mutate their hosts, which, with the already noted Weatherby exception, would be contrary to all observed evidence at this—"

"I'm not asking if it's likely," said Adam. "Just if it's at all possible."

Archibald puffed out his cheeks. "Given"—he counted briefly under his breath—"twelve or thirteen assumptions about things currently in the gray area of common understanding . . ."

"A yes or a no would be fine," interjected Adam as Archibald's thoughtful pause drew on.

"Yes," sighed Archibald, with the tone of an exhausted parent replying to their child's request with a strained *We'll see*. "It is theoretically possible. But—"

"That was all," said Adam, holding up his hands and backing toward the elevator. "That was all I needed to know."

"But I need to stress—"

"No stress!" He was in the elevator by now, repeatedly tapping the Close Door button. "Thanks for your time. Sorry to interrupt lunch."

Archibald looked forlornly at his sandwich. Something from a nearby flask had dripped onto the corner of the bread, and said corner was now rapidly growing a bright yellow fungus that Archibald knew for a fact would, if ingested, cause paralysis and a condition technically known as "horrific pregnancy." He clicked his tongue and resolved to eat around it.

16

"Diablerie spoke to an informant," said Elizabeth Lawrence, tapping her steepled fingers together over her desk.

Alison, feeling tired and breathless from her long recounting of the previous evening's events, could only boggle once again at Elizabeth's ability to summarize. "Um, yes. Mr. Chahal."

Elizabeth continued tapping her fingertips together in silence. Alison could only guess at the route being taken by the train of logic in her head. "Rajesh Chahal," she repeated to herself, before her hands moved to her laptop and she began to type with the measured, careful finger movements of a pianist. "We have a file under that name."

"We do?"

Elizabeth tapped the Enter key, and her eyes scanned a screenful of new information. "Occult scholar. File first opened in the Ministry era when he uncovered certain magical truths at university. Some feelers were put out to see if he could be persuaded to join the Ministry in some capacity. That went nowhere. Apparently he was vehemently against keeping magic secret."

"But magic isn't secret," said Alison. "Not anymore."

Elizabeth didn't seem to hear her. She kept reading, idly stroking an invisible beard. "There's no record of Chahal since he turned down employment. That was over ten years ago."

"Does that mean something?"

Elizabeth caught her eye. "It would normally indicate to me that he was part of another clandestine organization during that time," she said gravely. "Rajesh Chahal may be dangerous, Alison. He must know something about Diablerie's agenda, if he isn't directly involved. I need to be informed immediately if he makes another appearance."

"Okay," said Alison, nodding rapidly. "What about his information?"

"I don't see how a small-time faith healing outfit could be an urgent matter," said Elizabeth guardedly. "Still, there is clearly more to it, especially if Diablerie seems interested. I believe we shall wait and see if it appears on our radar again."

"Okay," said Alison, a little disappointed for reasons she would find it hard to explain.

"Alison," said Elizabeth, switching to her softer, mollifying voice. "You've done well. I believe I still owe you something."

"You do?"

"The information you requested, the last time we spoke. We were interrupted before I could deliver it." Elizabeth shifted in her seat, silently taking a long breath in through her nose. "What do you remember about the incident ten years ago, when the skies went dark for a week?"

Obviously what Alison remembered was every slightest detail, as was the case with every other time in her life, but something told her this was one of those short-summary situations. "It said on the news that there was a volcanic ash cloud descending on the country and we should all stay indoors." She took Elizabeth's silence as a prompt for more. "We played thirty-seven games of Scrabble—"

"The Shadow Crisis is the only known case of an Ancient attempting a hostile invasion of our world," said Elizabeth mournfully. "We can still only guess at its motives, but I'm certain it was a deliberate invasion. Because it started at the place that posed the biggest threat to it. Right here." She pointed downwards.

Alison fought the urge to look down at the carpet. "Here?"

"At the Ministry. The old Ministry headquarters under Westminster Abbey. A human in a dual consciousness with the Ancient in question allowed themselves to be captured and placed in the dungeons there for reeducation, as was policy at the time. Once there, they became a kind of living rift through which the Ancient entered our world."

From what Alison could remember of the old Ministry of Occultism bunker, it had mostly been old marble and unnecessarily ornate wall decoration. It hadn't looked much like a place that had been ground zero for an interdimensional conflict, even one from ten years in the past. "How big was it?"

"It wasn't what you're imagining," said Elizabeth, perceptive as ever. "No misshapen monster emerging through a hole in space, waving tentacles. Our people could have handled that. And occasionally did." She went back to hunting through her briefcase, still talking. "The Ancients are noncorporeal beings. It was more like . . . an influence. It influenced the Ministry staff the way magic normally influences people. Altering them, body and mind."

She produced a worn picture from her briefcase, a posed photograph of a large number of individuals. The focus was on a circle of seated elderly men dressed in the robes of the Hand of Merlin, the inner council of the old Ministry of Occultism that had ostensibly been in charge but which had become largely ceremonial in its last few decades and more concerned with getting together for elaborate dinners while the Administration team did the actual work.

Behind the Hand's chairs was presumably the Administration team themselves: a row of men wearing ordinary suits and ties, and one short young woman on the far right dressed in blouse and skirt. Who, on closer inspection, looked a lot like . . .

"That's me," said Elizabeth, noticing Alison's gaze lock on to the image. "At the time, I was assistant to the Swordkeeper. That's the man next to me."

"Swordkeeper" was the title Richard Danvers had held when Alison had first joined the Ministry. He had very swiftly changed it to "head of field operations" after the Ministry became the Department, and prior to that had always insisted on "Swordkeeper" being printed as small as possible on his business cards.

The Swordkeeper in the picture was a man Alison didn't recognize. He was tall with midlength gray hair and an expression that, while neutral, suggested that his tolerance for this photo-taking ritual had a very clear and hard limit.

That led Alison to realize that, while she recognized some of the long-standing Hand of Merlin members—Richard Danvers Sr., most notably—the administrative team were all strangers. Besides Elizabeth, not a single one had been with the Ministry at the time of Alison's recruitment. Between that and the sad look in Elizabeth's eye as she looked over the faces, Alison was getting a bad feeling.

"I never knew his real name," said Elizabeth quietly. "I only ever knew him as Mr. Teapot."

Alison gave a little spluttered cough on reflex. "What?"

Elizabeth's lip curled briefly with embarrassment. "The Ministry was still a government secret. There was a rather juvenile code name policy among senior staff. So the Swordkeeper was Mr. Teapot. The Scrollkeeper was Mr. Spoon. And the Master Apprentice was Mr. Sugarbowl."

She indicated them in turn. Mr. Spoon was one of the younger men, in that his stringy brown hair was only beginning to gray, and he was just about the only person wearing a genuine smile. Sugarbowl was a stocky, bald man, standing with chin up and hands behind his back as if doing everything he could to artificially increase his height without resorting to standing on tiptoe.

"Spoon was the first to die," said Elizabeth bluntly. "He began acting strangely after speaking with the prisoner. He started going through his research obsessively. He was convinced something terrible was about to happen. We came in the next morning and found him dead in his office."

Alison could only stare at the smile on the face of Mr. Spoon. It reminded her of Archibald Brooke-Stodgeley.

"I didn't know what was happening," said Elizabeth. "I was an assistant. No one told me anything. I tried to distract myself with paperwork. I only realized how serious the situation had become after Mr. Sugarbowl's death."

"But why were they dying?" asked Alison, looking up.

"I never learned what killed Mr. Spoon. I do know what killed Mr. Sugarbowl. It was when Mr. Teapot marched into his office and shot him eighteen times with a revolver."

Alison blinked. "Eighteen?"

"He reloaded twice." Elizabeth caught her look. "I saw the body. I saw what Mr. Sugarbowl had been turning into at the time. If it were me, I would have reloaded once more."

Again, Alison couldn't help looking down at the faces of the smiling dead men. Sugarbowl and Teapot were practically standing side by side like . . . well, like a sugar bowl and a teapot. She stared at the few inches of space between them and, in her mind's ear, heard the sound of eighteen bullets passing through it.

"They were our leaders, so the Ancient hit them hardest," continued Elizabeth. "But by the time of Sugarbowl's death, its shadow was already spreading beyond the Ministry. That was your 'volcanic ash cloud.' Teapot was able to get the government to issue the isolation order in time, but the worst was to come . . ."

She faltered when, with either excellent or very poor timing, a familiar sound of heavy footfalls faded into earshot, approaching from the elevators. When they became loud enough to make all of Elizabeth's stationery quiver, an ominous shadow fell across the frosted glass in the door.

Sean Anderson, the Department's occasional liaison to the British government, barged into Elizabeth's office with his muscular chest already inflated for a rant, but he had to switch gears in a hurry when he noticed Alison's presence, and his twin lungfuls of air escaped from his mouth as something between an animalistic roar, a cough, and a belch. "Ah!" he said, after he had recovered. "Good. Little Miss Muppet's already here. I don't have to start punching down the walls looking for her stupid arse."

Nita Pavani trotted into the office behind Anderson's bulk and demurely moved into the corner like a sniper taking position.

"Tell me," barked Anderson as Alison shrank to avoid his flying spittle. "After the last time the media went through your knicker drawer, did I or did I not advise you to keep your sodding head down?"

"Erm, you did not," said Alison, calling upon her eidetic memory.

Anderson frowned in bafflement, and his eyes rolled back for a few moments as he went over recent events in his head. "Well," he eventually said. "I was *implying* some very bloody emphatic things."

"What's this about?" droned Elizabeth. She had already put the photo back in her briefcase and was sitting with hands clasped before her, the emotional brick wall fully rebuilt.

Pavani stepped forward, her mouth set into a thin, disapproving line, and turned her tablet around to show an image of Alison looking like a deer in headlights as Beatrice Callum barked questions in the car park of the Builder's Arms.

"Yeah, what you're doing now, gawping like a blind goldfish looking for something to suck?" said Anderson, indicating Alison's open-mouthed expression. "That's what we call looking like a pranny, and you can do it as much as you want in your own time, darling, but not when you're in front of the media! Because that makes us all look like prannies!"

"I'm sorry!" said Alison, it being her default response. "They surprised me . . ."

"They're the media!" roared Anderson. "You expect them to call ahead and ask when would be the most convenient time to hound you to your idiot grave where they bury idiots?!" He was tottering a little.

"Hardly the mainstream media," said Elizabeth, who was examining the display on Pavani's tablet.

"Actually, these activism streams rate very highly with teens and young adults," said Nita. "This particular branch of LAXA has close to a million subscribers."

Elizabeth leaned closer. "These teenagers, who drive around the country in a van, solving mysteries."

"Yes?"

"With a dog."

"Yes!" said Nita, exasperated. "Why does everyone keep saying that like it's weird?"

"If you don't mind, we were having a meeting," said Elizabeth pointedly.

Anderson glared at her, looking her up and down. Clearly he was unhappy with the power dynamics in the room, with Elizabeth holding court in her executive throne. "Damn right we are. That's why we're going to have it in a meeting room." He stomped over to the door and held it open. "Come on! All three of you. Someone get Danvers as well."

"What is there to discuss?" asked Elizabeth, not moving.

"The department's taken some flak, or *damage*," said Anderson condescendingly. "And now we have to talk about how we're going to *control* the amount of damage we have to take. There's probably a quicker way of saying that."

17

"We need to take a closer look at these Modern Miracle people," said Adam.

"Uh-huh," replied Richard Danvers, not looking up.

"William Shaw was killed from life essence removal, and this faith healer two streets over is handing out mysterious reserves of life essence. It might not be a coincidence."

"Right . . ."

"I spoke to Mr. Brooke-Stodgeley and he agrees with me that she's probably a conduit. That's a life essence manipulator who can—"

"I know what a conduit theoretically is, Adam," said Danvers. "Sounds like you should be talking to Sumner about this. Isn't he running the Shaw case?"

"Ah, yeah," said Adam uncomfortably. "Sumner's kind of stuck on his own theories. Mr. Danvers, all I have to do is go to one of these Modern Miracle sessions, and I'll know exactly what kind of magic we're dealing with—"

"Adam," said Danvers sternly, finally giving up on being able to read his newspaper in peace. "Two things. First, I know the current structure is new for you, but it's very bad form to go over a colleague's authority like this. It can make for a hostile work environment."

"Oh," said Adam, adding, "Sorry," as an afterthought.

"Second," said Danvers, "this is a conversation I would prefer to have over my desk, rather than through a toilet door."

Adam leaned away from the door of the toilet cubicle as if it had become red hot. "Sorry," he repeated.

Danvers sighed in relief as the room outside fell silent, then focused on concluding what had been, up until now, the only part of his daily routine in which he could actually relax for five minutes. This done, he flushed, got his clothing back in proper order, and emerged from the cubicle to wash his hands.

As he was doing so, he glanced into the mirror and found himself locking gaze with Adam, who was still in the bathroom, standing expectantly by the door with hands in pockets.

"Was there something else, Mr. Hesketh?" asked Danvers, hands frozen in the act of washing.

"Oh. I thought you wanted to keep talking across your desk like you said."

Danvers pinched his eyes. Good management, Danvers reminded himself, was about being someone your employees wanted to follow, not just obey. He hadn't intended that to apply so literally, but the point was, this would be a bad time to snap. This was a time to offer guidance. "Adam, is everything all right? Any problems settling in at Investigations?"

"No. Yes," said Adam. "I mean, other way round. Yes to the first part and no to the second."

"Are you sure?" Danvers scrutinized Adam carefully while he waited for the roar of the hand dryer to stop. "I'm getting the sense that you feel . . . unchallenged."

"No, it's just . . ." began Adam. He tried to stop himself there, but Danvers made an encouraging movement with his eyebrows, and he resigned himself to finishing the sentence. "It's just, I feel like everyone thinks of me as if I'm a really useful magic-sensing power on the end of a stick, and I think I've got more to offer. As an investigator."

Danvers nodded. "Okay. This is good, actually, Adam. It's great that you want to expand your skill set. Very forward thinking. But . . . it hasn't even been a week since the restructuring. What you need to be doing now is listening to your senior team members and learning as you go."

"But I was with the Ministry before Sumner," said Adam, in a plaintive voice.

Danvers stared. "You were?"

The awkward moment ended when they both jumped at the sound of a fist like an oversized leather coin purse slamming against the outside of the door. "Oi! Danvers!" came the voice of Anderson. "Get wiped and trousered up. Meeting time."

18

"All right, quick summary for the latecomers," said Anderson as Danvers skulked into the meeting room. "Arkin got ambushed by some new-media scum, and now it looks like we didn't come down hard enough on some conjuring twat who was breaking X-App."

"The X-Appropriation Act," explained Pavani, the teacher's pet for the afternoon.

Danvers hadn't sat down yet. He paused with his hand on the backrest of a free chair. "This is the top priority, is it?"

Anderson threw out his hands. "Slow news week," he said, in what passed for an apologetic tone for him. "Believe me, if she'd waited till World Cup season to bugger something up we'd be laughing, but this is the flavor of the month. The narrative is that DEDA isn't taking X-App seriously. We need to counter that narrative. Nowish."

"We did set up a dedicated skepticism department," said Danvers idly, having now taken a seat and rested his chin on one hand.

"We definitely should not draw attention to that," said Pavani spitefully. "In case anyone notices that there are only two people in it." She glared briefly at Elizabeth, who returned a completely passive look. "I suggest going back and actually arresting this appropriating magician. Say we needed time to get a proper warrant written up, or something."

"Erm, we couldn't arrest him in the end anyway," said Alison nervously. Anderson had steered her into the meeting room's biggest, most central chair, and she was starting to feel like an extremely reluctant Jesus at the Last Supper as his disciples discussed the itinerary for his upcoming violent martyrdom. "Because he was using—"

"Because there wasn't enough to build a case," said Elizabeth quickly.

"Anyway," said Anderson, fed up. "The government did not establish this law so you jokers could round up all the stage magicians and get revenge for your shitty birthday parties. It was supposed to stop faith healers and the like taking advantage of thickos. Alternative medicine's exploding now it can associate with real magic. The prime minister's been very hot on this since his sister-in-law's dog choked on her crystal therapy kit."

"Admirable," said Elizabeth dryly.

Anderson looked at each person in turn, waiting for suggestions, and met nothing but polite blankness, indifference, and cringing terror. "All right, since you're all collectively as much use as a one-legged cat on the Palestinian border, I'll tell you what you're going to do. You're going to invite these internet snots to come watch you enforcing this law in a way that makes us all look good. Yeah? Come down on some hippie who made a cancer patient ditch chemotherapy to stick incense in his pisshole. That sort of thing."

"Couldn't we just issue a press release saying we do take the law seriously?" suggested Danvers.

Anderson looked at him with the usual contempt, then sighed. "Be nice to go back to those times, wouldn't it? When that was all you needed to do. No, people get so much smoke blown up their arses these days, they don't pay attention anymore. They just take it in and fart it straight back out. These days, you want a story to stick, you gotta do stuff, not just *say* you're doing stuff."

"I'm firing a message off to LAXA Updates as we speak," said Pavani dutifully, going at her tablet like a desperate window washer without a sponge. "They're easy enough to find. Very social media active."

"Right," said Anderson. "Now all we need is a bogus healer to arrest in front of them."

The moment the words left his mouth, an urgent knocking came upon the meeting room door. It wasn't particularly loud or hard, but it started slowly and gradually increased to urgent tempo as the knocker gained confidence.

"Bog off!" roared Anderson. "Senior meeting!"

A moment of silence as the person behind the door wrestled with their courage, then the door opened exactly six inches. "Sorry, sorry sorry

sorry, this can't wait," said a breathless Adam Hesketh. "I've got an urgent, I mean, I'm late for some . . . investigating I'm doing. I just need a quick answer on what to do about that *faith healer* I was investigating?"

"Adam . . ." said Danvers, tired.

"Get in here, shambles," commanded Anderson. Adam swiftly did so, and the moment the door fell shut behind him, he was pinned to it by the stares of everyone in the room. "You got a faith healer we can move against?"

"Oh yes," said Adam, nodding so rapidly his voice was distorted. "This online faith healing group called Modern Miracle—"

"Modern Miracle?" asked Alison, sitting up. She exchanged a glance with Elizabeth.

Anderson looked from her to Adam and back. "This name mean something to us?"

"It appears to be coming up a lot lately," said Elizabeth, her voice low with suspicion.

Pavani was going at her tablet again and reading from the results. "Looking up Modern Miracle. A few results. Are we talking about the streaming channel, the message board, or this . . . Cult of El-Yetch thing?"

"Yes," said Alison and Adam together.

"It's all the same thing," said Adam.

Anderson was clutching his head. "Look, I couldn't give the fluff on a monkey's bum for the details. You lot work this out after I bugger off to the next pack of cockheads on my list for today. I just need to know one thing: are we absolutely sure this is fake healing? 'Cos the whole plan is in the bog bowl if it isn't."

"Erm . . ." said Adam.

"Oh yes, pretty much all faith healing is fake," said Alison eagerly. "Because of how real magic healing works. Basically everyone who knows anything about magic knows that."

"Okay. Good." Anderson stabbed a sausage-like index finger in Adam's direction, and he unconsciously flattened himself against the door again. "It was your idea, so it's on you if this goes up the poo pipe, spotty. Can I leave you all to it now?"

Alison hadn't realized it was possible to flush pale, but Adam was making a spirited attempt. "Uh," he said. "Uh. Well. Yes, I suppose it's probably fake, isn't it."

"Okay! Good meeting! Where am I next?" Anderson was already stomping toward the door and checking his phone. "Oh. Department of Business. And Alan is swearing that he dumped his shares by coincidence, because he thinks my brain has been replaced with a pulled pork sandwich since the last time. Eff me. On second thoughts, eff him." He opened the door and left, hardly noticing that Adam was still pinned to it.

After waiting the customary amount of time for the sound of angry footfalls to fade away, Danvers coughed. "Well, the strategy seems clear. Alison, could you inform Diablerie that his new assignment has been decided?"

"Modern Miracle is having one of their public healing shows at their house this Friday evening," said Pavani, still staring at her tablet. "I'll make sure LAXA's people are free, but does that suit the two of you?"

Alison didn't have the slightest idea. She didn't have access to Diablerie's calendar, or anything so mundane as a phone number with which to reach him; she had simply grown reliant on his tendency to materialize when needed, or thought about. "I think so," she summarized aloud.

"You propose to put Doctor Diablerie in front of cameras," said Elizabeth, holding her clasped hands before her face.

"Yes!" said Pavani.

"To show that we're taking our work seriously," continued Elizabeth.

"Hm," said Danvers, tapping his fingers on the desk. "Alison, just . . . do your best to keep him reined in."

"Maybe I should go too!" said Adam, stiffly holding up an arm like a schoolchild asking to use the lavatory. "In case she needs help reining him in."

"I think not, Adam," said Danvers. "There are plenty of open cases at Investigations that would benefit from your input."

"But—"

"Alison knows Diablerie well enough to handle him now," said Elizabeth. "One suspects the only thing that would significantly help would be a straitjacket."

Text messages between Victor and Leslie-Ifrig, 11:00 a.m. to 4:30 p.m.:

Your private message history with Leslifrig6969
hey victor
thanks for joining the site
hey
you there?
oh i guess your probly at lunch
hey are you back?
hey
hey you there?
i know your there it says your reading these
i thought you wanted to be friends
> **You replied: For christ's sake.**
> **You replied: I didn't sign up here to be friends.**
> **You replied: I am keeping tabs on you because you tried to
> kill me.**

you tried to kill me too
see we've got a lot in common
> **You replied: I'm not going to respond any more after this.**

ok
hey
hey victor
hey victor
hey victor
victor
> **You replied: WHAT DO YOU WANT?**

hey victor
wanna go start fires in rainham quarry
> **You replied: NO.**

i think im going to
> **You replied: DO NOT DO THAT.**

well im going to soooooo
better come stop me

THE NEXT FRIDAY EVENING

19

The address that Modern Miracle provided on their website turned out to belong to a very nice detached home at the end of a curling side street on the west edge of Worcester. As Alison drove Diablerie's car around the curve, the house was directly ahead, standing against a backdrop of a rolling grassy hill with the houses to the left and right of it seeming to cringe at its obvious greater importance.

The house itself was two stories of flat-faced nondescript orange brick, and the front garden little more than a rectangle of green lawn bisected by a path, but it was a bustle of activity. People of all ages were standing around it in small groups, chatting indifferently, all throwing occasional glances at the front door of the house and the inexpensive Modern Miracle banner that had been hung over it.

There were so many vehicles parked in the small suburban road that driving Diablerie's ostentatious car through the space available would have been like working out a particularly antisocial kidney stone, but then Alison noticed the familiar sight of Beatrice Callum's LAXA van parked a good distance from the house and took that as the invitation to park directly behind.

"There lies the weasel den," announced Diablerie, the moment the car door opened and his polished shoes touched the tarmac. "Come, then. Glorified rat catchers we may be, but never let it be said that Diablerie—what is it now, girl?"

The moment Diablerie had thrust himself to his full height and begun talking at maximum volume, Alison had started urgently hopping from one foot to the other and shaking her palms at him. "Um," she whispered. "I was just thinking we could try to be subtle?"

Offended, Diablerie threw his cloak around himself. "Think you to lecture Diablerie on the subtle arts?"

"We are . . . trying to catch someone in the act," tried Alison. "Maybe we should try not to be noticed?"

Diablerie's gaze shifted to the small crowd gathered on the lawn in the distance, and his eyes narrowed slowly as his lips drew thin. "From the mouths of babes, perhaps," he muttered, before turning and rummaging around the back seat of his car for a few moments. When he turned back around, he was wearing a top hat that had a black band instead of a red one and was about an inch shorter. "Come! Let us melt unseen among the dark shadows that haunt this place."

Alison decided to let the matter drop, partly because she was trying to figure out if Diablerie had just said something racist or not, partly because, at that moment, the side door of the van opened, and Beatrice Callum became visible for about half a second before Alison's view was entirely filled by a flailing mass of brown fur.

"Sorry!" said Beatrice, grabbing the dog's leash just in time and hauling him back. "I think he remembers you. Down, Arby. Bad boy."

Arby pawed the air, thrusting himself forward again and again, it apparently taking quite a long time for his conscious brain to absorb the fact that he was leashed up. Alison leaned back as far as she could over the bonnet of Diablerie's car until her body resembled a question mark. "You brought the dog?!"

"Yeah, well, we were going to drop him off at Mum's," said Beatrice, quite casually, despite the frenzied, slobbering mass she was using all her strength to keep at bay. "But that didn't really work out because, you know, Mum doesn't technically know we have him yet. How've you been? You all right?"

Alison was making a courageous effort to will herself two dimensional. "Allergies," she explained, in what came out as a whispered squawk.

"Oh, right, sorry." Beatrice pulled the dog back in earnest, and the leash was taken by her dreadlocked boyfriend-cameraman, who had also emerged from the van. "So . . . we got the message from your lady at DEDA and I gotta say we're pretty pumped about this, Modern Miracle has been on our radar for ages, there was this whole thing actually where they poached one of the best moderators away from LAXA.com and it was all a load of drama llamas for a while so it'll be great to get some ammunition—"

"Bea!" shouted Beatrice's brother David from his usual spot in the driving seat of the van. "How long is this going to take?"

"I don't know!" replied Beatrice, fists clenching. "An hour or two!"

"You said that last time! This is gaslighting!"

"No it isn't! Shut up! We're streaming!" She turned to her cameraman, who was tying the dog to something hopefully secure inside the van. "Can we start streaming?"

"Oh yeah, let me get the equipment out," he replied, after he had finally successfully closed the sliding doors without a furry snout getting in the way. He then produced his phone from his coat pocket and held it up. "Okay. Ready."

"Roger, we need lighting," said Beatrice reproachfully. It was to be an evening sermon, and the last rivulets of daylight were dribbling down the chimneys of the houses.

"Oh yeah," said Roger. He fumbled with the screen for a few seconds, then activated his phone's inbuilt flashlight. "Okay. Streaming live."

For the second time, Alison had the privilege of witnessing Beatrice's transformation, this time in the opposite direction. After she had finished blinking away the afterimages, her posture and expression changed like a cinematic dissolve. Her loose shoulders tightened. Her sleepy gaze hardened into a gimlet stare. Her perpetually open mouth clamped shut and became tight with disapproval.

"This is Beatrice Callum for LAXA Updates," she said into the microphone that she had produced from her hip pocket. "Thanks for watching, remember to like and subscribe. We're here in Worcester to investigate the so-called Modern Miracle cult and their so-called claims of magical so-called healing." Her eyes rolled back for a few moments as she parsed her own words. "And we're very pleased to announce that LAXA Updates is now fully backed by the British government."

"Erm," said Alison as the phone light swung around to drill into her retinas. "Hello?" She glanced around for Doctor Diablerie's support, but he was a few yards away out of shot, doing a channeling routine that looked as if he was trying to rhythmically sweep his hands past his nose as close as he could without touching it.

"Donation from TimelyGonad," reported Roger, reading off his phone. "He wants to know if Ms. Arkin is going to use her mind-taking powers against Modern Miracle."

"I don't have . . . that wasn't . . ." said Alison, words sputtering in her throat like a dying sparkler. "Do I have to answer that?"

"He donated," said Roger, as if that resolved the matter.

"Okay, back to me," said Beatrice, beckoning with a finger until Roger turned the lens back on her. "Modern Miracle is holding one of their so-called healing services tonight for all their brainwashed followers, and we intend to uncover the truth in front of everyone they've misled. This is investigative journalism at its noblest and most serious."

"Donation from JizzFairy," said Roger. "He wants to know your favorite flavor of crisp."

"Thanks for your support, JizzFairy, I would have to say salt and vinegar," said Beatrice, not changing her tone of voice.

Beatrice continued establishing the scene and answering viewer questions as she walked slowly toward the house, Roger trying his best to lead the way facing backwards. Alison drifted along after them, far enough into the road to be safely out of shot.

By this point there was music coming from the front garden of the Modern Miracle house, and judging by the way the visitors were all now politely sitting cross-legged in the grass, this was apparently the signal that the show was about to start. The music was a powerful orchestral track that was somehow simultaneously very bombastic and very generic. In fact—Alison's eidetic memory suddenly kicked in—it was music that she had heard on no less than three epic fantasy movie trailers in just the last six months.

"Girl," said Diablerie, heart-stoppingly close to her ear. He had been strolling along at the rear of the party and had subtly slid into place beside her, marching with the ominous tilt of a pallbearer. "A storm brews here, girl. A metaphorical storm," he swiftly added. "For the sake of our mutual dignity, do not glance at the sky."

Alison's neck stiffened as she rushed to cancel the nerve impulse she had just sent.

"There's danger here." He sniffed. "Dark tendrils play at the edges of that house's aura like black fingers."

"This isn't a racism thing, right?"

"Keep your wits about you," said Diablerie, in about as serious a tone as Alison had ever heard from him. "Be ready to react to the unexpected." With that, he slowed his walking pace again and glided smoothly back to the rear guard of the party.

Between Diablerie's words and the dying sunlight projecting a flare of red sky against the looming silhouette, Alison felt a deepening sense of omen from the Modern Miracle house. Although that might equally have been coming from the fact that the trailer music had reached the part normally accompanied with a succession of quick cuts of increasingly intense action scenes.

By the time Alison had knelt down on an unoccupied patch of grass at the very back of the crowd and leaned against the perimeter fence, the music had reached a crescendo and faded out. The enraptured silence of the followers as they stared expectantly at Modern Miracle's front door painted a fresh layer of eeriness onto the scene.

Miracle Dad's entrance, after a few finely calculated moments of utter silence, left her rather underwhelmed, but perhaps she had spent too much time around Diablerie and his smoke bombs. Miracle Dad simply opened the door and bounded out. "All right, Miracle Mob!" he exclaimed. "Thanks for coming to another Modern Miracle stream!"

He addressed the second part to the camera rather than the crowd. Modern Miracle appeared to have a more advanced setup than LAXA, because their camera was a webcam sitting on a pile of books on a dining chair. It was connected by cable to a laptop being operated by a frail, meek-looking middle-aged woman who Alison assumed must have been the lady of the house, Miracle Mum perhaps. She seemed like the kind of person who would end up with someone like Miracle Dad, the way a small, pale moon gravitates to a large, boisterous planet.

"We've got a follower today who's come all the way from Inverness to receive El-Yetch's blessing," said Miracle Dad, rubbing his hands in a gesture combining prayer and excited anticipation. "But before that, let's remind ourselves about the story of El-Yetch."

He paused, smile wide and hands clasped, for long enough to make things awkward. Then, just as he was glancing desperately over to the woman at the laptop, the speakers began emitting a relaxing pipe tune. And from her position, Alison could clearly see that Miracle Mum's laptop was displaying a video thumbnail entitled "Ten Hours of Baby Sleep Music."

"Yes, El-Yetch!" said Miracle Dad, getting back into the swing of things. "Our adoptive mother. The Ancient who looked down at the little struggling specks of humanity and thought, hey, maybe there's more I could be doing for these guys besides giving some of them superpowers and making their faces go weird. Maybe I could do something to help. And so she came into my daughter, and now she's Miracle Meg."

Alison had only been half listening, as she was keeping one eye on Beatrice and Roger as they crouched stealthily behind the fence waiting to strike, but as she parsed the words of Miracle Dad's sermon, she found herself entertaining a few doubts. Miracle Dad had an authentic manner that would have been difficult to fake. He didn't have the overblown religious fervor that only played well to credulous cultists; he was very matter of fact. He spoke about his god not with starry-eyed, desperate, one-sided love but the way one would, say, recommend a relative's house-cleaning business.

Alison shook herself. Of course he seemed confident; hence the phrase *confidence trickster*.

"El-Yetch doesn't want your worship," Miracle Dad was saying, slowly drifting up and down the "stage" to give time to each segment of the audience. "She doesn't care if you've sinned or if you love thy neighbor. She'll never ask you to pledge your eternal devotion to her and her alone. She doesn't want you to sing hymns, and she doesn't want your money."

"Donation from Xyzyx," reported the woman at the laptop.

"Okay," said Miracle Dad as a subtle titter went through the audience. "El-Yetch doesn't want your money, but we very much do. All the money you donate goes toward producing these streams and helping us spread the important word of El-Yetch. Was there a question?"

"What is El-Yetch's favorite flavor of crisp?" read Miracle Mum from the screen.

"Oh, salt and vinegar, definitely."

Alison took a few careful looks around at the crowd. They didn't seem like brainwashed cultists either. They were from all walks of life. There were young people and old people, families with children and people in loosened business attire who must have come straight from work. The same kinds of people Alison saw every day in the streets of Whitehall and the corridors of the Department. The kind of people she worked with, socialized with, went to school with . . .

A realization hit her like an iron stake, going through her suddenly open mouth and pinning her to the ground. Rana was here. Sitting just a few rows away.

Rana had been Alison's closest friend back when Alison's eidetic memory had caused her to be erroneously enlisted in the government magic school. Rana had been there, studying at the desk next to Alison's, on the very day that Adam Hesketh had shown up and revealed her utter mundanity to the world.

Alison had been the rising star of her class. The other kids, the ones with real magic infusions, they had actually looked up to her. Her ears still burned with humiliation when she thought about that day. And then of course she had learned about the second school, the concrete prison where those with confirmed magical infusions were sent to be reeducated, to suppress all chance of dual consciousness. That was no longer policy, thankfully, but not because of any protest Alison had made.

Alison had occasionally wondered what she would do if she ever ran into one of her old classmates. She had eventually decided that it needn't be an issue, as long as she just turned on her heel at first sight and ran until her shoes melted.

She rose into a half crouch and began picking her way through the seated crowd to the garden gate. This was LAXA's show anyway. She and Diablerie were only here to make the arrest. Anderson would probably appreciate it if she retreated a little farther into the background . . .

Miracle Dad suddenly stopped sermonizing, which made Alison wonder for a moment if she was being called out, like someone going to the toilet halfway through a standup comedy act, but Miracle Dad was looking past her at the darkened street. The puttering of a motorcycle engine was breaking off from the background roar of distant traffic and growing in volume.

The sun was now almost completely down, and the figure on the motorbike coming up the street was a black shadow, the streetlamps not so much illuminating it as adding orange highlights. They reached the end of the street, pulled off a noisy full turn with a whine of tires, and then stopped in front of the Modern Miracle house, angrily slamming their foot to the tarmac like a suburban mother who damn well wasn't leaving without a refund.

"HEY! BELIEVE IN CHRIST!" yelled the rider, holding something up in one hand. Alison rose slightly to get a better view and recognized it to be a leather-bound Bible in the brief moment before they threw it.

It seemed to fly through the air in slow motion as Alison experienced a moment of perfect clarity, during which she realized two things: first, it appeared to be an extremely heavy volume with a cover reinforced with metal bits on the corners, and second, it was absolutely going to hit her in the face.

It was a perfect hit, depending on your perspective. One of the rein-forced corners landed an inch above Alison's right eye. An ice-cold stab of pain threw her head back, which slowly transitioned into a rather pleasant warmth that soaked through to the back of her brain. Something started humming soothingly in her ears. It was only after she felt blood streaming sideways along her forehead that she realized she was lying on her back.

"OH SHIT! SORRY!" yelled the biker, before gunning their engine and riding off into the gathering clouds of fuzzy pink cotton wool that were now surrounding Alison.

She felt friendly hands on her limbs and the sensation of being lifted, which made the fuzzy pink cotton wool spiral in faster. Snatches of conversation drifted through the pink and burst like bubbles in her ears.

"What happened?"

"Bloody Bible thumper . . ."

"Yeah, literally."

"There's a lot of blood."

"Come on. Get her inside!" That was Miracle Dad.

"Alison? I know her. That's Alison Arkin . . ." That was Rana.

"Noooo I'm nooot . . ." moaned Alison groggily, before the pink clouds engulfed her again.

She floated there in a state of warm bliss, far away from the troubles of the waking world with all its hurled Bibles, intrigues, and shouty Downing Street enforcers, before being rudely stirred back to partial consciousness by the feel of something cold and hard beneath her. She was sitting on a floor with her back to a wall.

Unbidden, her faultless memory felt the lines of the tiles beneath her and of the metal drain directly beneath her left buttock and reported that the floor they were on was one she had seen before. It was the bathroom floor in the Modern Miracle house, the very one from the video.

Someone helpfully pressed a cold washcloth against her forehead, which only served to remind her of the head wound, and with that, the pain crashed into her again like a fast-moving wave. Her entire body cringed and something roared in her ears, creating a harmony with the anguished moan that escaped, unbidden, from her throat.

A small hand touched her cheek. "Don't be afraid," said the voice of Miracle Meg.

A moment later, Alison was overcome by a sensation completely new to her. It started as a tingle in the pit of her stomach and swiftly exploded to fill her entire body to the tips of her fingers, chasing away all the pain and leaving only a mild, glittering coldness.

She felt a warm throb wash over the wounded part of her forehead, and then a rather alarming sensation of skin crawling, accompanied by a frenzied whispering in her ears. It reminded her of the chittering of the Ancients she had heard on her first and only attempt to draw a rune, but with all the voices hissing in unison.

When the whispering stopped, the pink fog went away. Alison was dropped unceremoniously back into full alertness. She was sitting bolt upright on the bathroom floor, her body fizzing with energy as if she were two coffees deep at a really productive meeting.

She felt at her brow. Some blood was still there, but she could sense with inexplicable certainty that her body had already manufactured a replacement quantity. The wound was completely closed. Nothing remained but a thin, unnoticeable Y-shaped scar that could have been several weeks old.

She looked up at Miracle Meg in astonishment, who was sitting on the toilet, just as she had done in the video. She definitely wasn't older than eleven and had black hair pulled tightly back into twin pigtails. She was smiling expectantly, as if waiting for the teacher to praise her work.

"What did you do?" was all Alison could say.

"I healed you," said Miracle Meg, frowning in confusion for a moment but smiling throughout.

Alison felt at her forehead again. "It's real," she breathed. "You really did."

"Miracle Meg does it again!" said the voice of Miracle Dad.

Alison looked to her left and saw that there were about seventeen people packed into the hallway that led up to the bathroom, several of them holding out camera phones. Miracle Dad was at the forefront, holding the webcam from his laptop.

"I think it's safe to say that El-Yetch has a new believer!" he said into the webcam before turning it on Alison again. "Alison Arkin from the Department of Extradimensional Affairs, you've just been magically healed by Miracle Meg! Anything to say to the people?"

Alison stared, suddenly exhausted, into the cloud of unfeeling black camera lenses, and thought about the people. Specifically, she thought about people like Sean Anderson, who would no doubt see this, and at this moment would probably be clutching the armrests of his chair so hard that his fingertips were three inches deep.

"Sorry," she said.

MEANWHILE

20

Victor Casin was spending that same evening exploring a gravel quarry, and his mood was only getting fouler the more convinced he became that Leslie-Ifrig wasn't there. He had walked all the way around six piles of gravel so far and had completely lost track of which ones he had already checked, so he was starting again from the yellow bulldozer. This time he made sure to give every gravel pile a savage kick so he could remember it, and so it would know who was boss.

Before long, his jeans were coated in gray dust from the knees down, which gave him a strange feeling of satisfaction. He pictured himself at the office tomorrow, being approached by a colleague asking why his clothes were covered in dust. Naturally, Victor would instantly reply: "Because I spent last night in a quarry looking for a dangerous possession, who was out causing trouble because I didn't kill them when I had the chance, because the new policy is to give the poor, misunderstood demigods smacks on the wrist when they try to incinerate people." And thus would said colleague hang their head in shame at Victor's devastating correctness.

Victor practiced the wording under his breath. Then, since the quarry was deserted at this time of night, he recited it out loud. Then he made his way to the top of the nearest pile, planted one foot higher than the other, and announced his devastating argument to the stars with one finger held high, then spent a moment to drink in the imagined applause.

A burst of magical fire appeared just over the next rise, and Victor flinched so hard that he toppled over and rolled back down the gravel slope, dusting the rest of his outfit with a layer of gray powder. He was able to translate it into a forward roll and stopped in an alert crouch that he imagined would probably have impressed someone.

Another yellow mushroom cloud unfolded into the sky, far enough away that Victor doubted it was being cast at him, or because of anything he had done. He crept toward the next rise and ascended it as slowly as possible, shifting his weight carefully to avoid making the gravel crunch.

Just beyond the quarry was a wild plain of unkempt grass and an oxbow lake that was murky and green with algae. Someone was standing with their back to Victor between the two arms of the lake, restlessly stirring the ground with one foot.

Their silhouette was made a little indistinct by a baggy hoodie that seemed to have been thrown on so haphazardly that it was only pure random chance that their arms had gone into the sleeves, but Victor could tell that it was Leslie-Ifrig. The big giveaway was when he or she summoned a gigantic boomerang-shaped wave of flame and sent it over the waters of the lake, close enough to the surface to send ripples that glittered impressively in the orange glare.

Victor continued advancing as slowly as he could, descending the gentle slope of gravel onto the grass. With Leslie-Ifrig unaware, he had the opportunity to end this swiftly and painlessly. All he had to do was superheat the three or four square feet around Leslie-Ifrig to the evaporation point of human bone. Using all his concentration, it should only take about half a second for a space as small as that, and they'd never have a chance to react.

No doubt the Department would kick up a stink if he didn't issue a warning first or offer a complimentary premurder beverage. But apparently the Department only saw Victor as good for killing things, and it would serve them right if he proved them entirely correct.

But something made him hesitate, and he wasn't entirely sure what. Maybe he was picking up danger vibes from Leslie-Ifrig's rather deliberate nonchalance. Surely they wouldn't drop their guard like this. They must have some sort of magical booby trap set up.

Maybe they already knew that Victor was there and were waiting for him to attempt the ambush, so they could turn it around on him somehow. Well, he wasn't going to fall for it. He held out a hand and sent a beam of fiery energy well above Leslie-Ifrig's head, but close enough that it added its own cascade of reflections across the lake.

Leslie-Ifrig immediately spun around, delighted. "You came!"

Victor stayed in a half-crouched combat stance, arms extended as if aiming an invisible sniper rifle at a nervous person in a vest of dynamite. "Of course I came," said Victor, maintaining fierce eye contact.

Leslie-Ifrig beamed. "Come on! If we both did one of these curved-line things, we could probably draw a big heart over the lake."

"I'm not here to play games," growled Victor, not moving. "I have to take you in."

Leslie-Ifrig frowned with the part of their face that was capable of doing so. "Why?"

Victor was getting more and more frustrated with Leslie-Ifrig's interpretation of events. As far as he was concerned, he was talking down a dangerous threat that could blow up on him at any second. Leslie-Ifrig seemed to think they were hanging out at the mall with a friend, endlessly passing the "What do *you* want to do?" buck back and forth. "Because we can't let you go around setting fire to things," said Victor.

"I'm not. I'm drawing hearts. *Trying* to draw hearts."

"You're upsetting people."

"Who?"

"ME!" Victor's sudden blast of rage sent sparks flying from the gravel near his feet. "I'm people! You're upsetting me!"

Leslie-Ifrig cocked their head like a poorly trained dog as their owner yells *sit* for the fifth time. Their lips parted and their shoulders sagged as an unpleasant realization hit. "You don't like me."

Victor didn't reply. He was too busy repeatedly chanting the word *de-escalate* in his head.

"Why don't you like me?" asked Leslie-Ifrig plaintively, their lower lip quivering.

Victor's arms dropped in exasperation. "Because you're Ifrig!" He gestured broadly. "You're the one who did this to me!"

Leslie-Ifrig stared at him, the furrows on their brow emphasized by glowing red lines. "When did I put dust all over your jeans?"

"You made me into this!" Victor could feel his anger rising and consequently his magic sparking and bubbling just behind his eyes and teeth. He screwed his eyelids shut and pushed it back inside himself. "I could have been anything. You understand that?"

"I understand," lied the increasingly concerned Leslie-Ifrig as the threat/negotiator roles reversed.

"I could've gone to university," continued Victor, shoulders shaking. "I could've been a businessman. Or a scientist. Or I could've learned a trade. Plumbing. Carpentry. I could've worked behind the till at the god-damn Morrisons." He swatted away a few strands of hair that had fallen in front of his eyes. "I could've finished school! Got my A levels! Finished maths! Figured out how trigonometry worked!"

"Doesn't sound that great," offered Leslie-Ifrig.

"Well, I'll never know!" yelled Victor, blue flame flaring at his eyes for an instant. "I will never know what any of that is like, because when I was eleven years old things started catching fire. And after that, every-thing went away. My toys, my computer, my Judge Dredd pillowcase . . . all burned. One by one."

Leslie-Ifrig gave a worried half smile. "Do you want to talk about it?"

Victor clenched his fists as hard as he could to stop his emotions rising. "That was the worst part," he said, no longer looking directly at Leslie-Ifrig. "That it happened when all my potential was spreading out in front of me. All of that got cut off. I had to go to the monastery, then the second school, then . . ." He held out his hands, then let them flop to his sides, as if unable to bear the weight. "This is all I can be, now, because of you. Just something that destroys and kills."

"I don't want you to kill things," said Leslie-Ifrig. "Doesn't your boss make you do that?"

Victor's anger came to a boil all at once, rising up and bursting out of him before he could stop it. He gave in and went with the flow, thrusting his arms out and roaring as everything in front of him whited out. The pounding of his heartbeat in his ears was like a door open to a thunder-storm, crashing rhythmically against a wall.

When the smoke and the steam cleared, the water level of the oxbow lake was looking a couple of feet shallower and the horseshoe shape had drifted into more of a serifed capital D. The area between the arms had been reduced to an obliterated mess, craggy with blackened glass.

Victor sagged, gasping for air, groaning with each breath to drown out the chittering at the back of his mind. Steam was drifting up from everything, and the entire scene wavered with a heat haze. He glanced around as his full thinking capacity gradually returned. It seemed that Leslie-Ifrig . . .

. . . was right next to his ear again. "Now do you want to talk about it?"

21

With the excitement of the impromptu ritualistic healing over and everyone already inside the house, Miracle Dad had turned on a playlist, cracked open a case of inexpensive beer, and made the evening change from "mass" to "house party." The congregation had scattered themselves around the ground floor and the front garden, mingling their little conversation groups to compare notes on all of this El-Yetch business.

The largest gathering was in the living room, where Alison had been helped into an armchair to recover but now found herself under the uncomfortable scrutiny of Modern Miracle's followers. They filled the room, sitting on the floor and perched on every available space like primary school children hearing a guest speaker. She hadn't seen Diablerie or any of the LAXA people since she had been brought inside, and it was hard to find an opportunity to make her excuses and leave, not when people kept coming up asking to touch the healed scar on her forehead. Alison was starting to feel like a statue of Buddha.

"You have many questions," said Miracle Meg, who was holding court from the arm of Alison's chair.

Alison looked at her. "I do?"

"You wonder why I look like this"—she gave a little shrug—"even though El-Yetch is in me."

"Oh yeah," said Alison. "We were all wondering about that."

"This realm has become more open to that of the Ancients," she said, in a slightly ethereal voice. "Now that magic is no longer secret and those whom the Ancients touch are not shunned as they once were. And at the same time, the Ancients are becoming more open to you."

"The Ancients are watching us?" Alison looked up and around absurdly.

"El-Yetch influences this world because she means to," continued Miracle Meg. "She has seen us and she wants to help us. That's why she didn't change the way I look."

"But why?" asked Alison, frowning. "What can she possibly be getting out of helping us?"

Meg seemed confused by the question. She looked to Miracle Dad, who was sitting on the near end of the sofa, nodding along to the things she said.

"Well, you don't expect to get anything out of keeping a hamster, do you, but you still look after it," he said bluntly, setting his beer to one side. "Maybe she thinks we're cute. Maybe she gets frequent-flyer miles hanging out down here. Whatever, she wants to give us free healing magic, so why ask questions?"

Alison thought uneasily about the Shadow Crisis, and the look on Elizabeth Lawrence's face whenever she talked about it. Whatever that Ancient had wanted out of the human realm, it may well have been the same thing motivating El-Yetch. And somehow Alison doubted that it was merely some Ethereal Realm equivalent of completing their Pokémon collection.

She looked at Miracle Meg again. While she gave every impression of being a perfectly mundane little girl on video or from a distance, there was definitely something inhuman about her when examined up close. There was a strange glimmer about her eyes, and when she spoke, her voice seemed to be coming from far away.

"But how does she provide free healing?" asked a member of the audience who was sitting on the floor.

"She, er . . ." Miracle Dad faltered. "Well, she touches them. You all saw."

The audience member pushed her large spectacles up her nose, and Alison tensed up when she realized it was Rana. She was focused on Miracle Dad in a very deliberate manner that unnerved Alison even more than if Rana had been sitting there staring daggers straight at her. "I mean, magic healing has only ever worked by giving up the healer's own life essence." She was leaning forward, enunciating each word carefully. "How do you make it work without that happening?"

"El-Yetch makes all things possible," said Miracle Meg dreamily.

"What she means is, El-Yetch has the power to create more life essence," said Miracle Dad, just quickly enough to make Alison's eyebrow raise.

"She can do that?" asked Rana.

"Hey, some people can create stuff from nothing, right?" said Miracle Dad. "That girl on the news could do it with salt." He pointed a chubby finger to Alison, and she tried to subtly dig herself deeper into the arm-chair cushions. "The one you, you know, did the brain thing to."

"She's a life essence elemental?" said Rana, fascinated.

"Could be, yeah," said Miracle Dad. "Look, I'm just a regular dad. I don't pretend to understand this stuff like the government experts do. Speaking of which. Ms. Arkin?"

Alison had just successfully snuck out of the armchair unnoticed and had made it a princely seven or eight inches toward the door when all eyes suddenly fell on her again. She winced, frozen in midcreep. "Yes?"

"Those Bible types, like the one that beaned you in the face tonight? They've been getting worse." His expression was suddenly dire and plaintive. "It was nasty emails first. Then letters. Then they started tying the letters to things and throwing them at the house. They don't like new religions. We're a threat to them."

"Okay," said Alison, glancing back and forth to the door as if she could will herself closer to it with eyeball movements alone.

"You have to go back to your bosses at the Department and tell them we want recognition. We're not some cult, we're not trying to brainwash anyone, we just want acknowledgment that we've got as much right to exist as any other religion. You tell them that."

Some stubborn part of Alison's mind—probably inherited from her mother—told her to ask to hear the word *please*, or perhaps for him to rephrase his words to sound more like a request and not a demand, but better instincts overruled it. "I will . . . go and tell them right now," she said.

To her relief, that seemed to satisfy the room, and all eyes turned back to Miracle Dad and Miracle Meg as Rana pressed them with another question about how the magical healing worked. Alison had to wonder why Rana was displaying such interest in the matter, but then again, back at school she had been Alison's chief rival for the teacher's pet posi-tion, and in any case, the exit door was open wide and inviting and this wasn't a question Alison felt was going to keep her awake at night.

Someone had set up a grill in the front garden to cook burgers and sausages for the lingering groups of El-Yetch followers, so by the time Alison had carefully navigated her way between the conversation groups, the healed scar on her forehead had acquired a colorful mix of ketchup and mustard stains from people wanting to touch it. The moment she was on the pavement and the garden gate had swung closed behind her, an enormous feeling of relief washed over her like a cool breeze on a stifling day.

It was augmented slightly by the appearance of Beatrice and Roger from LAXA, and even more so when she saw they weren't filming. They drifted over to her from their concealed spot behind a hedge, both with hands buried sheepishly in pockets.

"Wow, so they really healed it, huh," said Beatrice, admiring Alison's scar. "What is that, like, ectoplasm?"

Alison touched it with a finger and inspected it. "No . . . Dijon, I think."

Beatrice sighed. "Guess this whole thing was kind of a bust, huh. Still, it's pretty cool that it's real healing. Pretty cool to watch it happening as well. Bit gross, but overall cool. Just closed up like the zip on some trousers." She blew a raspberry and jerked a finger upwards to imitate the motion.

"Yeah," said Alison, glancing back at the house. *Cool* wasn't the word that would occur to her. There was a lot about the evening's events she was going to have to take away and process—or rather, tell Elizabeth about so that she could process it. All that Alison could say with confidence was that something didn't feel right about Modern Miracle.

"So, guess the Department isn't gonna be happy, since they wanted an arrest," said Beatrice, watching Alison's pensiveness.

"Yeah," said Alison, feeling ill.

"Yeah, that sucks." Beatrice offered a sympathetic wince and a half smile, then both disappeared in an instant. "Anyway, do you mind if we head off?"

"No, we should probably all go," said Alison, turning away from the noise of the impromptu party behind her one last time.

Beatrice blinked. "Don't you need to wait for your partner? Boss? Thingy?"

Alison shrugged. "He'll probably appear at some point."

"Oh sure, cool," said Beatrice as they began to walk down the darkened street to the two vehicles. "My uncle has a cat like that."

Beatrice prattled on, unheeded, as Alison worked her eidetic memory fit to burst. She was recalling every moment of the evening's events in sequence. There was no doubt that she had been genuinely, magically healed. She had been uniquely positioned to notice if there had been any tricks in use. So did that mean Miracle Meg really was possessed by an Ancient that had somehow become benevolent to humanity? It turned everything Alison thought she knew about Ancients on its head. It was like hearing that a passing black hole had decided to support a specific football team.

Her conscious mind registered the sound of a barking dog and filed it at first with every other generic sound of a nighttime suburb, until the sound grew enough in volume to register that something was up. "Isn't that your dog?" she asked.

"Oh yeah," said Beatrice. "Probably."

Arby was making distressed noises in a regular rhythm. Two or three barks, then a desperate whine, then a growl gradually transitioning into a fresh chorus of barking. As Alison drew close enough, she could see a hairy brown shape in the darkness at the side of the van, animatedly struggling against a very short leash and throwing itself against the van's door.

"Arby?" said Roger the cameraman, jogging forward to free the dog. The leash had been trapped in the side door, and Arby had been attempting to run around and seek assistance with about six inches of free range.

"What happened?" asked Beatrice.

"Someone must have shut him out," posited Roger, stroking Arby's fur and trying to calm him down until he forgot to be upset and attempted to jump around in excitement again.

"David!" yelled Beatrice, hitting the side of the van. "What're you doing in there?! There's no Wi-Fi! You'll use up all the data!"

Roger finally got the side door unlocked and hauled it open to free the dog, at which point David emerged. Or rather, gravity caused David to slump lifelessly into the street.

He was quite dead. It was only his LAXA T-shirt and ill-fitting jeans that made him recognizable. His hair had become pure white, and his skin was blotchy and sunken, as if a vacuum hose had been inserted into him and shrink-wrapped his bones to his skin.

"Oh my god," said Beatrice, after a shocked silence. "Wow. He finds a way to ruin everything."

LATER THAT NIGHT

22

It was past nine o'clock when Adam Hesketh received a call from Richard Danvers, commanding him to come in to the Department for an emergency briefing. After waiting about ten minutes to hopefully give the impression that he'd had anything better to do, Adam caught the next underground train to central London.

After hurrying through the deserted atrium of the Department's building—an area that was filled with ominous echoes when not bustling with activity—he reached the Operations briefing room to find three people gathered around the front desk, embodying three different interpretations of the word *sitting*. Elizabeth Lawrence sat behind the desk in a fairly traditional, conservative manner; Richard Danvers was perched on the end of the desk with one foot drawn up; and Alison Arkin sat on a chair in front of them so bound up with tension that her posterior must have been hovering an inch above the seat.

"Mr. Hesketh," said Danvers. He was in serious, no-nonsense chief inspector mode, as evidenced by having fastened his top shirt button. "Notice anything unusual about Ms. Arkin's forehead?"

Alison dutifully leaned forward to let him see. "No?" he said, before a quick double take. "You mean, besides the fact it's been magically healed recently?"

One of the layers of tension audibly vanished from the room as Danvers leaned back. "That'll do for confirmation."

"It definitely felt real," said Alison. "It definitely seemed like something hard to fake."

Adam was not quite prepared to internalize the notion that he had been called across the city at night to look at three square inches of forehead. He was an Investigator, and obviously he had been called to help Investigate. He leaned forward and dynamically raised one foot on the seat of the nearest vacant chair. "What happened? Fill me in."

"Another vampire victim has turned up in Worcester," said Danvers, after a moment's surprised hesitation. "This one right on Modern Miracle's doorstep—moments after Alison here received magical healing from someone who didn't appear to suffer any ill effects from granting it."

Adam's eyes popped wide with excitement. He thrust out a pointed index finger so quickly that everyone in the room instinctively flinched. "I told you! This is exactly what I said! She's got to be a cond—"

"Yes, yes, yes, I remember you raising that theory," said Danvers, waving a hand. "I'd be interested to hear your theory on how she was able to drain life from this poor young man from an entire street away."

Adam froze, jaw slack. With no conscious thought on his part, his defiant pointing finger slowly drifted to the top of his head and began scratching it. "It, er. Well. If they moved the body afterwards . . ."

"In any case, this girl was on camera, on multiple livestreams, clearly only touching Ms. Arkin and nobody else," said Danvers. "We had a little conference call with Mr. Brooke-Stodgeley while waiting for you. He assures us that life essence transfer depends on physical contact. It can work through a layer of clothing or two, but not solid walls and empty air."

"And, and," said Alison, "he said it wouldn't take a whole teenager's worth of life essence to heal one small head wound." This was something that had started particularly bothering her during the drive back to London.

"I'm inclined to agree with his theory that the girl is a genuine healer but uses scam-healing techniques most of the time and reserves the real stuff for very rare occasions, such as when someone in the government needs convincing," said Danvers, nodding to Alison. "I'm sure the aging effect wouldn't have been noticeable for a wound that small."

"So what happened to David?" asked Alison.

Danvers puffed out his cheeks and shrugged. "There must have been a separate vampire on the scene. One we don't know about. The same one that drained William Shaw."

"It can't be a coincidence," pressed Adam, reasserting his dynamic lean forward. "An entirely separate vampire just happening to be there on the very same night?"

"On the very same night of a large public event," said Elizabeth calmly. "Held by a group with a large percentage of extradimensionally infused members. Whose public message board appears to be a hotbed of magical extremism."

"Turns out it can be a coincidence," said Danvers tactfully as Adam's face fell again. "It can quite easily be a coincidence. What does this message board turn up?"

"There is a public discussion on the subject of tonight's sermon," said Elizabeth, opening the laptop in front of her. "Mostly general agreement that it was a positive evening. Some anti-Christian sentiment after Alison's wounding. After that, a lengthy sidetrack on Alison herself and an argument over whether what she did to Jessica Weatherby was justified—"

"Who thinks it was justified?" said Alison, suddenly buoyed.

"Nothing that seriously implies an intention to enact violence," finished Elizabeth, barely pausing.

"In any case, I'm going to put someone onto monitoring this site," said Danvers. "Someone in the Pacifications unit. They've been fairly idle lately—"

He was interrupted by the door flying open and Nita Pavani marching in. She was driving her heels into the floor as hard as she could, but she didn't have the mass to match Sean Anderson's effortless stomp energy. "Oh, excellent," she said, drawing herself to her full height and planting her hands on her hips. "You're all here."

"Ms. Pavani . . ." said Danvers.

Nita ignored him and went to Alison, placing a hand on her shoulder. "Alison, it's so good to see you all right. I saw the attack. It must have been very traumatizing. How do you feel?"

"Erm, fine?" said Alison, a little confused. While Nita had bent down to Alison's level and was looking her square in the eye with an expression of deep sympathy, Alison couldn't shake the feeling that Nita was actually addressing a point about six inches behind her head. "I got healed."

"I saw that as well," said Nita, straightening up and spinning on her heel to address the room. "And I don't know why, but I immediately had the funny feeling that the authorities would be doing everything in their power to take this flagrant hate crime against a marginalized group and find a way to blame the victims for it."

She glared at Elizabeth, which was, as ever, like attempting to mace a concrete barricade, and then Danvers, who told her everything she needed to know by immediately breaking eye contact.

"So, I assume we're discussing how to track down the terrorists that attacked an alternative religion's private worship and injured poor Alison here?" said Nita, striding back and forth.

"That isn't our remit," pointed out Danvers.

"Oh!" said Nita, with sarcastic surprise. "But we have made sure to file a police report, in that case?"

"Alison is perfectly entitled to do so at her leisure," said Elizabeth. "This briefing is to discuss a separate matter that does fit our remit."

"A body turned up right after the event," explained Adam, who had been feeling left out. "Killed by a vampire."

That threw Nita for a moment. She looked around at the others, eyebrows high and lips tight, before saying, "And I suppose we're going to blame Modern Miracle for that as well?"

"Their message board does seem to attract a radical element," said Danvers.

Nita did that thing she sometimes did that was halfway between a scoff and click of the tongue. "It's the internet, Richard. There are a lot of layers of irony at work. You wouldn't understand. Why isn't it just as likely that those terrorists did the killing?"

"Christian vampires?" said Elizabeth dryly.

"Well, it seems no one else is taking our obligation to represent the extradimensional community seriously," said Nita, folding her arms. "So you can either keep sitting around muttering about scary vampires or get with the march of progress, because I'm going to reach out to Modern Miracle and find out what I can do to support them. Alison, what did they say to you about that?"

Alison didn't see much point in lying, as it seemed likely that at least one of the streamers at the party would have captured her conversation with Miracle Dad, and Nita had the wide-eyed look of someone who had been doing a lot of Googling tonight. "They said they just want acknowledgment."

The floor began shaking to herald another new arrival, but the moment Sean Anderson stomped into the room and opened his mouth to bellow, he was frozen by Nita thrusting out a hand in a "stop" gesture. She didn't break fierce eye contact with Alison throughout. "What kind of acknowledgment?"

Alison glanced worriedly at Anderson's face and its deepening shade of crimson. The individual hairs of his crewcut bristled like an encroaching forest fire. "Um . . . they just want to be taken seriously, I think. Like all the other religions."

"Pardon me," barked Anderson. "But why are we talking about bigging up a bunch of weirdos who just completely humiliated—"

"SHUT UP, SEAN," barked Nita straight back, with such venom that actual fear registered briefly in his eyes, and everyone else present felt their eyebrows involuntarily leap to the tops of their heads. "This is bigger than you! This is bigger than whether it made the government look bad! Do you understand that?! This is about harmony between humanity and the Ancients! And why the hell shouldn't they be treated like every other religion? Why is their mother goddess any more ridiculous than water getting turned into wine by yet another mediocre white man?"

Anderson held up his hands mollifyingly. They looked like a pair of bulwarks made from salted ham. "Okay, Nita. Calm down."

Nita leaned even further into his personal space. "Oh, you'd like that, wouldn't you? Calm down, little people. Go back to sleep. Big Daddy Government will make sure everything stays nice and peaceful." She made to storm out, with Anderson only just managing to hop out of the way in time, then stopped and spun around at the doorway. "It won't go back to bed so easily this time! We . . . drank too much fizzy pop tonight!"

The others watched her go, stomping away down the corridor like a trotting show pony, until the sound of traumatized carpet and hoarse breathing faded into silence.

"Right," said Anderson uncertainly. "So . . . what were we talking about?"

"I think we were about to call this meeting adjourned," said Elizabeth.

"Hey!" Anderson glowered, pointing a meaty finger. "I'm the one who says that!"

"Then be my guest."

Anderson took in the four expectant faces of the people that remained, then sniffed self-consciously and bowed his head. "Uh. Meeting adjourned."

"Thank you," said Elizabeth, rising. "Alison, I'll give you a ride home."

"Oh!" said Alison, caught off guard. "You don't have to . . . I can just . . ."

Elizabeth caught her eye. "Alison," she repeated, not changing her tone of voice in the slightest.

"I mean, thank you, I'd really appreciate it."

Adam watched them until they had drifted out of both visual and audible range, then stepped close to Danvers's desk. "Mr. Danvers, you know if I went to one of these Modern Miracle services, I could tell you exactly how they're doing the healing trick. It might help . . ."

Danvers was rubbing his forehead. "Yes, all right, Adam, given the circumstances, I'm not against it." He gave Adam a piercing look that pinned him to the floor as he made to leave. "But you and I will have a meeting with Sumner in the morning to have a full and frank exchange of notes."

"Okay, thank you, Mr. Danvers," said Adam, rushing out the sentence as a single unbroken stream of syllables and then making for the door before anyone could have a chance to change their mind. He made brief eye contact with Anderson on the way and spent the rest of the trip to the door with his head dropped low and his face parallel to the floor.

Anderson, for his part, took one look at Danvers's tired but politely expectant expression, and what energy he had left visibly drained from his muscles. "I suppose . . . all of this can wait till tomorrow," he said. "I'll, er, I'll see you later." He began to leave, sheepishly trying to minimize his footstep sound.

"Anderson, small question," said Danvers softly. "It's past ten o'clock. How did you know we were having a meeting?"

Anderson's nostrils flared. "Oh, come on. Like I'm the only person who watches live security footage when they can't sleep."

23

Alison hadn't seen Elizabeth's car before. Somehow she had imagined that Elizabeth would drive some kind of terrifyingly large black utility vehicle, something that would reflect the vastness of the thinking and history behind her deceptively small form, but as could have been predicted from a small amount of thought, this was not the case. Elizabeth drove a car as seemingly unassuming as her: a simple family sedan, of a color that couldn't quite decide if it was gray or blue.

Nonetheless, Alison felt like a tiny child in the passenger seat as Elizabeth drove in the slow, contemplative way that went easy on her bad knee. It hadn't escaped Alison's notice that the interior was clear of all the usual debris that cluttered cars. Even Diablerie was guilty of having a couple of old receipts in his coffin-shaped drinks holders.

"Do you know where Diablerie went?" asked Elizabeth as she stared at a red light waiting for the change.

"N-no," admitted Alison. "I haven't seen him since I got hit by that Bible." She had called Danvers after the discovery of David Callum's corpse and had been forced to drive Diablerie's car back alone to make the emergency briefing.

"He disappears, and a body turns up," thought Elizabeth aloud.

"Well, he did send me a text thirty-two minutes ago," said Alison, commencing the ever-awkward dance of removing a phone from a hip pocket while sitting in a car seat, "saying the cost of his train ticket will be extracted from my soul one sin at a time." She hesitated when she noticed the frown Elizabeth was directing at the bumper of the car in front. "You think he might have been . . ."

"No, I think we learned our lesson the last time we accused him of murder," sighed Elizabeth. "He's not the killer. That would be far too straightforward. But . . ."

As Elizabeth's pause lengthened, Alison realized she was being prompted. "But he knows something. He knew something about Modern Miracle ahead of time. That's why he warned me."

Elizabeth nodded slowly in approval. "Either he knows something or Rajesh Chahal knows something about Modern Miracle's agenda. But we may gain the advantage if Ms. Pavani can get closer to the source."

Alison thought of the furious expression on Nita Pavani's face as she had been ruining the office carpet with her heels. "You really think she'll agree to be an informant?"

"No," said Elizabeth bluntly. "But the best informant is one that does not realize they are an informant."

Alison nodded slowly, unconsciously mimicking the action Elizabeth had made a moment ago. "Do you think there's any chance that Modern Miracle could be on the level? About Mir—about that girl being a life elemental, and dual consciousness, and El-Yetch wanting to help humanity . . . ?" She let the question trail off when she saw Elizabeth's knuckles turning white around the steering wheel.

"A couple of points give me pause," said Elizabeth measuredly, tapping the tips of her index fingers once, twice, three times. "First, of all the people who could have been wounded tonight, it was the one person who would be the most useful if converted. The one with government connections and the most open mind."

Alison was almost certain that open-mindedness was generally considered a virtue, but she wasn't getting that vibe from Elizabeth's tone. "You think it might have been set up?"

"Second, from the direct encounters with Ancients I have had, I find it hard to believe that an Ancient could even comprehend the idea of benevolence toward us."

Alison didn't reply but drooped in her seat, feeling faintly ashamed, like an unsavvy internet user finally accepting that the deal being offered by the Nigerian prince in her email inbox might not be as sweet as it first appeared.

Elizabeth sighed so gradually that it was barely audible. "Where were we on the story?"

"Story?"

"The Shadow Crisis."

"Oh!" Alison perked up, then tried to perk back down again when she saw the dark clouds gathering in Elizabeth's expression as she made to recall the memories. "Mr. Spoon died. The Ancient took over Mr. Sugarbowl, and Mr. Teapot killed him. Then Mr. Teapot made the government issue a shutdown order."

"Right," said Elizabeth. "Teapot was certain that Sugarbowl had come under the Ancient's influence and murdered Spoon. The trouble was, Sugarbowl had been passing for normal up until his death. Which raised the possibility that there may have been others who were influenced and passing for normal. So Teapot ordered the entire Ministry bunker quarantined. No one in, no one out.

"No members of the Hand of Merlin were there. They only ever came to the bunker for their 'meetings.' It was only the administrative team and a division of the Brotherhood of Merlin. You remember the monks?"

Alison remembered the Brotherhood of Merlin all too well: an ancient monastic sect that had a deal to work alongside the government to suppress magic and the magically infused, until they had been deemed politically toxic at the onset of the current era. Alison had no idea where they had gone since then, but a bald man with hauntingly familiar tattoos had glowered at her and Diablerie across the counter of a petrol station several months ago.

"At first, the atmosphere was civil, if tense," continued Elizabeth. "But disagreements began to rise. Some thought we should stay in large groups to keep each other under surveillance. Some thought we should avoid each other entirely. No one could agree on how to distribute the food stores in the cafeteria to be certain that no tampering occurred.

"On the second day, someone in the Scroll physically transformed and wounded a colleague. Either they'd grown impatient or the Ancient had. There was no obvious connection between them and Mr. Sugarbowl, or the possessed prisoner. Nobody knew how the influence was transmitted. Nobody knew who was already taken. In response, Mr. Teapot announced that he wasn't prepared to risk trusting anyone but himself. He shut himself in his office to coordinate the network of freelance operatives by phone. Barricaded the door. Even to me, his assistant."

"He abandoned you?" said Alison, horrified.

"He was correct to," said Elizabeth, with a hint of admonishment. "It was the most rational course of action from his perspective. I found that hard to understand at the time. And without leadership, everything went to chaos in the rest of the bunker. There was a faction of hard-liners—mostly monks, but with a few administrators mixed in—who took it upon themselves to enforce the quarantine. Beating up anyone who left their offices. It was that group that decided they couldn't trust whatever Mr. Teapot was doing to end the crisis. After all, he could have been possessed as well."

"What did they do?" asked Alison, fidgeting with her seat belt strap.

Elizabeth took another infuriatingly long sigh before answering. "They stormed the dungeon and killed the prisoner. It was a reasonable-enough assumption. Destroy the Ancient's original access point, remove their influence from the world."

"It didn't work?" deduced Alison.

Elizabeth's face hardened even further. "Either it only made the Ancient desperate or widened their access point. The rate of transformations rose. More people died."

"How did you get through all of this?"

"My office was in the antechamber that led to Teapot's office," said Elizabeth, with a small measure of guilt. "The facilities were good. A large storage cupboard in which to hide when I heard footsteps in the hall. It also meant I could talk to Teapot through the barricade on his office door.

"He made it clear he would never let me in, of course, but there were long hours when there was nothing to be done but pass the time with conversation, and it kept us both sane. In that time, he and I gained an understanding that went beyond friendship. There are parts of yourself you can only truly share when in the face of death . . ."

Her eyes flicked to a red stop sign at the next junction, and as she pumped the brakes to obey, a shudder ran through her, breaking her out of the brief reverie she had indulged. "The extremists became all the more irrational after their failure. Suspicion of Teapot's actions became hysteria. I'm certain some of them were possessed by then. There was talk of storming his office. So I passed him a warning, and he took measures to defend himself.

THE NEXT MORNING

24

Adam Hesketh arrived at the Department building clutching a brand-new manila folder bulging with fresh printouts and feeling extremely dynamic. So much so that, when he bought his usual latte from the snack stand in the lobby, he decided to go completely crazy and get a banana as well. This did mean that he had to show his ID to the security guard by holding it in his teeth, but even that couldn't sour his mood.

After Danvers had promised him a meeting to discuss the possible connection between the vampire case and Modern Miracle, Adam had made a special effort to write up his most compelling arguments. He had even gone through the Modern Miracle forums, taken screenshots of every suspect post, and printed them all out before he had allowed himself to go to bed. But he couldn't sleep, so he had gotten up again and gone over all the relevant lines with a yellow highlighter pen.

Nevertheless, he was brimming with energy that morning and was quite unable to stop himself from bouncing on his heels as he waited for the lift to reach the Department's main floor.

As he emerged, he saw the black-clad figure of Victor Casin hanging around the vending machines in the Department's bright reception area like some kind of gothic Christmas decoration and attempted to suppress his own excitement. He didn't want to irritate his oldest friend further by rubbing in his new status as a respected top-level investigator. Victor didn't handle jealousy well. Back at school, he'd swiftly been banned from playing Monopoly in any room without a sprinkler system.

"Well, if it isn't the superstar of the Hinvestigations Hoffice," said Victor loudly as Adam attempted to slip by unnoticed. "How's it going? Just back from meeting the Baker Street Irregulars?"

Adam was about to apologize on reflex, until Victor turned around to reveal the wide, slightly mocking smile that covered his face. There was a color to his pale cheeks that Adam had never seen before, like a pink stain in a snowfield from where a reindeer had been savaged by wolves.

"Victor?" said Adam, abandoning his attempt to speed walk past with an awkward faltering of his step. "Are you all right?"

"Sure!" said his former partner, swaying slightly. "Infused by an evil fire god. Can only masturbate in lead-lined rooms. Usual stuff, really."

"Why are you so . . . chipper?"

Victor's smile instantly vanished and his posture tightened up, ending his swaying movement as surely as if his shoulders had been pinned to the floor with wires. "I'm not chipper. I don't do 'chipper.'"

"You are totally being chipper."

"Ha—I am not!"

"Then why did you just laugh?"

"I didn't!"

"You did. You went 'ha.' That's what people say when they laugh."

Victor glanced furtively left and right but saw no obvious escape route from the conversation. His ears and nose had turned quite red. The savaged reindeer was proving to be quite the gusher. "Not necessarily. People say it when they're doing karate too."

Adam cocked his head. Victor was the person he knew best in all the world, and this was the first time he'd ever seen him in this mood. He knew Victor had been feeling alienated lately, but that was, if anything, his default state. The only explanation was that Victor had had some kind of new experience.

"Oh my god," realized Adam aloud, his eyes beginning to bulge.

"What?"

"Have you got a girlfriend?"

Victor forced himself silent, sucking his lips into his mouth, but it was pointless. An entire reindeer massacre was unfolding across the snow.

"You have! You've got a girlfriend!" shouted Adam, the tone of his voice wobbling with a complicated mixture of emotion.

"I haven't! It's not like that!"

"But there is an 'it'!" Adam took a step forward, and Victor had to flatten himself against the vending machine. "There has to be an 'it' for 'it' to not be like that! Who is she?"

"She's not a she! Or she might be. I haven't figured it out. Um." Victor looked past Adam and suddenly noticed that the Department's receptionist, who at this time of day would normally have their nose buried in social media, was looking directly at them with their gossip-collecting ears pricked up and primed for action. Victor grabbed Adam by the lapel and steered him a safe distance down the corridor, eventually positioning him between a secluded water fountain and a plant. "All right, yes, I have been . . . seeing someone, but it's not a girlfriend thing."

Adam's eyes and mouth were in a constant state of motion as he tried to decipher this. "But . . . when we were twelve, and you got really angry when I asked if you wanted to practice kissing . . ."

"Or a boyfriend thing! No romance or anything like that happening at all. It's more like . . . we get together now and again and try to kill each other for a few hours."

Adam's jaw dropped. "You've got an archnemesis?"

"It's probably a bit too early to put labels on it," said Victor, wobbling a hand. He was unable to stop himself breaking out into a stupid grin at the sight of Adam's face. "But I'm pretty sure there's a lot of archnemesis potential in this one."

Adam glanced in every possible direction, jaw still hanging open in disbelief, before returning his gaze to Victor. "We never had an archnemesis when we were partners!"

"So?"

"We spent years waiting for the right archnemesis to come along! We always said, if we ever got an archnemesis, we'd have one together! Now we stop being partners and within, like, three weeks you've got an archnemesis?" His lips were quivering.

Victor sighed in irritation. "Oh, come on. Don't take it so bloody personally. I wasn't gonna pass this up. They're possessed by Ifrig, for Christ's sake. They're, like, the perfect archnemesis for me. They probably wouldn't connect with you much."

"Well, I guess we can't know, can we?" said Adam, hurt. "Since I haven't even had a chance to meet them. Where did you meet them anyway?" His eyes widened. "Tell me it's not that pyrokinetic who was tearing up the docklands . . ."

"No, of course not," said Victor, his hands drifting nonchalantly into his pockets. "We . . . we met online."

"There's nowhere you can get matched with an archnemesis online," said Adam. "You know I know that. We checked together."

"It was on a forum. That Modern Miracle forum."

Adam's hands tightened around the folder of printouts in his hand with a snap of manila. "You're on Modern Miracle?!"

"Yeah." Victor shrugged. "A lot of people are on Modern Miracle."

"That's where all the magic extremists hang out!"

"Oh. Yeah. There's some of that," said Victor sulkily. "I don't really pay much attention to that stuff."

"Oh my god." Adam perched his coffee cup on the edge of the potted plant and started rifling through his folder. "We are having a meeting right now about their links to actual murder cases. I spent half last night printing out posts from that forum. Is this you?" He brandished a sheet. "ComradeBuggerov on the thread about 'all-time favorite explosions.' That's you, isn't it? Oh god. I had a feeling . . ."

"No!" Victor batted the paper out of his face. "I don't post. I just lurk, really. They've got a pretty good *Mogworld* subforum."

"I can't believe you," said Adam, shaking his head. "We stop being partners, and in less than a month you're meeting archnemeses and getting radicalized . . ."

"I am not getting radicalized!" barked Victor, suddenly angry. "It's just a bloody message board and I only lurk on it, so I don't even care that you think it's a terrorist group. Jesus, I didn't think you'd be so jealous about this."

"I am not jealous!" cried Adam.

"Look, it's no trouble. I'll talk to my archnemesis. They might have a friend who could be your archnemesis. Then we could all go on a double fight to the death. Happy?"

"I don't need—" Adam glanced at a nearby clock. "Gah. I need to get to my meeting with Mr. Danvers. And now I have to figure out how to explain that the Department's own special Pacifications agent is a potential person of interest."

"Fine! I'll be a person of interest! Suits me!" shouted Victor after him as Adam hurried down the corridor. "WHEN WAS THE LAST TIME A PERSON TOOK AN INTEREST IN YOU?!"

New face on the forums! :D
posted by NitaPavani1985 at 11:35 a.m.

Hi, Modern Miracle! I'm a "newbie" as you might say, I just made my account and wanted to post a topic to introduce myself! My name's Nita Pavani, and I work at DEDA (that's what we call the Department of Extradimensional Affairs on the inside) (actually I'm the head of public relations at DEDA, but I didn't want to boast!). I'm really interested in getting to know you all and finding out what more us "muggles" can do to be good allies to the extradimensional community!

Yours,
Dr. Nita Pavani

Edited by NitaPavani1985 at 11:38 a.m.
Edited by NitaPavani1985 at 11:43 a.m.
Edited by NitaPavani1985 at 1:25 p.m.

SpookyBlender replied
get banned

Xyxxy replied
deda is shit

InterstellarFunPirate replied
fuk u

MiracleDadHimself* replied
Hi Nita! This is Miracle Dad. I'd be very interested in having a private conversation about what you can do to help our community. Check your private messages plz.

Crazybob replied
post ur tits

THREE DAYS LATER

25

Nita was backstage at a television studio, leaning against a section of wall between a stack of plastic chairs and a snack table. This was the only place she could find to stand that wasn't dangerously in the path of the many runners and technicians that were constantly backing and forthing through the place like blood cells lost on their way to the heart.

Nita's agitation was growing, as there were minutes to go until tonight's show began, and the producer—the harassed-looking one in the white blouse who was clearly feeling threatened by another powerful woman in the room—kept making eye contact from across the room and tapping her watch meaningfully. Nita checked her phone again and confirmed that Miracle Dad would be there "any minute." He seemed to be sure of this, as he had texted as much six times over the last half hour.

Finally, mere minutes before airtime, when the studio audience was already settled and the producer had started making urgent phone inquiries as to what television comedians were within five minutes' drive and reasonably sober that night, Miracle Dad appeared. He was brought to Nita by one of the runners, who dropped him off like an armload of laundry before darting off on their next errand.

"Nice to meet you, Ms. Pavani," said Miracle Dad. He was wearing his usual Modern Miracle T-shirt and had applied something oily to his thinning hair. "Woo! Pretty psyched for this. This is gonna be a big step for the channel, y'know?"

"Yes, well, no thanks were necessary," said Nita, slightly pointedly. She leaned unsubtly back and forth to look around him, but he seemed to be alone. "Is Megan-El-Yetch here?"

"Oh, just call her Miracle Meg."

"Thank you, you must let me know if I'm using incorrect terms," said Nita. There was that slightly pointed tone again. "Is she not here?"

"Nah. School night."

"Oh." Nita clasped her hands behind her back, squeezing her fingers a little too hard. "I assumed you would want her to make some kind of demonstration . . ."

"Ah, nah, I thought about that," said Miracle Dad, keeping one eye on the activities behind him. "Don't want people to think we're a one-trick pony, do we?" He turned around, caught Nita's concerned look, and his tone of voice became serious. "I don't wanna treat El-Yetch like she's free healing magic on tap, you know? Gotta show a lady more respect than that."

"Of course," said Nita carefully. She was harboring a growing dislike for Miracle Dad in person, and his last statement cemented it. There was nothing specifically objectionable about what he said, just the way he spoke. He talked like everything he said was accompanied by a wink and a smack of the buttocks.

"Need to show her we're worth her trouble," he continued. "That we all want the same thing."

"And what does El-Yetch want?" asked Nita.

His answer was cut off by a call of "Quiet on the set please, *everyone!*" from the producer, who made sure to catch Nita's eye as she emphasized the last word. The lights were going down. Nita folded her arms and could only watch as a runner—possibly the same one as before, but it was impossible to tell with these media people—grabbed Miracle Dad's elbow and gently pulled until he was swallowed by the growing darkness.

A spotlight came on, illuminating the painted backdrop of London's skyline and the small collection of furniture arranged in front of it: a pink sofa, a tall potted plant, and a porcelain bathtub in a classical Victorian style. The audience was just settling into an interested hush when jazzy music started and they were instructed to applaud by a pair of gesturing technicians.

"Ladies, gentlemen, boys, girls, and miscellaneous," said a disembodied and altogether too-loud voice. "Please put your hands or closest equivalents together for your host: live from the bathtub, it's *Shgshthx Tonight!*"

The applause grew in volume and expanded into cheering as a large glistening, semitransparent blob with a pinkish, slightly terracotta hue slithered onto the set. It had arranged itself into a pleasingly smooth cone shape, on top of which sat a top hat whose brim had gone slightly out of shape from being partially digested.

"Hello, and welcome to the show," said Shgshthx, after they had decanted themselves into the bathtub and the applause finally died down. Shgshthx's mastery of human-style talking made them virtually unique among the amorphous fluidics, even if their name didn't. The cosmetic mouth that appeared just below their hat moved in perfect synchronicity with their words, and they had even outfitted it with a little set of buck teeth for additional cuteness. "It's that wonderful time of the week when you turn on your TV and listen to a greasy pile of slime in a chair. But then you get bored of *Newsnight* and switch over to me instead."

The audience laughed dutifully, but Nita felt herself tensing up. She wasn't a fan of *Shgshthx Tonight*. Much as it was good to see fluidics in prominent positions, the whole tone smacked a little too much of fluidixploitation to her. Granted, it was difficult to properly "exploit" a species that happily ate garbage and had no use for money, but people like the producers of this show were certainly giving it a damn good try.

"We've got a great show coming up for you tonight," said Shgshthx, tokenly. "Later on, Shgshthx and the Shgshthxes will be performing their new fart melody, 'Chirpy Burpy Life,' but first, let's bring on our first guest. What do you get if you cross religion with the internet? Well, first you'll get a comment section you won't want to touch with a ten-foot barge pole, but you also get Modern Miracle, which styles itself as the fastest-growing new 'online religion.'"

Nita was trying to retain a good view of the recording by bobbing left and right like a frustrated swan trying to get at the bread. Privately, she wondered how long Modern Miracle had been styling itself as that, and to whom.

"Joining us tonight is the high priest of Modern Miracle himself; please welcome Miracle Dad!"

The music went up again as Miracle Dad himself appeared stage left and made for the couch he was being helpfully pointed at. He was in no hurry, jogging along a wide curve that took him close to the cameras and audience, so he could wave with both hands and grin without a hint of embarrassment. He was completely at home in front of cameras. The kind of person who instinctively waves and pulls faces when finding themselves in the background of a live news report.

"So, Miracle Dad," said Shgshthx, after Miracle Dad had finally settled onto the sofa. "You're the father of the girl with healing powers who's the center of your religion?"

"Yep, that's my Miracle Meg," said Miracle Dad proudly, clutching his knees and bobbing in his seat. "She's got one hundred percent real healing powers and you can see them every week on our streaming channel."

"Nobody said they weren't real," said Shgshthx.

"Good! 'Cos they are." Miracle Dad darted a quick, slightly alarmed look to camera before visibly shaking himself back on track. "Sorry, Shgshthx, a lot of people think we're scam artists just 'cos there's never been a magic healer who can use their magic without killing themselves."

"And what makes Miracle Meg different?"

"Well, she's in dual consciousness with El-Yetch," said Miracle Dad promptly. "And El-Yetch didn't change the way Meg looks 'cos El-Yetch is the one Ancient who's on our side, you see."

"Hm," said Shgshthx, neatly encapsulating in one syllable their personal feelings. The Ancient that had possessed Jessica Weatherby had set out to torture and murder a large number of fluidics, and while Shgshthx themselves hadn't been among them, most fluidics still hadn't fully gotten to grips with the whole "individuality" thing. "And your movement actually worships El-Yetch as a god?"

"Yeah!" said Miracle Dad, grinning again. "People think we're a bit weird 'cos of that, too, but hey, does Jesus ever come down to kiss us better? My arse he does."

"Jesus kisses your arse?" said Shgshthx, turning his mouth into a cheeky smile.

"Hey, maybe he could!" said Miracle Dad laughingly, over the giggles of the audience. "Christians are the worst. They're the ones always sending hate mail. Chucking bricks at our house. And you know why they do it?"

Shgshthx wobbled with faint concern. He appeared to be doing the fluidic equivalent of exchanging glances with the offscreen producer. It was his responsibility to rein in the guests when they started saying things that might upset a general audience, but on the other hand, this, like a six-lane pileup, had the makings of great television. "Why do they do it?"

"Because they're afraid of us. And that's why I wanted to come on here: to show you why they should be." He reached behind him and pulled a rather damp and crinkled wad of papers out of the back of his waistband. "This is the lawsuit Modern Miracle filed today against them."

"Against the people who chuck bricks at your house?" asked Shgshthx uncertainly.

"Nope," said Miracle Dad triumphantly, holding up the papers for all to see. "This is the lawsuit Modern Miracle and the British government will be filing together against the Christian Church."

Nita, who was still leaning against a wall near the catering table with her arms folded, froze. Her arms tightened around her own chest so hard it felt like her lungs were being pushed into her stomach. On the other side of London, a small quantity of tea that had, up until this moment, been inside Sean Anderson's mouth arced attractively across his living room.

"The government is filing this?" said Shgshthx, giving voice to the wall of disbelief that now filled the entire room.

"They have to," said Miracle Dad smugly, pulling a specific piece of paper out of the wad. "See this? This is the X-Appropriation Act." He read out loud from the page like a messenger at a medieval court getting way too into their role. " 'It is an offense for any person to attempt to profit from any false claim that they or any entity they claim to own or associate with are in possession of extradimensional capabilities.' Now, is there anyone you can think of who's been going around saying they know someone who walked on water and knows when we're touching ourselves? It's not even a civil case. The church is breaking the law, and the government has to come down on them."

Shgshthx formed their "mouth" into a sidelong smirk. "I think the government could very easily just . . . not come down on them."

"You might be right," said Miracle Dad, with a sudden grave serious-ness. "But there's a lot of magically infused kids on the Modern Miracle forums who are scared about what's happening to them and their futures, and not a lot of them have much confidence in the Department of Extradimensional Affairs, not when their policy up to now was to kill them and brainwash them and stuff. So I'd say the government needs to take a look at this new generation of wizards holding the power of the Ancients and a sizable chunk of the votes, and then look at this pack of old fogies in dresses who've done nothing but hold us all back for centuries, and at some point they're going to have to figure out which side they're on."

Nita's phone was ringing. She trotted quickly toward the exit door as if going to answer it, but declined the call without even looking at the screen. Immediately, her phone rang again, and she declined that one as well, quickening her pace. By the time of the fifth call, she was sprinting.

THE NEXT MORNING

26

Richard Danvers didn't have much time for late-night television, and had a policy of only turning on his phone when he was safely behind his desk and ready to face the day, so he arrived at the Department without having heard anything about the night's events. Still, he could sense that something was off. The civil servants in the Administration department were eerily quiet, all sitting hunched forward over their work with the tight mouths and moist eyes of people who had recently been shouted at.

Richard glanced through the open door of the main meeting room on the way to his office and stopped in his tracks. The meeting table was absolutely groaning with food. There was a fruit platter, a cheese board, a pile of croissants and Danishes, a row of dispensers filled with a variety of breakfast cereals that must have been borrowed from a hotel, a stack of unopened pizza boxes, and more besides. Having only had his usual breakfast—a muesli bar and a mug of strong tea large enough to drown a ferret—Richard could feel his stomach falling in moaning love at first sight.

Elizabeth Lawrence and Nita Pavani were sitting on opposite ends of the table, both with arms folded as if afraid to touch anything. Spurred by hunger and curiosity, Richard took a step into the room. "Good morning," he said. "What's the occasion?"

The door slammed shut behind him. Richard spun around. Sean Anderson was there with a manic smile and eyes that couldn't have had much sleep. "I'm glad you asked," he said, in a dangerously quiet voice.

"The occasion is, no one gets to leave this room until we figure out the plan of action against these Modern Miracle twerps. I've canceled all your meetings and laid on breakfast, lunch, and dinner. No one has any excuse to leave."

"And what if someone needs to use the toilet, Sean?" asked Nita.

Anderson threw out his massive hands. "There's four perfectly good corners in this room, aren't there?"

"What happened?" asked Danvers, resigning himself to a seat.

"Modern Miracle are pressuring the government to apply the X-Appropriation Act to the popular religions," summarized Elizabeth.

"The prime minister called me this morning," said Anderson, leaning forward and planting his hands on the table, deftly positioning them either side of a large basket of Wagon Wheels. "He'd just had his meeting with the queen. She asked him if she should be concerned about being hand-cuffed and arrested in her capacity as head of the Church of England. She showed her characteristic grace and good humor, for which she is beloved, and everyone had a good laugh about it. The PM is sodding livid."

"Anderson . . ." said Elizabeth patiently.

"He also took a call from the American president," continued Anderson, not pausing. "Who, in turn, has been getting calls from several Christian groups over there. Certain phrases came up. Phrases like 'complete boycott of British products.' Just as soon as they figure out what this country even exports anymore . . ."

"Anderson," repeated Elizabeth sharply. "It was not us who passed the X-Appropriation Act."

Anderson sagged as if the string holding up his head had been cut. "Yes. I know."

"I recall advising against passing it." Elizabeth recrossed her legs. "Citing concerns with ambiguity in the wording that could be used against—"

"ALL RIGHT!" barked Anderson, head still bowed. "I'm not saying this is DEDA's fault. I am saying that a department that, let's face it, hasn't inched terribly far out of the toilet bowl in estimation since its last big cock-up might like to see this as a wonderful opportunity to get back in the PM's good graces and prove to him that this department is a professional and efficient part of the government team, deserving of all respect and dignity." He let his point sink in for a moment, then looked up. "Right. What dirt have we got on this Miracle Dad prick?"

Danvers, having been raised in a strict upper-class household that had drilled into him the importance of not wasting food, was resignedly buttering a croissant. He sighed. "For whatever it's worth, we have a double murder case in Worcester at the moment that one of my investigators seems to believe might be linked."

"All right, good start," said Anderson, nodding. "How concrete a link?"

"I sincerely doubt that anything at present could stick to Miracle Dad himself," admitted Danvers.

"No worries," said Anderson. "Shit like that, doesn't matter if it sticks. If you can chuck it and at least get him in the splatter zone, it might leave enough of a stink to put people off. Anything else?"

"Miracle Dad isn't your problem," said Elizabeth.

Anderson stared at her, mouth sarcastically agape. "Sorry, was there some other bugger on last night telling the world that Her Majesty's government is about to piss all over the corn flakes of the entire religious voting bloc?"

"I had Alison look over the Modern Miracle forums," continued Elizabeth nonchalantly, staring straight ahead. "She tells me there was a thread posted by Miracle Dad relating to his television interview, asking what he should say. Every line he delivered last night was fed to him from a different member of the forum."

"What are you saying to me?" asked Anderson.

"That Miracle Dad is just a willing mouthpiece for what you're actually up against—what may well be the entire online extradimensional community."

"Mm," murmured Danvers agreeably, through a mouthful of croissant. "I wouldn't be surprised if Miracle Dad himself is only in this for the publicity it brings his streaming channel. And then if you try to take him down . . ."

"We'd just be making a martyr," said Anderson gloomily. He half-heartedly punched the tabletop a couple of times. "All right then, what've we got on the rest of these internet twats?"

"Before you invest in a new fleet of unmarked vans," said Elizabeth, "it might be easier to simply amend the X-Appropriation Act. Include a clause that permits religious activities?"

Anderson had settled into a chair and was attempting to open the wrapper on a Wagon Wheel. He eventually resorted to pulling it apart with his teeth. "Ngh! Maybe. It was enough of a bastard getting it through in the first place. And anyway, no. Stupid. 'Cos half the buggers the act was supposed to target will just turn around and claim religious practice. All them crystal therapy and spirit medium shits. They'll just say it's Wiccan or something." He took a bite and proceeded to talk through his mouthful of Wagon Wheel, spraying biscuit crumbs. "Nita, don't just sit there like a plastic fanny. Contribute. Throw an idea out!"

"Well, I did have one idea," said Nita, slowly leaning back and folding her arms. "Give the extradimensional community what they want. Find a representative of the Church of England. Put them in front of a panel. Get them to publicly explain why Christian doctrine doesn't contravene the X-Appropriation Act."

Anderson rubbed his chin, creating a sound like leather being dragged up and down a washboard. "Right. I see what you're saying. Put it out in the open like that, so the public can see how stupid Modern Miracle is being. Still, the right message might not—"

"Message?!" interrupted Nita sharply. "Has it even occurred to you that Modern Miracle might be completely in the right?"

Elizabeth rolled her eyes toward the ceiling, and Danvers took a lively interest in the interior of his croissant. Finding absolutely no support, Anderson was forced to meet Nita's piercing glare. "You what?"

"This might be just what the human race has had a long time coming," said Nita, eyes manically wide. "Miracle Dad's absolutely right. Why do we let old religions hog so much power and influence? Why does God get a free ride? Worshiping the Ancients makes some sense! We know the Ancients exist, for one thing!"

"It's never been about whether God exists," said Anderson patiently, holding out one hand like a flesh-colored serving tray. "The fact that He doesn't just hang around on earth messing with people is one of the things we find most agreeable about Him."

"Are you a Christian, Anderson?" asked Danvers.

"What?" Anderson straightened up defensively. "No. Parents were pretty big into it, but I don't really . . ."

"This isn't going to just go away, Sean, no matter how people vote, no matter how many media outlets you manipulate," said Nita. "Religion has been offering make-believe magic for centuries. Now real magic is here. This was going to come to blows at some point."

"Look, don't be stupid, Nita," said Anderson. "The church is an institution."

Nita had picked up a single grape from the nearby fruit platter. "Slavery was an institution," she said, before crunching down on the grape as a devastating punctuation mark.

Anderson hissed in frustration, then turned to the other end of the table. "Look, could one of you sodding goldfish stop eyeballing us and get back in this debate?"

Danvers and Elizabeth, having worked together for years, had become adept at communicating nonverbally. Throughout the discussion they had been having an intense debate of their own entirely through subtle movements of the eyes and facial muscles. With one last nod of the head, Elizabeth nominated Danvers, the diplomat, to announce their conclusions.

"Anderson, I'm sorry," he said, clasping his hands in front of him. "This department's duty is to support the extradimensional community. And it appears that that's essentially what Modern Miracle is, at least online."

"Exactly!" said Nita, with a triumphant snap of the fingers.

"At the same time, Nita," said Danvers quickly, "we also realize that we are part of the government of England, and as such cannot reasonably be expected to participate in prosecuting the Church of England. If nothing else, it's a conflict of interest."

"Yeah!" said Anderson. "And you can bet your twisted-up knickers the Ministry of Justice will say the same. So let's have a bit less of this edgelord atheist shite."

"Edgelord?!" snapped Nita. "What's 'edgelord' about wanting . . ." She stopped suddenly, clamping her lips shut, and physically recoiled into a demure sitting position, like a dog being hauled back on the leash. She smiled at Danvers pleasantly. "You're saying, Richard, that the Department is officially declaring neutrality?"

"We have to," said Danvers firmly. "We cannot choose a side on this. I don't believe we *should*."

"That is completely fair, I understand, and I will not ask you to say anything more." Nita rose from her seat, still smiling beatifically. "I think we've all made our positions perfectly clear. I don't think there's any reason for me to stick around. I have things to get on with."

"Nita, I do hope you're not planning on going rogue on us," said Anderson, trying to look casual and unconcerned with his face still the color of a warning light on a nuclear reactor. " 'Cos I don't know if you realize how easy a thing it would be to just not renew your contract."

Nita smiled even wider at him, pinching her eyes with a sarcastic sympathy that unsettled Anderson enormously. "Don't worry, Sean, from this point forward I swear I will do nothing but my job and stop trying to escalate events." She turned to leave, then stopped and peered coquettishly over her shoulder. "After all, I have a feeling I won't need to."

Anderson glared silently at the door for some time after Nita left, only snapping out of it when Richard and Elizabeth both tactfully stood up. "Hey!" he yelled. "Where d'you think you're—"

"Anderson," said Elizabeth. "She was right. Our positions have all been made perfectly clear."

"We already said, the Department can't take sides on this," said Danvers, politely holding the door open for Elizabeth. "As in, we legally cannot. No amount of threatening or cajoling us is going to change that now."

"Fine," said Anderson, sulkily folding his arms as he was left alone in the meeting room. "All the more breakfast, lunch, and dinner for me."

He sat there for some time, stewing on the problem and what options were available. Central to his thoughts, like the eye of a particularly violent hurricane, was Nita Pavani, and that suspiciously placid expression she had had while leaving. To Anderson, that gleam in her eye had been the playful sparkle that gives away the position of a concealed sniper. He needed to make a move before she made her next one. And it would make things difficult if cajoling and threatening had been ruled out, as that accounted for about sixty percent of his playbook.

The meeting room door had been left open, and as he sat lost in thought, several civil servants on their various errands drifted past. Each one in turn slowed their pace to eye the buffet hungrily, noticed Anderson sitting behind it with a face like thunder, and swiftly moved on.

Eventually, Adam Hesketh walked past and hesitated to stare at the food for slightly longer than the rest. As the two of them made accidental eye contact, a little light bulb came on in Anderson's head. Perhaps, he thought, it was more a matter of cajoling and threatening the right person.

"Oi! Wait a tick!" he called as Adam made to keep walking. "You were the one looking into Modern Miracle, weren't you? Andrew, right?"

"Erm. Adam." Adam's body was already trying to move him on, so by this point only his head was peering around the door frame.

Anderson put on what he thought was his "approachable" face. "How would you like to make some very powerful friends, Adam?"

"Erm. I. I'm supposed to be . . . I can't."

Adam was pointing meaningfully in the direction by which he was planning to exit but was still lingering. Anderson swiftly deduced what his gaze was drifting to. "All right, shorter term," he said. "How would you like to eat some of these pastries?"

News Plus article:

DEDA TO CHURCH: YOU'RE ON YOUR OWN

The Department of Extradimensional Affairs has announced that it will do nothing to stand in the way of the proposed legal action by the online extradimensional religion Modern Miracle against the Christian Church.

DEDA's head of field operations, Richard Danvers, is quoted by sources close to the agency as saying, "This department's duty is to support the extradimensional community . . . we cannot choose a side on this."

Many commenters are already seeing this as a significant legitimization of Modern Miracle's campaign. "A branch of government not coming out in support of the religious establishment is certainly a watershed moment," said Devin Purcell, a professor of political theory at the University of Leeds.

Many are seeing this as a pivotal event in the ongoing debate over what role, if any, established religion has in a modern . . .

Please buy a News Plus subscription to continue reading.

Related Articles
  • "Magic vs. religion: why we don't have to choose a side"
  by Maureen Weaver
  • "Is this the conflict that will define our generation?"
  by Tom Winchester
  • "All right, fine, I suppose we DO have to choose a side"
  by Maureen Weaver

LATER THE SAME DAY

27

After lunch, Alison was at her desk, compiling a more formal report on what she was finding in the Modern Miracle forums. It wasn't the worst task she'd ever been given. Most of it was fairly mundane online discussion, although she had gotten absorbed by a rather amusing thread in which forum members speculated on what it would be like if *Lord of the Rings* characters had to fill out a standard DEDA extradimensional services request form.

At around two o'clock, she found herself unable to focus on reading any further, because Adam Hesketh was creeping very slowly into her work area, trying not to be noticed. He was lifting his feet high, clasping his hands behind his back, and looking everywhere except directly at her. He finally came to rest at a potted plant near Alison's desk and began carefully examining the leaves, feeling each one in turn between thumb and forefinger.

"Alison," he eventually said as his fingertips traced the veins of a particularly interesting leaf. "Don't look at me. Keep looking at the screen. Pretend we're not talking."

"Okay," said Alison, confused. "That should be easy. Because. I didn't think we were."

"Do you still have Doctor Diablerie's car keys?"

"Yes." Doctor Diablerie was still yet to reappear, and Alison hadn't had a chance to return them. The black key with the skull-shaped silver fob continued to look out of place on her key ring alongside her front door key and a small plastic Japanese cat.

"I'm on kind of a secret mission," admitted Adam. "I need to get to Modern Miracle's next service without Mr. Danvers knowing."

"I thought Mr. Danvers approved you checking on their next service?"

"He did, but I told him I wasn't going to go after all." He coughed. "Because now I have to do it secretly. For my secret mission."

Alison winced. She glanced around, to make sure that the terrible spirit of Elizabeth Lawrence's disapproval wasn't manifesting physically behind her shoulder. "And this is all fine, is it?"

"Oh sure, it's fine," said Adam. "It's totally fine. But I can't take any of the Investigations cars because they have to be checked out and monitored. They don't do that with Diablerie's car, right?"

"I don't think so." Alison wasn't sure, but it seemed safe to assume. She'd never had to sign anything when taking Diablerie's car out, and presumably neither did he; bureaucracy was one of the things that he deliberately kept shut out of his little world, along with most popular trends in culture and fashion. "But I don't know, Adam, I probably shouldn't . . ."

"Look, we'll just head out to Worcester on Friday and be back the same night," pressed Adam. His voice was casual and downplaying, but his fingers were massaging the leaf in his hand with greater and greater violence. "You don't even have to get out of the car. Plenty of people drive to Worcester and back for no reason. Worcester's nice. Very historic cathedral."

"Actually," said Alison, suddenly thoughtful. "Beatrice Callum at LAXA has been sending me emails." She went to the keyboard and clicked over to the relevant browser tab. "She says she's got new information on Modern Miracle and has been asking to meet up."

"Well, great! Perfect!" said Adam, looking over her shoulder, before remembering he was supposed to be doing this covertly and returning hastily to the potted plant. "You can go there as part of your official investigation, and you can tell everyone you didn't notice me in the passenger seat. No risk to you at all."

Alison eyed Beatrice's email uncertainly. She had been pretty inconsolable the night of her brother's death, once the shock had worn off and the matter had properly sunk in. She had been absolutely incoherent with sobs by the time Alison had had to leave and had created quite a large dark patch of dampness on her boyfriend's shirt. Looking at the text of her emails, Alison doubted she had yet returned to a healthy emotional space. It was something about the way she was ending all her sentences with at least four punctuation marks.

"I still don't know about this," admitted Alison.

"Please?" said Adam. "I'd really appreciate it."

Alison glanced toward Elizabeth's office door again and bit her lip. "Could you order me to do it?"

Adam blinked several times. "Erm . . ."

"You can do that, right? 'Cos you're a special agent and I'm a junior agent. I'd just . . . I'd feel a lot better about it if you were ordering me."

"Okay," said Adam uncomfortably as Alison reddened with embarrassment. "I, uh. I order you to drive me to Worcester on Friday afternoon. Will that do?"

Alison drummed her fingers on the keyboard, lightly enough not to press any keys, and tossed her head left and right, weighing up whether her feelings about it had changed. "Actually, could you write it down on something?"

Text messages between Victor and Leslie-Ifrig, 6:27 p.m. to 7:09 p.m.:

Your private message history with Leslifrig6969
   You replied: You've crossed the line this time.
sorry victor i was in the loo
what have i done now?
   You replied: That cargo ship that caught fire. The one on the news. That was you, wasn't it?
uh
you mean the one in cyprus
no that actually wasnt me
   You replied: Sure.
   You replied: I warned you what would happen if you didn't behave. I'm putting a stop to you once and for all.
victor
wheres this coming from
   You replied: It's coming from not turning you into vapor when I had the chance.
come on
what are you really angry about?
   You replied: Nothing!
   You replied: Just the usual stuff.
you mean work
   You replied: Mainly Adam acting like a twat.
   You replied: Which is the usual stuff, because he is one.
how is he acting like a twat?
   You replied: Dunno.
you dont know
   You replied: He's just being whiny because no one in his fancy new office respects him and he's jealous of me.
thats quite a lot of insight for someone who doesnt know

THE NEXT FRIDAY EVENING

28

After Adam had written down the order and signed it, and Alison had cosigned it and enlisted the fluidic who cleaned the bathrooms to sign it as a witness, and Adam had taken a picture of himself holding the order in one hand and a copy of that day's newspaper in the other, Alison finally felt comfortable about agreeing to help. It was a comfort that entirely deserted her when the time came to actually do it. The moment she climbed into the driving seat of Diablerie's car on Friday afternoon, she felt her entire body fold into a guilty cringe. She could only bear to cling to the steering wheel with her fingertips in case the white-hot sting of accusation bled through to her palms.

She didn't feel any better after she picked up Adam. Everything he nonchalantly did felt like another violation. He wasn't fumbling with the seat belt—he was fumbling with the seat belt Alison stole from Diablerie. He wasn't looking out of the window—he was looking out of the window Alison stole from Diablerie. The several rounds of effusive thanks he had made in the first five minutes of the journey had been no comfort, because the sound of his voice had had to drift through several cubic feet of stolen air.

"Look," said Adam, picking up on the tension in the car from the way Alison kept flinching at the blinking of her own indicators, "if any trouble comes out of this, I will take full responsibility. Just let me do the talking."

"So you'll say you ordered me," said Alison.

"Absolutely."

"To take you on your secret mission."

"I—well, obviously I can't say that. I'll think of something." He looked down. "Although the mission was a lot more secret before you made me print out triplicate copies of the order."

"Sorry," said Alison, eyeballing the cars in front. "I've never taken this car without proper permission before. I'm a little bit on edge."

"Yeah, I guess we've all had to deal with new experiences since the reshuffle," said Adam, glancing wistfully out of the window again. "I'm still kinda new to going on special investigations by myself."

"Right, how's Victor been doing?" said Alison, nervously embracing the change of subject. "Haven't seen him around lately."

"Victor? Oh, he's been getting really weird. I don't get what's going on with him."

"What's he doing?"

"He's, you know, feeling shut out by the Department so he's started hanging out with bad crowds because he thinks it'll make us jealous."

Alison nodded uncertainly. "That's, er, that's quite a lot of insight for someone who doesn't get what's going on with him."

The conversation proceeded to die the first of the many hideous drawn-out deaths it would suffer throughout the course of the journey, until Alison was finally able to get off the motorway and surround the car with livelier scenery. The discussion could then survive on weak life support as Adam repeatedly commented on how Worcester seemed nice, and Alison agreed that it did, indeed, seem nice.

Alison finally pulled up on the corner of the turn that led to the Modern Miracle house. "Okay," she said, with forced brightness. "I'll pick you up from here. Send me a text when you're ready."

Adam didn't get out immediately. He gazed up the sloping road toward the house, already feeling pangs in his legs. "You don't feel like getting any closer?"

"Erm, no, actually . . ." Alison pointed ahead. "Beatrice wants me to meet a little ways off. Around the corner."

"O-kay," said Adam, letting himself out. "Have fun."

"Have fun?"

"I mean, good luck," said Adam, now out of the car and talking through the six inches of gap left by the door he was partway through closing.

With him gone, Alison didn't exactly feel relief, because she was still driving a stolen car that was sprouting hot needles of guilt at every single point where her body touched it, but there was certainly a mental clearing of the air.

She double-checked the address Beatrice had given her on the GPS. It was literally the next street down from Modern Miracle's street, a cozy suburban cul-de-sac practically identical to the last, stacked with another row of expensive detached houses. The main difference being—as Alison discovered after she had parked under a willow she judged shady enough to conceal her crime—a public footpath running between two of the houses.

Alison checked Beatrice's message again. There was the address, and then the extra instructions: "Head down path. Stand between first two trees and make cuckoo noise."

The path was the start of a rough walking trail that ran behind the houses for a few hundred yards before snaking off into the picturesque grassy hills that gave the suburb its backdrop, occasionally touching base with light clumps of trees and foliage to give the dogwalkers something to besmirch. At the first of these, two thin trees stood over a thick bank of bushes as tall as a man, like two skinny Victorian ladies in ridiculously large hoop skirts.

It didn't escape Alison's attention, when she reached the spot between the two trees, that she now had a fairly clear view of the back of the Modern Miracle house. Even without her eidetic memory, the faint sound of chatting congregation drifting over from the front garden made it unmistakable.

"Cuckoo," she said aloud, not being entirely clear on what sound a cuckoo makes. "Cuckoo, cuckoo."

She flinched as the bank of hedges to her left burst open, revealing that it was, in fact, the LAXA van, covered in a thick camouflaging layer of branches and weeds that must have been gathered with the single-mindedness that only a disturbed brain can possess. Beatrice stood in the open side door, staring madly and pallidly like some kind of harassed creature of the forest guarding its cave, and Alison immediately noticed that she was wearing the exact same outfit she had had on at their last meeting.

"Alison!" she said, grinning widely. "Get in here!"

Alison thought it best to obey, only having second thoughts when the wave of stench hit her: a combination of unwashed laundry, bad breath, and dog fur, all percolating nicely in an atmosphere kept warm by several running electronic devices. Three laptops were scattered around the unmade sleeping bags in the back, one of which was connected to a whirring camera in the passenger seat with a very long lens pointing forward through the disguised windscreen.

"You're staking out Modern Miracle," said Alison, half asking, half realizing.

"Yeah, but it's okay," said Beatrice, squatting before one of the laptops. "I told Mum I was getting to the bottom of David's murder, and she didn't, like, directly tell me not to. Take a look at this."

Alison was moving to join her behind the laptop when the thing she had taken for a pile of unwashed laundry at the back of the van shifted slightly and revealed itself to be Roger, Beatrice's dreadlocked cameraman-boyfriend. And on closer inspection, the crumpled furry sleeping bag at his feet was Arby the dog, dozing.

"Oh, hello," said Alison on instinct as she made eye contact. "Have you . . . have you all been here this whole time?"

"Yeah," said Roger. He seemed quite placid and unconcerned in comparison to Beatrice, but he was still unshaven and wearing clothes that had become a few shades darker since Alison had seen them last. "It's cool, I had nothing on."

"Look!" insisted Beatrice, pointing at her screen. Alison obediently leaned in.

She was being shown a recorded video that must have been taken from the camera in the front passenger seat, as it was prominently focused on the back of the Modern Miracle house and the tall wooden fence that enclosed its rear garden. The footage had been taken at night and was bathed in night vision green.

"Where'd you get all this equipment?" asked Alison as nothing happened onscreen for several seconds.

"Oh, I had some savings," said Beatrice dismissively. "And Mum didn't directly tell me not to spend it. Ah! Look!"

On the screen, a gate in the middle of Modern Miracle's rear fence opened a few inches and a figure emerged. It took a few moments for Alison to identify it as Miracle Dad; he was barely recognizable with a bathrobe on over his Modern Miracle T-shirt, and with all the flamboyance and energy he reserved for the camera subtracted from his posture.

"So, this happened last night, and the night before as well," said Beatrice as the image of Miracle Dad furtively crept along the walking trail until he was out of shot. "The first time it was Miracle Dad, and yesterday it was Miracle Mum. Only ever one of them."

"Where do they go?" asked Alison.

"We don't know," said Beatrice, in a mysterious voice.

"Have you followed them?"

"Yeah, we tried, obviously." Beatrice pointed to the camera. "But that thing doesn't pan very far. And then they just go out of shot again."

"I mean, physically follow them," said Alison. "Like. Move."

"Oh." Beatrice scratched under her beret, which was now more brown than red. "No, I'm pretty sure they'd notice a van this size."

"I mean, leave the van and follow them on foot," said Alison, exasperated.

Beatrice stared at her, bleary eyed and confused. Then she looked to the others. Arby perked up, peeling his jowls off the floor of the van and letting his tail thump left and right, as if he didn't understand what was going on but was getting the vibe that it might be time for walkies.

"See, this is why I said we should bring the professionals in," said Roger.

29

In the time it took to walk all the way up the road to Modern Miracle, Adam concocted a cover story. He was Achilles Vanderberg, recently returned from studying overseas. His younger sister, who, to his slight embarrassment, practically worshiped him as a god, had been diagnosed with Creutzfeldt-Jakob disease. With her medical expenses having used up the last of the inheritance they had earned from their Swiss uncle, an eccentric inventor with a mysterious past, he had come to the Modern Miracle service to see if magical healing might provide the solution to their problems.

As he sauntered up to the front gate, he was mentally filling in the last few details. He could picture their uncle's mansion outside Zurich and the extensive grounds in which they had spent so many magical summers. He was prepared for any amount of questioning. So he was rather annoyed when absolutely nobody noticed or tried to stop him.

After Modern Miracle's televised PR boost, the congregation had expanded to the point of overflowing the front garden. As Alison had noticed, the people present were from all walks of life, naturally separating into conversational cliques. Adam's additional senses informed him that each clique had at least one magically infused person. The crowd was a fireworks display of multicolored traces. He even noticed a few dual consciousnesses, not that he needed enhanced senses to notice those; the nearest one had a face like a plate of day-old salad with eyeballs. For a brief moment he wondered if any of them would make for a good arch-nemesis, but he quashed the thought.

As he was scanning the crowd, he noticed a pink smear slowly growing larger and dismissed the vision to see a bespectacled girl of about twenty approaching him with open curiosity. He immediately pretended to take an interest in the strikingly regular brickwork in the nearest wall. *Achilles Vanderberg*, he reminded himself. *Achilles Vanderberg.*

"Hey, aren't you Adam Hesketh?" asked the girl.

"Er, no," stammered Adam, theatrically looking around so quickly that his arms flapped like tetherballs. "I'm. Er. My sister was a mansion in Switzerland—"

"I'm Rana," said Rana. "I've seen you come into the school once or twice. I was there that time you were kicking Alison out."

"O-oh," said Adam. It had started out as an *oh* of disappointment at being recognized, but he was able to head it off at the pass and strangle it into an *oh* of feigned interest. "How are you?"

"Good," said Rana, not breaking smiling eye contact. The way she spoke and looked at Adam implied a mixture of curiosity and total fascination. "I saw Alison here on the night she got the Bible in the face, but I don't think she noticed me. How's she doing?"

"F-fine," stammered Adam, feeling he was losing grip on who was doing the investigating here. "Have you been coming to these often?"

"Yeah, for a while," said Rana, taking a conspiratorial step closer and looking back to the house. "Don't worry, I'm not one of the weirdo El-Yetch cultist types."

Adam smiled weakly, taking another glance around. He had a strong sense that the vast majority of people present would say the same thing. "Right."

"I'm here mainly because I want to know how they control life essence transfer the way they do, with no one having to die." There was a sadness in her voice. "I guess you can see why I'd be interested in that."

Adam double-checked with his special senses and confirmed that Rana's magic infusion manifested as a pink glow around her. Pink was the color of both healing and vampirism, and for all Adam's gifts, there was no way of telling which one Rana had if she wasn't actively using it.

He recalled what Danvers had said, that as well as Miracle Meg being a conduit, another explanation could be that there was a murderous vampire among her followers. With that in mind, Rana's inquisitive look took on alarming notes of a hungry wolf, but she was by no means the only pink smear on the scene. Life essence transfer was actually a quite common infusion; you just didn't see it much in the wild, as it were, because they were trained not to use it. Adam could see at least six other pink infusions just from one scan around. He took a moment to carefully commit each face to memory but, by the end of that evening, would have forgotten every single one.

"You're here to investigate the cult, aren't you? Like Alison was," said Rana, smile widening as her excitement grew. "You're going to use your senses to figure out how they do the healing."

Adam let his head drop, defeated. "It's actually supposed to be a secret."

"Oh sure, don't worry," said Rana, patting him on the back. "You probably don't want to get a Bible in the face. Hey, is it true Alison's got, like, supermemory? That her memory's so good they put her in the school 'cos they thought she was psychic?"

"Yeah, that was basically it," said Adam.

"Man," said Rana. "She's so cool."

A small kerfuffle was unfolding on the part of the lawn that adjoined the driveway. A van had pulled up, and a man in the white clothing of a medical orderly was opening the side door while a second, practically identical man gestured irritably for the surrounding onlookers to clear a space.

Before long, the two men had gently decanted the van's occupant. He was a boy of about twelve, strapped to a wheelchair and trailing several tubes and wires from a forest of drip feeders and monitoring devices. A young mother, with the sad eyes and permanent half smile of someone who has already cried themselves through the worst of it, also emerged and helpfully guided her son's wheelchair down the ramp.

"Must be today's star patient," muttered Rana, only audible to Adam.

"All right, Miracle Mob!" said Miracle Dad, catching off guard everyone who had been watching the action around the van. He had emerged from the front door of the house and was bounding along the path to greet the newcomers. "Now this must be Jamie, is that right?"

"Yes, Miracle Dad," said Jamie's mother as Jamie himself boggled wordlessly over his mouth and nose tubes.

Miracle Dad bent down, bracing his hands on his knees. "Now, I think there must have been some mistake here. I was told Jamie had been feeling poorly lately, but you look like a pretty tough little warrior to me!"

Jamie replied with a weak little hiss from a nearby respirator. "Um, no, he's . . . he's been really ill," translated his mother, with humorless concern.

To his credit, Miracle Dad managed to not let the energy drop. He met her gaze with an utterly sincere expression of sympathy. "How ill is he now, exactly?"

"Well, the doctors say he's through the worst of it," she replied, moisture gathering in her eyes as she spoke. "But if he . . . survives the year, it'll be another year or so before he's even strong enough to get up by himself."

"Sounds like the doctors have worked a few miracles of their own so far," said Miracle Dad, nodding respectfully. "But let's see if the blessing of El-Yetch can give Jamie a little booster, shall we?"

"El-Yetch has got her work cut out for her," muttered Rana, leaning into Adam's ear, as Miracle Dad helped Jamie and his entourage into the house to prepare for the show. Adam gave her a curious look, and she responded with an embarrassed smile.

She's trying to impress you, thought Adam, the notion surfacing from the depths of his subconscious like a lady of the lake.

Why would she be doing that? asked another part of his mind, a less subconscious one.

Because you're a senior investigator for the Department of Extradimensional Affairs, and that's the sort of thing that impresses people who haven't gotten to know you properly. So make good use of this before that happens.

"Oh yeah," he said aloud. He coughed as Rana's confused expression began to unfold. "Uh. Yes. You've been coming to these 'for a while,' you said? You've seen this healing in action a few times?"

"Yep," she replied, eager to be part of the investigation. "And I'm pretty sure the healing magic is real. But here's the interesting thing." She raised an index finger and waggled her eyebrows. "It's usually something small. Sometimes it's a little flesh wound, like what Alison had. A lot of the time it's something more like, you know, what fake faith healers do. Get someone with an old ache and get them to think it's gone for a few seconds."

"I see," said Adam, thinking about Danvers's other theory that Miracle Meg might have been a genuine healer, but only doling out real life essence in small doses for special occasions. "And Miracle Meg definitely hasn't prematurely aged from the healing? Could she be faking it part of the time?"

"I thought the same for a while," said Rana, nodding rapidly. "But she's done the real thing enough times I'm pretty sure she'd have aged up a bit by now. And besides, every few weeks or so they do a really big heal. That's what they're doing today, I think."

Adam glanced at the now-closed front door. "The boy in the wheelchair?"

"About a month ago, it was a man who'd broken his spine and was never gonna walk again," said Rana, leaning in with her conspiratorial voice again. "He came out afterwards and gave his wife piggyback rides around the garden. It may have been staged though."

Adam gave a little nod he wasn't really feeling. Jamie's condition would have been difficult to fake, unless Jamie's guardians were prepared to keep him starved in a dark basement for months until his muscles had all but wasted away and his skin tone turned the right shade of deathly. And even if they did, how were they going to fake the miraculous recovery? Take him into a back room, paint him pink, and feed him two hundred energy bars?

"Any idea how they'd stage it, exactly?" he asked aloud.

As if in reply, the music denoting the start of Modern Miracle's sermon began playing. A hush fell over the congregation, and there was a gradual drift toward the front door, like impatient airline passengers who think their boarding call is coming next.

"Looks like we're about to find out," said Rana as the lock on the front door clicked open.

30

The gate in the rear fence of the Modern Miracle house opened directly onto the walking trail, which reflected the traditional suburban values of convenience and complete lack of security concerns. It opened slowly and Miracle Mum emerged, wearing an overlarge dark coat and carrying the kind of ragged tote bag that one of the nearby supermarkets would probably stubbornly refer to as a "bag for life." She grabbed the gate before it could swing shut behind her and gently guided it closed, cringing slightly with every creak and click.

Alison, crouched behind a bush twenty yards away, sorely wished she had known she was going to be stealthing through the undergrowth that evening. She would have worn something other than her work blouse, the one that now seemed to possess the shining, lustrous whiteness that it always lacked while under harsh office lighting. Then again, when it came to going unnoticed, it was the least of her worries.

"Donation from Lakichew," whispered Roger, holding his phone out. "He wants to know if this is the first time Alison has gone commando in the jungle."

"Do you have to keep reading those out?!" hissed Alison, not looking away from Miracle Mum.

"He donated," said Beatrice and Roger in unison. Alison was getting the unpleasant sense that she was the designated adult for the evening.

Miracle Mum frowned directly at their position, and Alison froze in the act of rubbing her forehead in exasperation. A tense handful of silent seconds drifted by before Miracle Mum finally shrugged and began to walk away from the house. Alison let all her breath out in a long sigh, slow enough to mingle with the sound of the trees swaying in the wind. "Come on," she whispered, carefully sliding herself out from behind the bush.

She stayed off the path and behind the low fence that separated it from the grassy hills. If Miracle Mum turned around again she wouldn't notice Alison as long as she could do a convincing impression of a plank of wood. She endeavored to keep Miracle Mum's diminutive figure in the center of her view, assuming that Beatrice and Roger were staying close behind from the sound of rustling grass and whispered donation acknowledgments.

They followed Miracle Mum as the path split from the houses, curved widely around a hill, and began to slope downwards into a denser section of forest. The branches overhead clenched together more and more as the sun slipped ever farther below the horizon. Before long, Alison was having to squint to keep track of Miracle Mum's movements.

"Lot of comments saying they can't see anything and if we can turn the brightness up," whispered Roger.

"We cannot turn the brightness up, because the brightness is the sun," said Beatrice firmly. With the camera rolling, she had slipped into her businesslike, on-the-record persona.

"Maybe you should stop streaming," suggested Alison over her shoulder.

"There needs to be a record of what we find," said Beatrice firmly.

"Yeah," said Roger. "No point of activism if no one can see you doing it."

There was no hint of expression in his voice. Alison wondered, not for the first time, exactly how many layers of irony he was operating on. "Apparently, no one can see you doing it anyway," Alison pointed out.

"Donation from JankWilliams," said Roger. "He'd like to know why we didn't take the night vision lens off the camera in the van and bring it with us."

"Great question," said Beatrice, who apparently hadn't been listening, as she was busy extricating herself from a particularly thorny part of the undergrowth. "These are the questions for which today's youth demand answers."

Alison decided she was doing a poor job of being the adult. She stopped and turned on the two teenagers. "I would really like you to stop livestreaming this," she said firmly, feeling her status as "one of the cool ones" draining away as she said it. "I'm just worried we're going to get distracted and lose the suspect."

She turned back around and discovered, inevitably, that she had lost the suspect.

"Oh, figs," she muttered, before hurrying to the specific bush she'd last seen Miracle Mum disappearing behind.

When she reached it, there was nothing beyond but another cloud of foliage surrounding another section of overgrown trail, so Alison continued in the same direction, already concocting apologies and picturing the unsympathetic faces of Adam, Elizabeth, and the people of a disappointed nation as she made them. She pushed through the next wall of leaves and almost ran straight into the cave.

The ground was beginning to rise into yet another grassy hill, but this one cracked open at the base as if frozen at the most critical point of stifling a yawn. A wide black zigzag led into a passage running underneath, made all the more obvious by the way the plant life had been pushed aside at the entrance, probably several times in the recent past.

"She must have gone down here," said Alison, crouching to peer into the darkness. She produced her own phone and turned on the flashlight. "There's a tunnel. Maybe an old abandoned sewer or underpass or something."

She glanced back to get Beatrice's perspective and discovered at that point that she was alone. There was nothing behind her but crowding bushes and the trees that loomed overhead like disapproving playground monitors discovering an illicit game of marbles.

Alison had always been mystified by the concept other people referred to as "being lost," and of the way it was spoken of with such fear and omen. She was incapable of not knowing where she was. Her eidetic memory ensured that she had a perfect three-dimensional map of her surroundings at all times. At that moment, she knew that Diablerie's car was parked precisely two hundred and thirteen meters away in a roughly east-southeasterly direction.

And yet, while she didn't feel "lost," it was moments like these that made her think she could at least hum along with the idea—with the dwindling daylight barely penetrating the encroaching branches and the dark tunnel entrance in front of her like the expectant grin of a giant monster.

Precious seconds had passed, with Miracle Mum getting farther and farther away into the tunnels to do who knows what, and the teenagers were still nowhere to be seen. Alison had to press on. The alternative was having to explain to Elizabeth that she did nothing to prevent another death because she had felt a little bit scared. She ducked into the cave, keeping one hand over her head to brush away the spiders.

31

It had been ambitious of the Modern Miracle front garden to try to contain the entire congregation, but it was a stonehearted pragmatist compared to the interior of the house. Still, Adam and Rana were able to get inside by being among those members of the crowd with the foresight to politely speed walk closer to the door the moment they noticed signs of the ceremony beginning.

"Shoes off," said the person directly behind them, mere picoseconds after Adam's boot made contact with the living room carpet.

"What?" Adam turned to see that everyone coming through the front door behind him was removing their shoes and adding them to an increasingly monolithic pile under the hat stand. The person who had spoken was a young man wearing the inevitable Modern Miracle T-shirt and giving Adam the evil eye through thick spectacles.

"You have to take your shoes off when you come in," said Rana, who was pulling off her own trainers as she spoke. "Miracle Dad's rule. You know. Dads."

Adam conceded that this was indeed characteristic of Dads, and reached for his boot zippers with sad reluctance, knowing it'd be an undignified couple of minutes sitting on the front step when it came time to squeeze his feet back into them.

He glanced around the living room. It was a large space bare of furniture—except for one old couch shoved right up against the far wall—although there were marks, scratches, and outlines on the wallpaper indicating the places where a television and some shelving units might once have stood. The carpet was an inexpensive beige affair that had already been worn down to the depth of a piece of paper, so the no-shoes rule seemed a little academic at that point.

Adam followed Rana's lead by sitting cross-legged in the middle of the room, allowing the more devout attendees to fill up the front and provide cover—the "front" in this case meaning the part of the room that adjoined the main hall, at the end of which could be seen the door to the ground floor bathroom that served as Miracle Meg's "altar." Several identical floor lamps with much of the IKEA about them had been set up to form a walkway to the bathroom door. Each one was wrapped in Christmas lights.

It was all rather tacky, and even more so with Jamie in his wheelchair at the near end of the hallway. It was like watching a cancer patient having to go onto a high-energy Japanese game show to receive chemotherapy.

"All right, Miracle Mob!" said Miracle Dad, breaking off from the little huddle around Jamie to address the audience. "Make yourselves comfortable, we'll be ready any second to change Jamie's life." He turned to one of the orderlies and did a very poor job of lowering his voice. "Can he come out of the wheelchair?"

"Does he have to?" asked the nearest orderly, after the two men took a moment to exchange disbelieving looks.

"Well, you know how it is," said Miracle Dad, with the usual forced nonchalance of someone realizing in the moment that they had unthinkingly said something horrendous. "El-Yetch, nature goddess. Technology rubs her up the wrong way sometimes, you know. Maybe you could hold him up?"

Both orderlies simultaneously directed their disbelieving looks at Jamie's mother, who in turn looked to Jamie. Who must have become quite accustomed to communicating through eyes alone, as even from across the room, Adam could read the expression: *Do whatever he wants. Please don't screw this up for me.*

His mother gave the nod and gathered up an armful of drip stands like a poorly organized golf caddy as the two grumbling orderlies gently took Jamie under the arms and lifted him up, letting his legs dangle.

"Hang on," said Miracle Dad, looking down. "He's got shoes on."

The orderlies stopped, both clearly fighting the urge to throw what they were carrying to the floor in exasperation. "Does El-Yetch have a problem with shoes now?!"

"No, but the carpet might," said Miracle Dad, unable to stop himself. Jamie's mother squatted down and smoothly pulled Jamie's shoes from his unresisting legs before the argument could draw things out any longer.

"All right, time for Jamie to take the Walk of Worship!" said Miracle Dad to the crowd, hesitating only momentarily at the word *walk*. "Let's introduce him to Miracle Meg!"

Adam readjusted his sitting position, leaning a little farther forward as he prepared to use his special senses. If nothing else, his first glimpse of Miracle Meg would immediately confirm whether she had any kind of magical infusion, which would go a long way to eliminating possibilities.

Miracle Dad had stepped to one side briefly to toy with a nearby laptop, and generic soothing music began playing over the home sound system as Jamie's cluster of puppeteers began to escort him along the Walk of Worship. "Oh, I forgot to mention," said Miracle Dad as he returned to the front of the "auditorium." "Today's blessings of El-Yetch are also happening in recognition of Breast Cancer Awareness Month."

He flicked a switch on a nearby cable, and Adam's vision was flooded with pink.

All the lamps that made up the two sides of the Walk of Worship were pink, as were all of the Christmas lights wrapped around them. Pink gels had been placed on all the ceiling lights. There was a tiny light on the side of Miracle Dad's laptop to show that its power cable was plugged in, and he'd even put some pink tape over that.

And it wasn't just any pink—it was the exact shade of pink that indicated the presence of life essence transfer magic to Adam's senses. Exactly as he usually described it: like the color of Barbie's car if it was parked outside a strip club.

When Miracle Meg finally made an appearance, emerging from some side room to walk to the bathroom in a vaguely floaty, mysterious manner, Adam's senses reported that she was, indeed, infused with healing magic. As was the toilet she was sitting on, the U-shaped mat on the floor, Jamie, Miracle Dad, and absolutely everything in Adam's field of view.

He looked at Rana. She was pink, too, and the pink magic inside her that he already knew about was completely indistinguishable from the light that bathed them all.

She caught his open-mouthed look. "I know," she whispered. "I had no idea it was Breast Cancer Awareness Month either."

32

Again, Alison was wishing she had been forewarned about a couple of things before she had set out that afternoon, such as that she was going to be stealthing through the undergrowth, and that later on she would be pursuing a possible suspect in a muddy tunnel, illuminated only by the flashlight on her phone. Had she known all of that, she would have worn something more camouflaging, and waterproof shoes, and charged her phone to the full. Or, perhaps more likely, she would have decided to stay home and spend her evening cleaning out the fridge.

She had been making the effort to step lightly and carefully along the damp ground, but this had only drawn out the excruciating process of cold water seeping into her socks. Her phone was only illuminating the ten or so feet ahead. The point where it ended was an omnipresent wall of darkness, waiting to pounce at any moment. She couldn't say if it was that or the ever-diminishing battery icon on the phone's screen that made her most anxious.

She had switched to Airplane Mode to preserve battery life, and that meant she couldn't call anyone if she ran into trouble, just to add another layer to her continued lack of forethought. At any rate, there was slim chance of getting a signal down here. There was nothing Alison could do but press on and hope to run into Miracle Mum. At which point, she could either make an arrest or ask to borrow her phone.

From what she could see, the brickwork was ancient. Whatever this tunnel was, it probably hadn't been in official use for a few hundred years.

Maybe a disused sewer or dungeon for some castle or estate that no longer existed. She wondered if it might even have been an ancient Roman underground aqueduct, but she was half certain that wasn't a thing.

The tunnel forked off into other passages and chambers, but most of them were blocked off by rubble. Some of the blockages were because the ceilings had collapsed, but others consisted of bricks and stones gathered from elsewhere. That meant some passages had been blocked off deliberately. Whoever had repurposed these tunnels apparently had a specific use in mind for them.

Alison had paused to inspect a small, square room off the main tunnel with a gnarled tree root emerging from the broken ceiling when she heard a wet footfall in the tunnel ahead. One that couldn't have been coming from her, because it sounded like the source was wearing sensible footwear. She glanced ahead and saw light spill across an upcoming turn in the tunnel.

She quickly killed the light on her phone and pressed herself against the nearest wall of the chamber, where she could still see the doorway.

The noise of calm, businesslike footsteps grew in volume until Alison thought, deliriously, that they must have been coming from the inside of her own head. The light coming through the doorway became brighter in time with every step.

Then, as fear surged up Alison's throat and grabbed her by the tonsils, the light rose to a crescendo and the silhouette of Miracle Mum in baggy coat and undersized Wellington boots drifted across the doorway.

"Greedy," she muttered as she went, apparently addressing herself. "Greedy, greedy, greedy."

Alison waited until every trace of Miracle Mum had disappeared from her senses. First the last dregs of Miracle Mum's light flickered away down the tunnel, then the sound of muttering faded, and finally the last dribbling echoes of wet footsteps.

Alison let all her breath out in a sigh of relief. She was alone again in the silence. In pitch darkness. In a potentially unstable ancient tunnel containing an as-yet-unconfirmed number of murderous vampires. With that thought, she sucked her entire sigh back into her throat.

She carefully poked her head out into the main tunnel again, confirming that it was still pitch black and silent in both directions. Now that Miracle Mum had apparently doubled back, following her suddenly felt less important than investigating where she had just come from and what, if anything, she had been doing there. Maybe Beatrice and Roger were still near the tunnel entrance and could take over tailing Miracle Mum. Assuming they hadn't hurled themselves off a cliff because a donor told them to.

Alison looked pointlessly up the darkened tunnel to where Miracle Mum had come from. She decided not to turn her light back on for the moment, there being no reason to think a murderous vampire could see her any better than she could see them in the darkness. She pressed on, carefully lifting her feet to avoid the puddles and fallen stones in her path that her eidetic memory had diligently cataloged the last time there had been light.

When she reached the point where the tunnel turned ninety degrees, a new point of light appeared. Another fifty or so yards ahead, something was lit up in flickering red and yellow. Alison immediately hopped back, took cover around the corner, and carefully peered out.

Fortunately the source of the light was not, as she had briefly thought, the yawning gullet of a hideous fire-breathing monster. It was another square chamber like the one she had taken cover in, lit by candlelight.

At first, Alison was inching forward, ready to turn and bolt at the first sign of monster or vampire coven. But as more and more of the candlelit room became clear, all thoughts of fleeing drifted from her mind like leaves in the wind. By the time she finally entered the room, her feet were moving on their own, and her jaw hung open like an unresponsive chat window.

The room was a shrine of worship, lit by a perimeter of candles of varying shapes and sizes running along all four walls. In the center of the room was a low wooden table with more candles covering its entire surface, except for a circle about a foot wide. In the middle of that was a single framed photograph of Miracle Meg in the uniform of some local primary school.

But behind that, a colorful mural of what Alison assumed was supposed to be El-Yetch dominated the far wall of the chamber and a good portion of the ceiling. It was a chaotic collage of patterns with the vague sense of a female figure emerging from it, with curving rainbows for hips and spirals for breasts. The bulk of the "head" was on the ceiling—a mass of leaf-shaped prints for the face, blue spirals for eyes, and a perfectly round, pouting black mouth.

Alison was still slowly drifting into the room, fixated on the artwork. It took a few moments for her to notice that she no longer had to stoop; the ceiling was a fair bit higher here. A foot or so of brickwork and soil had fallen or been carved away before the painter had gotten to work.

Alison might not have had much faith in her own deductive skills, but her gut was telling her that she was not looking at the product of a sound mind. The finger painting alone had been performed with the careful, determined precision of someone who thought they were doing something far beyond interior design.

Her foot nudged something soft as she took another step closer to the painting, and she froze. Her gut began telling her something new and unpleasant. She lingered for one last moment on the calming blue spirals of El-Yetch's eyes, relishing the last few moments of her life with its current number of complications, then looked down.

The corpse was female, lying full length across the ground with their skinny arms wrapped around their torso. They were wearing a Modern Miracle T-shirt and a dark green skirt, and Alison conservatively estimated that they had the body of a ninety-eight-year-old.

The difference between the corpse of someone elderly and someone who had been prematurely aged by vampire magic was one piece of esoterica Alison could have done without, for all her eagerness to learn. And yet, having found her second vampire victim, she was picking up on the signs. Their skin, while deathly pale and clinging to their bones, lacked the spots and laughter lines of skin that had been naturally weathered over time. There was a sheen of sweat on them that hadn't fully dried.

Which meant they had died extremely recently.

Which meant the vampire was probably still close by.

Alison had been doing an excellent job of focusing on the fine details in order to drown out the part of her that wanted to indiscriminately run around the room waving her arms and screaming. But those last two deductions cut through to that part of her like a scythe to the skull.

She jumped away, suddenly conscious of the big, empty tunnel directly behind her and its currently unknown quantity of murderers, and pinned herself against the wall beside the door. She took some deep breaths and tried to think. Miracle Mum had to be the vampire. She'd just come from here. But there was no reason she'd return, as by some miracle of good fortune, she hadn't spotted Alison. Had she?

Alison strained her hearing for any sound besides the terror ringing in her ears, but all remained silent. Safe to assume that Miracle Mum wasn't coming back. But that brought a fresh wave of guilt and horror, because she'd last seen Miracle Mum heading back toward the place where Alison had last seen Beatrice and Roger.

Alison broke into a run, heading back down the pitch-black tunnel and relying solely on her eidetic memory to keep her from running headlong into walls and fallen bricks. She wondered for a moment if she was running to Beatrice or running away from the corpse, but since neither option felt like a worse idea than standing still, she focused on the running.

The tunnel had seemed quite long when being navigated at a stealthy creep but rushed past in less than a minute at a full sprint. Soon, Alison could see the exit, a ragged rectangle of dark blue mottled with what specks of moonlight could penetrate the trees. She rolled under the lip of the cave without slowing, remembered at the last moment the possibility of spiders, and emerged into the open air waving her arms madly above her head like a semaphore operator speaking in tongues.

A cold breeze blew upon her face as she stopped, bringing a moment of perspective, along with a strong smell of something burning. She looked around, blinking, as if having just been shaken awake from a traumatic dream.

With her eyes still adjusted to the darkness, she spotted Beatrice almost immediately. She was crouched behind a mossy rise with her hands over her head.

"Beatrice?" asked Alison.

"Oh!" said Beatrice, looking up. "Have they gone?"

"Who? Miracle Mum?"

"No . . ." Beatrice frowned. "The fire person?"

"What fire person?"

Alison noticed the fire person just in time. They had been slowly approaching their position from the forest ahead, silhouetted against a blurry shaft of moonlight. They were clearly a person, but the "fire" part only made sense a moment later, when they held out a hand and sent a pyrokinetic blast roaring through the trees.

Alison ducked out of its way, then lost balance and fell onto her posterior. A streaming yellow funnel of magical flame was cast brilliantly against the night sky, passing by harmlessly above her, then abruptly vanished, taking all her night vision with it.

"Victor?" she mouthed to herself, it being a level of pyrokinetic power she had only seen once before. She blinked rapidly to dispel the blue smudge in front of her eyes and peered out from behind her smoking cover.

The silhouetted figure was looking around, apparently just as blinded by their own fire as everyone else, trying to determine if their targets were still there or atomized into grease stains. Alison could get a longer look at them but still couldn't tell if they had the build of a man or a woman. They either had a massively misshapen head or were wearing a motorcycle helmet.

"Where's Roger?" whispered Alison, covered by the hiss of cooling scenery.

"He made a run for the van," replied Beatrice, still clutching the back of her head. "I-I think he made it. I think I'd like to make a run for the van too."

"Don't run for the van!" suggested Alison.

The fire person took a step toward their cover, blackened vegetation crunching beneath their feet.

"Okay, I'm making a run for the van," said Beatrice, before hopping up in a shower of leaves and beginning to sprint away, waving her arms and screaming just to remove whatever atoms of a chance remained that she might go unnoticed.

"Hey!" said Alison, instinctively leaping to her feet as the fire person leisurely extended their hand toward Beatrice's retreating back. "Um. Hello. Do you know Victor Casin? Because if you don't, erm . . . you'd . . . probably get on."

The fire person stared at her, hand still outstretched. Then their torso slowly rotated around like the wheel of a torture device until their hand was pointing at Alison instead.

Alison's instincts hadn't been producing the best results lately but now had the chance to redeem themselves. She ducked and dived back into the cave, returning to the cool darkness just as the next fireball splattered against the cave mouth's shaggy upper lip. She was back on her feet and running down the tunnel within seconds, barely even registering the spectacular new range of mud stains her work trousers acquired.

She glanced back after a few yards and faltered to a stop when she noticed that the fire person wasn't chasing her. They had stopped at the cave entrance, bending down to peer curiously into the dark.

Realization seized Alison as she saw them extend that terrible hand again. They didn't need to pursue. Not when Alison had just voluntarily stepped into an impromptu pressure cooker.

Alison opted to sprint even further down the tunnel, pushing herself until her breath was rasping in and out of her like a serrated knife through stale bread. She had no idea if distance was even a factor. If the tunnels had no big vents or outlets, then surely the fire person could just keep pouring power into them until every square foot of air was super-heated. Couldn't they? Alison had once seen Victor bring a section of ocean the size of a tennis court to a boil within a matter of seconds. That amount of energy could probably make all these stuffy tunnels hot enough to at least give Alison a new appreciation for the plight of a potato in a microwave.

She was pushing her thinking to the limit, raking through her eidetic memory for anything about heat and science that might help. In her panic, the only mildly relevant fact that she could summon was that shepherd's pie should be baked for about twenty minutes, then put under the broiler for another three or four minutes to get a nice crispy top.

Something made a hissing sound behind her, and she stopped and turned just in time to see the fireball burst into life. The far end of the tunnel became a rectangle of churning yellow-orange light that was roaring toward her like the headlights of an express train.

Alison froze. At the pace it was coming, the fire was going to hit her in seconds and was showing no signs of dissipating. Time slowed down as her brain went into survival mode and cataloged every detail in her field of vision, searching for a way to live on. The tunnel was ninety centimeters wide and one hundred and eighty centimeters tall. There were two thousand two hundred and fourteen bricks currently in sight. She was four feet away from a tunnel that led to a small side chamber with no exit. There were now one thousand nine hundred and eighty-five bricks in sight because the fire had advanced farther . . .

She was so occupied by updating her brick count for the third time that she barely noticed the arm clamp around her chest or the hand grab one of her wrists. She was pulled back with a strength that lifted her off her feet. Her senses overwhelmed, she went limp, and her assailant dragged her unresponsive form into the nearby side chamber.

A moment later, the fire arrived, tearing unfeelingly through the air like a swarm of locusts, and Alison was surrounded by what might as well have been orange-tinted television static. Every muscle in her body tensed. After several seconds of her body very conspicuously not being lashed with agonizing tongues of searing heat, she opened one eye.

The fire was still raging mere feet away but couldn't seem to encroach any closer. It was splattering uselessly against an invisible wall that surrounded her.

She looked down. She had been pulled inside a very familiar circle of white tape, adorned with a very familiar sequence of runes. By her side, a very familiar cell phone was chanting the circle's associated sequence of syllables in a disinterested computerized voice.

Alison looked up.

"Ah, girl," said Doctor Diablerie, still holding her wrist and raising his voice to be heard over the roar. "I assume you are here to return my car."

33

A few minutes later, the fire stopped. The fire person would have made the obvious assumption that everything in the tunnels was now dead, but just in case they were the incredulous sort, Alison opted not to head to the tunnel entrance straightaway. Instead, she hurried to the innermost part of the tunnel, as she had the horrible feeling that everything she had found would be . . .

"Gone," she said aloud, tottering into the mass of ash-blackened matter that had been the El-Yetch chapel and the body of the vampire's latest victim.

"How unsporting," said Doctor Diablerie, just behind her. "This accursed vampire must have had the bizarre notion that a vampire-stricken corpse might act as evidence against them."

He was wearing the exact same clothing he'd had on the night Alison had abandoned him in Worcester. Alison knew for a fact that he had several identical copies of the same outfit—dinner suit, cape, and top hat—but these were definitely the same specific garments. He was also sporting several days' growth of beard.

"But you know there was a body down here, right?" said Alison, growing flustered. "You could tell everyone about the vampire too!"

Diablerie drew himself up with a sneer. "Do not think to dictate what Diablerie knows, girl. Diablerie's knowledge is to your understanding what the deepest oceanic abyss is to the understanding of a fruit bat."

Alison frowned. "Wait, you didn't know?"

He broke eye contact and appeared to be addressing the blackened ceiling. "When Diablerie chooses a temporary lair, he concerns himself not with the antics of his next-door neighbors."

"How can you say . . ." Alison bit the end off her protest. Whether Diablerie was lying to obfuscate his real agenda, or lying to provoke her, or lying because he'd somehow derangedly convinced himself it was the truth, it didn't matter. Diablerie was lying. There was very little point in pressing the matter. "So you've been here since we drove down here together?"

"Few other options remained." He glared hard enough that Alison thought his closer eye was going to pop out. "I was relieved of my transportation by a ridiculous chit with devilry on her mind."

Alison was far too tired and overwhelmed to dredge her guilty feelings back up. She sighed. "I thought you caught a train. You sent a text saying you caught a train."

"As was Diablerie's intention when that missive was sent!" said Diablerie, twirling on the spot and raising an index finger in time with the exclamation mark. "But destiny had another path in store. As I was repairing to the station to flee this land, a sign fell upon my path. Two sticks, arranged in an arrow, pointing in the direction where the fates would have me go."

"So . . ."

"Pointing to the station," continued Diablerie. "And so, I turned on my heel and went in a completely different direction. For Diablerie is no plaything of the cosmos. And behold! You return. The correctness of Diablerie's arcane instincts need go unstated. Now, shall we leave this fetid place?"

"I have to pick up Adam," admitted Alison, anticipating Diablerie's reaction but unable to summon the effort to try to avoid it.

"Ah?" He flashed an intrigued look. "So, after stealing my car, you proceeded to use it to entertain boys. As much to be expected of your generation, I fear, but know this, girl: Diablerie checks his upholstery most diligently, and every sticky patch I find shall be visited upon you tenfold."

Alison blinked a few times. "Okay."

"Come, then. Let us find your paramour and tarry no longer. Diablerie will tolerate a carload of sexual tension if it means I can finally escape this tawdry little suburb."

"Adam's . . . at the Modern Miracle service," said Alison, dread making itself comfortable in her stomach yet again as she realized aloud. She glanced back down the blackened tunnel. "The vampire was going back there too. We've got to make sure Adam's all right."

"Very well," spat Diablerie. "Clearly Diablerie's abandonment is less important than an inamorato of yours being drained any further of their virility." By the end of his statement, he was attempting to maintain his dignity while holding his top hat in place and jogging to keep up.

Beatrice and Roger were nowhere to be seen in the forest at the tunnel entrance, nor did Alison see the LAXA van at any point on her way along the walking trail back to the road. She had to assume they had gotten away or massively improved the van's camouflage, either of which implied they were at least alive.

Alison left Diablerie at his car, grumblingly sniffing the passenger seats, and continued on foot to the Modern Miracle house. Her concerns about Miracle Mum enacting horrors there gradually faded as she ascended the road and passed numerous satisfied servicegoers chatting amiably on the way back to their cars. It wasn't the kind of atmosphere one associated with the aftermath of a vampiric death orgy. Not one that knew anything about projecting the right image anyway.

She saw Adam sitting in a little cloud of gloom on the edge of the pavement just outside Modern Miracle's front garden, laboriously working his feet into his boots. Behind him, a few stragglers from the congregation were still hanging around, watching a red-faced young boy in hospital pajamas delightedly sprint around the front lawn, making airplane noises.

"Hey," said Adam, when he saw Alison trotting up. "How'd things go on your end?"

"Um, it turned into kind of a mess actually," said Alison urgently. "Another vampire victim turned up and we got attacked by—"

"Yeah, things didn't go well here either," said Adam spitefully, worrying at his boots and not really listening. "But I'm pretty certain that girl's got to be a conduit now. Why else would they have put all that pink light up?"

"Pink?" asked Alison, confused.

"Because there's something about Miracle Meg they didn't want me to see," continued Adam, holding up an index finger while making a knowing look he'd been rehearsing for the last ten minutes. "What I want to know is how they knew exactly what shade of pink to use. There aren't very many people who know that. Me, Archibald, Victor—"

"Victor!" Alison found her opportunity to get a word in edgeways. "Adam, we just got attacked by a pyrokinetic. Like, a Victor-level pyrokinetic."

That seemed to break Adam out of his prepared statement. He looked up as his foot came down, devastating the back of his left boot. "Victor attacked you?"

"Um. Someone did." Alison could only say with certainty that the fire person had been humanoid, wore a motorcycle helmet, and spewed fireballs like some kind of theoretical opposite of a sprinkler system. "I don't know if it was Victor. I mean, I haven't known him as long as you, but I'm pretty sure he wouldn't just kill me without warning." She fiddled with her earlobe, thinking about her own words. "Not on purpose anyway."

"I think we're all learning that maybe we didn't know Victor as well as we thought we did," said Adam bitterly. He met her gaze. "Did you know he's been hanging around on the Modern Miracle forum?"

Alison looked up at the Modern Miracle house. With the moonlight behind it, it loomed over her with a dangerous omen, and the effect was only slightly lessened by the young boy in the front garden, who was now running back and forth blowing raspberries with a coat over his head to the delight of the remaining adults. "You don't seriously think Victor . . ."

"Can't overlook the facts," said Adam gravely, sitting up straight. "That's something you need to learn when you're an investigator. This fits together a bit too well. Modern Miracle suddenly knows things only Victor knows, and then there's a mysterious pyrokinetic trying to stop you from . . ." He frowned. "What did you find again?"

"Er, the vampire killed someone else," said Alison, before remembering that this was probably important and repeating the statement in a more urgent voice.

"What?" Adam stood awkwardly, nearly fell over again because his left foot was hanging out of his boot, and straightened up. "Who?"

"I don't know, but there was a dried-up body, back there, in some, like, old tunnels." She pointed vaguely toward the hills.

Adam frowned in the direction she was pointing. "I think you'd better show me."

"Oh. It all got burned actually." She caught his incredulous look and instinctively added, "Sorry. But I saw it. It was in this whole creepy shrine to El-Yetch and Miracle Meg. Like the vampire was worshiping them or something."

"That's . . . a theory," said Adam. "Was there any sign that Miracle Meg had been there? Maybe sucked their life out a short time before the sermon tonight?"

Alison's eyes widened as Adam's question raised another pertinent detail in her mind. "Oh! Miracle Mum was there. I think she's the vampire."

"You actually saw Miracle Mum draining the victim?"

"Well . . . no," admitted Alison. "But I didn't see anyone else and the body was pretty new, so . . ." Her gaze flicked over to the Modern Miracle house again. "Has she come back here? Could you use your thing on her?"

"I don't see her," said Adam, scrutinizing the collection of joyful faces in the front garden watching Jamie express his newfound lust for life. He took on the slightly fish-eyed look he always had when he was using his magic senses. "There is someone with pink magic just over th—oh, never mind, it's Rana."

A single short yelp blasted from Alison's lungs, and she dropped into a crouch. Adam looked down at her, baffled, as she attempted to insert her entire head into a spherical section of hedge that was close to the ground.

"Hey, Mr. Hesketh!" said Rana, jogging up. "I was able to talk with Miracle Dad, and he's agreed to let me have some one-on-one time with Miracle Meg to ask about how her powers work, so . . . is that Alison?"

The quivering hedge froze. Adam winced. "Er. I'm not sure she wants me to say."

"Oh," said Rana, stirring the grass with one foot. "Okay. I'll . . . go back over there now." She turned and slowly walked the five or six feet back to the thinning circle of onlookers, glancing back several times as she went.

"Alison," said Adam, crouching beside the bush. "Miracle Mum probably isn't the conduit. Everyone here saw Miracle Meg doing a big heal tonight. There was nobody else in the room. Nobody touched the patient but her." He nodded to the patient, who was by now loudly commanding his audience to keep watching while he worked on pulling off a cartwheel properly. "And it was a very big heal. Probably enough to drain a person to death. The only explanation is Miracle Meg must have somehow drained the body you found before the sermon."

The part of hedge containing Alison's head tilted quizzically. "So what now? Call in the body?"

"Er, no," said Adam quickly. "I should take a look at where you found it. I might, er, notice something you missed. And then, I suppose I'd better have a little talk with Victor."

"Right," agreed the hedge. "Do you need anything else from me?"

"Just to . . . show me where this body was," said Adam patiently.

"Ah. Yeah. I assumed." The hedge quivered again. "'Cos in that case, would you mind helping me pull my head out of this hedge?"

Call between Sean Anderson and Adam Hesketh beginning at 9:56 p.m.:

SEAN ANDERSON: This is Anderson.

ADAM HESKETH: Hello—

SEAN ANDERSON: What've you got, Hesketh?

ADAM HESKETH: Oh. Uh. I only just got back. I mean. I literally just closed my front door.

SEAN ANDERSON: What've you got?

ADAM HESKETH: Actually I thought I would send you an email. Do you mind waiting? I'm not good with phones.

SEAN ANDERSON: Funny, I could've sworn I asked you a question twice, and I'm pretty sure you're saying things in reply, but all I'm hearing is a load of useless drivel. Maybe it's the phone. *[Three loud bangs of phone being knocked on something hard.]* WHAT. HAVE. YOU. GOT.

ADAM HESKETH: Okay. Um. About Modern Miracle?

SEAN ANDERSON: No, about the other faith healing outfit I sent you to get dirt on tonight. YES, ABOUT MODERN MIRACLE. And quickly, they're doing another interview tomorrow and I'm calling the producer in ten. Did you figure out how they're pulling the scam?

ADAM HESKETH: Um. No. I-I think they might've known I was coming. They had a whole bunch of pink lights set up.

[Long pause.]

SEAN ANDERSON: Pink lights.

ADAM HESKETH: It's, er, the thing is, when I use my senses that detect magic, healing magic shows up as pink. So I couldn't see if they were using any. Because the whole room was pink.

[Long pause.]

ADAM HESKETH: Because, I have these senses—

SEAN ANDERSON: Yes, yes, I understand. I'm just suddenly remembering why Extradimensional Affairs is my least favorite department. So you still don't know how the scam works.

ADAM HESKETH: No. Ooh! But Alison says she found a corpse.

SEAN ANDERSON: Okay. For future reference, you should've led with that. Tell me about this corpse.

ADAM HESKETH: Apparently it was in a cave not far from their house.

SEAN ANDERSON: But it was definitely killed by someone in the cult, yeah?

ADAM HESKETH: Apparently.

SEAN ANDERSON: I'll tell you what's worrying me, Hesketh, it's this word "apparently" that keeps dropping out of your mouth like a greasy nipple. Did you see this corpse yourself?

ADAM HESKETH: Uh. I didn't. Appa—er, Alison says there was a pyrokinetic on the scene as well, and by the time I got there, they'd basically totally carbonized it. Nothing left but dust.

SEAN ANDERSON: Right.

ADAM HESKETH: I got her to draw a picture of it though.

SEAN ANDERSON: So if I could just summarize this ammunition you're loading me up with here: you've got pink lights, you've got some dust that might have been a corpse that might have been killed vaguely near the subject, and you've got Alison's crayon drawing. Would that be about right?

ADAM HESKETH: I think she used colored pencils actually . . .

[Rustling sound, continuous sound of clipping scissors.]

SEAN ANDERSON: Hey, can you hear that?

ADAM HESKETH: What?

SEAN ANDERSON: That cutting sound. Are you hearing that too?

ADAM HESKETH: Um. The thing that sounds like scissors?

SEAN ANDERSON: It is scissors. It's MY scissors. Because I'm officially cutting you loose.

ADAM HESKETH: Mr. Anderson, I'm sorry, but it's not my fault—

SEAN ANDERSON: Snip!

ADAM HESKETH: They knew we were coming, and—

SEAN ANDERSON: Snip!

ADAM HESKETH: I think someone on the inside—

[Clipping noise intensifies.]

SEAN ANDERSON: Can't hear you over the sound of me cutting you loose! Stick to going cross-eyed at bullshit, kid, 'cos investigation isn't working out.

ADAM HESKETH: But—

SEAN ANDERSON: Cutting you loose now! Cutting you loose like this cord!

ADAM HESKETH: What cord?

[Clipping noise.]

Call ends 9:59 p.m.

Call between Victor Casin and Adam Hesketh beginning at 10:09 p.m.:

VICTOR: Yeah?

ADAM: What did you do, Victor?

VICTOR: Adam? Why are you calling me?

ADAM: W-what did you do?

VICTOR: You hate talking on the phone. You can't even call in a pizza 'cos you're afraid they'll judge you if you order pineapple.

ADAM: I've, I've asked a question two times now, Victor, and all I'm hearing is words coming out of you, and—

VICTOR: Yes, there are words coming out of me, Adam. It's this amazing new fashion trend called "talking."

ADAM: Were you in Worcester tonight?

VICTOR: Why would I be in Worcester? Why do you care? ·

ADAM: The pyrokinetic that was trying to kill Alison! Was that you?

VICTOR: Why would I kill Alison? On purpose, I mean. You know there are other pyrokinetics in the world, right?

ADAM: She says this one was at your power level.

VICTOR: Power level? That's not a thing. That's only a thing in *Dragon Ball Z*.

ADAM: Victor, would you please just answer me . . .

VICTOR: What are you expecting here? Even if that was me, do you really think I'd say so if you asked? You think I'd crumble under interrogation by the butternut squash that walks like a man?

ADAM: Whuh . . .

VICTOR: You actually thought it was me. You actually jumped to that conclusion. What happened to trust?

ADAM: Oh! Oh! Trust? Like how I, I trusted you with all my, my colors?

VICTOR: Sorry, you're going to have to run that through the butternut-squash-to-human translator for me.

ADAM: How did the Modern Miracle people know exactly what shade of pink to light the room with so my senses couldn't tell who had healing magic?

VICTOR: Oh, come on. I can't be the only person you've told that to.

ADAM: I told you and I told Archibald. And Archibald only leaves his basement when his tea urn needs filling. Be honest. Did you tell someone at Modern Miracle about my pink?

VICTOR: I told you I don't even post on the forum!

ADAM: Have you told someone who does?

VICTOR: I . . . um.

ADAM: You bastard!

VICTOR: Well, maybe I didn't realize it was classified information! You were always pretty sodding free with it. Usually whenever I wasn't the slightest bit interested. And it doesn't mean I was out murdering Alison or whatever.

ADAM: You pass information to suspects, and then there's a pyrokinetic on the scene destroying evidence for the suspects. What am I supposed to think?

VICTOR: You could always just believe me when I say it wasn't me, because we've been friends for years and that actually means more to you than trying to suck up to the boss.

ADAM: Victor . . . you do realize, if anyone other than me found out about this, you'd probably be fired, like, instantly.

VICTOR: Oh. What a threat. Whatever will I do if I can't sit around the cafeteria all day. I'll have to go to a Starbucks to make sculptures out of their sugar packets instead.

ADAM: Be serious.

VICTOR: I'm being totally serious. Because it turns out I can splatter monsters for the government for years and it absolutely counts for bugger all the moment something can get pinned on me.

ADAM: Oh, come on . . .

VICTOR: No. It's all been made perfectly clear to me now. Tell Danvers and the rest that they don't have to worry about keeping me on anymore, I quit. Tell them the next time you have one of your meetings. If your voice isn't too muffled.

[Long pause.]

ADAM: Why would my voice be muffled?

VICTOR: Because you'll be kissing their bottoms the whole time. Should've made that clearer. So yeah, good luck dealing with the next big monster attack. Maybe you could kiss its bottom till it dies.

Call ends 10:13 p.m.

THE NEXT EVENING

34

"That was Shgshthx and the Shgshthxes," said Shgshthx the TV presenter, effortlessly oozing charisma, as well as another substance that was becoming very smelly under the studio lights. "Playing their hit fart single again. Always great to hear the noises that come out of those boys." He was stalling expertly as a small platoon of off-camera technicians wiped off the other part of the stage.

"Now," said Shgshthx, turning to camera as his close-up began. "It's the debate that's sweeping the nation, and it started right here with one man asking one simple question: Can religion and magic get along? If they can't, what should we do? Build an ark? Have a crusade? To answer all these questions, we've invited two guests to hash it out once and for all. First, please welcome back to the show the man who was the start of it all, the high priest of the Cult of El-Yetch, Miracle Dad!"

The camera cut to one end of the couch, where Miracle Dad grinned and waved in acceptance of the token applause. His colorful T-shirt and the way he bounced eagerly in his seat made him look like a contestant gearing up for their chance to totally humiliate themselves in some kind of brightly colored teatime game show.

"And representing the Anglican Church, and religion in general," continued Shgshthx, "please welcome Miracle Dad's own parish vicar, the Reverend Simon Frobisher."

"Good evening," said the vicar, with a nod. He was the same thin white-haired vicar that Adam had spoken to after William Shaw's funeral.

He smiled nervously to the camera as his eyes darted around, looking like a weak-willed teacher realizing only in this moment that he had been volunteered for the ducking stool at the school fair.

"Reverend Frobisher, let's start with you," said Shgshthx, arranging himself into a rather abstract shape that somehow successfully evoked an interested cross-legged, cocked-head pose. "The church has had a lot of harsh things to say about magic throughout history, hasn't it? What's the official position now?"

The vicar laughed good-naturedly. "Yes, we've had a pretty poor record on that, haven't we? Don't worry, I don't think the church will be starting up any witch trials in this day and age, ha, ha." His laughter trailed off into silence, broken only by a single embarrassed cough from the audience. "You'd actually be surprised to see how up on current thinking the modern church is. We believe there's room on God's earth for everyone. Magic and, er, not so much."

"What a load of bollocks," declared Miracle Dad, proudly sitting fully upright as he spoke.

Shgshthx broke the surprised silence that followed. "Miracle Dad?" he prompted, after quickly glancing at the offscreen producer and seeing an enthusiastic double thumbs-up.

"It's bollocks," said Miracle Dad, still grinning chummily. "They do this every time. Everyone starts liking something religion doesn't like, and, oh lo and behold, turns out God actually likes this thing because it's popular now. They're doing it with magic. They did it with gays. And Muslims. And women voting."

"Well, the, the, interpretation of God's will has always been an ongoing process," said the vicar. "It's like a science."

"Never had that problem with *my* god," said Miracle Dad. "Interpreting the will of El-Yetch is easy. I just ask her. 'Cos she lives in my daughter. If I wanna know if she wants Weetabix for breakfast, she can just tell me. I don't get a team of experts to go over her nappies from five years ago and argue about it."

The vicar laughed at Miracle Dad's joke for slightly longer than the audience did. "Well," he said. "That certainly does sound a lot more convenient. But just because El-Yetch is in easier reach doesn't change the fact that our church has been around for many hundreds of years, and that many millions of people all around the world take a lot of comfort from their faith in the Lord, whether or not He truly exists."

"What do you think of that, Miracle Dad?" pushed Shgshthx. "Is there room in the world for both your god and the gods that are more, shall we say, existentially challenged?"

"Hey, I'd say we're all entitled to believe whatever rubbish we want," said Miracle Dad charitably. "But it's not up to me, is it? It's a matter of the law now. The X-Appropriation Act says you can't say you've got magic powers or that you worship something with magic powers if they aren't really magic. So I'm just asking questions on behalf of all those people getting arrested now for saying they believe in crystals and homeopathy and all that. And for all the magic kids who remember when the law was to keep them all locked up. How is the church *not* breaking the law?"

"Reverend?" asked Shgshthx as the vicar's terrified silence dragged on. "I think what Miracle Dad is asking is: how can you prove that God exists?"

"The, the Lord is all around us," said the vicar, sweat visibly beading on his brow. "You can see Him in the beauty of trees, the faces of children . . ."

"Mmm," said Shgshthx. "But let's say you have to prove it in a court-admissible sort of way."

"Well . . . obviously we can't," said the vicar sheepishly. "B-but you can't prove that He doesn't exist either."

"Oh yeah, that's the usual line, isn't it," scoffed Miracle Dad. "Unfortunately we're in the world of law now, and in law there's this lovely little thing called 'the burden of proof.' And the burden of proof is first and foremost on the party claiming, not the party refuting the claim." He winked to camera, and in the living room of a faraway apartment the Modern Miracle forumite who had typed up four paragraphs explaining this concept to Miracle Dad felt extremely gratified. "So I'll ask you again. Where's your proof?"

"I mean, it's," stammered the vicar, looking from Miracle Dad to Shgshthx before finally hunching his shoulders and leaning close to Miracle Dad. "Come on, Gus, why are you doing this to me?"

"What did you call him?" asked Shgshthx as Miracle Dad's eyes and mouth popped wide in astonishment.

"Gus. It's his name. Gus Arkwright." The vicar looked around in bafflement as he took in the shocked faces of every person in the crew and audience. "What's the matter? I'm his parish vicar. I officiated his wedding."

"Did you just doxx me?!" exclaimed Miracle Dad, recoiling in horror. Someone in the audience shrieked in affronted disbelief.

"We may just have had a doxxing on air," muttered Shgshthx into the earpiece mike that had been subtly draped over the side of his bathtub.

"I can't believe I just got doxxed by the church!" said Miracle Dad, rising from his seat. A growing hubbub was developing. Several people in the audience were booing, and a distant producer was yelling at someone.

In the middle of it all, the vicar sat flinching like a meerkat on a busy traffic roundabout. "What? What did I do wrong? How can it be doxxing to say what someone's name is?"

"Someone cut his mike!" yelled the producer.

"If you're just joining us, I'm afraid we have just experienced a live doxxing," said Shgshthx to camera. "Miracle Dad, on behalf of the show, let me extend my full apologies and assurance that we will strive to be better."

"Thanks, I suppose," said Miracle Dad, arms folded. "Not like that's going to undoxx me, is it?"

"Er, we'd better end the debate there. Why don't we get Shgshthx and the Shgshthxes back on to play us out?" The technicians on the other end of the stage, still holding mops, collectively palmed their faces.

Before long, the chaos and the hubbub were drowned out by the rhythmic squelches of the fluidic band, and the audience settled down. By then, Miracle Dad had already stormed out, and the only lingering trace of the debate was the Reverend Frobisher, who was tactfully led out of the building by an uncommunicative runner, all the while politely requesting that someone explain what doxxing was.

Posts from Twitter (names redacted):

N—— posted:
Complete insanity. They seriously want to put Jesus Christ on trial? What's the plan after that, prosecute Mother Nature for Hurricane Katrina?

F—— posted:
I'm with Miracle Dad. It's high time we reexamined the place of the church in modern society. What better way to do that than a public trial? Seems only fair after what they did to Galileo.

W—— posted:
What I'm taking from all of this is that this new generation of magic-using kids is pathologically incapable of respect. They don't respect tradition, they don't respect ancient institutions like the church, they don't even respect the laws of physics.

F—— replied:
If only the magic users would show the church all the respect and dignity the church has shown magic users over the years. Maybe they could politely and respectfully pull out a nice comfortable ducking stool for it to sit on.

L—— replied:
yeah plus I heard they doxx people now

THE NEXT DAY

35

Richard Danvers and Elizabeth Lawrence had lately gotten into the unspoken habit of sharing an office for the first few hours of the day. This was mainly for defense; it minimized the chances of either of them getting cornered by Anderson. That morning, Richard was taking up space on the couch in Elizabeth's office, going through the first few reports of the day on his laptop. His free arm was propped up on its elbow, holding aloft a steaming mug of tea like a lighthouse in the mist.

"Seen the school report?" he said. "Enrollments went up ten percent in the last six months."

"Mm," said Elizabeth, staring at her own computer screen and only half listening. A few moments of thought later, she sat back, tapping her index fingernail upon the desk. "That might call for further analysis."

Danvers raised an eyebrow. "You think?"

"We're seeing an increase in magical infusions in young people," said Elizabeth. "That may be a cause for concern."

"Or an increase in young people willing to admit they have magical infusions," said Danvers. "Now it's declassified, and legal, and dare I say, fashionable."

"Even so, I'd expect the increase to plateau sooner than this," said Elizabeth, typing a note to herself. "I'll ask Archibald to monitor the situation."

There was a knock on the office door. A short and timid knock, the kind of knock that would like to be heard if it wasn't too inconvenient but half hopes to be ignored or mistaken for some other sound so that it can go away for a while and come back when it felt slightly readier to face the day.

"Come in, Alison," said Elizabeth. "And close the door."

Alison did so, although at first she only poked her head in to get a quick lay of the terrain. Some of the tension noticeably disappeared from her muscles when she saw Richard Danvers. There was something immediately reassuring about the way he was lounging on the sofa with his cup of tea, looking as if he'd only temporarily mislaid his dressing gown and slippers.

"Sorry I'm late," said Alison, after closing the door carefully enough that it barely made a sound.

"Don't apologize, almost everyone's late today," sighed Danvers. "Take it your train was delayed by a protest? Or was it a counterprotest?"

"Um. Counter-counter-counterprotest."

Elizabeth glanced up from her monitor. "Hm?"

"Well, it started with some religious people protesting at the Ministry of Justice," said Alison, standing in the middle of the room and fidgeting with her fingers as she spoke. "Then some pro-magic students counterprotested them. Then there was a counter-counterprotest from, you know, some of those online right-wing people? The ones that might be doing it ironically?"

"The ones wearing Pilgrim hats and carrying around witch-burning stakes," said Elizabeth, nodding.

"Um. Yeah. It was the counterprotest to them that delayed my train."

"At the risk of sounding immodest," said Danvers, "I'm very glad we declared neutrality as early as we did. Both sides seem to be respecting that."

"That may change if the protests become less civil," pointed out Elizabeth.

"True," said Danvers, swallowing tea. "But we're not in with-us-or-against-us mode yet."

Alison had taken the seat in front of Elizabeth's desk. "Um. Anderson's in the building," she said. When Danvers's mug froze midway to his lips she quickly added, "I saw him in the lift, but he got off at a different department."

"Thanks for the warning," he muttered, before taking a long gulp.

"He was shouting into the phone about that last Miracle Dad interview," continued Alison. "The person he was shouting at, he was saying that he could put them in touch with someone who could 'give Miracle Dad a run for his money.'"

"His exact words?" said Elizabeth.

"He said another word between 'Miracle' and 'Dad,' but I didn't want to say that one," reported Alison dutifully.

"Hm," said Elizabeth. "It probably won't be relevant."

"Still, it's useful to be abreast of all the details," added Danvers, with a hint of reproach toward Elizabeth when he saw Alison's eyes drop.

"In any case." Elizabeth tapped her Enter key with a slight flourish to signal the completion of her current task, then pushed her laptop to one side. "You said Diablerie has resurfaced?"

Alison leaned forward. "Yes. He was hiding out in Worcester for the last week or so, keeping an eye on Modern Miracle, I think."

"Any specific reason?" asked Elizabeth.

"I'm not sure, but he was living in a tunnel right next to the little shrine where the third vampire victim was."

Elizabeth's change of expression, and the gesture with which Danvers set down his mug of tea, might as well have been accompanied with the tolling of an ominous bell. Alison flinched.

"What third vampire victim?" asked Elizabeth, the words firing one by one from her mouth like poison darts from a blowpipe.

"Oh," said Alison, unconsciously drawing her legs up into a fetal position as the two administrators bored into her with their stares. "Adam said he would call it in. After he looked at the scene. Did he not do that?"

Danvers closed his laptop as if turning over the last page of a very disappointing book. "No, I was not aware of a third body," he said, rising to his feet. "Neither was I aware that Adam was in the field."

Whoops, thought Alison as Danvers walked stiff-leggedly across the room to the door, opened it, and scanned the visible offices and cubicles as if standing on the prow of a battleship. "Mr. Hesketh!" he yelled, seeing his prey.

"Oh, hi, Mr. Danvers" came Adam's voice from across the office floor. "Sorry I'm late. My train was delayed by a counter–counter–counter–counter—"

"My office, now," commanded Danvers as he slipped out and closed Elizabeth's office door behind him. There had been a very uncharacteristic but very slightly Anderson-like harshness to his voice.

"What do you make of Diablerie's actions?" asked Elizabeth.

Alison looked at her. She had placed her hands behind her desk and was somehow displaying even less emotion than usual. Her eyes were fixed upon Alison in total scrutiny, like two searchlights mounted to the top of a sheer prison wall.

"Uh," began Alison, immediately looking to the floor. "I . . . I'm pretty sure he was lying about not knowing about the chapel. Or the body."

"Good," said Elizabeth charitably. "Disregarding everything he says is a good start. So what do his actions suggest?"

The thought that immediately amplified Alison's anxiety was that this was a test, one that she was losing points on for every moment her mouth hung open in silence. "Uh."

"Feel free to think aloud," prompted Elizabeth.

Finally, Alison found her voice. It helped to try to imagine the sort of thing Elizabeth would think. "There's something significant about Modern Miracle. Or he thinks there is. He thinks they're going to be in the middle of something important."

"Which they are now," pointed out Elizabeth. "But what makes you think this?"

"It was Rajesh Chahal who tipped us off about them. But from the way Diablerie has focused on it, it makes me think, maybe he already sort of knew about it? And . . . wanted to investigate? And . . . Chahal just . . . gave him the excuse?" She was scanning Elizabeth's face for the slightest sign of encouragement, drawing her words out longer and longer. At the moment the question mark dropped, she winced like a bomb-defusal expert snipping a wire.

"Good," said Elizabeth softly, putting her out of her misery. "But what was the point of that little piece of theater in which Chahal passed on the tip, if both of them already knew about it? Are you sure it was Diablerie being given the excuse?" Alison's face remained blank, so she helped her over the last hurdle. "You were there too, Alison."

Alison's brow furrowed. "Me? But . . ." Realization smoothed out her frown, then stretched it in the other direction. "He knows I talk to you."

"He wanted the Department to investigate officially," confirmed Elizabeth, with an almost imperceptible nod. "That was my conclusion. So."

"Why would Diablerie want that?" finished Alison, Elizabeth somehow effectively prompting her with nothing but a pause and a shift of glance. "Maybe he needs the Department's help?"

"Or there's a danger he's not willing to risk himself," said Elizabeth, looking off to the side with one finger to her chin. "Or he's trying to distract us from something else entirely. The only way to know for sure is to keep investigating."

"Right," said Alison, sitting back with relief. The exam was over, and it didn't seem like she was going to have to take summer school this year at least.

"Perhaps some more background would help," said Elizabeth, shifting back in her seat to take a storyteller's posture. "Where had we gotten up to?"

Alison sat up like a Labrador hearing the sound of kibble hitting the bottom of a metal dish, then almost as quickly dropped her gaze when she remembered the answer to Elizabeth's question. "Uh. The, er. The knee thing."

Elizabeth glanced down at her crippled leg as if it were that one remaining dinner party guest who just refuses to leave. "Ah yes," she said. "I insisted upon being rescued from the Ministry bunker, and in response, Nicholas Fisk shot me in the knee. Then he took my mentor, Mr. Teapot. I never saw him again. My last memory of him, he was being held face down on the back seat of the car, with a gun to his head, as it drove away."

She was recounting the memory the way a bored waiter would read aloud today's specials. Not a single shift of the eyes or twitch of the facial muscles indicated any emotion that she was harboring about these events. Then she stopped talking and didn't resume for several seconds of frozen silence. She stared straight into Alison's eyes throughout, but somehow wasn't looking at her.

"So what happened next?" prompted Alison.

"I remained where I was for some time," said Elizabeth, turning her eyes to the ceiling. "I had not been outside since the shadow had first appeared. The sky was black. Not with night. The air felt thick, as if I was breathing in dust. It was clear that any measure we had taken to prevent the shadow's influence from leaving the bunker had been futile.

"Somehow, I was brought to a hospital. Some kindly passing soul perhaps. It was in chaos. They couldn't handle the patient load. My knee was bandaged, and I was left on a stretcher in a corridor for two hours, nothing to do but listen to passing snatches of conversation. The shadow had brought hysteria and road accidents, as well as magical incidents that no one knew what to make of. Mass possessions, attacks from infused ferals, all over the country.

"I decided to leave. I couldn't be sure I wasn't spreading some terrible magical infection. And I was haunted by thoughts of the remaining survivors in the Ministry bunker, still quarantined without news or hope. I stole a crutch and some pain medication and made my way back to the Ministry.

"When I returned, the complex was silent. There were numerous bodies strewn about the connecting hallways. Some dead from Fisk's assault. Others from . . . other ways." By now, her voice was like the sound of a distant stream at the center of a rocky, impenetrable mountain range. "But it was finally peaceful at least. Everyone who was still alive was confining themselves to their offices in small groups. It seemed the major agitators had been shot, or had killed each other. The remainder were . . . waiting for someone to take charge. I could sense them watching me from cracks in their doors as I limped back to Mr. Teapot's office."

As she stared at the ceiling, lost in memory, Elizabeth's hands came up from under the desk and subconsciously gripped the armrests of her huge chair.

"I realized there that it was up to me to decide on a course of action," she continued. "Staying in the bunker no longer had a purpose. I planned to unite the survivors. Leave the city. Split into discrete units to minimize the damage that could be caused by possessed members. And do what we could to oppose the influence of the shadow.

"But as for that evening, I was exhausted. I needed a clearer head to make plans. I took enough pain medication to keep my mind off my ruined knee and fell asleep in Teapot's chair. I awoke to the sound of a looping radio broadcast, reporting that the volcanic ash cloud had moved on, and that everything was back to normal."

"I remember that," said Alison, somewhat redundantly. Her interjection finally stirred Elizabeth from her trance, and she met her gaze curiously. "Five days after the ash cloud came down, that broadcast was on every TV channel and radio station for, like, six hours. Mum complained because she'd wanted to watch the repeat of *Neighbours*."

"Yes," said Elizabeth, after a moment's awkward pause. "I went straight back up to the surface, as did most of the staff, and by then the skies were completely clear. The possessed ones that were too far gone had simply died where they stood. The rest returned to normal, with no memory of their time under the influence. The world moved on. The media and the public accepted our lame explanations for the carnage, and the Hand of Merlin returned for their regular meetings within a week." She caught Alison's look. "Yes, it felt just as much an anticlimax at the time."

"But why did the shadow go away?" asked Alison. "What defeated it?"

Elizabeth heaved a sigh. "Ten years and I still have no satisfactory answer. Taking over the administration of the Ministry was my main focus, but every effort I could spare went toward investigating that question. Nothing but dead ends."

"What do you think happened?" asked Alison. "I mean, what seems likeliest to you?"

Elizabeth met her gaze again, her eyebrow raising a fraction of a centimeter in pleasant surprise. "Good question. I want to believe that it was Mr. Teapot. Either by combining forces with Fisk or in spite of him, he found a way to defeat the Ancient. Of all the occult experts and operatives in the country, he had the best chance. He was the most knowledgeable, the most qualified, the most connected. But as I said, I never saw him again. And Fisk was no help, the next time I saw him."

Alison frowned. "You saw him again?"

"Oh yes. As I said, I was making every effort. I found him just a few weeks later."

"And what did he say?"

Elizabeth was still scrutinizing Alison. The merest hint of a smile stretched the corner of her mouth for a moment, like a glimpse of a drowning person's hand amid calm seas. "Alison, do you think you're improving as an investigator?"

Alison had been gradually leaning forward in rapt attention throughout the story, but Elizabeth's question sent her leaning all the way back as surely as if she'd been shoved in the chest. "Oh. Um. I don't know."

"You have made achievements," said Elizabeth, fighting a losing battle with the tiny smile her face was trying to make. "As I recall, it was you who first deduced the identity of the Fluidic Killer."

"Oh yeah, that," said Alison, flushing. "It was only because I had all the facts before everyone else. I think someone else could have put them together quicker."

"Why do you say that?"

"I just think . . . there are a lot of people who are . . ." Alison made a sweeping gesture that, half unconsciously, ended with her pointing at Elizabeth. "Naturally smarter than me."

Elizabeth gave a little wince of sympathy. "In my experience, Alison, ninety percent of what people call 'intelligence' is learned skill. It can be taught." She pinched her chin between thumb and forefinger. "Why don't we create a learning opportunity here."

Alison blinked several times. "Um?"

"Find out what happened to Nicholas Fisk," said Elizabeth, placing her hands on the desk. "If you can do that by yourself, with your own capacity for research and deduction, then I will fill in the remainder of the details."

"Okay," said Alison, thrown for a loop. "Is it . . . are there records? On the department server?"

"You'll have access to everything you need," said Elizabeth, suddenly cold and turning to her laptop. Alison must have burned through the small allotment of humanity Elizabeth had reserved for her that day. "Your standing orders remain the same. Assist Diablerie with whatever he asks. Report his actions directly to me. And if you have time, continue monitoring the Modern Miracle online community. Keep abreast of the wind direction."

"Right," said Alison uneasily. "What about the vampire? Or the conduit or whatever it is?"

"You ascertained that real healing magic was in use during your first encounter with Modern Miracle," summarized Elizabeth, with not even a hint of a question mark.

Alison remembered the sensation of her head wound being closed by magic, with the usual fondness that people have when they recall their impromptu surgical procedures. "Yes?"

"Then it's no longer a matter for the Office of Skepticism. Investigations can handle it from here. But you will have to write up a witness report for Mr. Hesketh."

The floor shook slightly at the sound of a door slamming, coming from somewhere around Richard Danvers's office.

"Or someone else," added Elizabeth.

36

The anger of Richard Danvers was more of a precision instrument than the anger of Sean Anderson, but no less to be feared. It was like the difference between a sledgehammer and a scalpel.

"Mr. Danvers, I was just about to report the new victim . . ." said Adam, the moment he sat down, as Danvers was stomping his way behind his desk.

"Really?" said Danvers sharply. "And why didn't you do so the moment they were found? Thought the evidence could stand to mature for a couple of nights first? Did it not occur to you that the family of the victim might be going insane wondering where they are?"

"We don't know who it was!" blurted Adam. "Actually, I'm—I'm not even completely certain there was another body," said Adam. "Alison's the only one who saw it. And then the whole crime scene got destroyed by pyrokinesis, and, and . . ."

Danvers didn't interrupt him. He simply stared, his eyes flashing from under his lowered brow like hidden spikes in a clenched fist, until Adam's voice faltered and died.

"Alison has perfect recall," said Danvers steadily. "She wouldn't make it up. She's got no imagination. She's never needed one. And besides, there's plenty an investigator can deduce, even from ash. Have you even mentioned anything to Sumner? This is his case!"

"I just . . . wanted to be sure," muttered Adam.

"No. You wanted to prove you could crack the case by yourself. That's not how it works, Adam. This is a team. If you can't work as part of the team . . ." He leaned heavily onto one of his armrests and pinched his eyes. "Maybe this is my fault. I thought you were ready to set out on your own."

"I am!" said Adam, half rising out of his chair. "Mr. Danvers, I'm so close to proving that girl's a conduit. The way they used pink lights . . ."

"This is exactly the problem, Adam!" barked Danvers, pushing him back into his seat with a sharp glance. "You aren't looking for the truth. You're trying to prove your theory. You're supposed to get all the facts in front of you and find the theory that fits them all, not latch on to the first idea that . . ." He suddenly stopped ranting and leaned back, releasing the rest of his breath in a sigh. "I shouldn't have to explain this to a professional investigator."

"I am sorry," said Adam, although his tone of voice implied to Danvers that he had been mentally preparing the word *but* and had lost his courage at the last moment.

Danvers felt himself soften as he watched Adam stare at the floor, his knees vibrating slightly as he fought the urge to draw them up to his chest. His anger had completed the necessary deconstruction; now it was time for the not-angry-just-disappointed voice and the partial reassembly of Adam's self-worth. "Look, I think I get what's going on here," he said tactfully. "I think you might have gotten too used to being part of the superstar team-up. It's hard to go from that to having to reinvent yourself at the ground level. Is that fair to say?"

Adam nodded, still staring at the floor.

"Perhaps I should pull Victor off Pacifications and partner the two of you together again as a distinct unit, and . . ." The sudden, alarming change in Adam's expression gave him pause. "What's the matter?"

"Victor . . . he quit," admitted Adam.

"What?!" Danvers's not-angry-just-disappointed voice was forced to rapidly return to the bench. "He quit? Since when?"

"The other night." Adam saw no point in lying anymore. Better a prolonged bollocking now than the prospect of an additional bollocking at an uncertain point in the future. "The . . . crime scene that got destroyed by pyrokinesis? There was a slight, slight possibility that it was Victor."

"How slight?" asked Danvers, aghast.

"Er, not sure. I didn't see them. Alison did."

"Alison again," Danvers leaned back in his chair like the arm of a medieval trebuchet winding up for another fling. "Maybe I should have a long talk with Alison. She might be interested in an upcoming vacancy in Investigations. So he quit because you confronted him on it, I take it?"

"Yeah," said Adam, barely audibly.

"And what made you think it was him? Because if we have to bring in the world's most powerful pyrokinetic, we're going to need a lot more than an arrest warrant."

"He's been . . . posting on the Modern Miracle forum."

Danvers blinked. "And what has he been posting?"

Adam sank in his chair even further. With his red hair in its usual ponytail, he now resembled a pile of crumpled black laundry with a squirrel sitting on top of it. "I don't know."

"You don't know," repeated Danvers slowly. "Well, thank goodness. There was me thinking you didn't have a good reason to alienate our most powerful asset."

"Mr. Danvers, I . . ."

Danvers was covering his eyes. "Adam, I can't deal with you right now. Get out. Clear whatever belongings you have out of the Investigations office. Go and sit in the cafeteria, and I'll figure out where to put you later."

Adam slowly stood on wobbling legs, turned to leave, then a strange surge of emotion caused him to turn back around, lean forward, and urgently slam his hands on Danvers's desk. "Mr. Danvers. I swear I can crack this case. Just give me twenty-four hours."

Danvers gazed back in astonishment. "I . . . cannot believe you actually said that."

The two men stared each other down in silence for an increasingly awkward few seconds, until the tension was finally broken by the ever-familiar sound of Anderson's heavy footfalls in the hallway. His bulky silhouette appeared behind the frosted glass that separated Danvers's office from the rest of the building.

Danvers and Adam both closed their eyes in anticipation and simultaneously relaxed when Anderson's footfalls continued straight past the door and moved on to harass some other civil servant.

"Sometimes I think we should build a railway crossing in the corridor for when he turns up," muttered Danvers.

37

None of the senior staff at the Department of Extradimensional Affairs could remember which cubicle had been officially assigned to Nita Pavani, nor indeed assigning her a cubicle at all, and yet, she had undeniably carved out a section of the work floor for herself. Her workspace was like a carefully curated shrine to decorative rain sticks and animal figurines, and the collection of inspirational printouts was seriously encroaching upon the workspaces of her assistants. Some of whom hadn't even realized they were her assistants until several months after she had started issuing orders.

Nita Pavani herself was sitting in the middle of the explosive display, typing away at her computer like a bored church organist. When she came into view, Anderson slowed his noisy freight train advance, clasped his hands behind his back, and continued approaching in what he thought was a casual saunter, kicking his legs up high with each step and sending a fresh wave of tremors through the floor every time his feet came down.

"Hello, Sean," sighed Nita, not looking around, already tired from the effort of pushing those two words through her glumly pouting lips.

"All right, Nita?" said Anderson chummily, standing behind her and rocking on his heels in a manner suggestive of an oil pump jack. "Still saving the world one tweet at a time?"

"I suppose," she muttered.

"Boy, that Miracle Dad friend of yours," continued Anderson, rearing back and folding his arms. "Really knows how to work a crowd, eh? Kicked up quite a stink with that last interview."

"So I hear."

Anderson was beaming happily at the ceiling, not even acknowledging her responses. "Pity he doesn't realize he's swimming with the barracudas now, eh. Oh, he did a lovely job dunking on that cardboard-cutout vicar you set up for him the other night, but oh bugger me, is he in for it when he comes on *Evening Issue* tomorrow. The bloke the church has got lined up . . . blimey. Miracle Dad'll be like a holiday camp entertainer warming up for Aerosmith."

Nita finally looked at him. "Why are you telling me this?"

Anderson grinned like a freshly polished cemetery. "Just hoping that Modern Miracle realize what they're getting themselves into," he said with relish.

Nita returned to her computer screen and gave the Enter key a vicious swat, as if trying to kill a fly. "And why do you assume I have any insight into what Modern Miracle do or do not realize?"

Anderson's smug pose and expression didn't change, but after a few seconds of frozen silence, an air of awkwardness began to creep in like the smell from a poorly covered septic tank. "I . . . thought you were doing their PR," he finally said.

"Well, I'm not," she said, spitting the words.

"Oh" was all Anderson could say.

"And for the record, it wasn't me who set up that last interview," said Nita, seemingly addressing her keyboard. "That was the idea their other PR person had. And now it seems Miracle Dad has decided he only needs one PR person." She smashed her Enter key again and sniffed deeply, hoisting her nose high. "Perhaps I had a few too many X chromosomes for his liking."

"Right. I get you." Anderson took a step closer. "So who is doing their PR?"

Nita rolled her eyes. "Nice try, Sean, but I'm not giving you any ammunition. Even if they do think showy media stunts are more important than real societal change."

Anderson realigned his posture and gave a little huff to get his energy back. "You know what? Great. Now I know you're not actively plotting against the state religion, maybe this government can go back to working together as professionals. Just as well, really; my budget for contract killers was running low." He rubbed his hands together theatrically, but deflated again when he saw Nita still refusing to pay him the slightest attention. "Oh, bollocks to you people. I'm gonna go yell at Education. They're good for a decent punch-up."

THE NEXT EVENING

38

In contrast to *Shgshthx Tonight*, *Evening Issue* was a serious political debate program scheduled to air just after dinner, right when the audience was fully energized and about to start drinking.

As the severe drumbeats of the opening theme faded, the spotlight came up on one of four leather swivel chairs arranged in a semicircle against pitch blackness. The presenter, Pippa Mormont, dressed in a dark gray pantsuit with lapels sharp enough to pierce an apple, looked to camera with a severe but curious look. "Good evening," she said. "On *Evening Issue* tonight, the ongoing question of magic and religion. With new protections for extradimensional citizens made law, should the Christian Church be held accountable for magical appropriation?" She spun with dazzling grace in her chair to face a different camera, one that was framing her with the two chairs on her right. "Arguing that it should, we have Miracle Dad, the high priest and chief spokesman of the online extradimensional community Modern Miracle."

A light came up on the nearer chair to reveal Miracle Dad, who had been forced to exchange his usual T-shirt for a featureless button-down dress shirt by the wardrobe department. He was sweating uncomfortably in this more formal setting and was clutching his legs hard enough to leave dents in his kneecaps. "Hello."

"As well as Modern Miracle's chief public relations adviser, Mr. Rajesh Chahal."

"Good evening, Pippa," said Chahal as his spotlight came on. He was dressed in a suit jacket and tie and was sitting comfortably with his legs loosely crossed. He offered the camera a confident smile, briefly flashing his teeth like a glimpse of a concealed dagger in a sleeve.

"And arguing that it should not, we have Pastor Thaddeus Barkler, chairman of the North American Evangelical Fellowship for Christ," said Pippa, turning the other way.

The man sitting to her left looked into camera as if it had just been introduced to him as his daughter's new girlfriend. He was tall and slightly overweight with no discernible chin and an angular mass of gray hair sculpted harshly around his ears to frame his features. His lips were tight, puckered, and constantly twitching, as if he was extremely unaccustomed to keeping his mouth closed. "God bless you," he said, the sentiment of his words at extreme odds with the naked fury blazing in his eyes.

"If I might start with our guests from Modern Miracle," said Pippa, turning away from the American pastor with undisguised relief. "Your organization has been the source of this debate since it began. What exactly is it that you want the church—or indeed, any of the world's leading religions—to do?"

Chahal smoothly took the lead, anticipating the plaintive look Miracle Dad was about to give him. Miracle Dad was clearly out of his element without an admiring audience to work off. "Pippa, I would argue that this debate began with the X-Appropriation Act, or at least should have done," he said in a calm and measured voice. "What we want hasn't changed. We want organized religion to be held to the same standard to which the law holds everyone else. To either prove that their figures of worship do exist and exert extradimensional influence upon the world or stop claiming that they do."

"Pastor Barkler," said Pippa, with an enormous inward sigh of depressed anticipation. "Do the beliefs of the Christian Church violate the X-Appropriation Act?"

Barkler's lips were already quivering with rage so hard that it took him quite a lot of effort to sneak a few words past them. "This television show is an affront to the LORD," he seethed, with eyes like peeled grapes rising to the top of a pot of boiling water.

"Hm," said Pippa, nodding interestedly with one hand supporting her chin. "But if I could press you to address the specifics of the question . . ."

"The LORD is all things, and all things are the LORD," clarified Barkler. "The LORD cannot violate the law of MAN. It is only the law of MAN that violates the LORD. You are all GUILTY of crimes against the unassailable WORD of GOD." It was clear what his favorite words were from the way he heaved them from his mouth like corpses being dumped over the side of an overloaded boat.

"What do you say to that, gentlemen?" asked Pippa, to break the suddenly frozen atmosphere.

"Er," began Chahal, before getting back on track and opting to direct his words at Pippa. "We at Modern Miracle certainly aren't trying to antagonize religion, or any religious person. We want the law enforced in its original spirit. To protect extradimensionally infused people, and to ensure that people seeking extradimensional services, such as Modern Miracle's healing practice, know that they're getting the real deal."

"The LORD is the real deal," countered Barkler, jerking forward as if he'd just sat on a hedgehog. "There is no power but the LORD's power!"

"Oh, is that right?" said Miracle Dad, perking up now the discussion was turning combative. "I think El-Yetch might have a couple of things to say about that. There's a little boy who was gonna die inside a year who the LORD didn't seem to be coming through for. He came to us, and he was doing cartwheels in the garden after ten minutes."

"Pastor Barkler, I understand that you conduct faith healing sermons at your own church in Missouri," said Pippa, feeling the need to stir the pot.

"The LORD rewards those of us who have FAITH," said Barkler, raising a pointed finger as if erecting a cross. "You peddle in the droppings of SATAN. All those you taint are DAMNED to BURN in HELL. Suffer not a WITCH to LIVE!"

Chahal blinked. "I'm sorry, did you just say that extradimensionally infused people deserve to be killed?"

The tactic of appealing to Barkler's sense of shame immediately proved ineffective. "I am just a deliverer of the LORD's message," he declared, folding his arms. "It is not our place to question the WORD."

"Is this a joke?" asked Miracle Dad, addressing Pippa. "How are we supposed to debate this nutcase? He's off his trolley." He looked Barkler up and down. "Probably thinks trolleys are the work of Satan."

"Do not mock the LORD," countered Barkler. "The power of the LORD is greater than you can possibly imagine. You must end your rituals of SATAN and BEG the LORD for forgiveness or be DAMMMMMMNED." He kept the *m* in *damned* going for a full three seconds.

"All right!" said Miracle Dad, sitting forward. "Since it sounds like the LORD's up for a proper fight, why don't we cut to the chase? Let's have a contest. The LORD versus El-Yetch. Whenever you like."

"Er . . ." said Chahal, staring at him.

"What are you proposing, Miracle Dad?" asked Pippa, recrossing her legs. "A contest of what exactly? Faith healing?"

"Yeah!" said Miracle Dad, his energy fully restored. "We'll line up two sick kiddies, put them in the same room—he can have one, and my Miracle Meg can have the other. We'll see who gets healed first. Do it all scientifically and the like. Sound good?"

"Do not test the LORD," warned Barkler, shifting uncomfortably. "The miracles of the LORD will not appear for the unfaithful."

"El-Yetch's do," pressed Miracle Dad. "We've got them on video. Livestreamed and everything. And they work on pretty much anyone. Turns out it's, like, pretty useful for miracles to work on the unfaithful as well, because they tend to become faithful really bloody quick. Come on, don't you want to show the world how powerful the LORD is?"

"I won't let you drag the LORD down to your level," said Barkler, determinedly refusing to make eye contact.

Miracle Dad was leaning forward and pointing at Barkler provocatively. Chahal leant in and nervously plucked at Miracle Dad's outstretched sleeve. "Perhaps we should get back on topic . . ."

"Oh sure," said Miracle Dad, sitting back and folding his arms smugly. "If he's not up for it, he's not up for it. Guess he doesn't have as much faith in his LORD as we thought."

Barkler had been starting to slouch in his seat and cringe a little bit, but he instantly sat fully upright again with an audible pop of bones. "How DARE you?! My faith in the LORD is unshakable!" The pointing finger came out again. "The LORD will meet your challenge. And He shall strike you all dumb with the power of FAITH."

"W-well, it seems both sides are amenable to a . . . contest," said Pippa, adjusting quickly.

"Yes, but realistically," interjected Chahal, trying to lean back into the center of the shot, "something like that would require some kind of unbiased judge, and I don't think you're going to find—"

"Ooh! What about DEDA?" said Miracle Dad, pushing him back. "They declared neutrality when this all started. We'll get someone from there to organize it. Sort out a venue. And we'll broadcast it around the world. And whoever loses has to stop pretending they're really doing magic."

"I welcome it, for the LORD will come through," countered Barkler, with a little burst of spittle.

"It seems this debate will be continuing," said Pippa, turning to camera with the kind of confidence one can only have from knowing that everyone else's mike has been cut. "Will the Department of Extradimensional Affairs agree to arrange a televised contest of magical healing? Will El-Yetch or the LORD emerge victorious? Could this really be the only way to settle the differences between magic and religion? I'm Pippa Mormont, and this was *Evening Issue.*"

The moment the cameras cut, Rajesh Chahal left Miracle Dad and Barkler to exchange contact details at maximum volume, nimbly dodged between a couple of technicians, and exited the studio. He hurried straight down a hall and out into the garage, where he clutched his head and screwed up his eyes in frustration.

The moment the door behind him fell closed, all the stress disappeared from his face and posture. He glanced around to assure himself he was alone, then ducked behind a convenient shelving unit against the nearest wall and dug out his phone.

His call wasn't picked up, but he wasn't expecting it to be. He tapped his foot with increasing excitement as he waited for the automated voice to finish inviting him to record a voicemail.

"Hey, it's me," he whispered, powerless to stop a smile spreading across his face. "You will not believe how well this is going."

THE FOLLOWING MORNING

39

Elizabeth Lawrence was making her way into the DEDA building to begin the day's work. She dodged the now-inevitable protest outside the front entrance—this time it was the turn of the pro-religion side, waving banners depicting cartoon-bearded wizards with crosses through them—and paused with her hand on the door when she spotted Anderson. The orange bristles of his hair were drifting through the crowd toward the building like a shark's fin at a crowded beach.

Elizabeth paused for less than a second to emit a microscopic sigh, then pretended she had seen nothing and proceeded into the building. She was showing her ID to the guard at the front desk when the doors flew open and she heard Anderson stomp his way up to her like the unfeeling inevitability of death.

Without turning around, she threw up a finger. "Anderson, before you say anything, we are obviously not going to organize or encourage a televised faith healing contest between two cults. You can calm down."

"Yes you bloody are," said Anderson calmly.

Elizabeth finally looked at him. His eyes bore the usual degree of balled-up tension and fury, but his mouth was pulled into a mischievous smile.

"You're not seriously saying . . . that you want this to happen?" asked Elizabeth, scrutinizing every inch of his face.

"O' course," he said.

Elizabeth waited patiently for the gotcha, probably in the form of a clarification like "as soon as hell freezes over" or "as much as I want to shove my face into a bucket of used hypodermics," but he silently returned her gaze. Anderson took the opposite approach to Elizabeth when it came to concealing his true feelings: he usually expressed himself as loudly and aggressively as possible so that the truth became lost in the noise. As such, his calm demeanor came across as total sincerity.

"You left me four voicemails last night," said Elizabeth levelly. "I only understood about half the words, and most of those were obscene."

"Yeah, well, I've had a bit of time to think since then," he said, embarrassed. "And now I think it's worth doing. You see that?" He cocked a head toward the entrance, outside of which several protesters were now performatively praying in front of an inflatable Jesus. "The gridlock from that shit is sending the city down the economical poo pipe, and it isn't going to stop until they get closure. Preferably sooner rather than later. And this would be sooner."

"I thought you were on the side of the church," said Elizabeth.

"I am!" His smile twitched. "I mean, obviously I and this government are unbiased and only want security and happiness for all the people of this nation." He glanced behind him and lowered the tone of his voice. "But off the record, yes, I am. So what?"

"Anderson, you know what will happen," said Elizabeth, in the concerned tones of someone chairing an intervention. "Modern Miracle uses actual healing magic. My agents have confirmed that to our full satisfaction. The church is going to be totally humiliated."

"*A* church," corrected Anderson, grinning wider and waggling a pointing finger. "That sect of snake-handling weirdos Barkler runs across the pond. No one in the Church of England thinks he represents them. Hell, most of the nutters in America don't either. Bloody country's got more denominations than people with basic health care."

Elizabeth looked away, attempting to hop onto his train of logic as it steamed through her station. "Even so . . ."

"But it's all the same to the magic weirdos, isn't it?" He tapped the side of his head meaningfully. "They'll chalk it up as a win for their side, calm down, and forget about this stupid suing-the-church idea. And then the whole country can come back together in solidarity over a bunch of mouthy nutjob Yanks getting taught a lesson."

"And you're certain of this?" asked Elizabeth skeptically. "You're certain the church will be happy about the existence of God being disproved on live television?"

"Lizzie, they won't be disproving shit," said Anderson, with a flash of anger. "Like I said. No one seriously expects God to come down and work miracles in person. He'd lose all his mystique. All his plausible deniability. No one is gonna stop believing because of something like this. They'll say God wouldn't lower himself to our level. Or Barkler didn't ask nicely enough. Or whatever else they need to get it to make sense in their own heads. Because it's never been about proof, has it?"

Elizabeth nodded slowly. "And what about maintaining the dignity of government?"

Anderson scoffed on reflex. "You don't spend a lot of time on social media, do you, Liz? Guess you haven't noticed that dignity's kinda out of fashion in politics these days."

Elizabeth checked the time by the clock on the wall. She was late for the morning briefing, which was now going to go quite differently to how she had planned. She opted to start walking, and to her complete lack of surprise, Anderson kept pace right by her side.

"You are doing this," he affirmed. "Figure out the details today. Date. Venue. Invitations. As much media as possible, yeah? And keep me informed. I'll get the treasury to spare you whatever budget you need. They're a stubborn lot, but they usually give up if I stamp on their fingers enough times."

"Such generosity," said Elizabeth dryly, nearing the lift.

"Yeah, well, believe it or not, DEDA's a few points up in the polls over all this, and we're gonna wring out as much goodwill as we can. Your boy Danvers did good, declaring neutrality. People respect the principled stance, yeah? He comes off well. Real leader-y vibes. In fact, why don't we get him to referee?"

"And there it is," muttered Elizabeth, stepping into the lift and pressing the button for DEDA's main floor. "It was a brief dalliance with the concept of dignity, but I suppose you mustn't exhaust yourself."

Anderson smartly held out a flattened hand as the lift doors made to close, and they grumblingly returned to the open position. "I'm serious. Loop him in."

Elizabeth unsubtly pressed the Close Door button. "Mr. Danvers is a respected asset of this department, not a celebrity judge for reality television."

Anderson thrust his hand out again to block the doors. "So let him wear a tie! You're behind the times, Liz. It's not reality television anymore. It's television reality."

Elizabeth opened her mouth to make one last attempt at getting the final word, but at that point the lift door alarm went off, and both she and Anderson jumped back like two competing bulls discovering an electric fence between them.

A FEW DAYS LATER

40

Yet another protest was rolling along the streets of London like a mass of prickly caterpillars. The early protests had had some organization: someone had been leading them, they had a specific destination in mind to march upon, and someone had taken the time to draw up a logo for the social media event page, but by this point the city was riddled with a network of small directionless protests that had all formed from the breakup of larger ones.

The protests in the city were now akin to a weather system, little scraps of cloud breaking off and swirling around the main roads, joining into clumps until they became large enough for roving squads of police riot control officers to notice. It didn't seem to matter which protest a protester joined; there was a lot of mileage in joining an enemy protest ironically and taking pictures of the really crazy members, a significant percentage of whom were also protesting ironically.

Victor had been trying to get to a specific car park near Tottenham Court Road for close to two hours. Moving against the protesting mass was like trying to get three supermarket trolleys up a gentle slope. In the end, he had had to randomly join protests that seemed to be moving in roughly the right direction and pick his moment to tear away, like a lone kayaker in swirling rapids.

Finally, he made it to the car park. It was at full capacity. A lot of out-of-towners had come to the city center to participate in some protest tourism as a wholesome day out for the kids, and each level of the car park was a labyrinth of Range Rovers and sedans. None of which mattered to Victor; he had never learned to drive and was legally prevented from doing so. There had been an incident with a sarcastic instructor who seemed to have great difficulty grasping the idea that a perfectly competent and intelligent person might fail to notice a stop sign or two.

He took the lift to the top level, which was the roof, the last resort for late-coming vehicles parked by people who had had to adopt a philosophical attitude toward bird excrement. He took a few faltering steps into the forest of towering sports utility vehicles, as "roof of the car park" was all the direction Leslie-Ifrig had given him.

"Show yourself," he commanded, clenching his fists.

"Hiya!" said a cheerful voice from nearby. "Victor! Over here!"

He turned a corner and saw Leslie-Ifrig at the far end of a corridor of oversized family cars, which wasn't the most epic backdrop for a final duel to the death, but probably the best they could hope for. They were leaning on the parapet at the edge of the roof, admiring the crowds below.

"Hey, you kept me waiting," they said, without malice. "I got to watch the protest get counterprotested, like, five times. It's like a wave pool."

"Shut up," said Victor, planting his feet and letting his power glow at his fists. "This is our final battle."

"You always say that," complained Leslie-Ifrig, turning and leaning their elbows on the barrier. "Not every date has to be an archnemesis battle. It's okay to just hang out."

"Did you attack my friends?" Victor advanced slowly, glowing hands splayed out by his sides like a gunslinger ready to draw. "A pyrokinetic was hanging around the Modern Miracle sermon the other night. Was it you?"

"I only go sometimes," said Leslie-Ifrig, emphasizing the last word playfully. They turned to watch the crowds again.

"Adam said they attacked," said Victor, still advancing. "He said they were guarding something. What was it?"

Leslie-Ifrig clicked their tongue. The mutated half of it emitted sparks like a flint being bashed against metal. "How should I know? When there's a service they ask on the forum for volunteers to guard behind the house. It's sensible. People get weird. Someone threw a Bible once."

"So you expect me to believe you were guarding their house, from the woods," growled Victor.

"Yeah," said Leslie-Ifrig, kicking the parapet with the back of one foot. "They don't want people coming into their house. All their stuff is in it. Underpants and . . . stuff."

"I'm done playing nice with you." Victor took a particularly ominous step forward. "You took everything from me. It's time to end this."

Leslie-Ifrig sighed with boredom, propping up their chin on one fist. "I don't remember taking anything from you. I remember giving you stuff. I gave you fire powers."

"How about my job?!" snapped Victor, sparks forming in the air in front of his face. "I don't have that anymore! They kicked me out because of this!"

Leslie-Ifrig finally turned around again, intrigue flashing in their good eye. "They kicked you out?"

Victor hesitated. "I kicked myself out. They were just about to."

"I can't believe they kicked you out. Haven't you worked there for, like, ever?"

"Yes! So let's add it to the list!" He counted off his fingers, sending a fresh burst of sparks each time one of his fingers touched another. "School. Family. Every aspect of normal life. And now my job, the only thing having fire powers actually made me better at. You've taken everything. I've got nothing left."

Leslie-Ifrig had turned to watch the crowd again halfway through Victor's speech. When he was finished, they suddenly straightened up and pointed across the street. "I think I'm going to see how this looks from that roof over there."

"What?" asked Victor, hands poised to begin dueling.

With a single effortless hop, Leslie-Ifrig was standing on the parapet, one foot still in the air, arms out to maintain balance. Then, still staring at the opposite building, they hopped again, into thin air.

Victor ran to the spot where Leslie-Ifrig had been standing just in time to see them arrest their fall with a blast of fiery energy directly below them. They splayed out their skinny arms and legs like a flying squirrel and bounced prettily off a spreading translucent mushroom cloud.

They made their way across the expanse of the street that way, by throwing out their arms and generating another puff of fiery air to fling them skywards every time gravity appeared to be taking hold. A portion of the crowd below stopped midchant and glanced up to watch the unfolding fireworks.

Leslie-Ifrig made one last extra-large fireball and cleared the department store opposite by a good six feet before landing face first on the roof with eye-watering force. Victor watched, baffled, as they shakily rose back into view and waved their arms happily.

". . ." called Leslie-Ifrig.

"WHAT?!" replied Victor. Some of the gawkers below turned to look at him, and he instinctively backed away from the roof's edge, out of view. "I CAN'T HEAR YOU! OBVIOUSLY!"

Leslie-Ifrig pouted. The demonic half of their face looked for a moment as if it was trying to eat its own nose. Then they dived off their new roof without a moment's hesitation and boost jumped back across the street, tucking their knees up to their chin at the apex of each bounce like a platforming video game character. On the last jump, they pulled off a little somersault at the top of the bounce before, again, crashing face first down onto the tarmac next to Victor.

"What did you say?" asked Leslie-Ifrig, after they had peeled their face off the ground.

"I said, I couldn't hear you," said Victor, feeling stupid.

Leslie-Ifrig stood up and dusted themselves off. "Why didn't you come closer then?"

"Because . . ." Victor rubbed his forehead in frustration, sending little sparks running along each of his hairs like the wires coming out of cartoon dynamite. "I can see what you're trying to do."

"What am I trying to do?" asked Leslie-Ifrig, smiling innocently through the several pieces of grit now embedded in the cracks of their face.

"I've tried to do the hover thing, but it takes loads of power to keep going. And if I . . ." Victor stopped himself.

"If you use too much power at once, what happens?" prompted Leslie-Ifrig.

"You know what happens!" Victor scowled. "It makes me open to being possessed again."

"The only one who can possess you is me. Is Ifrig," pointed out Leslie-Ifrig. "What if I told you I have absolutely no interest in possessing you?"

"I'd . . . completely not believe you," said Victor, folding his arms obstinately. "Because Ifrig trying to possess me was, like, the background noise of my entire teens."

"That was before I'd gotten to know you," said Leslie-Ifrig, leaning forward, clasping their hands behind their back and batting one set of eyelashes at Victor, like an affectionate cat trying to solicit pets from a marble statue. "Maybe I prefer you from the outside. Come on. Don't you want to fly?"

"I *want* to start this fight to the death," said Victor, returning his hands to the gunslinger pose and conjuring two palm-sized fireballs.

Leslie-Ifrig stared at them sadly, then promptly hopped back onto the parapet with a single twitch of one leg. As always, they moved as if they weighed less than a birthday card. "Then it sounds like you're going to have to chase me!"

Without another word, they fell backwards into the street, catching themselves with a daringly low blast of firepower that made an entire regiment of protesters instinctively duck and shield themselves with their placards. It looked as if everyone down below had given up on the idea of protesting and had paused to watch the impromptu magic display, although a couple of minor arguments were breaking out over which side of the debate must have organized it.

Leslie-Ifrig performed a spectacular backflip and swan dive with each bounce, each time delaying the boost as long as possible to make the crowd gasp, which juxtaposed nicely against their usual extremely clumsy landing on the opposite roof. This time they landed on their back and ended up lying there twitching with all four limbs in the air like a dead cockroach.

Victor leaned forward slowly to peer down into the street again, just to make sure it hadn't lost a story or two since he'd last checked. Some people in the crowd were applauding Leslie-Ifrig's performance, but a few had noticed Victor and were now watching in open-mouthed excitement to see what this next performer was going to do.

Victor retreated from the edge and began to walk away. He was either making enough distance for a decent run-up or making his way back to the lift in order to go home. Victor himself didn't know; he hadn't decided. The time to decide would be the point when he had reached the maximum necessary run-up distance.

He reached it. He stopped.

Well, said a little voice in the back of Victor's mind, which Victor couldn't help notice sounded a lot like the voice of his dad. *This will probably shoot right to the top of your list of terrible decisions in life. It might even eclipse that moment when you were twelve and wanted to see if it was possible to boil an egg without using water.*

Victor slowly turned around and planted his feet. He stared up into the cloudy sky with half-closed eyes and let the little voice make its point and fade away.

Of course he knew how to use his powers to project himself, bodily, with blasts of hot air. He'd done it before, back when he was experimenting, right after his powers had first manifested. That was probably the last time he'd been truly happy, spending his summer holiday playfully flying off the cheap swings in the back garden of his family home.

But that was before he'd started hearing the voice of Ifrig, and before the men from the Ministry had come to tell him exactly what would happen if he listened to that voice and didn't exercise his power with the proper restraint. How he would end up . . .

. . . well, like Leslie-Ifrig. Being erased as a person and replaced with some monstrous clash between humanity and Ancient. Victor had never been entirely sold on the inherent worth of humanity, not since his teens, so he could only imagine what kind of monster Victor-Ifrig would be. Human Leslie must have had the disposition of a cartoon teddy bear to keep Ifrig's impulses in check.

The point was, he already knew how to use his powers to fly. He'd been a lot lighter back then, of course, and had mostly only been exploding monsters in the intervening time, so he was out of practice with the more delicate stuff.

Experimentally, he jumped straight upwards and summoned a blast directly beneath his feet, boosting his jump by a good eight or nine feet. As he rose, he felt a sensation like his head was bursting through a pink layer of bliss, but the feeling disappeared when he glanced down and saw the tarmac of the car park roof rushing up to reacquaint itself with him.

He fired off a gentler blast to slow his descent but stumbled awkwardly on landing. When he had regained his balance, his heart was pounding in his ears.

He took another look at the abyss that was the street. Leslie-Ifrig was visible in the distance, watching him with head cocked. Could this really be some sinister plan on Ifrig's part to get Victor to use too much power and open up his mind to possession? It seemed as if Leslie-Ifrig would have had plenty of opportunity to do that during the fiery magical duels that had taken up most of their previous "dates."

Victor winced, kicking the tarmac like a bull contemplating a charge. Could an Ancient possess more than one person at a time? It felt likely that they could. There were only a certain number of Ancients, and in Victor's professional experience, there was never any shortage of possessed buggers to deal with.

So I get possessed, said another little voice in Victor's head. *So what? What else was I going to do, now I'm unemployed? Sit around in the apartment and wait for my savings to run out? It'd at least be funny to see the landlord's face if he showed up and it was Victor-Ifrig to meet him.*

And besides, imagine how much it would tick Adam off.

Victor judged that he had sufficiently distracted himself. He broke into a sprint and leapt off the roof before his mind could register a misgiving.

He outdid himself with the first launch. An almost perfectly spherical blossom of magical heat sent him flying forward and upward, one leg back and one knee thrust forward, like a gothic Peter Pan. The wind rushing through his hair was as cold and refreshing as water.

He launched himself again when he reached the apex of the first jump, having no intention of dropping as low as Leslie-Ifrig had. He climbed higher and higher, alternately kicking his legs forward as if leaping up a giant, invisible staircase. Before long, he had ascended to double the car park's height.

He was already feeling the hot sensation in his head that told him he was using too much magic in too short a time, but he didn't care. Against the cold rush of air against his face, it was like the spark of a lighter with no gas. Dreamily he allowed himself to spin around, to see how far he had come, and he heard the crowd "ooh" in appreciation of his pirouette. His coat spread out around him like the petals of a flower.

He was past the halfway point. The roof of the opposite building, and Leslie-Ifrig, were practically below him. It was time to come down. He held his legs together and dropped his arms by his sides, and let himself drop like a melting icicle from the edge of a roof. His coat flew up around his ears and pulled on his armpits.

Leslie-Ifrig was gazing up at him, head still cocked and with a faint smile of admiration. Then they held out an arm as if inviting a high-five, and the air directly beneath Victor exploded into flame.

Victor saw it coming at the last moment and set off a blast of his own just above it, but he was panicked and his aim was off, so it pushed him to the side, sending him into a tailspin. He felt the heat from Leslie-Ifrig's flame as he passed it, already dissipating into the air but still hot enough to leave a burn on his face and hands.

He concentrated on burning energy in the opposite direction to his spin until the world stopped tumbling madly around him like a kaleidoscope falling down a spiral staircase and he was able to reorient himself. There was the building in front of him, there was the sky in its appropriate place above him, and there was the police car he was about to slam into at terminal velocity.

With a yelp, he pointed all four of his limbs downwards and channeled all his power along them until his vision was entirely flooded with churning yellow-orange light. His fall was arrested, and he changed vertical direction so rapidly that every joint in his body audibly clicked. By now, the magic was screaming inside his mind. He could only just differentiate it from the screaming of frightened onlookers and nearby car alarms.

The next thing Victor knew, he was clinging to the edge of Leslie-Ifrig's roof by his hands. Some instinct, apparently one that was generally a lot more on top of things than his conscious mind, had caused him to scrabble for it as it had come into reach. He dug his boots into whatever paltry toeholds they could find.

His mind was in a magically induced haze. The ringing in his ears was blocking out all other sound. The edges of his vision swam with orange fog. But Leslie-Ifrig was clear enough, in the very center of his vision, smiling down at him and extending their hand again.

All of Victor's clarity of sense returned in an instant, just in time to report that he was completely helpless. Spitefully, his senses were going to make sure to soak in every agonizing moment of his death.

Leslie-Ifrig paused when they saw the change in Victor's look, then cocked their head the other way, grabbed him by the wrists, and hauled him up and into safety with a completely illogical degree of strength.

The moment he was on relatively safe ground, Victor snatched his hands away as if, appropriately enough, from a fire and put a suitable distance between himself and Leslie-Ifrig, stopping with his feet apart and his hands primed for battle. "Come on then," he said, bouncing on his toes.

Leslie-Ifrig still hadn't put their hands down from when Victor had snatched his away. "What are you doing?"

"We're fighting to the death," said Victor.

Leslie-Ifrig glanced down at their hands, hanging limply from their wrists, and took a moment to try to gauge the manner in which they were fighting Victor to the death. "Since when?"

"Since you just tried to kill me!"

"I didn't. Sorry. I just thought you could use a little boostie." They held out their hands in a gesture of placation, but under the circumstances, it didn't convey the intended meaning.

Victor spat, "You expect me to—"

An explosion rang out. Victor ducked behind the parapet. Something made of red-and-blue plastic that looked like it belonged on the top of a police car briefly rose into view, then fell back down.

Victor hooked his nose over the edge of the roof to see. The police car that had very nearly broken his fall (and no doubt various bones) was now a mangled pile of blackened metal. One of the tires was still rolling away, apparently pursuing a fleeing crowd of mixed protesters, whose individual allegiances or levels of irony were now entirely secondary to the matter of getting the hell away from the place where cars explode.

Cars were honking in the distance, as several motorists, already angry about being held up by protests, became doubly angry at the fleeing protesters climbing over their cars to escape. But from scanning the area, it didn't seem as if anybody had been hurt. That was a relief. Although Victor doubted the owners of the police car would see it his way.

"Oh good, god damn," he said, breathing heavily. "We have got to get out of here."

"Why?" asked Leslie-Ifrig, appearing beside him and leaning their elbows on the parapet interestedly.

"Because that was a police car!" said Victor, already backing off and looking for the most survivable route to ground level. He gestured frustratedly at Leslie-Ifrig's uncomprehending expression before continuing. "And that means more police cars are going to come along to find out what happened to the first one!"

Leslie-Ifrig frowned at the smoking debris in the street below. "And . . . those ones will be explosion proof?"

MEANWHILE

41

"All right," said Richard Danvers, standing at the head of the Operations briefing room with a clicker in one hand and a pointer in the other. "After a great deal of exhaustive negotiation between Modern Miracle and the North American Evangelical, et cetera, a venue has been agreed upon for the upcoming televised faith healing contest, and yes, apparently, this is a thing that we do now."

He pressed the clicker, and an image was projected onto the screen by his side. It was a photograph of a cluster of modern buildings that had been constructed around an old theater like an arm around the shoulder of an uncomfortable first date.

"The Flash Microsystems Hotel and Convention Centre," he revealed, sweeping his pointer across the image grandly. "Incorporating the Pelican Theatre. We needed a lot of space for visiting media, and Modern Miracle insisted upon a proper stage. This was the most suitable facility that wasn't booked at any point in the near future." He pressed the clicker again, and the image changed to a floor plan of the theater, around which he drew an invisible circle with his pointer. "This is the main stage and auditorium where the contest will take place. We will need all our people on the ground ensuring the facility is secure."

"How much trouble are we expecting?" asked one of the agents in the front row.

Richard paused for a moment to allow the faint sound of protesters outside to drift in through the windows. "Hear that? That, but concentrated into an indoor space with all the people they hate. There will be police on hand to deal with the usual sort of trouble. Our responsibility is to handle the extradimensional kind of trouble."

"And how much of *that* are we expecting?" asked someone else.

"Modern Miracle attracts a radical extradimensional element," said Danvers smoothly. "Hopefully the sheer obviousness of the fact that Modern Miracle is going to win this contest will keep the magically infused attendees from lashing out, but we can't count on that. Mr. Hesketh will be on the ground to direct agents to any flare-ups that arise. And do nothing else." He glared directly at the table at the very back of the room, where Adam was doing everything he could to avoid making eye contact with anything even vaguely eye-like. "Mr. Sumner?"

"Thank you, Mr. Danvers," said Sumner, rising from his seat and smiling in a manner Adam considered very oily. "The main concern is obviously the as-yet-unidentified vampire who has been hanging around Modern Miracle's sermons lately. They've claimed either two or three victims so far. Still a bit of a question mark over the third. There was a suspicion that Modern Miracle itself was directly involved, but no conclusive evidence has been turned up by, ah, independent inquiry."

He directed a little smile toward Adam's spot at the back of the room, where the ambient humidity was increasing to an alarming degree.

"My own investigation indicates we may not have anything to worry about." Sumner had a tendency to imitate Danvers's accent in briefings, but with a hefty dollop of smugness layered on. "The MO so far has been to go after isolated individuals away from the view of witnesses, and there won't be much opportunity for that with the crowds we expect. Still, be aware this person may be present. Try not to get distracted."

He looked directly at Adam again for his last sentence, then nodded confidently to Danvers, who responded with a distinctly unimpressed raised eyebrow. "All right," he said as Sumner sat down again. "Regarding the contest itself. Rawlins has been in touch with a local retirement home willing to provide some volunteers for magical healing. Rawlins?"

After the agents had collectively decided which of the chronic patients on offer seemed the most sufficiently detached from reality to have no possible bias against either side of the debate, the briefing rolled along, covering a few more specific items of logistics, and then tailed off with some small assignments unrelated to the contest. These didn't take long. As far as the world of Extradimensional Affairs was concerned, everything was on hold until the weekend's outcome.

The meeting broke up, and the agents returned to their individual concerns. Most left the Operations room, but a few hung back to discuss lesser matters in small groups, or to catch up with some research or paperwork of one kind or another.

That appeared to be Adam's intention. He had his laptop open and a few scattered file folders in front of him, and was staring forward with a disturbing focus that made Alison unable to concentrate on her own work. She had to attend these briefings too, partly to pass on anything relevant to Doctor Diablerie, partly because it saved money on hiring someone to take the minutes.

After ten minutes, almost all the other agents had drifted away. She came to a decision, stood up, and carried her laptop over to Adam's table. "Hi, Adam," she said, with forced brightness. "You doing all right?"

"Alison," said Adam, looking at her with slight bafflement. "Yes. Fine. Does it seem like I'm not?"

"Well, it's just . . . I thought you've been getting a hard time from everyone today."

"Do you think so? I didn't really notice," said Adam, returning his gaze to his laptop screen. Alison noticed a slight quaver of emotion in his voice that he attempted to disguise with a bored sigh.

Alison hefted the laptop she was still holding open with both hands. "Can I sit? Study buddies?"

Adam didn't reply with words, but he inelegantly scooted his chair a few inches to the right with a thrust of the hips.

As she moved behind him to take the spot he had cleared, Alison couldn't help noticing Adam's laptop screen. He had at least ten windows open, each displaying a different piece of information relevant to the vampire case. There were witness reports, photos of the shriveled bodies of David Callum and William Shaw, and two windows were simultaneously playing Miracle Dad's two most recent televised interviews.

"The . . . vampire case?" asked Alison.

"Just putting all the facts in front of me," said Adam, interlacing his hands just beneath his nose. "There's a way all of this fits together that makes sense. If I keep looking, it'll jump out at me."

Alison leaned over his shoulder and watched the cacophony for a few moments. "Anything jumping?"

"If it is, it's not jumping very high," muttered Adam. He seemed to break out of his trance and gave Alison a searching look. "You saw Miracle Mum back there, right? In that tunnel where the third victim was?"

"I don't think you're supposed to be still investigating this, Adam," said Alison, wincing.

"Someone from Modern Miracle's inner circle was right where a vampire victim was!" Adam's eyes were wild. "And now we're just going to dismiss that?"

"Actually, I have been thinking about that." Alison played with her fingers in idle angst. "And . . . if Miracle Mum had been the vampire, and she sucked the life out of that body, wouldn't she have looked young? And all refreshed? Because she didn't, when I saw her. She looked like . . ." Alison shrugged. "She looked like somebody's mum."

Adam clutched his head in one hand. "She could . . . she could absorb the life and then give it to Miracle Meg, so Miracle Meg can—"

"So they're both conduits?" said Alison. "Magic isn't genetic. Wouldn't that be, like, super, super rare?"

"I can figure this out!" insisted Adam, clutching the other side of his head with his other hand and holding his face closer to his screen. "It's got to make sense somehow!"

Alison gave a little sympathetic shrug and turned to her own laptop. "My work's not going very well either. I don't suppose you remember Nicholas Fisk?"

"No," said Adam, the syllable coming out a little distorted from the way his hands were stretching his mouth.

"No, I thought there'd be more in the old Ministry records," sighed Alison, indicating the old document scans currently displaying on her own screen. "But there's just a couple of invoices from back when he was a contractor before the . . . see, I'm supposed to find out what happened to him after . . ."

She trailed off sheepishly when it became clear that Adam wasn't paying her the slightest attention. She scrolled down through a couple of the pages she had up, but it was hopeless to try to focus on it through the cacophony coming out of Adam's laptop. It was like trying to fix a grandfather clock by hitting it with a second grandfather clock . . .

Then.

Something jumped out from the muddle of mixed audio tracks. It was the moment in the *Shgshthx Tonight* interview when the vicar mentioned Miracle Dad's real name. Gus Arkwright. That name caused some kind of blockage to fly out of one of the grandfather clocks, and a hitherto-stalled wheel began to click.

"Gus Arkwright," she said aloud. "So Miracle Meg would be Megan Arkwright."

"Uh-huh," grunted Adam.

"Arkwright, M." The revelation made Alison jerk forward and grab Adam's shoulder. "I've seen that name before."

Adam's hands came away from his face with a sound like two wet slugs being peeled off a garden wall. "You have?"

Alison took a deep breath to calm herself and arrange her thoughts into an orderly line before speaking. "Back when they took me to the school. 'Cos they thought I was psychic. There was this whole first-day-meeting thing where I had to go to the headmaster's office. They took down some details and made a file folder for me."

"Right," said Adam, frowning. "They did that with everyone."

"But I saw them put my file in the shelf with the rest of them, and the name on the folder right after mine was Arkwright, M. That might have stood for Megan."

"I guess," said Adam. "Probably some other Arkwright."

"But if it was her, and Miracle Meg went through the school, then the Department would have a file on her." Alison's hands flew to her keyboard, and she brought up the shared database folder that contained all of the Department's unclassified data.

"Maybe," said Adam skeptically. "But they still haven't finished digitizing the records, and some were lost after declassification—"

"Found her," announced Alison, turning her laptop around in beaming triumph.

Name: Arkwright, Megan Louise
Next of kin: Augustus and Sarah Arkwright (parents)
Place of birth: Worcester, Worcestershire
Infusion group: LET-A
Ancient: El-Yetch

Background: Subject was discovered by agents when her family began offering her healing powers online as a paid service.

Outcome: Subject and parents were informed of the nature of magic and the degenerative effect of her healing powers. Subject was enrolled and given standard education on magic suppression and possession prevention. After demonstrating full understanding, subject was released from occult education and returned home.

Adam leaned back, jaw hanging. "It . . . it might still be someone else," he said, his complete lack of faith in his own words reflected in his slurred consonants.

Alison frowned at the screen. "You think so? It's the right name. Right father's name. Right town. And the right Ancient. What's LET-A?"

"Life essence transfer A," said Adam distractedly. "That means healing. Vampirism is LET-B. But hang on, wait a minute." He clutched the side of his head again. "She does have healing powers. So she really is possessed by El-Yetch. Could she actually be a conduit after all?"

"Dunno about that," said Alison. "I still don't see how she could have had a chance to drain David Callum. Or the one in the tunnel."

Adam's gaze was sliding back and forth across Megan Arkwright's data as if he was trying to paint it with invisible brushes attached to his eyes. After four or five run-throughs, his gaze settled on a small collection of numbers in the top right. He poked at it with one pudgy finger, leaving a greasy mark on the screen. "Look at her date of birth," he said.

"Is that what that is?" Alison peered at it. "Oh. Because . . ."

"If it's accurate, then Miracle Meg is nineteen years old," said Adam, finishing his thought.

Alison tapped her lower lip with one extended index finger. "Maybe it isn't accurate."

"No," said Adam. His posture straightened as his mood brightened. "This means she has to be the conduit! She must be draining enough life force to keep her young, and that's why she still looks like she's ten years old!"

Alison screwed up her face as she tried to lever this into her thoughts. "Is that how it works though? I thought magic healing just, you know, refreshes you. Brings you back to peak health. I didn't think it made you age backwards."

"But you have to realize . . ." Adam stopped himself before he could say something condescending as a vision of Richard Danvers shaking his head in disapproval suddenly flashed across his mind's eye. He deflated, and when he spoke again, his voice seemed to be coming from the very bottom of his stomach. "You're right. Life essence doesn't literally turn you back into a child. We can't just throw a fact away because it doesn't fit the theory. We need to throw the theory away and find a better one that fits the facts."

"Yeah, I suppose," said Alison, nodding slowly. "That's really smart actually."

"Well, it's just the way you need to think when you're an investigator." He frowned at the date of birth again to double-check he hadn't misread it the first five times. "Let's think about this. How would it make sense for Miracle Meg's file to have this date of birth?"

Alison put a finger to her forehead. "The file could be wrong?"

"Hm. Possibly. But the thing is, almost everyone who gets admitted to the school is in their teens, or older. It'd be really, really unusual for Miracle Meg to be admitted at the age she looks now. And this record is from a couple of years ago, so she'd have been even younger. Nineteen would make a lot more sense."

"Okay," said Alison, undeterred. "Maybe she is nineteen, and she just looks really young?"

Adam stared at her. "So, what are you saying, Alison? She's got dwarfism or something?"

"It's possible!" She tapped her chin again. "I suppose there's no way to know for sure."

"Um, there might be." Adam coughed. "We could check the medical report that's attached to the file."

He pointed, and Alison noticed for the first time that the database entry had a second tab. She reddened. "Sorry."

The medical report didn't contain any reference to Megan Arkwright having any condition that might restrict her growth. But that became a moot point fairly swiftly, because it did have photographs of Megan at the time when she was admitted to the school, just to make Alison feel even sillier.

She and Adam both leaned in simultaneously when they saw the pictures. There were two: one in profile and one head on, fully lit and in high resolution like a police arrest photo. As such, the conclusion they both drew as they simultaneously leaned back was unmistakable. It was Adam who voiced it first.

"That's not Miracle Meg," he said. "That doesn't look anything like Miracle Meg."

Alison kept staring. It was true. As well as being in her late teens, the Megan Arkwright in the database had a different hair color to Miracle Meg and a generally different facial structure. Plus, the wall markings in the background indicated that she was about five foot six inches in height. At first look, the girl in the photo was totally unfamiliar to Alison. But then a creeping thought darted across her mind, and she clutched the side of her head as if to stop it from falling out. "Ow."

"What is it?"

She looked to Adam with frightened eyes. "I'm getting this . . . it's like, I saw something in the past, but I can't see it in my head exactly the way it was when I saw it."

Adam glanced to the side, then back. "You mean . . . you're remembering it the way most people remember things?"

"Is this what that's like?" She grimaced. "How do you live with it? It's really weird. There's something really familiar about this girl's face, but . . . I just can't place it."

Adam placed a hand near Alison's mouse hand and made awkward testy motions with his fingers until she let him use it. He clicked back to the previous page, then quadruple-checked the details again. "There can't be more than one Megan Arkwright with healing powers in Worcester. There's something behind all this we're missing. This is why Miracle Dad threw such a fit when his name came out. He knew sooner or later someone would look up . . ." He sighed. "If I could just pursue the investigation a little bit longer . . ."

"Well, you can't, can you?" said Alison brusquely. She was still disturbed by her inability to remember something and was internally debating whether she should call her doctor. "Mr. Danvers took you off the case."

"Whatever they're doing, they're going to be doing it again, this weekend, at the contest," said Adam, into his chest. He looked up. "You believe they're up to something, right? You saw them in that tunnel!"

"One of them," said Alison, uncomfortably looking around the room for eavesdroppers and playground monitors. "Adam, please don't go after them at the contest. You'll get in even more trouble."

"I can't anyway, I'm supposed to be watching out for magical rioters or something." Adam turned his brownest and moistest puppy-dog gaze on her. "But . . ."

"I can't either!" Alison deflected the gaze with a sweeping gesture. "I have to be on hand to help out with, you know, the administration and stuff. I already told three people I'd remember their agendas for them."

Undeterred, Adam cranked up the puppy-dog power by a couple of cocker spaniels' worth. "Alison, I've . . . I've messed up. I've basically thrown my whole career away chasing one stupid theory. But I get it now. I get how I'm supposed to do this. And now we're so close to finally figuring this out, and if I can push it just one tiny bit further I know I can turn everything around. There's never going to be a better chance than this weekend. They're exposed. Away from their home turf. If we let them get away after this . . ." He left the point hanging.

Alison was hugging herself, staring at the picture of Megan Arkwright on her laptop screen. There was a sadness in the eyes that made Alison think of the body she had seen in the shrine to El-Yetch underground. She wondered if there was anyone out there still waiting for them to come home.

"You just want . . . someone to watch them, right?" she asked, uneasily passing the words like kidney stones.

"Yes!" He nodded so fast that his ponytail started whirling around his head like a morris dancer's ribbons.

"I think I might know someone who can help out."

MEANWHILE

42

On the roof of a small terrace of apartments in one of London's lower-rent districts, Leslie-Ifrig lay on their front, supporting their chin on their fists. They were looking down on a small beer garden that was bestowing the surrounding neighborhood with the gift of its ambient rock music as the owners of several nearby windows with twitching curtains showed a complete lack of gratitude.

Leslie-Ifrig bobbed their head left and right in appreciation of Twisted Sister, their smile never wavering throughout. When the song was over, they called back over their shoulder, "Still no sign of police!"

"Shh!" replied Victor, who was huddled under a tarpaulin in the middle of the roof.

Leslie-Ifrig pouted at the beer garden, decided they weren't interested in listening to "Message in a Bottle" for the third time, then hopped gracefully into a standing position and sauntered over to Victor. "No sign of police," they repeated, in a quieter voice. "Just some people having a lovely time. Do you want to come out from under there?"

"No," said the tarpaulin as the mass underneath pulled it closer around itself. "The helicopters will see."

The skies were completely clear. The only sound was the music and the occasional muffled argument between middle-class homeowners trying to decide who was going to go out to complain about the noise. Leslie-Ifrig looked down. "No helicopters either."

"They'll come."

Leslie-Ifrig sighed tolerantly. "You want to know what I think, Victor? I think you keep going on about the police coming to get you because you secretly want it to happen."

"Why would I want that to happen?" asked Victor contemptuously.

"I dunno, I think maybe you think you deserve it because you hate yourself."

"I hate *you*."

"Aww." Leslie-Ifrig rubbed the part of the tarpaulin they assumed was over Victor's head. "I hate you too."

Victor finally poked his head out from under the tarpaulin like a green plastic turtle. "Why are you still here?" he spat. "Haven't you caused me enough trouble?"

Leslie-Ifrig hung their head, then turned and sat down with their back to Victor, bringing their knees up to their face. "I'm sorry," they said. "I didn't mean to get you in trouble. And I'm sorry if you lost your job because of me. I didn't know you liked having it so much."

"Like it?" Victor scoffed. "I haven't liked a single aspect of my life since the day I started setting things on fire. And I liked my job less than I liked getting my prostate checked."

Leslie-Ifrig smiled in bafflement, brow furrowed. "So why are you so broken up about losing it?"

"I'm not! I mean . . ." Victor dropped his gaze. With his face pointed down and just his hair visible at one end of the tarpaulin, he looked to Leslie-Ifrig like a gigantic discarded bobble hat. "They only wanted me around to blow the tits off monsters when they needed it. But that was something! At least I was useful to them. It's the only place I ever belonged!"

Leslie-Ifrig cocked their head as they thought about this. Then they leaned back, pointed a hand skyward, and allowed power to flow out. Instead of a blast of fast-moving conflagration, they created a curved line of glowing air that slithered lazily upwards and outwards like a fiery caterpillar, before curling back in. When it had stopped moving, it had taken the form of half a heart symbol.

"You could be useful here too," they prompted, nodding toward the empty air where the other half of the symbol belonged.

Victor stared up at the artwork with an unimpressed scowl. Then he looked Leslie-Ifrig directly in their good eye, wriggled one hand out from under the tarpaulin, and pointed.

His caterpillar of fire was a little redder and a little more erratic than Leslie-Ifrig's. Its edges were jagged and wavered constantly as it crawled across the air beside Leslie-Ifrig's contribution, but it still formed a coherent line. When it stopped moving, Leslie-Ifrig's half heart was forming one side of a crude line drawing of a penis and testicles.

Leslie-Ifrig burst out laughing. It sounded like a child's laughter mingled with the huffing of a labored steam engine. The cracks on their face expanded, increasing the orange glow coming from the molten substance in between. At length they pulled themselves together, then glanced at the airborne graffiti again and launched into a fresh round of smoky guffaws.

"It's not funny," grouched Victor.

"Then why are you smiling?"

Victor's head disappeared under the tarpaulin again. "I'm not!"

"Looked like you were."

"I say I wasn't, and I would know best," said the tarpaulin pointedly.

"Fair enough."

Leslie-Ifrig sat in silence for a few moments, watching the remnants of the giant fiery penis gradually dissipate into an incoherent but considerably less puerile blob. Then they pulled out the phone from their back pocket, flicked through to a messenger app, and examined their last few pieces of correspondence.

"Would you be feeling better if you still had a job?" they asked, giving the tarpaulin a sidelong look.

"Obviously" came the reply.

"I think I might know someone who can help out."

THE FOLLOWING SATURDAY

43

The contest of faith healing had been scheduled for Sunday morning, as this was a typical time for a religious service, and Miracle Dad was keen to give Pastor Barkler the best possible fighting chance. Or more accurately, the least possible room to make excuses because the conditions weren't one hundred percent perfect.

In preparation, the Flash Microsystems Hotel and Convention Centre had been locked down since Friday night. Alison arrived on Saturday morning, enjoyed the usual thrill of self-importance that came of flashing her DEDA ID to be allowed through a police cordon, and started making her way through the car park.

The complex consisted of one tall building, the hotel, and a number of lower, broader, more architecturally creative buildings, and the convention center. The bland rectangle of the hotel combined with the other buildings' artful diagonal lines gave the effect of an incomplete domino fall-over.

And then there was the Pelican Theatre, a Victorian-era building in the middle of it, which for heritage's sake had been permitted to exist unmolested by present-day trends, except for a couple of covered walkways that connected it to its more modern fellows. Its somewhat more disheveled look gave it the air of a wiry terrier sitting in the wreckage of the domino fall-over pretending to know nothing about it.

The massiveness of the car park was emphasized by the small number of vehicles in it, most of which were clustered around the hotel entrance.

There were a few of the "official" DEDA vehicles with the purple markings, and near those Alison recognized the expensive but sensible car belonging to Richard Danvers and a few of the flashy sports cars driven by those field agents who were less secure in their masculinity. Besides those, she hazarded a guess that the severe black town cars belonged to Pastor Barkler and his entourage, and the beaten-up family sedan with the hilarious bumper stickers was Miracle Dad's transportation. Farther away from the hotel entrance were the vehicles belonging to the various media outlets that had been invited to set up for filming. The BBC was here, as were a couple of old, beaten-up cars that probably belonged to the tabloid reporters Miracle Dad had invited. And finally, in the farthest corner of the main car park, Alison found what she was looking for: the LAXA van.

Beatrice and Roger had left a few parking spaces of distance between them and the next vehicle, probably in accordance with Alison's request that they be as discreet as possible. It was rather a futile gesture, however, as the huge, beaten-up van stuck out like a hulking, incontinent bloodhound at a dog grooming show. It still had some of the forest camouflage clinging to it.

Alison sidled up to the van's side door, did a quick check for onlookers, and then knocked gently with two knuckles.

"It's all right!" squawked the voice of Beatrice from inside the van. "We've got a press pass! We are supposed to be here!"

"It's Alison."

The van slid open, and Beatrice was there. She had either had a chance to launder her LAXA T-shirt or changed into a completely identical one, but the bags under her slightly manic eyes showed she was still sleeping roughly. Alison was able to take this in for all of about half a second before a large brown furry mass streaked across the space between the two women, causing Alison to fall back in surprise.

Roger immediately dived out of the van and was able to grab the end of Arby's leash before it flew out of reach. Arby was forced to abort his quest to comb the hotel car park for bottoms to sniff and hands from which to solicit pets.

"Sorry," said Roger, lifting an uncomplaining Arby back into the van. "He's really excited today."

"Did you have to bring him to this as well?" asked Alison, still sitting on the tarmac.

"Viewers like it," said Roger flatly. "They keep saying, it's not solving mysteries with a dog if you don't have a dog."

"Yeah," said Beatrice. "Plus, I kinda, technically, still haven't told Mum that we have him yet."

Arby made another bid for freedom, forcing Alison to abort her attempt to stand up, and Roger had to haul on the leash again. "Sorry," he said. "It's the old people."

That remark left Alison in a state of complete bafflement until she looked in the direction Arby was lunging and saw that a minibus had arrived on the other side of the car park, adorned with a logo for something called the Broken Boughs Retirement Hospice. A couple of elderly people of indistinct gender were being helped down by a pair of orderlies in white.

"Oh yeah, Arby loves old people," said Beatrice conversationally. "We rescued him from an old people's home originally."

"Rescued him?" asked Alison, standing up. From the way Arby's tail was wagging like the rotor of an attack helicopter, he didn't seem to have any negative associations with elderly people.

"Yeah! Our first big exposé actually. There was some absolutely shameless magical appropriation going on there. Isn't that right, Arby the Psychic Dog?" She fondly scratched Arby above the tail. "They let us have him if we promised to go away."

"Anyway," said Alison, brushing herself down to firmly signal a change of subject.

"Oh yes!" said Beatrice, clapping her hands together. "Thank you so much for sorting out the press pass. We sent a message to DEDA for one a while ago but didn't hear back. Roger thinks using Twitter might have been too informal . . ."

"You understand what I need you to do here?" whispered Alison, checking behind her for spies.

"Yeah, yeah," said Beatrice, nodding. "Keep investigating Modern Miracle."

"Keep *watching* Modern Miracle," corrected Alison, maintaining fierce eye contact to drive the point home, waggling her eyebrows as she emphasized the word. "Don't confront them or anything. Just watch. And report back if they do anything . . . worth reporting on."

"We're not, like, new to this, you know," said Beatrice. "We've done a whole, like, three investigations now."

"I know," said Alison uncomfortably. "I just don't want to be responsible for getting you guys into danger again. Like what happened with that pyrokinetic."

"Trust us," said Beatrice, thrusting her chest out. "No one goes into online streaming without learning to live with a little risk."

"But you will only keep an eye on them, right?"

"Sure, sure, we'll be completely professional."

"But only professional watchers of things," pressed Alison, still trying to urgently maintain eye contact. "Not a professional anything else. Right?"

Beatrice seemed to have stopped listening and was now fiddling with the electronic recording equipment in the front half of the van. Alison noticed that there had been some additions since she had last seen the collection. "What? Yeah, totally."

That would have to be enough. "I have to stay at the hotel tonight to be ready for the contest in the morning," said Alison. "I'll text you my room number once I've checked in. So you can get in touch at any time. Okay? If absolutely anything happens."

"We've got it!" said Beatrice, looking up from her work with a hint of testiness. "We're on the job. You can go do yours."

"Just chill," offered Roger.

Alison sighed. In her mind, the itinerary for the day stretched ahead of her like a crematorium conveyor belt, and it didn't seem like "chill" was going to comfortably fit in anywhere. Unless she squeezed it in between "worry about riots" and "afternoon general worrying time."

LATER THAT DAY

44

The entrance doors to the Pelican Theatre were a grand affair. Ten-foot-high oak slabs that wouldn't have been too out of place on a church, adorned with carved wooden decorations evoking ribbons, bunches of grapes, and theatrical masks. They were designed to immediately impose upon incoming visitors the grandness and sheer occasion of a night at a London theater. And no doubt would do so, had they been opened at any point in the last thirty years.

The current owners of the Pelican Theatre felt that the brief journey across the threshold just didn't offer enough chances for user engagement. Now, the theater lobby could only be accessed by one of the newly built side corridors, which marked the end of a circuitous path that started at the main car park, wound through the convention center's main entrance plaza, and passed two food courts.

At the point where the walkway left the main entrance plaza, it passed under another, elevated, walkway that connected parts of the business center on the second level, and this was where Richard Danvers had set up DEDA's temporary operations center. He had fully commandeered the largest meeting room and had already scrounged up several desks, a whiteboard, and most of the building's coffeemakers.

The place was already abuzz with activity when Adam Hesketh arrived. The moment he rode the escalator up to the second level, he spotted Danvers through the main meeting room's large windows, standing over a floor plan of the complex with his sleeves rolled up and his least approachable look on his face. Agents with smartphones were in constant motion around him, giving up-to-the-minute reports on what persons of interest were on the scene and what interesting things they were doing.

Danvers glanced up briefly when he saw Adam approaching, then immediately glanced down and impatiently gestured to Sumner, who was standing at his elbow looking like a smug cat next to a fish pond. Sumner looked at Adam, then made an identical gesture to the general throng of agents beside him.

Adam was on his way to the office door when a junior agent came out and very firmly pulled the door shut behind him. He was one of the new Administration hires who was still showing up every day with perfect hair and a buttoned-up suit jacket that hadn't yet accrued any stains from running errands to Archie's laboratory. "Hi! Adam, right?" he said, getting between Adam and the door. "I'm Jake. Nice to finally talk."

"Just checking in with Mr. Danvers," said Adam, awkwardly using two pointed index fingers to suggest a direction Jake might like to move in to get out of Adam's way.

In response, Jake placed a hand gently on Adam's arm as if about to spin him around. "Yes, he said you'd be showing up, and he said we should take you to your special spot as soon as you arrived."

"Special spot?" said Adam, warily intrigued.

"Yes, you've got a special spot just over here."

Not letting go of Adam's arm, Jake gently pulled him over to a spot near the footbridge that went over the main walkway. There was a small seating area with a couple of soft chairs, from which one could get the best possible view of the main entrance plaza below.

"Just here," said Jake, trying to point to both chairs with one hand. "Either one. All the crowds will be coming through here to get to the theater. Just do your magic-vision thing and let us know if you see anyone magical and dangerous."

"Right," said Adam, eyeing the nearer chair. "Can I have a computer? Or a desk?"

Jake glanced around nervously, then pointed to the two chairs again. "Either one's fine. Literally, just watch out for trouble and give someone a shout if you see any."

Adam plopped his backpack down beside one of the chairs, then plopped himself down. "Right," he repeated. "I did bring my own tablet . . ."

"Oh, good idea," said Jake as Adam pulled a rather scratched and elderly tablet out of his bag. "Play some games or something. Probably be a quiet time for you. I'm jealous!" He nodded back toward the meeting room behind them, then noticed that someone at the door was irritably beckoning him back, so he took off without another word.

Adam let a deep sigh bubble up from the depths of his gut like gas from a volcanic vent. Of course he hadn't expected to be back in the inner circle of top investigators so soon after being benched, but still, it was galling to know he had been unofficially demoted to security camera.

He cast a token look over the convention center, but the big crowds wouldn't be coming until tomorrow, and at the moment there was just a handful of hurried assistants from across the spectrum of politics and journalism running errands. He switched on his magic vision anyway and determined to his satisfaction that no crazed water elementals were gearing up to flood the building.

He turned to his tablet. Ever since the minor breakthrough of finding Megan Arkwright's file from the school, he had redoubled his attempts to solve the case by staring at the evidence. He had even created a custom app on his tablet that immediately opened sixteen different tabs for him to stare at in turn. He was actually starting to find it relaxing. And he knew that sooner or later it would all come together. He could feel the truth behind it all jiggle like a loose tooth under pressure.

After thirty minutes, the loose tooth wasn't coming any looser, so he cast another idle glance over the plaza, only to see a pink trail making its way up an escalator toward him. He shook off his enhanced vision just as it came into talking range.

"Hi, Adam!" said Rana. She was wearing a Modern Miracle T-shirt. "I wondered if you'd be here."

"Rana!" said Adam, pushing his tablet to one side as he mentally assessed his posture for natural-seeming nonchalance. "Are you . . . are you here with Modern Miracle?"

"Yeah, I'm volunteering for them now. Sort of general-assistant thing." She looked up at the bustling office behind them. "This is where I pick up our security passes, right?"

"Yes, yes it is," said Adam quickly, not wishing to reveal that his colleagues had clued him in to the logistics of the situation as much as they had the potted plant to his immediate right.

"What're you working on?" said Rana, suddenly leaning forward when she caught a glimpse of Adam's tablet. "Oh. The vampire killings?"

Adam gave up trying to casually cover the screen with his sleeve. "Yes," he admitted.

"Is Miracle still a suspect in all that?"

"There's just . . . a lot of unanswered questions still," he mumbled unhappily, although he did pick up on her use of the shorter, more familiar name. "You think they shouldn't be?"

"Well." Rana gleefully dropped into the other chair and leaned in as she took on a hushed tone. "Obviously when I first joined them it was partly to see if I could learn any more about that."

"And?"

"And I've seen Miracle Meg working enough times that I'm pretty sure she's on the level. They're nice people. Really. I don't think they're killing anyone. It has to be a random vampire who hangs around after the sermons. A lot of magic kids do."

"Right," said Adam, nodding slowly.

She frowned at his unconvinced response. "You have new evidence?"

"Well, it's just this." Adam fingered his way to a specific tab. "Me and Alison found a file for a Megan Arkwright in the school database. Graduated two years ago."

"Ah?"

"Except it doesn't look anything like Miracle Meg." He brought up the photograph. "And it says she's nineteen years old."

"Well, it . . . can't be the same person, can it?" said Rana, shrugging.

"It can't. But it has to be." Adam rested his chin on his hand. "And there's still that tunnel Alison found in the woods. Where she found the El-Yetch shrine. And the third victim. She says she saw Miracle Mum there as well. Which would suggest that Miracle Mum is the vampire. But . . ." He waved his hands.

"I'm pretty sure Miracle Mum's not a vampire; she makes me packed lunches," said Rana, smiling nervously. She leaned over the screen again. "So that database, you've got a file for everyone who's been through magic school, right?"

"Some of them haven't been digitized yet, but most of them, yes," said Adam. It occurred to him that this was probably information the government didn't want being passed to civilians, especially ones working for suspect organizations, but he was finding it hard to care that much.

"Have you tried searching for Miracle Mum's name? Or Miracle Dad's? Just to completely pin down who does and doesn't have superpowers?"

"Yeah," said Adam. "No luck."

"Oh yeah, I guess that would've been obvious," said Rana, leaning back into her chair. "Probably the first thing you do in official investigations, right? Look up every person of interest on all the government databases and make sure all the facts line up?"

"Pretty much," muttered Adam.

Rana gave him an encouraging half smile. "Well. I should get back to work. Hey, do you want to hang out after this is all over? Go over your notes properly? This is actually really interesting to me."

"Sure."

She touched his shoulder as she walked away, but he didn't react. He was back to fiercely staring at the screen. He didn't look up until her footfalls had entirely faded into the background noise, when he glanced around to make sure she was out of view.

Then he hurriedly opened the database application, flipped over to the records for the school, and began searching for names. He started with Miracle Mum, which a moment's beating the side of his head with a fist caused him to remember to be Sarah Arkwright. No results found. Then he tried Augustus Arkwright. Nothing.

So, there were no conduits or vampires among the Miracle parents, at least none the government knew about. Could they have honed their powers by themselves without help from the school? Without getting possessed? Unlikely. Adam dropped the thought. That was just more speculation. From now on, he worked only with hard facts.

He was about to settle back down, disappointed, but he determinedly kept his shoulders tensed. He wasn't going to let this little trickle of momentum go. *All the government databases*, Rana had suggested. She was right. There were a lot of nonextradimensional records he could pull information from as a government employee.

Shortly, he brought up the online database for the most recent UK census and searched for the name Augustus Arkwright. There were several, but only one based in Worcester.

"Arkwright, Augustus Peter," read Adam aloud. "Caucasian. Male. Two children. Sep—"

He froze up as that relevant nugget of information shot up his conscious mind and pinned it to the top of his skull. Two children. Miracle

Dad and Miracle Mum had two daughters, according to this. Megan Louise Arkwright, nineteen, and Phoebe Rose Arkwright, eleven. Eleven felt a lot closer to a feasible age for the girl who was currently being presented as Miracle Meg. So if that was Phoebe, where was . . . ?

Adam pressed his palm against his forehead. This was it. He could feel it. He was tumbling down the hill toward the truth, and now nothing could stop him. He had the last piece in his hand, and any moment now he was going to rotate it the way it was supposed to go to fit in the space. He was going to figure it all out.

THE NEXT DAY

45

At just after seven o'clock in the morning, Adam figured it all out.

"Oh shit," he said, sitting bolt upright in his ridiculously large hotel bed. "Rana's about to be killed."

MEANWHILE

46

Alison was also having a moment of revelation. She was realizing she'd accidentally left her phone on silent for the entire night.

She discovered this only by pure chance, when she was lying half awake just before seven and saw it on the charger on her bedside table, lighting up with an incoming text message. Adding to a lengthy ladder of text message prompts that had already arrived.

Alison thrust out an arm to grab it, knocking a glass of water all over the thick hotel carpet, and sat up in bed with her knees drawn up to read the messages.

The last few were from Roger. Just after midnight, he'd sent a text asking Alison if she'd heard from Beatrice, as she hadn't returned to the van. Every text after that was just the phrase *see above*, with about an hour between each one for politeness's sake.

Above that, there were two messages from Beatrice. The first one read *Check your email :)* and had been received at around nine o'clock yesterday evening. The second, just a few minutes later, read simply: *Help :(*

Feverishly, Alison navigated her way to her email app. Sure enough, there was something from Beatrice. No text, just a link to a video file on the cloud.

It was a low-quality cell phone video taken in profile, which showed only darkness for the first few seconds before a strip of whiteness slid into view. After a moment for the camera to balance the light and find the focus, Alison was looking at the interior of a hotel room extremely similar to her own. The image was sandwiched thinly between two strips of dark brown, implying that the video was being recorded from inside a cupboard with the door slightly ajar.

"Oh, Beatrice," muttered Alison to herself in frustration. "Nobody was telling you to hide in their cupboard!"

The first recognizable figure was Miracle Meg, or at least the girl most of the world knew as Miracle Meg. She was sitting on one of the two beds in the room, wearing silk pajamas and greedily attacking an elaborate dinner on a room service tray. The camera moved slightly to get a better look at the other bed, on which Miracle Mum was daintily bent over a dinner tray of her own. She was wearing one of the hotel bathrobes.

The phone centered on Miracle Meg again as she scooped up the last few specks of something chocolatey. The moment her dessert bowl clattered emptily to the tray, she locked her gaze on to the as-yet-untouched dessert on Miracle Mum's tray and stretched out a hand. "Can I have your cake?" she said, still chewing the last mouthful.

Miracle Mum flinched. "What?"

"I want more cake. Can I have your cake?" It was voiced more like a demand than a request.

"Oh, but . . . I was actually going to have that," said Miracle Mum in a weak voice. "I was looking forward to it."

Meg slapped her hand against her dinner tray in anger, grabbed the knife from the wreckage of the main course, then held it in front of her face. "I'll cut myself."

Miracle Mum was frozen, apparently in terror. She slowly brought up her hands and held them out to placate. "Please. Don't."

The knife didn't move. "Can I have your cake?" Her voice was more plaintive, less threatening.

Miracle Mum looked down sorrowfully. "You've already had your cake. You had—"

Miracle Meg stabbed herself in the head with an unflinching force that made Alison's jaw drop. From the way the camera jiggled, Beatrice had been taken aback, too.

The knife clattered down, and blood began to pour down Miracle Meg's face, mingling with the free-flowing tears. Miracle Mum, panicked, was trying to press her dessert bowl into Meg's hands, but Miracle Meg was only clutching her face and howling.

A few moments later, there was the sound of a hotel room door opening. Beatrice tried to move the camera to capture the newcomer, but there apparently wasn't much space to shift position inside a hotel wardrobe. Not that it mattered.

"What's going on here?" came the unmistakable voice of Miracle Dad. "What've you done to yourself?"

"I fell!" wailed Miracle Meg, barely intelligible through a foam of various bodily fluids.

Miracle Dad clicked his tongue. "Oh, dear. We can't have Miracle Meg looking like that for her big day tomorrow, can we?"

"No," agreed Miracle Meg, at full volume.

There was a meaningful pause, after which Miracle Mum hung her head. "You . . . you said I wouldn't have to anymore," she said, on the verge of tears herself. "She did it to herself!"

"Come on, love, this is for family," said Miracle Dad. "There's nothing more important than family. It's just a little cut, you'll barely feel it."

From Miracle Mum's slumped posture, it was clear that she knew there was no point in arguing. She reached over and placed the tip of her index finger against the part of Miracle Meg's brow that she wasn't covering with her hands.

Even through video footage, Alison could sense the magic at work. There was an ethereal glow about Miracle Mum's fingertip, and the garish red line on Meg's brow disappeared like a pencil mark being removed with an invisible eraser.

"Now, what do you say?" prompted Miracle Dad.

"Thank you," said Miracle Meg tokenly, already helping herself to the second dessert bowl. Miracle Mum appeared to have gone into a state of catatonia.

"All right, we've got to be up nice and early for the big show," said Miracle Dad. "So you can only play games on your handheld for two more hours, okay?"

"Yes, Dad."

The video abruptly ended there, and Alison slowly lowered the phone from her face with shaking hands. She had been right. She had seen the face of Megan Arkwright before. It was the face of Miracle Mum. And that's why she hadn't quite been able to grasp that in her memory, because the photo in the file was of Megan before she had been prematurely aged by about twenty years.

The screen on her phone powered off, but she couldn't stop staring at it. Too many thoughts were crowding in her head. Had it always been

Miracle Mum doing the healing? How? Could she be a conduit as well? And what had happened to Beatrice after she'd recorded and emailed this? Was she all right?

Her hands were shaking so hard that it took a few moments to realize that her phone was vibrating with an incoming call. It was from Adam. Who wasn't high on Alison's list of who she should probably talk to at this point, but she took the call anyway.

"Alison, are you awake?" said Adam, flustered.

"Um, possibly," replied Alison, equally so.

"I think I might have figured this whole thing out. I just need to—"

"Miracle Meg isn't Miracle Meg," interrupted Alison. "Miracle Meg is Miracle Mum. Miracle Mum isn't Miracle Mum. I don't know where the real Miracle Mum is."

". . . Yeah, I figured something along those lines," said Adam, after a surprised pause. "I looked up the census. Miracle Dad has two daughters, and he listed his status as 'separated.' I think the real Miracle Mum's been out of the picture for years."

"So they were sisters this whole time!" said Alison. An absurd random thought told her that this was no conversation to be had while wearing pajama bottoms, and she began hunting around for her clothes while keeping the phone pinned to one ear. "Does this mean Miracle Mum . . . I mean, the girl we thought was Miracle Mum . . . was she doing the healing?"

"No! I don't think she was!" said Adam. "That's the other thing I figured out. But I need to confirm. You've got eidetic memory, right?"

"Um, yes, still."

"That cave you found. In the woods behind Modern Miracle's street. How far, exactly, was it from the street?"

Alison felt suddenly energized, as she often was when someone actually wanted her to provide exact details about something. "The cave was one hundred and forty-three yards from the street."

"Right. Now. After you entered the cave. How far did you travel down the tunnel before you got to that little shrine where the third body was?"

Alison thought about the answer and opened her mouth to reply, but then her words died as the two broken grandfather clocks being smashed together in her head both began ticking like dervishes. "Oh. I think I just figured the whole thing out."

"Right?!" said Adam.

"So that must mean . . ."

"Yes!"

"And that's why Modern Miracle insisted on . . ."

"I think so!"

Alison was fastening the button on her jeans, holding her head sideways to hold her phone against her shoulder. "So . . . that must be how Miracle Mum . . . I mean, Megan, was doing the healing!"

"No no no no no," said Adam excitedly. "She can't have been. She'd have been completely aged to death by now. See, I had this idea to look up all the suspects on all the databases we have. That's how I found out about the two-daughters thing. But then, late last night, I thought of looking up the two victims as well."

"And what did you find?" Alison was now fully dressed and searching for her room key.

Adam told her.

Alison was in the process of finding her room key in the back pocket of the jeans she was currently wearing, and Adam's revelation made her freeze in midpat. "Rana's about to be killed," she realized.

"I know! I've tried calling Mr. Danvers, but—"

"Everyone'll be busy," said Alison, now hurrying down the hotel corridor. "They'll have started letting the audience in already. But maybe if we can just get to Rana before the contest starts . . ."

"Right," said Adam. "Let's meet up in the basement."

47

The contest was due to begin at eight o'clock, and both levels of the Pelican Theatre's main auditorium were already full to capacity. There hadn't yet been a major violent incident, largely because the two sides of the debate had been requested to queue up at opposite entrances. Now that they were all in one room together, peace was being maintained by a rather conspicuous fence running down the middle of the auditorium, manned by plainclothes police officers.

It was a fragile peace. Richard Danvers had done his best to screen out the audience members with protest signs that were a touch too bellicose or had too many misspellings, but there was still an audible tension crackling between the two sides of the grumbling theater. It was like standing on a floor covered in primed mousetraps, waiting to erupt into chaos at the slightest disturbance, and he flinched every time someone yelled a slogan or threw popcorn over the dividing fence.

He tugged the curtain aside and stepped out onto the stage. The house lights were still up and there were no spotlights on, and no music played to signal the beginning of the event. For the sake of everyone's safety he was going to do his damnedest to make this whole morning as bland and dispassionate as possible. He was, after all, a civil servant.

"Erm, good morning, everyone," he said. He gave his lapel mike a few taps, and the bustle of the audience swiftly died down. "My name is Richard Danvers, I am the head of operations at the Department of Extradimensional Affairs."

"SUCKS," yelled someone from the pro-magic side of the audience.

Danvers directed an admonishing glare toward the source of the sound, and to his surprise, the initial titters of the oncoming wave of mocking laughter instantly died. He had spent his entire life being raised by one stern overseer after another and had a natural gift for tapping into the primal part of the brain that doesn't want to be sent to bed without supper.

"As I'm sure you're aware," he continued, "we are here today to conduct a . . . comparative effectiveness test. Of the healing services offered by Modern Miracle and the North American Evangelical Fellowship for Christ." His eyes rolled back for a moment as he mentally checked that he had said all the words in the right order. "We will be approaching this as scientifically as possible. Both representatives will be assigned one patient, each suffering roughly equivalently from chronic physical difficulties related to old age, and who will be fully assessed by a medical team both before and after the healing. There will also be a third subject, as a control."

He glanced into the wings, where Jake the junior administrator was holding a bucket of warm water and a sponge.

"The event is being recorded and livestreamed from multiple angles." He nodded to the front row, which was a forest of lenses of every shape and size. "But those of you in the live audience should feel free to make your own recordings; we are inviting total scrutiny here." Privately, he hoped this would keep a few more restless minds occupied. "I'd also like to take a moment to acknowledge the online audience watching the streams from all over the world, who number in the several millions, I've just been informed."

He blinked silently into the camera lenses before him for a few moments, fighting the urge to let his thoughts dwell on the situation, as he feared he might never come back mentally. He fancied he could sense the children of the future watching this moment in school history class for centuries to come. And then cutting clips of it to make into hilarious memes he didn't understand.

"Clearly, there is a lot of . . . popular investment in the outcome of this event," he said. "Both participants have requested to be allowed to make a public statement before the competi—I mean, test." He felt his fists clench. "I will invite them to do so now. I would like to stress, beforehand, that I want this morning's events to take place in an atmosphere of mutual respect, and with all the dignity warranted by the occasion."

"All right, Miracle Mob!" cried Miracle Dad as he bounded onto stage waving both hands. "Who's ready to piss off Jesus?"

48

Even with the auditorium completely full, crowds were still packed outside the Pelican Theatre at both entrances, trying to catch a glimpse through the open doors or holding out hope that some unwary person might make the mistake of leaving their seat to use the bathroom.

Adam, arriving from the hotel at a full sprint, stopped when he reached the edge of the crowd. He hopped from foot to foot, looking for an entrance point from which he could politely plow his way through, but it was hopeless. It was like trying to push a tomato through a keyhole.

Instead, after a searching look around, he headed for a gray, unfeatured emergency door that was doing everything in its power to be unwelcoming to passersby, and after bursting through it he found himself in the alleyway that led to the theater's rear entrances. Dumpsters, pipework, and old shipping crates roamed freely, safe in the knowledge that they weren't expected to look appealing to a modern public the way the rest of the theater was.

Adam found an unlocked door and was reassured by the sight of cold cement floors and unfeeling brickwork. Nobody was around. He was in the maintenance part of the theater behind the main stage, which nobody usually needed to see except technicians and actors, whose opinions on decor apparently didn't matter much.

He checked a few doors, and after finding a couple of unused dressing rooms mainly being used to store enormous cardboard cutouts of space heroes from the last time the complex had hosted a science-fiction convention, he found a stairwell leading down to the basement.

It was only when he had thundered halfway down the steps two at a time that he noticed that the basement lights were all on, the bare light bulbs really bringing the sickly unpleasantness out of the yellowing paint on the walls. Someone had gotten here first. He stopped dead on the middle step with a noisy clatter of footwork, then carefully tiptoed the rest of the way down.

The tunnels down here were even less welcoming than the floor above. The distant noise of the crowd in the auditorium was like the low, barely audible moans of a submarine hull as it descends to a depth it has never been officially rated for. An ancient wooden sign on the nearest wall pointed Adam in the direction of the trap room, and he began to follow.

He turned a corner and stopped. The way ahead was blocked by a darkened silhouette, standing with arms held out in a way that suggested the exact opposite of a friendly embrace. Adam flinched, and his startled instincts activated his special vision, obscuring the figure in front of him with the kind of bright blue smear he associated with pyrokinetics.

He shook his head to dispel it, just in time to see his attacker's hands begin to glow orange.

Immediately, a keen instinct in the center of his mind suggested that he wet himself and cry. Then another, even keener, instinct took control of his legs and made him dive sideways into the wall. He only discovered after the fact that the wall contained a door, but he wasn't one to question providence.

He threw himself into what was almost certainly a laundry room—going by the way his head bounced off the circular window of an ancient front-loading washing machine—just as a rectangular mass of flame thundered along the corridor like a speeding train down a tunnel.

He slammed the door closed behind him and began looking for things to barricade it with. There was nothing to be found but multiple washing machines, far too heavy for him to move in time, and a prop that must have been left over from the last science-fiction convention. Some kind of plastic alien rifle that had had its last shreds of dignity spray-painted away to resemble a specific gun from *Interstellar Bum Pirates* or whatever. Useless as a weapon, but it might make someone pause for thought.

Adam grabbed it and pinned himself against the wall beside the door, aiming the barrel of his fake gun.

His magical senses reported that the blue smear was still in the corridor outside, moving unhurriedly toward the laundry room. Then they stopped and appeared to be staring at the door handle, making no effort to reach for it.

After a few confused seconds, the one sharp instinct in Adam's mind came through again. *Hey*, it said. *The interior walls down here seem a bit flimsy, don't they?*

Adam was already flinging himself to the ground when he noticed the section of wall that his head had been touching begin to sizzle and turn glossy. A moment later, he was showered in paint flecks and plaster dust as another gigantic fireball burst through, sailed over him, and caused a severe amount of future inconvenience to the next person who needed to do laundry in this room.

Adam shook the debris off his face and saw his tormentor looming through the dripping hole they had made in the laundry room wall. They were wearing a motorcycle helmet that concealed their features and appeared to be quite a petite person physically. But then they raised their hand to send another blast and became, to Adam, the size of the entire universe.

Then they hesitated, cocking their head to one side. "Is that a water pistol?" they asked, in the strange overlaying voice of a person of dual consciousness.

Adam glanced down at the plastic gun that he was still aiming at his attacker. "You wanna take that chance?" he asked, voice quavering with adrenaline.

"I can see the little valve where the water goes in."

Adam took another look and noticed a stopper at the base of the bulbous thing he had taken for a futuristic magazine. "Maybe it shoots poison," he tried.

"Hey!" said a new voice, coming from the direction of the stairs. "I found us breakfast. They had a bunch of those mini cereal boxes in the hotel restaurant. Do you want the Shredded Wheat or the—"

"Victor?!" yelled Adam, sitting up.

Victor Casin appeared at the shoulder of the person in the motorcycle helmet, carrying miniature cereal boxes in each hand and a couple of pastries under his armpits. "Adam?! What the hell are you doing here?"

"Erm, I was just . . . getting murdered, by this person, I think," said Adam.

"Story checks out," said Leslie-Ifrig quietly.

Victor glanced back and forth between the two of them, confused. "Did you join the cult?"

"What? What cult?" said Adam, getting back to his feet.

"The . . . fundamentalist cult," said Victor. "The ones running this contest thing."

Addressing them through the dripping, sizzling hole in the wall was starting to feel awkward, so Adam shuffled to the side and let himself through the door back into the corridor, keeping his hands in plain view. Leslie-Ifrig kept one hand primed and aimed at him throughout. "Er," said Adam. "This is a DEDA event. DEDA is running it."

"What?!" Victor turned to Leslie-Ifrig. "Is that true?"

Leslie-Ifrig clicked their tongue. "You don't work for them anymore anyway, so what does it matter? We're just making sure no one gets into the trap room."

"We're trying to get to the trap room because Modern Miracle is about to kill someone in there!" pressed Adam.

"Is *that* true?" repeated Victor, still staring at Leslie-Ifrig.

"I dunno, I don't keep their agenda for them," said Leslie-Ifrig sulkily. "I just guard things they tell me to guard."

Victor was rubbing his eyes, trying to get his thoughts in order, when Alison appeared at the far end of the corridor, having found an alternative staircase. "Adam?" she called, jogging forward. When she noticed the others, she froze, with a look on her face like that of a shrew barging into an owls-only changing room. "You!"

"Oh, hey," said Leslie-Ifrig, sticking out their other hand to keep both her and Adam covered.

"You were at Worcester!" cried Alison. "You tried to kill me!"

"Kinda assumed I had," said Leslie-Ifrig, confused.

"So that *was* you?" said Victor. He was trying to glare Leslie-Ifrig down and was getting more and more frustrated from the way they kept dodging eye contact.

"I never said it wasn't," they mumbled.

Adam had been watching in a state of complete confusion, but the way the two pyrokinetics were interacting made something click inside his head. "Oh! You're the archnemesis I've heard so much about. But . . . why are you working together?"

Victor made a frustrated hissing sound through his teeth. "You said Modern Miracle was being challenged by mad Christian fundamentalists," he said, eyes flaring.

"I said mad Christian fundamentalists *or something*," corrected Leslie-Ifrig.

"You said this was one of those things where archenemies have to work together against the bigger enemy," said Victor accusingly. "It's not that at all, is it? It's just straight corrupting me."

"Vic-tor," wheedled Leslie-Ifrig. "Why does it matter? You keep saying you hate the Department. You hated the work. You hated how they only wanted to use you to blast things and then tell you off for blasting things. You hated the weird smell in the cafeteria fridge."

"Oh yeah, that's a pretty weird smell," said Alison.

Leslie-Ifrig took their helmet off and gazed piteously into Victor's eyes. "I thought I could show you how you could be free of all of that," they said softly. "That . . . you don't need to think of your power as this . . . heavy thing that weighs you down. It's a gift. It can make you fly."

"Wait a minute, wait a minute," said Victor. "Let me get this straight. You know I hated being used as a weapon by the Department. And your solution, to get me to move on from that, is to . . . let someone else use me as a weapon?"

"You're your own weapon now, Victor," said Leslie-Ifrig.

The air between the two of them seemed to be literally crackling. "And what if I don't want to be any kind of weapon?" said Victor.

Leslie-Ifrig clicked their tongue again. "What else can we be? Barbecue lighters?"

"Um," said Alison. "We actually need to be getting on with something, so perhaps we could leave you to your conversation . . ."

She took a single step in the general direction of away, and Leslie-Ifrig's head snapped around. Their arm came up again as the air between them and Alison began to waver with heat haze.

Victor also snapped out an arm, grabbing Leslie-Ifrig by the wrist and slamming it against the wall. Pyrokinetics didn't actually project fire out of their hands—it was just a mental technique for directing it that skilled ones could learn to do without—but the surprise was enough to break Leslie-Ifrig's concentration. The flare fizzled out.

"Look, just go do the thing you came down here to do," said Victor, glaring at Alison.

"Okay," she said, adding, "Thanks!" before trotting away.

"Thank you, sorry, 'scuse me," said Adam as he squeezed through the narrow gap between Victor and the wall.

"Right," said Victor. He turned back to Leslie-Ifrig, and his words died when he noticed that his face was mere inches from theirs. "Erm. Right."

"Victor," said Leslie-Ifrig chidingly.

"Leslie. Ifrig," said Victor.

He had become momentarily lost in their one human eye, but he was stirred from the moment by a sensation of pain. He looked to his hand holding Leslie-Ifrig's wrist and saw the heat haze rising again.

"Victor," said Leslie-Ifrig again. "It's not working out. I think we should try to kill other people."

49

"We beseech you, oh LORD," intoned Pastor Barkler, his eyes reverently closed. His voice would have filled the theater even without the lapel mike. "Shine the light of your infinite mercy upon your daughter, Ethel."

"Hello, dear," said Ethel, his elderly patient. He had placed his hands over her eyes, but she was smiling throughout.

"We beseech you, oh LORD, to cast the demons of pain from Ethel's earthly form," continued Barkler, shuddering with devotion. "Out! In the name of the LORD you are cast OUT!" He placed one palm over Ethel's forehead and slapped it with the other.

"Ooh, that'd be nice," said Ethel, tottering.

"We should let the winner of the contest offer to heal all the patients who take part," muttered Richard Danvers, watching from the wings. "I worry this will seem in questionable taste otherwise."

"Yes, sir," said Sumner, standing beside him and mimicking his posture. "Do you . . . do you think he actually believes he can do it?"

"Hm." Danvers had a finger to his lips.

"I mean, you see a lot of these faith healing churches on TV where the priest is really slick and asking for donations, and you can tell that *they* know it's a scam," continued Sumner, emboldened in his attempt to be chummy with the boss. "But Barkler . . . well, I guess he wouldn't have let it come to this if he didn't really believe he could do it."

"Mm," muttered Danvers uncomfortably.

"It's like those guys who say they know exactly when the world is going to end, and then get in tons of debt." Sumner attempted a laugh that died swiftly when nobody joined in. "You have to wonder, do they listen to their own followers too much and forget they made it up, or are they just naturally crazy?"

"I feel uneasy about mocking anyone for deeply held beliefs," said Danvers, from the side of his mouth.

"Oh yes, of course, sir," stammered Sumner, restraightening his posture hurriedly. "I was just. You know."

A smattering of applause from the pro-religion half of the audience, as well as the way in which Pastor Barkler was standing arms aloft like a totem pole in a high wind, suggested to Richard Danvers that the ritual was complete. He stepped back onto stage. "Thank you, Pastor," he said, before addressing the smiling old woman in surgical garments. "How are you feeling, Mrs. Radcliffe?"

"Oh, just fine, thank you, dear," she replied. "How are you?"

Danvers gestured to the paramedics who were waiting beside the makeshift medical laboratory in the wings, and two of them hurried over to take Mrs. Radcliffe's arms. "We'll have you medically assessed as soon as possible. It's time for Modern Miracle's turn."

"The LORD has spoken," said Pastor Barkler ominously, before turning and striding offstage to join the small cluster of pale, undernourished figures in black that were his entourage.

The moment they were out of public view, Miracle Meg came onto stage carrying a stool with a businesslike air, set it down at a very deliberate spot near center stage, and primly took a seat. Miracle Dad appeared at the same time, waving with both arms. "All right, Miracle Mob!"

Danvers waited politely for the cheers from the audience to die down. "Bearing in mind that you have already addressed the audience . . ."

"Oh, right. Sorry, boss." Miracle Dad turned to Danvers, offering the audience one last cheeky wink and roll of the eyes.

"I believe your patient's initial medical check is just wrapping up," said Danvers, eyeing the wings. "What do you need them to do?"

"Just have a seat or kneel in front of Miracle Meg, and let her do her stuff. Easy-peasy."

"Right. Just sit."

"On the prayer mat," added Miracle Dad, turning back toward the wings for a second.

Danvers looked down. Miracle Dad was now holding a thin rectangular plastic mat about a yard across. It was printed colorfully with the words "Man's Best Friend," and above that were two black circles, apparently designated for a food bowl and a water bowl.

"Prayer mat," repeated Danvers.

Miracle Dad jiggled his head toward where Pastor Barkler and his followers had left the stage. "Well. We don't all get tax breaks, do we?"

50

Adam and Alison made it into the trap room just as a lively and quite literally fiery exchange of views commenced in the tunnels outside and yanked the door closed behind them. A moment later, a couple of jets of hot air puffed out from under the door and through the keyhole.

"Is Victor going to be all right?" asked Alison.

Adam shrugged. "I think he'll need some space, but he'll eventually be ready to start meeting new people."

Alison blinked. "I meant physically."

"Alison?" said Rana.

The trap room was the area directly under the stage, the destination for many a magic act participant through the ages, but it had been a long time since the Pelican Theatre had had that kind of booking. Currently, the room was mainly being used to store items left behind after cosplay contests—boxes full of random sci-fi props, loose bits of plastic armor, the occasional massively impractical hat.

It also contained, at that moment, Rana and Miracle Mum, who were both sitting on a wooden bench in the middle of a space that had been cleared in the debris.

"Adam?" added Rana, frowning at the two newcomers. "What are you doing here?"

"Rana, you have to get away from her," said Adam carefully as Alison tried to shrink into the background. "She was about to force you to use your powers."

"What?" Rana looked to Miracle Mum, who was sitting with shoulders hunched and legs crossed and seemed to be generally trying to be as small and unassuming as possible. "Are you?"

"No, I . . . wasn't going to do that," said Miracle Mum quietly.

"She says she wasn't," said Rana.

Adam coughed. "Well. Um. We're pretty sure she was actually."

"No," said Miracle Mum, shaking her head lightly.

An awkward pause followed, until everyone jumped at the sound of a sarcastic clap of hands. From the shadows at the far end of the room came the figure of Doctor Diablerie, marching into the center of the conversation with a slow, leisurely pace.

"That," he declared, "was pathetic."

"Doctor?" said Alison, bewildered.

"In all my voyages in the mindspace, my struggles with the demons of falsehood, Diablerie has never witnessed a poorer excuse for a parlor scene." He turned dramatically to Adam, snapping his cloak around himself. "Where is the gathering of the suspects? The buildup? This is the detective's moment to shine, boy! You don't leap straight to accusations like a dog glimpsing an unsmelled behind!"

Adam was struggling to pull his thoughts back onto the rails. "Doctor, I'm trying to . . . to . . ."

"You didn't even open with the seemingly irrelevant question!" He spun on his heel, making his cloak fly up around his chest, and pointed at Miracle Mum, who dropped her gaze immediately. "My lady. Enlighten us. Does Miracle Dad still insist that visitors to his home remove their shoes before entering?"

Miracle Mum looked up, confused. "What? Yes!"

"A seemingly innocent, common-enough request," said Diablerie smugly, making a slow circuit of the room. "A perfectly proper peccadillo for a patriarch proud of his personal palace." He paused to make eye contact with Alison. "Who could have dreamed that it would be the key to the sinister truth at the black heart of this villainous scheme?"

"Um, this is my case," said Adam weakly.

"On the contrary!" cried Diablerie, leaning into his personal space. "I represent the Office of Skepticism! The deliberate peddling of false magics falls within the mighty remit of Diablerie. Even if the illusion requires real magic to succeed."

"Okay, seriously, what the hell is going on?" asked Rana. "What's he trying to say?"

Diablerie responded by sharply pointing a gloved index finger upwards. "Only this. That the little girl who walks the stage above our heads, promising to dole out a goddess's touch like a fishwife peddling jellied eels, has no more magic inside her than does a crab paste sandwich."

Rana looked up at the boards above them. "Miracle Meg? But . . . I've seen her heal people. In the Modern Miracle house. She's the only one in the room."

"Ah! But what is a room?" Diablerie looked from baffled face to baffled face, enjoying himself immensely. "Four walls and a floor, yes? But sometimes these matters are not so straightforward. Girl! You remember that floor, don't you? You were sitting upon it as you received the bounty of our lady El-Yetch. I'm sure you remember every detail of it as if 'twere carved into your ample buttocks."

"There was a drain," said Alison impatiently. "It was a tile floor with a little circular metal drain that I was sitting on."

"When is a floor not a floor?" crowed Diablerie, looming over Miracle Mum, who was cringing harder than ever. "When it's also a ceiling. The ceiling of a certain underground chamber accessible via hidden tunnel in the forest? A ceiling adorned with a painting of El-Yetch's most benevolent face? With a mouth suspiciously round and bathroom drain shaped?" Diablerie turned from Miracle Mum with a little scoffing noise. "As any scholar of the mystical arts knows, magical healing requires physical contact but can still work through clothing. Or indeed a thin metal drain full of holes. Probably the 'holiest' aspect of this whole sordid affair, hah. The sole of a shoe is far taller an order, of course. Hence the house rule for stockinged feet."

"No," whimpered Miracle Mum, shaking her head and staring at the floor.

Alison was thinking back to her experience of being healed in the Modern Miracle house. She recalled how she had felt the power rising up within her from the pit of her stomach. In retrospect, she should have thought more about that. After all, why would the sensation be coming from below when Miracle Meg had been touching her forehead?

"My god," said Rana, eyes wide. "Someone was under the bathroom? Doing the real healing? Who?"

"Who indeed?" Diablerie suddenly spun around and addressed Adam, notching the dramatic tone of his voice down. "I hope you're taking notes, boy. This is how one does a parlor scene. Behold the captivation in their eyes. The room is primed for the next explosive reveal." He spun back around. "Who indeed! There are no conduits here, no divine blessings of the Mother Goddess. Only mundane healers, suffering in darkness as their very lives are traded for Miracle Dad's likes and subscribers. Is that not true, Megan Arkwright?" He inhaled sharply, making a little hissing sound to punctuate the reveal.

"Yeah, we figured that out," said Adam sulkily.

"What?!" said Rana, addressing Miracle Mum.

Alison coughed. "She's the original Miracle Meg. The one with the real healing powers."

Rana frowned. "So she was the one under the floor?"

"No!" said Adam urgently. "Maybe at first. But they've been luring in other people with healing powers and making them do it. Like the first vampire victim, William Shaw. Last night I found an entry for him in the school records. He had healing powers too. He—"

"No, no, no, no, no, no!" roared Diablerie. "It's far too soon for another reveal! You're supposed to prevaricate. Prevaricate!" He slapped his own face. "By all the damned spirits of the Otherworld, this is a farce."

"Oh my god," said Rana, backing away from Miracle Mum, who was madly shaking her head at the floor. "You were going to . . . you were going to make me . . ."

"Yes, well," said Diablerie, straightening his suit. "With the facts clumsily established, the whole sorry saga unfolds. A father of the gutter class, his ambition outweighing his scruples, discovers to his infinite glee that his daughter is possessed of miraculous healing powers and wastes no time attempting to exploit her. Until the first of many inconveniences comes knocking at the door of the Arkwright home. The Ministry of Occultism, taking Megan away to teach her the downsides of her extraordinary gift. The premature aging. The ever-present sword of Damocles of demonic possession."

"Dual consciousness," mumbled Alison quickly.

Diablerie made a slow circuit of the room as he spoke. "Not that it stopped your father's ambitions right away, did it, Miracle Meg?" He spat the words. "Just gave him a new angle for the con. The Cult of El-Yetch, the Mother Goddess, with a smile and a lollipop for every child of Adam. In truth, El-Yetch is as any other Ancient. Far away in their own cold, unreachable dimension, with as much concern for humanity as an oak tree has for an ant upon its leaves."

He paused to stare down his nose at Megan, the merest trace amount of pity in his usual permanent sneer. "What did he tell you, that a little heal now and then to gull the masses couldn't hurt? But it did. And bit by bit, daddy's girl doesn't look quite so girlish anymore. Was that when your mother left? Or perhaps she never left at all? Perhaps more skeletons than we know haunt the crannies of your father's house?"

Megan finally looked up, eyes wet and upper lip running freely with mucus. "He didn't!"

Diablerie put two fingers to his lips, gauging her reaction. "Perhaps even a man of such low breeding balks at some levels of depravity. After all, he eventually shied from the thought of aging his own eldest daughter to death. Perhaps he would have shelved the Cult of El-Yetch notion altogether. Until one fateful day."

Rana, by now, had backed all the way over to Adam's side, and the way she had fearfully taken hold of his elbow gave him a shot of courage. He stepped forward, resolving to wrest back control of the parlor scene. "It was when magic got declassified," he said. "Suddenly lots of people want to know more about magic and still don't trust what the government tells them. That's when Modern Miracle started really taking off."

"Indeed!" exclaimed Diablerie, making a single stomp toward him like a gorilla trying to scare off a rival alpha male. "A fresh batch of gullible plebeians, including many harboring the ethereal taint themselves, seeking a place to belong. And that's when the new scheme strikes Miracle Dad. One evil enough to chill even Diablerie's blood."

"William Shaw," interjected Adam. "He posted on Modern Miracle. And he was a healer. He probably wanted to know the secret of healing without draining himself, just like you did." He looked to Rana, and the look she gave him back addled his thoughts enough that Diablerie was able to seize control again.

"I doubt Shaw was the first victim ensnared by the honeyed tentacles of Modern Miracle's promises, but he may well have been the first to escape them." Diablerie rounded on Megan again with a maniacal smile. "If only for long enough to breathe his last upon a stranger's doorstep. What was the lie, girl, when you brought them to that shrine you and your family decorated so crassly? Reach up, wretched sinner, lay thine hands upon the mouth of El-Yetch, pour thy power upwards, and know at last the embrace of the Goddess? Or were they not all so naive? Was that your task, down there in the tunnels? To coerce, by force, if all lies failed?"

Alison had been watching Megan Arkwright with growing concern. She had spent much of the parlor scene staring at the floor, trembling or silently crying, but was now resentfully staring Diablerie down, sitting dangerously still like a trapdoor spider. The tension hung by a thread for a silent moment, then she rapidly threw a hand into her coat and pulled out a revolver.

"Yes, possibly using that!" said Diablerie, impressed.

Megan shot him.

51

Victor didn't know where he was. He was finding it difficult to piece together his recent memories. He knew that he had come to some theater to help Leslie-Ifrig with some bodyguarding job—or, wait, wasn't this a DEDA job? Wasn't he here with Adam? When he thought back, all he could remember was pain. A lot of pain. It hadn't lasted long, but now it seemed to be obscuring a lot of his memory, like a large ink stain in a book.

So he remembered pain. He also remembered that at one point he had been able to move his arms and see out of both eyes. That didn't seem to be the case anymore. He also seemed to remember weighing a lot more than he currently did.

At least his legs were functioning. He was upright, tottering forwards, letting himself be guided by the walls he was bumping against. Eventually, he stopped bumping into walls and sensed, dully, that he was bumping into hanging curtains instead, and his one remaining eye was seeing a lot of red.

Red curtains. So he was still at the theater. Things were starting to make more sense. Encouraged, he kept pushing forward. The curtain resisted, but eventually he felt it fall away, to be replaced with bright lights.

Bright lights and noise. And people. There were people all around, all of them yelling. He was hearing it as if he had cushions pressed against his ears, but it gradually became clear that most of the yelling was directed at him.

Realizing that, he began to feel quite overwhelmed. It was all quite tiring, having to stand up and get yelled at. That was another thing he remembered: that remaining upright used to be a lot less exhausting. It was probably about time for him to get some sleep anyway.

Victor promptly collapsed in the middle of the Pelican Theatre's main stage. His head hit the floorboards with a worryingly hard impact, but at that point, it was the least of his problems.

Richard Danvers hurried back onto stage and knelt beside him. He could only recognize him from the roughly one-quarter of his face that wasn't completely charred. "Mr. Casin? Victor?!" he yelled. "Dear god. Medics! Medics, now!"

Two of the paramedics ran onto the stage, clutching whatever equipment they could grab in an instant, and fell to their knees either side of the smoking ruin that was, for the moment, still Victor Casin. "Still getting a pulse," said one. "I think. Erm." He stopped himself from saying that it was difficult to find a spot where there was enough unburnt flesh to read a pulse. He called back to the wings. "Get an ambulance ready! And get some wet towels!"

"Wet towels?!" said Miracle Dad, taking a step toward the center of the unfolding drama. "He's not at the sodding hairdresser! He needs help!"

Richard Danvers, trying to get a reaction from Victor's one fluttering eyelid, flashed a hateful look. "This is not the time for—"

"For what?" Miracle Dad was addressing both him and the hushed audience equally. "I'd say it's time to drop all your both-sides bullshit, because you know damn well there's only one thing here that's going to save that poor bugger now. A touch from my Miracle Meg."

Danvers locked eyes with him. Miracle Dad had set his mouth and eyebrows into an expression of grim seriousness, but there was a smugness to his bearing that left Danvers instinctively repulsed. Nevertheless, he was a pragmatist and always did his best thinking under pressure, and all of his thoughts were pointing the same way.

"All right," he said. "Do it."

"Come on, get him on the prayer mat," said Miracle Dad. As he supervised the two sweating paramedics trying to lift Victor gingerly enough that nothing significant flaked off, he tapped his foot on the floor once, twice, three times. Very few people noticed it, and those that did took it for either impatience or a discreet attempt to knock something nasty off his shoe.

52

Megan Arkwright, still pointing the gun, flinched and glanced up at the floorboards. "It's time," she said, flustered. "Dad says you have to do it now."

She took aim at Rana, who was trying to hide behind one of Adam's raised arms. "I'm not doing anything for you! Adam, tell her!"

Adam wrestled his gaze away from the terrifying metal object in Megan's hands and focused on meeting her gaze. "Megan. Think about this. Are you really gonna shoot all of us?"

"She's set the precedent, boy," slurred Diablerie, from the floor. "Diablerie might suggest directing the conversation elsewhere."

"Stop talking!" wailed Alison, who was by his side, applying pressure to the ugly wound in his stomach with both hands.

Another three impatient knocks came from above. Megan jumped and redoubled her grip on the gun. "You, you have to do it now," she stammered, trying to sound intimidating as the muzzle of her gun shivered like an orphan in the snow. "They're on the trapdoor. Come on. You have to do it or . . ."

"Or what?" asked Rana as Megan struggled to find the words. "You'll shoot me? You'll shoot me if I don't kill myself? That doesn't make sense!"

"She's right! It doesn't make sense!" said Adam as Megan looked away in uncertainty. "Because . . . because this entire building is full of DEDA agents! You really think we're the only ones who figured this out?"

"Dad knows," said Megan, lips quivering. "Dad will know . . ."

"It's over, Megan," said Adam, suddenly remembering that that line had proved effective in a Harrison Ford movie he had seen once. "Rana isn't going to heal whoever's up there. Miracle Dad's going to be exposed. Even if he isn't, that shrine under your house has been burnt to a crisp, hasn't it? You really think you're going to keep finding healers? How long before he's making you do your part again?"

"We can help you," pleaded Alison. "Just come with us. Tell everyone what Miracle Dad was doing. You won't be in trouble. You won't have to hurt yourself for him anymore."

Megan was now staring at nothing, every part of her face moist and trembling as she fought the urge to break down. Her gun arm continued to waver until, inch by inch, she was aiming at the floor.

"Now!" cried Diablerie, trying to sit up in a burst of effort. "Overpower the harlot!" Blood squirted from between Alison's fingers, and he fell back down with a grunt.

The surprise broke Megan from her reverie, and she pointed the gun at Diablerie. "Get away from him."

Alison was desperately slapping Diablerie's suddenly unresponsive face in an attempt to provoke a reaction. "He's dying!"

With a small movement, the gun was pointing to her. Megan wasn't trembling anymore. "I said, get away from him," she barked, clearly and decisively.

Alison threw her arms up so quickly that she sprinkled Adam and Rana with droplets of wet blood from her hands. Diablerie's wound began to freely vomit blood all over the floor like a broken chocolate fountain.

"Please," said Alison, meeting Megan's determined stare. "He—"

Another three knocks on the floor above silenced her, louder and more impatient. This time, Megan didn't flinch. She looked up once, smiled philosophically, and returned her gaze to Alison. "You know," she said, with a faint quaver. "You were wrong about one thing. None of them ever needed much coercion. Neither did I."

Then, in a single, fluid action that no one was prepared to stop, she fell forward, threw aside the gun, and slapped both hands around Diablerie's ankles.

Adam clutched his head as a violent burst of magic overloaded his senses. Even Alison felt she could detect something—a sudden heaviness in the air that made all the hairs on her body prick up. There was a glow around Megan's hands as if she was trying to cover the end of a flashlight.

The flow of blood from Diablerie's wound stopped. His entire body convulsed, throwing his head forwards, and each time, when he settled back down, his bullet wound was a little smaller. The blood remained, but within seconds, there was nothing beneath it but a small cross-shaped scar in Diablerie's gut that could have been years old.

At the same time, Megan Arkwright's skin faded from pale to sepulchral, tightening around her bones like shrink-wrap and making her rapidly graying hair stand on end. In the matter of seconds it took Alison to wrestle with her conscience and try to shove her away, Megan must have aged at least sixty years. She made no resistance and fell back as lightly as a cardboard cutout.

"Because doing it feels so good," whispered Megan, going limp and grinning like a skeleton. "It feels so good."

Her words trailed off. Life swiftly faded from her milky eyes. When Alison felt her for a pulse, her gray skin had the texture of rice paper. "She's dead."

"It seems she made her choice," said a perfectly healthy Diablerie, rising to his elbows. He winced at the sight of the large quantities of drying blood that soaked his clothes.

"Is there . . . anything we can do?" asked Rana, staring with her hands partially covering her face.

Diablerie brushed himself down. "Yes. We can see if the hotel offers a dry cleaning service."

53

"Dad, she's not there," whispered Miracle Meg, or rather, Phoebe Arkwright. "Meg's not there."

Miracle Dad had tapped his foot on the stage boards so many times he was having to pretend that he suffered from a nervous leg spasm. "I know, love, I know," he hissed.

"Well?" asked Richard Danvers irritably. "A man is dying!"

"Yeah, we know!" snapped Miracle Dad. He caught himself and forcibly reinstated his confident voice. "Don't stress, boss man, give El-Yetch a second or two to, to, gather her energies."

"Daaad," said Phoebe.

Miracle Dad hurried to her side and muttered directly into her ear. "I know. I know, love. Just . . . put your hands on him, all right? Your dad'll think of something."

Obediently, Phoebe leaned forward and spread her hands over Victor's scorched torso, one on his stomach and one on his neck. She glanced at Miracle Dad for approval, then closed her eyes and put on her "serene and mysterious" look.

"All right, here we go," said Miracle Dad, bounding to his feet and addressing the audience. "The power of El-Yetch is real. It's here right now. But I have to say, this fella might be too far gone even for her power. She's gonna try, but considering Barkler only had to deal with some granny with a slightly achy back, it's not exactly fair that we're expected—"

"It appears this is well within El-Yetch's abilities," said Danvers.

Miracle Dad's voice died when he realized that most of the audience were staring straight past him with eyes like saucers. He turned around.

"Da-ad?" said Phoebe, her voice weak and plaintive.

Victor Casin's skin was regrowing in sheets. His burned flesh healed and puffed back up into a healthy state, like a reversed video of a pizza being cooked. The glow from beneath Phoebe's hands was brighter than it had been under Megan's and seemed to spark violently with every slightest twitching of her fingers.

"DAAAAD!" she cried. Her skin was tightening, and her hair was drying out and fading to white as it fell out of its pigtails. Her back arched as convulsions ran through her, but she couldn't pull her hands away. Soon, she was screaming.

Miracle Dad took a single step toward her, then stopped, frozen in incomprehension. A moment later his knees gave out, and he collapsed onto his hands before the stiffening body of his youngest daughter. The entire theater was silent but for the abortive sputters that came out of his mouth as he failed, again and again, to find words.

Groggily, Victor sat up, looking down in confusion at the skeletal white hand still draped over his stomach. Most of his hair was gone, but his skin was as smooth and pink as a baby's. He stared at the audience.

He coughed. "What, did I miss a party?"

54

There was no more protesting after that. The feeling shared by much of the audience, both in the theater and online, was one of shock, and of shame at having encouraged things as far as they had gone. Both sides of the debate filed silently out of the theater, protest signs hanging loosely from their hands, resisting the urge to make eye contact.

The mood surrounding the participants and DEDA agents was mainly confusion. There was a general sense that they should probably arrest Miracle Dad, but as for what crime, no one had a clear idea. That was until the hotel cleaners checked his room and found Beatrice Callum, alive but gagged and bound to a chair, at which point Richard Danvers told the police to start the ball rolling with kidnapping and see where the mood took them as the whole story came out.

Alison Arkin and Doctor Diablerie found themselves in front of the theater, watching an unresistant Miracle Dad being led away by two uniformed police officers. He still hadn't spoken a word since his stage performance, or indeed, closed his mouth. Rana and Adam had already left, as she had volunteered him to drive her home.

"And thus," said Diablerie, "the Office of Skepticism marks its first of many triumphs. The quill inscribes in the book of fate one last line to close the sorry tale of Modern Miracle."

"It does?" said Alison. "Doctor, there's . . . so much that still doesn't make sense. How could both daughters have been healers? And how did nobody know that about Phoebe until now?"

"Surely at least the first rule of paranormal investigation has penetrated your fog of ignorance by now, girl. That there is a universe of difference between 'unlikely' and 'impossible.' Healing is a by no means uncommon infusion among the tainted."

"I suppose," said Alison, scratching her head in worry. "But what about David Callum? The second victim. He wasn't a healer. And he wasn't anywhere near the tunnel."

Diablerie scoffed. "Life is no teatime detective drama, girl! Where there is but one killer and one rooftop showdown between them and their compression betwixt the thighs of justice! We know that Modern Miracle exploited the confused tainted ones that suckled at its electronic teats. They were luring in the healers and enlisting pyrokinetics as guard dogs. They must also have employed a vampire to engineer a killing meant to throw us off the scent. Little dreaming that one thwarts the nose of Diablerie in vain." He wrapped his cloak around his face, letting his nose peer over the top to illustrate his point.

"So you think there was a second killer?"

"Indeed, and since genuine vampirism was involved, one that falls outside of our remit as skepticism officers. We shall leave it in the ketch-up-stained hands of our colleagues in Investigations and prepare for another enigma we can call our own."

He turned with a flourish, letting his cloak swish around him like a peacock's feathers, and began stalking away toward his car. Alison realized to her slight shame that she had begun to meekly follow behind with no conscious decision making on her part. She was very far from satisfied that all questions were answered—when had Diablerie figured it all out? What had he even been doing all that time he hadn't been around?—and she felt her inclination to press him on those questions dissolve with her confidence as he walked determinedly away.

The impulse frustrated her. People like Diablerie were the ones who defined reality, she thought, the ones who simply push forward, never explaining themselves or acknowledging other views, until everyone around them was too cowed or too exhausted to call them out. She thought about Megan Arkwright, the way she jumped at her father's commands and came unglued outside of his presence. That's what happens to people caught in the wake of these human steamrollers. It was just that, in her case, the draining of her life force hadn't been a metaphor.

She took a deep breath and speed walked back into talking range. "Doctor, can I ask you something? Something unrelated?"

"All things are related in the tapestries of fate," he halfheartedly barked.

She took that as a yes. "Do you know anything about Nicholas Fisk?"

That made him stop short. He half turned, one intrigued eye glittering over his shoulder. "So. With what nonsense has Elizabeth Lawrence been filling your copious ears?"

"Is he still around?" said Alison, determined not to get sidetracked.

"Ha!" Diablerie's wide-eyed grin was terrifying. "Nicholas Fisk is as far away as any man can get, girl."

"He's dead," interpreted Alison aloud.

"Indeed. One of Lawrence's victims. She's an unpredictable killer, but her modus operandi never changes. Her weapon of choice is the illusion of trust."

"Right," said Alison, watching him intently.

Diablerie turned to face her properly with a little swish of the cloak. "Lawrence pulled no trigger and swung no blade, but she killed Nicholas Fisk nevertheless, by the simple method of allowing him to believe that she valued his life. Do not make the same mistake, girl. The moment you cease to be useful, she will cast you aside like a disposable razor that has lost its edge. Now!" He spun on his heel again. "Your task this eve is to deduce the esoteric ritual by which one pays for parking in this facility."

THE NEXT MORNING

55

"Come in, Mr. Hesketh," said Richard Danvers when he saw the trench-coated shadow hesitate behind the frosted glass of his office door.

Adam shuffled in, his mouth set into a glum line and his eyes directed downwards. He pulled out a chair to sit on as slowly as he felt he could get away with, in order to draw out the time before he had to look Danvers in the eye.

"You inspected the girl?" asked Danvers, the moment Adam was settled in the chair.

"Um, yes," said Adam unhappily. He had just returned from the morgue, and although his magical senses had needed mere seconds to work, any amount of time was too long to be in a cold room with the desiccated corpse of an eleven-year-old. "She definitely had a healing infusion."

Danvers grimaced. "I would be prepared to swear that this came as a complete surprise to Miracle Dad."

"It might have come as a surprise to her," said Adam quietly.

"What do you mean by that?"

"Nothing," mumbled Adam into his stomach. "It's just a theory. I don't have any facts to back it up."

"Sometimes that's as good a starting point as any," said Danvers gently. "Why might it have been a surprise to her?"

"It's just . . . when I use my senses on someone with a magic infusion, I see, like, a blob. Of color. That gets kind of blurry around the edges. And blurrier in, like, old people who've had infusions for a really long time."

"And?"

"And the girl, Phoebe Arkwright's infusion, it wasn't blurry at all. Completely clean lines. I've never seen anything like it."

Danvers frowned, one crooked finger over his mouth. "And what do you theorize that that indicates?"

"I just get this feeling that . . . maybe her infusion was really, really new. Like, she didn't have one up until the moment she drained herself."

Danvers leaned back in his chair, scrutinizing the worried lines on Adam's face, and let out a harrumph. "That would certainly make her actions easier to understand. Her father's, too. I just fail to see how such a thing could be possible."

Adam tried to shrug and cringe at the same time. "Maybe . . . maybe it was the wrath of El-Yetch?"

"I'd keep that theory to yourself, especially around the chief administrator. She doesn't respond well to the thought of hostile Ancients." Danvers stared at his own desktop for a few moments, thinking. "Not long ago, we noticed a mysterious increase in magical infusions worldwide. When I brought this up with Archibald, he mentioned there has been some reported . . . anomalies. Magic manifesting in ways that go against our current understanding of magic. This may well be part of that pattern."

"Ah," said Adam, eyeing the door. "Was there . . . nothing else?"

Danvers pinned him in place with a look. "Did you really think there'd be nothing else, Adam?"

"Um."

"The last time we spoke, I seem to recall removing you from the Investigations Office," said Danvers conversationally. "From the Modern Miracle case in particular. I don't recall there being much room for ambiguity in my language."

"Um," said Adam again. "Er . . . um," he went on to clarify.

"And yet, you continued investigating." Danvers's voice was flat, but his gaze was needle sharp. "You went over me, and you went over the investigator in charge. And you ended up in a deadly situation without backup."

"Alison was there," said Adam promptly.

"And you ended up in a deadly situation without backup," said Danvers, in precisely the same tone as before. He let his disapproval hang over Adam like a cold fog for a few seconds, before his next word cut through it like a lighthouse. "But. You solved the case when nobody else did. And by acting in time, you saved an innocent life."

Adam kept hanging his head, but glanced up hopefully with his eyes, like a wretched puppy checking to see if its overt guilt was slowing the incoming rolled-up newspaper.

"I suppose," said Danvers, rubbing his hands as he thought, "in the light of your success, there may be an argument for reinstating your previous position."

Adam looked up, clasping his knees. "Are you going to . . . ?"

"No," said Danvers, with devastating flatness. "No, I still don't think you're suited for the Investigations Office."

"Oh," said Adam, sagging in his seat.

Danvers had opened his laptop and was hunting around his desktop files with the mouse. "There's going to be another reorganization soon. You're going to be attached to a new division."

"Oh . . . ?" Adam glanced up again, wretched puppy eyes on standby.

"Like I said, there's been an increase in reported magical infusions, and that means an increase in graduates at the school." He winced a little as he read the reports on the screen. "Most magical infusions aren't particularly useful, as I'm sure you're aware, or no more so than, say, a well-trained agent with a gun, but a few individuals have been flagged as . . . standouts."

Adam just stared. He had no idea how to respond to this development. The wretched puppy had seen the rolled-up newspaper go away, only to see it replaced with a rubber chicken.

"Now they're graduated, there's really only one established career path for people with extradimensional infusions on this level." He caught Adam's eye. "A lot of them have been asking about you and Victor. You're something of a role model."

Danvers had turned his laptop sideways, and Adam was inspecting the profiles on display. "So you're putting together, like . . . a . . . powers team?"

"We're stopping short of code names and spandex," said Danvers dryly. "And I want you there as senior agent. Victor as well." He held up his hands as Adam frowned. "I know. But I'm willing to bet he hasn't filed any official resignation paperwork. So I'm leaving you the task of getting him back onboard. Tell him there's a young person graduating from the school next month who is very keen to know if he has a good source for fire-retardant underwear."

56

At the same moment, Alison was sitting in front of Elizabeth Lawrence's desk, undergoing what was technically her own debriefing, although so far it had consisted only of sitting in silence while Elizabeth skimmed through Alison's lengthy written report.

Alison scrutinized Elizabeth's expression throughout, feeling the same anxiety she always felt when a teacher had been marking her work in front of her. She could tell from the way Elizabeth was widening her eyes and idly scratching her temple that she had reached the part about Phoebe Arkwright.

"Both sisters had healing powers," she summarized.

"Y-yes," said Alison. "It's really unlikely. But it's not impossible."

"Quite," said Elizabeth coldly. "I note, in your report, that Diablerie assured you as much."

Silence resumed for several seconds, during which Alison felt unaccountably stung. She made up her mind to deliver the statement she had been practicing in her head all day.

"Doctor Diablerie is Nicholas Fisk," she said. "Isn't he?"

Elizabeth looked up, eyebrows climbing. The top part of the paper in her hands flopped forwards. "What brought you to this conclusion?"

"It was when he said that Fisk was as far away as anyone can be," said Alison, staring at her hands as they fidgeted. "I remembered you telling me not to trust anything Diablerie says. So it made sense for the opposite to be true. That Fisk was actually as close as he could possibly be."

After a few moments of tense staring, Elizabeth reached down into the leather briefcase she was keeping behind the desk and produced a single photograph, which she placed on the desktop and pushed across to Alison.

It was an old picture, apparently cropped from a larger scene, which depicted a man standing beside a car. He was wearing a practical army jacket over a generic T-shirt and holding an old revolver that he was either placing in or withdrawing from the front of his jeans.

"Recognize him?" asked Elizabeth.

The picture was a little overexposed, but Alison could see that the man had dark hair and a relaxed expression about his unremarkable jawline. He was probably around his early thirties. He also looked precisely like a young Doctor Diablerie, albeit without the top hat, curled mustache, or insane glint in the eye.

Alison's eyebrows shot up. "This is Fisk?"

"From twelve years ago, when he was a freelance troubleshooter for the Ministry." She took the photo back, dragging it slowly along the desk with one finger as she processed her memories. "He was found just a few weeks after the Shadow Crisis ended. Wandering along the side of a road. Ranting, gibbering, injured in strange ways. I had him brought to a Ministry hospital and treated.

"When he had been given a clean bill of health, I went to interview him. That was the first time I met Doctor Diablerie. The voice, the mannerisms, the . . . poses. He has changed very little ever since."

Alison stared in bafflement at Elizabeth's walking cane, leaning on the side of her desk. "And after everything . . . you hired him?"

Elizabeth rotated her chair until she was staring at the wall. "Somewhere, deep inside Doctor Diablerie, the mind of Nicholas Fisk holds certain information, vital to the security of the human race. He knows how the shadow was driven away. He knows what happened to Mr. Teapot. This is information I need. Eventually, I will find a way to extract it. Until then, it is important that I keep him close to hand."

"Can I . . . go?" Alison was already half risen out of her seat, bracing herself on the armrests. "I have to . . . dinner."

"Dinner by all means," said Elizabeth, snapping out of it and returning her attention to the work on her desk.

As Alison walked slowly to the door, one foot at a time, confused thoughts swirling in her head, she began to realize that there was something she needed to ask, and that if she didn't ask now, she might never work up the courage to do so again. But at the same time, she knew that Elizabeth's answer would change things in Alison's mind. Perhaps in ways that could never change back.

She was three steps from the door. Behind her, she heard Elizabeth begin typing something and heave the light sigh of someone moving on with their day.

Two steps.

One step.

Alison thought about what Diablerie had said to her.

She stopped, and felt the tension in the air begin to grow. The sound of typing paused.

"Who were Diablerie's other assistants?" asked Alison, turning around.

Elizabeth had been watching her, fingers splayed out and paused in the act of typing. "Hm?"

"You told me that you gave Diablerie assistants before me," said Alison, embracing the point of no return. "Could I ask . . . who they were?"

"Does it matter?" said Elizabeth. "None of them lasted nearly as long as you have, Alison."

The door handle was cold beneath Alison's grip. "I suppose it's not important."

Call between Victor Casin and Adam Hesketh beginning at 1:18 p.m.:

VICTOR: Adam.

ADAM: Hey, Victor. Uh. Thanks for picking up.

VICTOR: Whatever. I could spare you a few minutes between my busy schedule of doing bugger all.

ADAM: How're you feeling?

VICTOR: Perfect. Peachy keen. Just grins and smiles the whole day long over here.

ADAM: That bad?

VICTOR: I mean, it's not like I just got dumped by my archnemesis who very nearly killed me and burnt most of my hair off so I look like Dr. Robotnik, is it? What do you want?

ADAM: Oh. I just wanted to know if you'd be interested in coming back to work soon.

VICTOR: Oh no. Is my seat in the cafeteria getting cold? Did all my sugar packet sculptures fall over?

ADAM: Actually, Mr. Danvers wants us to be partners again.

VICTOR: Seriously? What about you and Investigations?

ADAM: It, um. It didn't really work out. I'm getting reassigned either way.

VICTOR: Aw, poor Adam. Well, I suppose if you desperately need my shoulder to cry on, I might as well come back.

ADAM: Great. So, what's going on with you and your archnemesis now?

VICTOR: We're not archnemeses anymore. Probably gonna kill them if I see them again, but it'll be more of a casual thing.

ADAM: Sorry it didn't work out.

VICTOR: You know what, I don't really care. I was gonna break it off soon anyway. I've decided I'm not really an archnemesis kind of person.

ADAM: Hm. And, er, how do you feel about teen sidekicks?

THE NEXT DAY

57

The police and DEDA presence at the convention center had finally thinned out enough that Rajesh Chahal felt it safe to retrieve his car. He had managed to fade away in the chaos after the events of Sunday morning, but he was certain that the police and the media were going to have pointed questions for anyone close to Modern Miracle for some time yet.

He had made it through the outdoor parking area without being stopped, and as he made his way past the ranks of empty parking spaces, he concentrated on walking in such a way that successfully balanced "nonchalant" with "too busy to talk about recently unveiled murder conspiracies."

Why the hell had he agreed to be on a TV interview? He should have stayed behind the scenes. It was just that Miracle Dad had gotten cold feet about doing a "serious" debate without backup, and there might not have been a better chance to escalate the situation, so he'd given in.

Rajesh reached his car, tucked away in the nice big shadow created by a pillar and a broken ceiling light, and grimaced at the memory of his own actions. He'd been played masterfully of course. Somehow, even after all these years, he was back to throwing himself into trouble just to please . . .

"Hello, Raj."

. . . him. The man who was sometimes Doctor Diablerie. He was leaning against the dark side of the pillar.

Rajesh froze, then slowly straightened his posture and folded his arms. "How long have you been waiting for me there?"

"I was here on another errand. I saw you arrive."

"Just admit it. You stood there for hours hoping you'd get to see an impressed look on my face."

"What do you make of the incident onstage?" said the man, taking a step forward to punctuate the way he was stabbing directly to the heart of the matter.

"I've been going back and forth between horror and self-loathing," said Rajesh, slowly circling around the car to the driver's seat, not taking his eyes off the man in the shadows.

"A girl with no infusion, no healing powers, nor the necessary maturity to have harnessed them, suddenly acquires them at an oddly convenient moment during a livestream to the world. What does that tell you?"

"That you've acquired a really weird fixation with dead young girls?"

"The Third Way, Raj. Our theory is confirmed."

Rajesh's hand was on the car door handle. He closed his eyes and took a deep breath. "Not necessarily. It's still possible that she did have the powers and was hiding it—"

"You don't believe that," said the man, adding a sharp edge to his normally placid voice. "This was the whole point of the exercise. Don't resist the truth."

Rajesh hung his head and bared his teeth. "Maybe I don't want to live in a world where the Third Way is a thing. Maybe I hate that you were right. It's not a rational feeling, but hey, some of us still have those, you know? Feelings? Some of us still feel a bit uneasy about manipulating people and getting innocent children killed for our science experiments?"

He was ranting by that point, with his hands balled into fists and his head jutting forward. The man in the shadows watched, unmoved, and waited for him to finish.

"There's no walking away from this now," he said eventually.

Rajesh released a sigh as his entire upper body went limp. "I know. God damn you, I know."

"I'll be in touch about the next phase," said the man, carefully placing his hands in his pockets and beginning to walk away. "Alison is starting to ask the right questions. I want to move forward with her recruitment soon. In the meantime, drop out of sight."

"Yeah," said Rajesh, seething. He glanced up. "You've seriously still got business here?"

"Yes," said the man, not looking around. "The last loose end, I hope."

58

Beatrice Callum was none the worse for her kidnapping ordeal and had just been released from prolonged, exhaustive interviews with the police that had only ended when they had finally gotten her to stop talking. A police car dropped her off in front of the hotel, near where she had left Roger, Arby, and the LAXA van.

It didn't surprise her at all that Roger and the van were still there. She knew Roger found it hard to motivate himself when left to his own devices, especially when the devices had a decent capacity for video streaming. Beatrice knocked on the van's side door, expecting about two minutes of waiting time before he would summon the energy to stand up.

"Hey, babe," she said, folding her arms and leaning on the van. "Phew. Sorry it took so long. Miracle Dad wouldn't let me use my phone. And he tied me to a chair. Then the police gave me my phone back, but they said I couldn't livestream the questioning. So we've probably got a lot of donations backed up . . ."

Something thin and white fluttered around her body and dropped to the ground. She glanced down, frowning, to see that she was now standing in a circle of white tape, adorned with a sequence of black symbols.

Runes, she realized, remembering her first meeting with Alison back at the Builder's Arms. Before she had time to process this revelation, she heard a droning computerized voice chanting incomprehensible syllables from somewhere nearby, and then felt a sensation like a velvet foot pressing down on her brain. She promptly collapsed, snoring, to the ground.

The man who was sometimes Doctor Diablerie appeared unhurriedly from the van's rear, holding up his cell phone as it repeated the runic chant. He scanned Beatrice's sleeping carcass for a moment. The ritual he had used was a relatively harmless one, and she would wake up within a matter of hours with no lingering effect, assuming she hadn't just concussed herself on the tarmac.

He silenced the phone with a brusque tap, then returned it to his hip pocket. At the same time he reached inside his jacket with his free hand and drew out the contents, examining it with interest.

It was a sausage. An individually wrapped piece of cured sausage he had purchased from a nearby petrol station. In cash, naturally. He ripped open the wrapper with his teeth as he fished around in yet another pocket, from which he produced a black extendable baton, and flicked it out to its full length.

He took up position at the van's side door, his feet on either side of Beatrice's oblivious form. He took a moment to hold the sausage and baton together in the same hand, then hauled the door open.

Arby the dog immediately leapt up from his slump on the floor of the van, lowered his head, and began to growl in warning.

"Hello, Arby," said the man, unperturbed. He peeled the sausage away from the baton and held it up. "I'd like to be friends. Can we be friends?"

He flicked the sausage away into the corner of the van. Arby ceased to growl and watched it go. He took a single sad glance at the floor of the van, and at what he had felt was important to defend, before realizing that a free sausage upended his entire list of priorities. He bounded after it, leaving behind Roger's gray, dried-out corpse.

The man looked at the body without emotion before glancing quickly around to confirm that Beatrice was sleeping peacefully and that nobody else was present. Satisfied, he returned to his pockets and produced one of Doctor Diablerie's white gloves, which he placed on the end of the baton.

Arby had finished the sausage and was checking around for the next development. When the glove was waved under his nose, he took a cautious sniff. His tail flicked.

"There, now we know one another," said the man. He was now holding a magazine clipping, from which he read aloud. " 'Arby the Psychic

Dog.' That's you, isn't it? 'The resident pooch at the Sundown Care Home for the Elderly has been making headlines with his uncanny ability to predict which resident will be the next to pass on. Whenever he chooses a new friend and begins resting on their bed at night, staff members know that their days are getting numbered.'"

Arby cocked his head, sticking out his tongue uncomprehendingly.

"Except it wasn't precognition, was it?" said the man, tucking the clipping back into his jacket. "It was your power. Who's going to notice the last few drops of life being drained from someone already old and gray?"

Arby glanced down at Roger's body and lowered his head in guilt, as if it were merely a chewed-up sofa cushion. He let out a brief whine.

"I know you didn't mean to," said the man gently. "You haven't been taught to control when the power strikes. We have a lot to learn from each other. I've never met an animal that could resist possession. Perhaps some dogs truly are incorruptible." He carefully worked the end of his baton under the dog's collar and began to inch the dog forward. "Come on. I have a forever home in mind for you, Arby. Or should I call you Harbinger?"

Arby jumped down onto the tarmac and trotted a few steps away, sniffing the evening air and giving a little huff of excitement. The man took one last look at Roger's corpse, then gently closed up the van.